The Confession of Gentry

This book is a work of fiction. The story's characters, incidents and dialogue are drawn entirely from the author's imagination. Any resemblance to any persons living or dead is completely coincidental. All described situations, conversations, and encounters are purely fictional.

THE CONFESSION OF GENTRY

Published by Karen G. Berry.

Printed by CreateSpace in the United States.

Available through Amazon.com and other bookstores and online stores.

Cover design and artwork by Mark Ferrari.

Original photos from pixabay.com are CC0 Public Domain.

The Confession of Gentry

Karen G. Berry

Other Works by Karen G. Berry

The Gentry Books, one through three –
The Temptation of Gentry
The Confession of Gentry
The Reconciliation of Gentry

Other novels –
Love and Mayhem at the Francie June Memorial Trailer Park
The Iris Files: Notes from a Desperate Housewife

With Shannon Page as Laura Gayle –
Orcas Intrigue
Orcas Intruder

For my sister Cat, who came to get me.

There is no sinner like a young saint.

—Aphra Behn

I. RECKONING

It's morning, Sunday morning. This is Your day, and God, I have a question. Why am I awake? I generally try to sleep through the death agony of my murdered brain cells.

God, send me back to sleep. Please. Amen.

The phone. That's why I'm awake. It's ringing. The ancient answering machine switches on upstairs. I think this answering machine was a clumsy prototype for all the better answering machines that came after, but I'm too broke to replace it. I can hear my voice through the cardboard walls. "This is Gentry. Um, please, um, leave a message. Bye."

That is some of my finest work.

She starts to talk, and I spring from the cocoon of my sleeping bag. And then I groan as I stumble up the stairs. Ouch, my head. The receiver gives me an earful of feedback before I can get the machine to stop recording. And she's shouting because she's of that generation that shouts into answering machines.

God, do You hate me? I think You hate me. Not that I blame You, but still.

"This is Gentry." I hate it that I answer my home phone like I answer the phone at work. "I mean, hey. Hey, Mrs. Hirsch. I'm here."

"Gentry, is that you?"

No, it's an impostor who wants to take over my exciting life. "Yes, it's me."

"I was just leaving you a message, and there you are." She sounds flustered. Maybe I should hang up and put her at ease. "Gentry, are you still there?" I don't know, am I here? Did I disappear between the answering of the phone and the verification of my identity? Or is that a philosophical question?

"Yes, I'm here." As far as I can tell.

"Can you *hear* me all right?"

This one seems obvious. I've answered all the questions. "Yes, I hear you."

"Just a minute. Let me fix this." She is, I'm sure, manipulating the volume control on her phone. "Well. We never hear from you."

"I'm sorry about that." Another long pause, because whenever I talk on the phone there are long pauses. What to say? Oh, yes. "How are you? And Mr. Hirsch?"

"Well, he just has that same trouble with . . ." and I switch off, because all I have to do during this litany of ailments is make the appropriate noises. I don't need to participate. I only need to "hm." While I hm, I run the coffee grinder that only works if I bang it on the counter. I set up the coffeepot that occasionally won't start brewing, flip the switch and wait for the gurgle. "But he's *better*, he's *better*."

"I'm glad to hear that." Come on. Gurgle.

"We just do as well as expected. Which is I'm sure how it is for you, too. I'm sure you're doing just as well as expected."

As expected. If there are expectations, I am fairly sure I'm failing them. Still no gurgle. Please, God, I need some coffee. Amen.

"Gentry? What are *you* up to these days?"

"Me? Um, working, mostly." And praying for my coffee pot to gurgle in direct violation of my pledge to stop all unnecessary prayer. I hate myself for that, but the truth is, I hate myself for everything these days. But I definitely hear a gurgle.

"Yes, of course, working." She sniffs, loudly. "How are you, Gentry?"

How am I? I am alone. I find myself living in a solitude so complete that I wonder why I bother to go on living. I have no idea how to end it.

The solitude, I mean. Not the living.

"I'm fine, just fine."

"Well, I'm glad to hear it. I'm just glad to hear you're *fine*." She's crying. Because I said I was fine? People ask me how I am, I say I'm fine. That doesn't mean I am, it's just what I say.

I swallow hard enough that my throat aches. "Hey Mrs. Hirsch? Is it this weekend?"

"Yes. Do you understand why we decided to have it at our house?"

"Yes. Of course. I think it's a good idea." It's a very good idea because I don't think all those people who were sitting around in this house last year watching me make a spectacle of myself would be happy with having nowhere to sit this year. They'd have to stand while waiting for the show to begin, shooting bitter looks at me and chewing food with their mouths open, waiting for the show to begin. The show being the Drunk Catholic show, starring an idiot who starts yelling at everyone, takes off his jacket and falls down the stairs, locks himself in the garage and sits in his Jeep, drinking and singing until the house empties. I'm not sure how to top that performance. Maybe this year I can wet my pants. I haven't done that yet, but give me time. I'm probably just working up to it.

"So, Gentry, we'll see you on Sunday? Around ten?"

"Yes. Do you want me to come over early to, um, help with anything?"

"Everything's taken care of, but if you come over early I can make you some breakfast."

"I'd like that. Mrs. Hirsch? Hey to Mr. Hirsch. I, um, have to go. Bye."

I hang up the phone and lean on the counter, my head on my arms, my heart in my throat.

God, change this. Do something. Anything. Whatever You send, whatever it looks like, I will submit and obey if You just change my life.

Amen.

I raise my head to look out the kitchen window. It's 82 degrees, a beautiful Sunday morning in Oklahoma City. On Sunday morning I used to rise, shriven and empty, ready for my personal favorite of the seven sacraments. It was a beautiful thing, Sunday morning.

The phone rings again. I don't know who it is, because it's the Sabbath and the only other person who used to call this house is busy with Mass.

The machine picks it up, and I listen to the message. It's a bill collector. Bill collectors don't usually call on Sunday morning. They call here every other hour of every other day of the week, but not on the Lord's day. I erase the message, pour my coffee and return to the cool basement and my broken-down couch, where I climb into the sleeping bag Mel mailed me last Christmas. It's blizzard-rated, like the bag I used while driving from Detroit to North Dakota at Christmas time, when Bosco and I wrapped up in the Jeep.

God, I miss Mel. I miss Bosco. I miss my Jeep.

I sip my coffee. Rather than pining over what's lost to me, I should work on my guilt. Guilt is a fine Sunday pastime. Let's see. I can feel guilty about being a lousy friend. I owe everyone at least one letter. I owe Paige three. I should write to her, or better yet, call her. She never minds my long pauses. So, letters. What else? What else could I feel guilty about?

Dishes. I left dirty dishes upstairs. One bowl. One spoon.

I think the dishes can wait.

The grass. I can never figure out how the grass grows with this eternal drought, but the grass always needs cutting. If I don't go out into the killing heat and mow the strange, broad, sharp-bladed grass every week, the neighbors wage a war with me. Their weapons are dirty looks and concerned inquiries. "Everything all right, Gentry? How're y'all getting along these days? Gosh, that yard sure gets away from a person, don't it?" I can't muster any guilt over my yard, or dirty dishes, or unanswered letters. But I could feel guilt over my true sins, which are too many to count at this point.

God? I think this is a low point.

My life is primarily composed of low points. How I acted a year ago, that was a low point. That's one to confess, except I'm so ashamed of what I said, of how I acted that I find I can't talk about it with anyone. Not even Mel.

Mel used to yell at me. Occasionally I yelled back. We argued. Now when he calls, his voice is patient and controlled. We exchange careful and meaningless email through my work account. We have general and safe phone conversations every month. All our interactions are carefully sanitized so we never make the mistake of talking about anything important.

He did ask me last month, "Gentry, do you need me? Do you want me there?" And I replied, "No, Mel. I'm fine, just fine." And I don't want him to know what I've become, what I've done with the life he saved twenty years ago.

I need absolution. I need a penance. But I've committed acts so unspeakable that they've sealed themselves up inside me and begun the slow process of poisoning me to death. I'll die with them in me, and then I'll go to Hell.

Hell is a basement. Even though it's scorching outside, on the way to an inferno, it's cool down here. I turn on the television and look for a sport I don't care about. No soccer, no fishing, absolutely no basketball or football. This leaves baseball and bowling and golf.

This is my life: the couch, something brown to drink, a boring sport.

But against my better judgment, I'm drawn into the human spectacle of a talk show featuring a brave group of people with a condition called Tourette's Syndrome. Aside from a little twitching and jerking, they look like normal people, but every so often they erupt into profanities. Like Lorrie Gilroy, but not on purpose. It's the most painfully unfair thing I've ever watched on a talk show, and God, to be honest, it makes me wonder about You. How could You do this? On the screen, they swear and blurt and twitch, and they speak movingly about their hopes for a normal life. I have a small epiphany, there, about myself and my desire to be normal. Is that what I prayed for? To be normal?

You laughed at me, I bet.

I used to wonder what the laughter of God would sound like. Now I know. I hear Your laughter in the deep silence that surrounds me as I go through my daily life.

~

Sleep never comes, but daylight does. Monday morning starts the less Godly part of the week. I stand in the shower and hate myself. Hating myself is part of the morning system I developed because I start so many mornings feeling like this. Every morning, in fact.

I have a session of self-loathing in the shower, and then I have a cup of coffee. I have a shot of poison in the coffee. And then another. I knock back a little from the bottle because the coffee is too hot. And then I drive to work in the rattling Toyota coupe.

It's possible, I know, that one day I'll kill myself driving this way. But not soon enough.

There's the workplace. How do I describe it? It resembles a Hieronymus Bosch painting. Souls on the wheel, wailing victims with spikes sticking out of their backsides, recombinant monsters, blood. And bad coffee.

As soon as I enter the main door, the receptionist fixes me with glittering, hungry eyes. Today she has on an acrid perfume that I can actually taste. She smiles. This woman has scary teeth. "Good morning, Gentry."

"Good morning, Fanny." I don't use that word, but it is her name.

"Did you have a good breakfast?" While she waits, her smile shifts from hopeful to desperate.

"I, um, need to get to work."

Her face falls. She props it up again with that ghastly smile. "Jesus loves you, Gentry!"

Once that's over with, I go into my office and shut the door. Most people here don't shut their office doors, but I've convinced my boss that I have to. Something to do with dust. I mumbled about it, the dust, the door, my mysterious dust-affected computer doings. He pretended to understand, so I get to close my door.

I hate this job.

I start the tick sheet I use to keep track of how many times a day I think "I hate this job." I start it with a nice long string of ticks, because I thought "I hate this job" when I walked in the door. I thought it when the scary receptionist said "Jesus loves you, Gentry!"

I hate this job.

When I sit down, my message light is flashing. Jesus, I thought you loved me.

Then tell me, Jesus, why is my message light flashing? I'm here early, Jesus, and who could need me already?

Jesus, I hate this job. I sit down. My line rings. "This is Gentry."

It's Fanny. "Silly Gentry, remember to listen to your messages."

"I will."

"If you don't, I'll *call back*."

I hang up. The message is from May in payroll. She says she needs to see me.

I hate this job. That's how many in three minutes? I'm on a roll, here. Maybe today I'll break my record of two hundred and nine ticks.

I'll die, someday. But not today. I have to sit in this office ignoring May's message and wondering what to do about the stupid balloon payment that's due on the house in three months.

I need a snack. A snack helps everything.

I have a challenge here. The challenge isn't getting past Fanny. Fanny is an impassable wall of chain-smoking faith, assaulting me with Jesus' great love for me and the heady aroma of menthol every time I pass. No, Fanny is not the challenge.

The challenge is to see if I can get to the break room and back without encountering any kindness. I can suffer pain, I can take cruelty, but if someone is nice to me, I'm undone. The women in this office have banded together in a Kill Me With Kindness Campaign that started a year ago and continues indefinitely. I'm not sure how much more I can take.

They sit in the break room and wait for me to come out of my office. There is a schedule, or maybe a lottery, like in the Shirley Jackson story. Somehow they figure out whose turn it is, and she stands up and accosts me at the coffee pot with something like, "Gentry, are you doing okay?" I look at whomever this is, and I think, yes, I was, I was okay until you were kind, until you were concerned, and now I'm not.

Unmanly tears well up in my eyes. I say "I'm fine, just fine." And whoever this is wraps her arms around me in clear violation of office policy on touching in the workplace that we all read and signed a few months ago, she pulls me close and I'm pressed against breasts, from very small to very large and everything in between. I have too much tactile information about the breasts of my coworkers thanks to these hugs. Some are too hard, some are too soft, and some are just right.

I don't hug back. I stand there frozen, unable to blink because the tears will fall. I'm ashamed of how good this feels and embarrassed about crying and relieved that I'm completely useless, or things could be awkward. Once released, I return to my office to drink my bad coffee and eat my processed, chemically flavored snack. They go back to the break room to decide who will do it tomorrow.

Today, the way looks clear. Fanny lobs up a "Gentry, Jesus loves you!" before I make it into the break room. But I appear to be safe from the huggers. Now, I have to hope that Terence from downstairs hasn't invaded the upper floor break room and purchased all the chips I like. He must have run out of quarters. I bag the last Ruffles, pour myself some coffee and get back to my office, sensing Fanny's ravenous gaze on my chips.

I made it this time. But I'll be back out, and they'll get me.

I appreciate the ladies in the break room. They don't just give me hugs, they give me food. Soup, casseroles, pie, cake, cookies. I keep it going in, even the sweet crap. I eat so I don't drink at work. I tried that for a month or two and I don't think my boss appreciated it. So I mark out my day in snack increments. That's my work survival system. So far, I'm still alive. But I'm fat. I look pregnant.

Oh well, at least my belly keeps me company.

Back in my office, my belly and I play computer solitaire and eat chips. That's basically what I do here. I started here almost two years ago. For the first year, I was so busy that I worked twelve-hour days fixing all the mistakes made by the last person who held my position. Now, I have very little to do. Most days are spent praying for a quick death.

When I first took this job, I was urged by my boss to "Move in, bring things from home." I brought in a newspaper every morning, wasn't that enough? But my lack of personalization was noticed and remarked upon, so I've culled items from empty desks to simulate habitation of my work environment. I'm hoping that a stress ball, a mouse pad that says "Is it Friday yet?" and a dusty cube of sticky notes present a successful masquerade of personal investment in my current position, but anyone who looks in my door can probably tell I'm a flight risk.

I hear my boss yelling out in the reception area. I used to believe Mel was the world's yelling champion. Then I met a woman who took the yelling prize until I came to work here and put on the yoke of Mr. Ben Hogan. He's the grand prize winner in the I Yell the Loudest Sweepstakes.

My phone rings. I hold it a foot away from my ear in case it is, indeed, Ben.

"This is Gentry."

It's not Ben. Whoever it is on the other line can't get something to print. How is she supposed to get the Whatever to print? The other Thingy worked well, why did I Monkey Around with her Thingies? She tries to print and it Spews Out Wherever.

I'm impressed with this woman's grasp of technical terminology.

"Um, you probably have the wrong printer selected. Would you like me to tell you how to change that?" No, she wants me to come out and just do it for her. "But I can teach you how to do it in about thirty seconds." She doesn't want to learn anything. "Please?" I would like to teach someone something, anything. No one here ever wants to learn anything. Ever. Oh, all right, if I have to, she'll allow me to get out there and show her the Thingy.

She will. Oh, and I leap, I scramble to get to her desk before she changes her mind.

She's grudging, but she listens and watches. While she's receptive, I show her how to access a spreadsheet she's avoiding. She's been emailing me data and asking me to enter it for her. I send it back and tell her I'll show her how to do it herself. She sends back snippy little refusals. This extremely important report has gone without updating for a month, now. But since no one in the company reads it but her, I think that's all right.

I open the spreadsheet. She grudgingly tries to use it, and after a time of my sitting with her, she's successful. "That's all there is to it?" she asks. "I don't have to do the math?" I explain about the formulae, how they do the math for her. "Oh. Well, that's handy." She smiles. She says thank you. My fingers tingle. I remember when my entire day was spent showing students how things worked. I can crest this wave of happiness for at least an hour, so long as I avoid my boss.

I stop in the reception area to find a magazine. I have my choice between a recently deceased old man, a pretty blonde and an overweight Republican. I choose the blonde.

"That's a good one," says Fanny.

I consider asking her if Jesus loves this magazine.

I won't read it, but I need it. I've developed a habit of putting a magazine over my lap as a shield for my useless and inert equipment. The magazine keeps it all warm, and keeps it all safe. When I don't have one on my lap, I fight an urge to keep my hands cupped over myself. If I start to do that on my way to the break room, that will really give the Kindness Ladies something to worry about. I wish I had one of those lead aprons that they put over you in the dentist's office when you have X-rays. I wish I had two, one over the front and one over the rear. That would work. But heavy, that would be heavy.

I get more and more weird every day. I won't be able to make the balloon payment on my mortgage, I'll become homeless, and I'll be one of those dirty, crazy men who wear athletic supporters outside their filthy clothing and sleep in the streets.

My boss bangs opens the door to my office. "WHAT THE HELL IS GOING ON WITH THE WEEKLY REPORTS!"

"What do you mean, what's going on with them?"

"WHERE ARE THEY?"

"They're due at ten?"

"Well they better not be LATE." He slams the door.

I look at my watch. It's eight-thirty. I go back to my card game.

I don't yell at my boss. As he reminds me every single day, he signs my paycheck. I need my paycheck. I sit here and play solitaire, obsessed with making the cards dance. That's what I consider my job duties to be, now, covering my lap and making the cards dance with occasional side trips out to the break room to amuse the staff and get more food.

I've been worrying about something weird lately. I'm afraid I'm getting fat all over, not just my belly. What if the back of me is getting as fat as the front of me? How would I know?

I could ask Phyllis. Phyllis. I can't figure out what she's doing in this office. She understands my jokes. I still tell a joke, once in a very great while, to Phyllis. She knows about the Sensitive Plant.

I win. The cards dance. I decide to generate the weekly reports in celebration. That takes seven minutes. I send them to print, and there's nothing to do.

Oh, I guess I could work on the SPAM problem. My boss is personally insulted by the amount of penis enlargement mail he's getting. I keep my face very still when he rants about it, I don't laugh, but I do need to figure out how this is getting through.

I take a moment to scan the subject lines. "Your woman will cry with pleasure." I remember that. "Ram her all night long!" One invites me to "Break the limits of ardor."

Fairly poetic for junk mail.

Sometimes at work I do more than eat, or play games, or bother Phyllis, or let myself be washed over by sexual nostalgia while setting the SPAM filters. Sometimes I sleep. But the phone rings or my boss barges in like he owns the place, he actually does own the place, but I think he could knock. Some of us are trying to sleep, after all.

He must wonder what to do with me, this employee who keeps the LAN running smoothly but never does any work. What can I say? I did it right and now I have to wait for things to go wrong? So I try not to sleep at work, because he'll come in and wake me and I hate that. Worse is when our demented Born Again receptionist comes in. She never knocks either. She thinks the best way to wake me up is with a rousing "Jesus Loves You, Gentry!" I wake up flailing, terrified she'll lay her hands on me.

I used to fear Baptists. I apologize for that, God. This Pentecostal receptionist makes me admire the open-minded tolerance of Baptists.

Bosch. I hate this job. Tick.

But now I have to go down to payroll to see May.

∽

There's something in a human being that makes a miserable person happy at another's misfortune. A cold comfort, but a comfort nonetheless, to see that these people have to work in the basement, and they have to work in cubicles.

At the very least, in my office I have a window with a panoramic view of the parking lot. I have a door. I can shut the door and stare out the window at the Harley dealership across the way, wondering what an apprentice bike mechanic makes per hour, and wondering if I could survive on it. Maybe. If I could go bankrupt.

The basement people are trapped in a rat maze. I'm disoriented. Where is May? How do these people do this? I keep poking my head in the wrong cubicles.

"Hey, Gentry."

"Hey, Terence." He snickers because I'm lost. At least I don't spend eight hours a day in the catacombs. Please stay down here, Terence. Please don't come up to the break room on my floor and leer at the women and loot all the good chips out of the machine. Eat the catacomb chips for a change.

I'm full of brotherly love today. And lost.

Maybe next time I have to come down here I should bring a ball of string and unroll it behind me so I can find my way back. Or some pebbles, like Hansel and

Gretel. I could use chip crumbs, but Terence would suck those up. “Hey, Gentry.”

“Hey again, Terence.” I refuse to ask him for directions.

Finally, I go into an empty cubicle, climb up on top of a desk and look over the top of the labyrinth. I see May’s long, curly hair. I sight out the path and set my system for getting to her, a left, two rights and another left, and there you go. “Hey May? You, um, wanted to see me?”

May raises her face. She has such a perplexed, serious expression. Her gap-toothed smile usually cheers me up, but she doesn’t smile at me today. She’s very, very stern with me in her lisping way. “Sit down, Gentry.” She says it like “Thit.”

“I, um, prefer not to.” I avoid sitting down here because I fear that somehow I’ll be restrained. I never eat anything down here, either. Not that I’m paranoid.

“Suit yourself.” She stares at me. “Gentry, what’s wrong?”

I stare back at her for a moment, think about my life, wonder where to start. And then I realize that she didn’t really ask me that. “You, um, called me. You’re supposed to tell me what’s wrong, May.” Things go wrong with the network, I get yelled at. That’s how it works around here. Doesn’t she know the system?

She gives me a look of disapproving sympathy. “Gentry, I do payroll. I know how much money you make. And I got a judgment filed, a garnishment, and I have to take it out of your check. This is serious.” And even though when she says it, it sounds like “Thith ith theriuth,” I don’t laugh. Because this is serious. The balloon payment on the house is due in three months. I’ve let them come in and take away everything. What more do these people want? They take away the stuff but they still want the money.

But this is a *judgment*.

I remember a Saturday morning, a man knocking on my door asking to talk to me by my full name. He wouldn’t hand whatever it was over to me until I showed him my driver’s license, the initials. I stashed the blue packet of paper with all the other bills I can’t pay. I don’t even look at them anymore. I just stash them. Once in a while someone calls to threaten me, and I send off a huge amount of money. Then, one envelope stops arriving at my house. That’s my current system for handling the bills. But the phone company is turning off my phone today, which is a good thing because the money is gone and now no one can call and demand any.

“Who is it?” She reads me the name, the amount. The stupid doctor. None of that was covered by insurance and I pay what I can, and they sued me anyway, they *sued* me, and I don’t know how I’m supposed to live if my checks get taken because I have to pay the stupid payment on the stupid house, I hate that house. "How much will they take?"

She tells me, and I feel the blood drain out of my face. I sit down and put my head between my knees.

God, this is bad. God, help me. I need help. Amen.

May pats my back, makes some sweet clucking noises. "You make lots of money, Gentry, way more than I do. Why do you have a debt judgment filed against you?" May sits upstairs in the break room and talks about her poverty in the most unabashed way. She's so poor that it's criminal. She once borrowed eight cents ("thenth") from me to buy a newspaper, and then made a point of paying me back. May can't understand why I have no money. Neither can I.

My money system has failed.

I make my way back to my office, Fanny shouts at me about Jesus, I go in and shut the door and sit down and contemplate my ruin. Because there's no money, none, I've sent it all away and I won't even have a stupid chance, now.

Someone knocks.

I push my hair out of my face. "Come in."

It's Fanny with a plate. "I brought these cookies home from church and thought you might like some, silly Gentry." And this is why I'm fat, now. Instead of telling her to go away and take her church cookies with her, I smile. I want the food. I'll eat anything, even Pentecostal cookies. But not in front of her, I can't eat in front of her.

As soon as she leaves as I shove one in my mouth.

Peanut butter.

I'm sick, I'm so sick. As I run to the men's room, I hear her voice behind me, "Jesus loves you, Gentry . . ." I'm sicker, then, at that. Why don't I sniff before I bite, anymore? I used to be so careful. I gag into the toilet, nothing comes up but just in case I stand there gagging until it stops. While I gag, I worry.

There has to be someone I can ask about this, some way to get advice, but every single friend I have is a priest or an English major. They think I'm pulling down a fortune here. Can I put in a quick call to the monastery? Ask the brothers for financial advice? I'd have to call the Vatican to find anyone with money in my church.

Who? Who have I ever known in my life who knew anything at all about money and how this all works?

No. No, I couldn't call him, I couldn't.

I always have a toothbrush in my jacket, always, and I put it to work with cold water, brushing until my teeth ache. I go back to my office and get that plate of cookies and take it into the break room. My fellow employees emerge from their areas like zombies, so demoralized they'll eat anything, even Pentecostal peanut butter cookies.

Fanny smiles at me. "Did you like the cookies?"

"I decided to share."

"Good idea, because you're getting a little tummy on you." She smiles. "Jesus loves you, Gentry!" I wonder if Jesus will still love me fat. I return to my desk to brood. Who can I call?

No. I couldn't call him, not him, no, never. Of all the people in the world, this is the last man I'd ever ask for help. I despise him. I know that's a sin, but God, throw it on the pile with all the others, the sin of hating this pompous, egocentric, patronizing, condescending, godless and unforgivably successful jerk.

Okay, I'll just get his number.

I have no idea where he works, though. Some place where he makes mountains of money, an office, a bank? I dial directory assistance. Even though I expect it to be unlisted, I get the home number. I write it down and stare at it. All right. I'll call the house and get his office number, but I won't use it. I'm only calling to get the office number. To have it. Not to dial it. Because I won't call his office.

"Hello, Michael here."

Why is he home? Idiot, because it's only seven AM there, that's why he's home.

"Hey Mike?"

"Gentry? Is that you?"

"Yes."

"How are you, fella? How the heck are you?"

"Um . . ."

"I can't believe it's you. It's been, what four years?"

"Almost."

"How are you? Eve, it's Gentry!" I hear her saying something, imagine her scary white teeth, rows of white stone, Arlington, is she smiling? I shudder. "Well, Gentry, answer me. How have you been?"

"Well, um, not . . ."

"It's so damn nice to hear your voice." When is he hearing my voice? "Gentry? Gentry, how are you?"

How am I? I'm useless, broke, in debt over my head and alone. I'm so desperate that I'm calling you, Mike, you of all people. "I'm fine, Mike, just fine."

"Great! That's good to hear. Any kids yet?"

"No."

"Well, you keep trying."

"What?"

"You keep trying, because Gentry, you were meant to be a father."

I'm undone.

"Gentry, are you okay?"

"Mike? No. I'm not okay. I'm in some trouble, here, this balloon payment on the house and I don't know what to do, someone's taking my paychecks, a debt judgment, and this stupid, I have no, I, this stuff, it's money and I don't, I can't . . ."

I can't talk any more, I can't choke it out.

There's a long silence. "Gentry?"

"What?"

"Are you asking me for help?"

"Yes."

His voice sounds undeniably pleased. "All right. I can help."

"You can?"

"Sure. Don't worry. Don't worry, Gentry. Who has your mortgage?" I tell him. He asks a few more questions, and his voice sounds like that night after graduation. "Okay. I'm going to make a couple of calls, see what I can get handled from here, and then I'll come right down there and we'll get the rest of it taken care of. Don't worry."

"You'll come down here? To Oklahoma City?"

"I'll fly down tonight." Why? Why would he do this? Why would he help me? "Just keep your cheese on your cracker. All right? I'll be there tonight."

My boss enters my office. He opens his mouth, then closes it. "Hey Mike? I, um, have to go. Here's my number at work." Ben's face gets redder and redder as I give Mike the number.

"I'll call you back with my flight information."

"Okay. Bye."

Help is on the way.

I sit, calm, while the yelling commences. "I DON'T PAY YOU TO MAKE PERSONAL CALLS ON MY TIME!" I listen, the boss yells about my excessive personal calls (this is the first one in a year) and moves on to something I've never even heard of. I think, what is he talking about? None of what he's talking about can possibly be my fault. His face turns scarlet, his forehead gets sweaty, the vein at his temple pops out, and then, it hits.

What did I do? I called MIKE.

The blind panic in my face temporarily disarms my boss. "What the hell is wrong with you?"

"I, um, have to cycle the backup tapes."

"Well, get to work, then." He leaves, and I try to figure out how to call Mike back and tell him that this was just a joke, just a very strange practical joke, ha ha, and the last thing he needs to do is come down to Oklahoma and bail me out.

And then I think about the balloon payment and the debt judgment.

My phone rings. I pick up my line. "This is Gentry."

"I brought you a sandwich, hon."

"What kind?"

"London Broil."

I groan a little. "How's the meat done?"

"Rare and juicy."

"Is there A1 on there?"

"Lots of it, and mayo."

"Phyllis, there are no words for my appreciation."

"My reward is to watch you eat."

We hang up.

∽

I spend part of the morning bothering Phyllis while she's working by signing into her computer and writing things she isn't expecting in her Word document while she's working in it.

Get out of here, she types.

Make me, I type back.

She laughs too loud so I have to stop. Mr. Hogan hates it when his employees aren't miserable. I make her cursor go crazy, and then she swears and I'm the one who laughs too loud. I let her work.

At lunchtime, I meet Phyllis in the break room and she feeds me. I give thanks for the sandwich. I give thanks for Phyllis. And then she quotes poetry to me in an elitist and literary fashion. Beef and poetry. To quote Lorrie Gilroy, it doesn't get any better than this.

I get away with training Phyllis about once a week. I've explained to our boss that as an English major, Phyllis has a difficult time with technology and needs all the help I can give her. We look as miserable as we can during the training sessions until he's out of sight. Then we play computer blackjack, and we play with the toys she keeps on her desk, and we eat. After snacks and games, I go back to my office.

We email all day long. We send each other letters of resignation written in English Major High Style. We critique each other's work. Phyllis found this one moving: "Mr. Hogan, Your obeisance to the gods of Mammon revolts me. You sign my paycheck, but your name is not written on my conscience, my heart, my soul. Yours no more, Gentry." She also liked, "Mr. Hogan, The unending chain of monotony that shackles my days here is broken only by the sting of your capricious and malicious tirades. Exeunt Gentry." My favorite of my own letters went something like this: "Hey Ben. The sky is not falling and I quit. Gentry."

Phyllis uses swearing and alliteration. "That we can hear the hideous howl of your harangues is a miracle, considering how deeply within your ass your head resides." "Bully me all you want to, you bilious bastard, you bombastic blowhard, but understand that my final check must legally be ready within twenty-four hours once I leave this shithole." I told her the contrast between high and low language added a dynamic quality to her sentiments, and was Shakespearean in its ability to communicate to a varied audience.

This is how we spend our time. Neither of us is in imminent danger of being named Employee of the Month.

Today we spend most of our lunch hour arguing over Lysistrata, which she wants to interpret through a modern filter. The conversation veers into denigrations of critical reading approaches. She accuses me of not being text-centered, and I say I've never been convinced that close reading is enough, that there has to be some consideration of political and historical context. I'm sure we sound pretty strange in the context of the break room, but all this is interrupted when Terence leans his perspiring face in to mine. "Hey, Gentry."

"Hey."

He stares at me. "You know, I can tell you hate coming downstairs, don't you."

"Pardon?"

"I can tell you think you're too good to come downstairs."

"I, um, don't like basements." Especially a basement with Terence in it, but I leave out that part.

"Well I'll tell you what. If you look out that fancy first floor window of yours and see a funnel cloud, I bet you hightail it down there pretty fast. You'll be praying for a basement if there's a tornado."

"If there's a tornado, I'll run outside and pray it takes me."

Phyllis laughs. Terence scowls. I'm serious.

This ends my lunch hour.

I pass Fanny's desk. "Hello, Gentry. What did you have for lunch?"

"Food."

She forces out an artificial giggle to disguise the gravity of her need. "What *kind* of food, silly Gentry?"

That was a direct question. I try to answer those. "Some type of sandwich. I, um, have to go."

Her ravenous face falls, disappointed by my vagueness. But she recovers. "Oh! Gentry, you have some mail." She holds out an envelope. Her bony hand, her acrid perfume, her hunger. I'm afraid to approach. But she has a letter, so I smile at her. She smiles back, oh, shudder, her scary teeth. I hold out my hand for my mail. Here it comes. "Jesus loves you, Gentry!" She smiles and hands it over.

This is the price of a letter.

I should be nicer, but I can't stand it. Fanny never eats. She feeds vicariously on food descriptions. Fanny smokes her lunch. She stands in front of the building, smoking and smiling and lobbing out praise grenades. She's on a Chain Smoking for Jesus Mission. Phyllis told me that she used to try to talk to Fanny because no one else would, but Phyllis soon realized that Fanny only has two conversational topics. She likes to talk about the Ritalin conspiracy, and she likes to talk about how all "the gays" are moving away from San Francisco to Oklahoma City. Why they might do that, we have no idea. Maybe Fanny envisions some sort of a hyperactive homosexual migration to Oklahoma, this tolerant and culturally vibrant slice of the heartland, this land of milk and honey, oh Paradise, Oklahoma.

I sit down at my desk, smiling as soon as I see the return address.

Dear Gentry,

Here's a joke. Why was Helen Keller a bad driver?

Because she was a woman. Hah. Hah.

Wanted to let you know that we are headed up to Canada at the end of the week to visit Vicki's people and do some camping, etc. All the usual bullshit, pardon my French. Speaking of, boy do I get sick of French up there, believe you me. Wish you could come with and speak English and catch more fish than me. Hah. Hah. Maybe some summer you can. We will be up there for the rest of the summer. So don't look for a letter until September. But we'll send postcards. I'll try to find you some good ones. Hah. Hah.

Vicki sends her mushy wishes. Walter and Renata are little shitheads as usual. We are expecting number three. Just wanted you to know. You're playing catch up now, little buddy. Time to get busy. Are you shooting blanks? Hah. Hah.

The best to Miriam.

Sincerely,
Lawrence Gilroy

Lorrie always signs his letters in this formal way, "Sincerely, Lawrence Gilroy." I can see why. I know so many Lorries that I might get confused and not know who sent me these letters full of profanity, obscenity, and vulgarity.

I miss him, God. My stomach aches with it.

I usually write back to Lorrie and Vicki, filling the page with words that reveal nothing, lies of omission. God forgive me.

I fold up the letter and throw it away. My phone rings. I let it go to voice mail. The only problem with voice mail is that eventually I have to listen to it. Back in the days when Miriam would call me, that could be grim.

Miriam called me for a variety of reasons. Sometimes, she called to talk to me about her health problems. She ate healthily, drank sparingly and exercised compulsively. During the first two years we spent together, she had a relentless and vigorous constitution. Hangovers aside, I've never been sick a day in my life that I remember, and she made me feel wan and sickly in comparison.

But after her surgery, she called the office to share symptoms with me. I particularly enjoyed this when the symptoms involved any kind of a bodily fluid or discharge, any drainage from anywhere, especially before lunch.

Sometimes she called to tell me about an argument she was having with someone. She had a few arguments every day just to stay in practice, I think. I could actually lay the receiver down on my desk and still cringe at the volume of her voice.

Sometimes she called because there was a home repair problem. She liked to describe household malfunctions in apocalyptic terms. She would call to say, for instance, "THE FUCKING DISPOSAL IS SPEWING!"

"Spewing? What do you mean, spewing?'

"WHAT THE HELL DO YOU THINK I MEAN! WATER IS JUST SPEWING ALL OVER THE KITCHEN! IT WILL JUST TOTALLY FLOOD THE FUCKING KITCHEN IF I DON'T GET SOMEONE IN HERE RIGHT NOW!!!"

"Turn off the water under the sink and leave it. I'll do it."

"THAT'S JUST LIKE YOU TO TELL ME TO WAIT! YOU DON'T UNDERSTAND!! THE HOUSE WILL FLOOD IF I WAIT FOR YOU!!"

If I were lucky, at this point she would hang up.

The problem was not with my home repair skills. I fix things once, and I fix them right. That was the problem. If I fixed things, I deprived her of one of her great joys in life. She engaged in heated battles with service people, battles pitched at top volume, involving accusations, withheld payment, warranty claims and threats of litigation.

Eventually, the service people would call me at work to tell me that they wouldn't set foot near my house again, ever, under any circumstance, litigation or not. The man she hired to clean our gutters actually threatened to burn down the house. So I would apologize, and send off some money, and then go home and fix whatever it was.

I don't mean to imply that Miriam called me at work about unimportant things. Sometimes, she would call me for something critical, something crucial, enormous, something of magnitude. Those conversations went something like this:

"I need you stop at the store on the way home." She would dictate a list to me. It had to be a very specific list, because if she were vague, I was likely to come home with some pretty odd things. "Are you LISTENING? Did you write it DOWN? Read it BACK."

I would read it back, a review, I guess, and we would discuss the finer points of brand names and ounces. "Hey, um, is that it?"

"Yes, that's IT. Just get it RIGHT."

"Hm. I, um, have to go. Bye."

I kind of miss those tender, meaningful conversations we used to have about was it supposed to be skim or one percent this time, or exactly which type of sanitary protection it was that she needed, depending on whatever was draining at the moment. And being told not to "fuck it up." "You're such a FUCKUP, Gentry."

I don't miss that.

I listen to my message. It's from Mike. He'll arrive after midnight. I'd better take a nap. God, I need a little rest, all right?

My head on my desk, and oblivion.

~

"Gentry?" I fly to wakefulness. Phyllis says, "Sh, sh. It's okay. I'm going home now."

"I wasn't asleep."

She smiles. "Of course you weren't. Are you staying late?"

"Yes." I have a small amount of work to do, and I've managed not to touch it for the last eight hours. Nine, actually, because in the words of my boss, "I DON'T PAY YOU TO EAT YOUR DAMN LUNCH!"

Phyllis puts a plate of hot something on my desk. "Here's your dinner, hon."

"You're too good to me."

She shakes her head. "Try to get some sleep tonight?"

"Okay. Bye." She leaves.

I say my grace. God, I want to say thank You for her, too. Thank You for Phyllis. Amen. I eat, too fast, too good, too full, too fat.

I need to import an enormous database, so I go out and get that started. I should put the server in my office, but I put it in a locked closet out by Phyllis to have more excuses for proximity. Then I stand in the kitchen area to thoroughly wash and dry the plate. The office is empty. Everyone in here strains toward the clock at the end of the day. The last fifteen minutes are spent in silent contemplation of the minute hand. I think everyone joins in a common prayer, Catholics, agnostics, Baptists, atheists and even Fanny. We pray fervently for deliverance, we pray in unison, and God hears our prayers and makes the workday end. There is a stampede of grateful souls to the door, and the office is deserted by 5:01. Amen.

I scrub the sink, rinse the sponge, leave it beside the clean sink in accordance with the wishes of whoever it was who cared enough about it to have taped up a note that says, "Please don't leave sponge in sink." This note has been altered with a marker to read "Please don't leave spooge in sink." Terence probably did that.

I put the clean plate in Phyllis's desk drawer.

The empty office frightens me. I feel like I slept through a nuclear attack and the whole world is like this, I am desolate and alone, except for maybe a band of snake-handling, gun-toting, survivalist Pentecostal Jesus Freaks.

This is Oklahoma, after all.

All right. Get a grip.

This import will take a few minutes. I'm not paranoid, but I hide in my office. I hide partly in fear of the imaginary freemen, and partly in fear that Fanny will sneak back and shout at me concerning Jesus. Fanny did that one night when she supposedly forgot something, she snuck up here and scared me to death, "JESUS LOVES YOU, GENTRY!" echoing in this graveyard. I thought the rapture had come and we were the only two left behind. Me and Fanny. I find myself listening for the hoof beats of the horsemen of the apocalypse.

God? Why does Fanny do this to me? She assaults no one else. Why, God? I love You, I hope You love me even though I don't give You many reasons to love me. But still. Does she think I need the comfort of her reminders?

I'm tired. I curl up under my desk.

∽

I wake up confused, as usual.

The cleaning lady is in here, startled at finding me compressed into the leg space. I scramble to get out of her way before she hits me with an electric broom. "Look, mister, you in the way. My job is to get clean here." She's impatient and Vietnamese, and in my experience this is a dangerous combination. "You need to get going, mister. I have to get clean."

Me too. But how? I can't confess.

I notice on my way out the door that thanks to my nap, my cheap suit looks like it was tailored from wadded up brown paper grocery sacks. Great. I check my cheap watch and I see that I don't have time to go home to change. Oh well, Mike will see it all, soon, this wrinkled suit, this swingy haircut I have, this fat stomach. The mess of the bills. Why did I call him?

I kick myself all the way to the airport. Hard to do in a manual shift. I consider crashing the car on I-240, but instead of a fiery, cleansing death, I'd become a mentally alert but physically paralyzed charity case. The state would hire someone like Fanny to care for me. Jesus loves you, swallow your pureed spinach like a good little lamb, oh the horror.

The plane gets in at midnight. It's been four years. Do I remember what he looks like? I remember him as being very selfish. I look around the airport for people who look selfish. And here he comes, silver in his hair, as tall and arrogant as ever. He looks right through me. His eyes scan the crowd, then return to me. He lopes over.

He's ten feet tall.

Oh, Mike, why this mauling and shaking and hugging, I don't know why I called you, why you, and you have to put your stupid hands on me, and then I realize, I'll submit to this man's stupid hands on me, because of all the men in the world that I know, this is the man who can help me.

"Gentry, you look great."

"I look like crap." I don't sleep, I have poison for breakfast, I drink a hundred cups of coffee a day, I eat too fast and worry too much. It all shows.

"Fine, you look like crap."

That makes me laugh. "Mike, you look great."

"I always look great. I pay money to look this great." And we both laugh. "How old are you, anyway?"

I have to think. "I'm thirty-one, almost thirty-two. Do you have another suitcase?"

"No, this does it." He hefts a bag that probably costs more than I made last month, and we walk out to where the ancient Toyota waits at the curb. The look on his face. I think he's trying not to laugh out loud. "Where's the Wrangler?"

"It's a CJ5."

"Where is it?"

"Broken."

I don't help him with his bag, and he maintains a straight face as we putter down the road, never exceeding fifty, even on the freeway. He looks out the windows. "It's flat here." That would be an understatement. Oklahoma is no great scenic wonder.

"Hey, Mike."

"What."

"No, I mean, I forgot to say Hey." He nods, looks out the window.

There's a Man Etiquette rule, here. Having had my heap of a car commented on, I'm supposed to inquire about his. It's the rule. "Do you still have the Saab?" Please, Mike, have some mercy.

"No. I got rid of that. I thought about giving it to one of the kids, but the damn thing was always in the shop. The transmission. I have something else, now." Thank you, God, that he spares me the particulars of what he drives, because something tells me it's not a thirteen year-old orange Toyota coupe.

This is incredibly awkward. "Hey Mike?"

"Are you saying 'hi' again or do you have a question?"

"I have a question. About Kathryn." My throat constricts, but I choke it out. "I wonder if things are still okay. With her . . ." I have to swallow and try again. "With her health."

"Kathy's in great shape health-wise. It was a little bit of a scare but she's all fixed up. Don't worry about her."

Don't tell me not to worry about her, Mike. Just because you never did. I'll always worry about Kathryn. I grasp the steering wheel tightly so as not to punch him in the mouth.

This is going great.

"Gretchen was sorry she missed your call."

"Hm."

"How long has it been since you talked to her?"

It's hard to speak with my throat like this. "Four years."

"You haven't talked to her once since you left Oregon?"

"No."

"Do you want to talk to her?"

Oh yes, Mike, the last words I heard her say still echo in my head. I never, ever called, I had too many problems letting go, calling and tearing open my heart was all that I needed, I wanted to stay hardened up and scarred over, but I'm no longer afraid to feel it, and I would, so much, Oh Dear God, after four years, I'd love to hear her voice.

"I'd like that."

"Well, I know she'd like that. She still talks about you. She misses you. She's grown up." I can feel his eyes on me as I drive. "So, I thought maybe you'd bring Miriam with you to the airport."

"Um." I swallow. "Miriam is gone."

"Gone? Is she out of town?"

"No. She's, um." I swallow again. And then I clear my throat. "She's dead."

"She's *dead*?"

"Yes."

"Are you *serious*? What the *fuck*? I mean . . . I'm sorry." It's silent for a couple of minutes. "When did she die?"

"A year ago."

"She's been dead for a *year*?"

"Almost."

"Have you had the unveiling?"

I am surprised. "You know about unveilings?"

"I've been to a few. I'm in finance, remember? I know lots of Jews." There's a pause while I concentrate on driving and how much I hate him. "Gentry, that was a joke."

"Oh."

"Sorry."

I still hate him. "The unveiling is Sunday."

He nods. "You know, it's a real shame you never had any kids. But you're still young."

"Pardon?"

"You're still young, you can try again for kids."

"Hm." That might be difficult, since I'm dead, too.

I drive him through Nichols Hill, the neighborhood Mike would live in if he lived in Oklahoma City. But of course Mike is too smart to live in Oklahoma City. "So, you live here?"

"No. I drive through to keep the Neighborhood Watch alert." He makes a sound like a drain clearing. It may be a laugh.

The nice neighborhood ends long before we enter mine. I pull in the driveway and cut the engine. I want to say something before we get out of the car. I want to tell him that I'm a terrible person and I deserve the worst. I deserved Miriam. But I don't think I deserve this house.

"Hey Mike? I always hated this house. I never wanted to buy it."

He nods.

The front door takes us into a quandary. We have to decide whether to go up or down. When Miriam was alive I used to stop here and listen for her, listen for one of her exercise tapes or the sound of her shouting into the phone about what a failure I was. Wherever she wasn't, I went.

Miriam is dead, now, so we go up. The living room is empty except for some shelves and a massive but useless hearth. The hideous drapes are always shut against the heat. When Mike sees them, he jumps back a little. "Jesus Christ."

"There used to be furniture in here."

"Did it help?"

"Not really."

He nods.

Don't look at the shelves, Mike, please, don't notice the shelves. I distract him by showing him the kitchen, a symphony of bile organ colors. He looks at the room. He looks at me. I lift a hand, let it drop. "We were going to redo the kitchen. But we were, um, too broke."

He nods.

I show him the bathroom off the dark hall. "You have to jiggle the handle after you flush." I used to think I could fix anything, but I can't fix that. "This is the only bathroom."

"You bought a *one-bathroom* house?" The way he says it.

The bathroom is the high point on the ugly tour. I switch on the light fixture that resembles the stylized heads of two small French poodles, sprinkled with gold dust and hanging from chains. The fixtures are a flesh-toned, Band-Aid color. He looks at the patterned tub enclosure that resembles faux vomit, the Formica countertop that looks like gilded vomit, the buckled vinyl flooring that appears to be flattened vomit. "It's a great place to throw up."

He nods. I switch off the poodle heads.

I stop at the hall closet and extract some fuzzy blankets. I find a pillowcase figured with what look like decaying banana peels and shove a flattened pillow in it. There are photos in frames in the hallway. Mike looks at these, looks at me. His expression.

"She's dead," I remind him.

He nods.

We stay out of the bedrooms. There are two. They're empty, but they used to be furnished. One was furnished with an ironing board. The other was furnished with Miriam.

And now, it's time to take him downstairs to the family room. I have a deep and personal aversion to the term "family room."

We step into the spongy pile of the high/low multicolored sculpted shag carpet. It's dark and cramped and gloomy down here. The ceiling is low, not so low that he can't stand at his full height, but Mike ducks reflexively. I pull my sleeping bag off the remaining couch, the one Miriam had when I met her. "Hey Mike? This is all I have to offer."

Somehow, it's the lack of a bed that shames me most.

"I like to sleep on the sofa. Don't you? Being married makes a man appreciate sleeping on the sofa." He sits down. He looks at the television. He looks at the ironing board. He looks at the wet bar. "Do you have anything to drink?" I go behind the bar and pour a couple. "Do you have any ice?"

I'm past ice at this stage in my life, but I go upstairs to find some. "Here you go."

"Cheers." He takes a sip, nods. "Nice." I have a crappy car and an ugly house, but I buy good poison. He has one more sip. I have a gulp. The burn and bliss and comfort. I will live.

"Gentry, can I ask you something?"

"Anything."

"How do you feel about selling this house?"

"I'd rather burn it down."

He nods. "Arson is risky. Safer to sell it."

My turn to nod. We say goodnight.

I undress in my study. The closet is the size of a gym locker, but I keep my clothes down here so I don't have to go into the bedrooms. Mike is already snoring lightly. I sit down to play some games at the computer, because I know I won't sleep. I never sleep at night.

My arms stiffen with anxiety, and my heart races. I forgot to iron my shirt. Every night, I iron a clean shirt. It's part of my system. I need to iron a shirt.

Well, forget the system tonight. I can't iron a shirt and I can't stare at the television all night, either. And I can't go out there and have another drink, because I can call the man and whimper at him until he comes to help me, I can give him a guided tour of this pit I call home and make him sleep on a couch, but I'm not going to creep out there and get another drink. I'll stare at the computer until my eyes burn and shoot infiltrators until my hand hurts.

And that's what I do.

Eventually, it's time to hit the carpet. I roll up in my sleeping bag and put my face in the pillow and pretend it still smells like the woman who gave it to me. Miriam had no idea where this pillow came from. I kept it hidden in the closet down here.

God? Why? How did I do this to myself? How did this become my life?

I left Oregon and I wanted a clean start. I wanted to start over. I was going to do things differently. I wanted a life with nothing to be ashamed of, nothing to regret. And what did I do?

I need to confess. Will confession cleanse my soul, God? This is attrition, not repentance. I'll never repent what started all this. I feel shame, despair, guilt. But as for regret, I feel none, none at all.

I know what You want. I submit.

I'll remember.

II. REMEMBERING

Every person to whom awful things happen responds in the same stupid way. We blame ourselves. We do this because it's preferable to see yourself as a self-destructive idiot than to see yourself as a victim, a punch line in the joke of life.

So I decided the things I'd suffered were my own fault. I was a self-destructive idiot who had deliberately ruined my own life. I had morally bankrupted myself so that I was unfit to teach. I'd also subconsciously arranged to have myself beaten to death. I could come up with no explanation for why I'd done this, I didn't remember how or why it happened, even who did it to me, but I derived some comfort from the idea because it put me back in the driver's seat. And things were going to be different, yes sir. I was starting over.

I drove south and east, because I wanted to see Sandy and Paige and their kids, Lucy Rose and Byron. As I have said, these are English majors. Paige was pregnant and if this child was a boy his name would be Shelley. I needed to get down there to avert this name and to start a new job, because the last new job had been such a great idea.

The trip was calming and terrible. Calming because all I had to do was drive. Terrible because of the agony of trying to get something in my stomach. Calming because the further south I went, the more I could take the top off my Jeep, my old CJ5 that had never, ever let me down. Terrible because the pain medication for my broken parts made me groggy, so I stopped taking it and my pain sharpened. So did my mind.

It hurt to move, it hurt not to move, but it hurt most of all to think. My mind wouldn't leave it alone. I went over all of it, one mistake after another, every error, every moment of drunkenness and longing and stupidity that put me on the road that led away from Gretchen and Bosco to wherever I was headed.

It hurt and hurt and hurt. I pretended it was the ribs.

At a drugstore somewhere in the heartland, I stopped for Ace bandages to bind up things. Lorrie told me how to do it before I left, after the doctor in Astoria told me that to immobilize my ribs would be to risk pneumonia. Lorrie told me I wouldn't be able to stand it, and he was right about that, just as he was right about everything. I felt like I'd die if I didn't have something holding me together, so I bound up my midsection with the help of a kind drugstore clerk who started to cry when she saw my bruises and wouldn't take my money.

I had plenty holding my mouth together. I had so much rubber and metal in there I couldn't take it sometimes. My breath went shallow and I had to pull over and stick scissors in my mouth and cut it all open and concentrate to make myself breathe. I'd grab a handful of the rubber bands and lace it all shut again, tight, until the next panic attack.

Breathing hurt. Moving hurt. Remembering hurt.

Once I taped my ribs, the pain dulled. The road and sun and flatness conspired to hypnotize me. I slept in the Jeep when I had to, but there was so little difference between asleep and awake that usually I kept going.

My inability to drink anything sweet made caloric intake difficult because as the days stretched on, everything began to taste sweet. Tomato juice first, but that was understandable. Tomato juice was always right on the edge of undrinkable for me. But then it was milk. Plain iced tea. I knew I was in trouble when beef broth tasted sweet. All that remained were water and coffee, but at a certain point, even water tasted suspicious.

Not good.

I drank whatever I could through a straw, and let out alarming amounts of whatever I drank. Why did so much more come out than went in?

I tried to keep my teeth clean as I starved, but digesting your internal organs gives you bad breath. I spoke as little as possible, and attracted interest only in that I looked so filthy and deranged that I always had to pay for my gas up front. When my debit card was snatched up by a zealous mini-mart employee, I drove 160 miles out of my way to get my account unfrozen. I took out enough cash to buy another car if that became necessary, and put that in my wallet.

I probably wasn't thinking too clearly at that point.

I've mentioned Oklahoma. I know Oklahoma is closer to Oregon, both in the alphabet and on the map, than Georgia. But I went to Georgia first because it is gentle and rolling and humid, and I needed to see her. I needed to look in her eyes to see if the betrayal was still there. When I left her last, it was.

In Becca's eyes.

I was what's called a late bloomer, but blooming requires certain conditions and my adolescence had lacked a key environmental element. There were no girls.

I started my all-boys high school as a small kid, both in age (12) and stature.

Small but fast. I stayed small until the summer I turned fifteen. I spent my senior year of high school growing. It was dramatic enough to start the school year at 5'3" and end it at 5'8", but it was good training for the summer, when all my parts got together and said, "Hey, Gentry starts college this year! Let's give it one last push and make sure he looks like an idiot before he gets there!" My arms and legs stretched to ridiculous lengths. My chest and shoulders expanded until I felt like I couldn't fit through doors. My neck got long and thick and dumb-looking, as did a certain other part of me. That grew from respectable to remarkable, proof that God has a sense of humor because what did I need all that for?

My oversized addition rose and fell according to its own priapic whims, further humiliating me. I couldn't tell where my arms and legs ended, and this unfamiliarity with my points of termination meant that I crashed around, knocking over chairs and tables. I'd become the kind of bony geek I'd run circles around. A true confidence booster, that growth spurt.

"You'll grow into yourself," Mel assured me. But I had to buy clothes. Mel and I didn't know when it would end, the expansion. He made a rare allusion to my genetic origins, saying, "You might be headed for 6'4" and 220, so we'd best be prepared."

I never wore anything that fit again.

Yes, I had the Ichabod Crane thing going on, with my baggy apparel and my big Adam's apple. But the dorm food was starchy and bountiful, and I started to fill in. I located my hands and feet again, so the windmilling and flailing around lessened. The girls thought I was sweet, and my Dear God, I never thought anything was as sweet as those girls. All those girls, to a recent graduate of a Jesuit boarding school.

We'd all arrived early for a week of orientation. I spent it walking around in a state of mild short-circuiting because half of the students on campus were female. This miracle of gender math. I was content to look at them, to watch how they moved and hear their laughter and enjoy the limber, modest way they picked up things from the floor. Most of all I wanted to position myself downwind and smell them. If one brushed against me in a hall, it sent me in search of solitude for a good half hour.

I would be lying if I said I didn't want more knowledge than was offered by observation and occasional hallway collisions. But I was young and profoundly ignorant. I had no idea what I wanted from those girls until I saw Becca.

Becca was Botticelli's Venus, except she appeared to me clothed at a drinking fountain, not naked on a clam shell, propelled across the sea by the gentle breath of Hesperus. I followed her into an upper-division poetry class and sat down, a tall, shy boy of sixteen with high SATs and low social skills who hadn't taken a class with a girl since I was ten years old. I kept my lips tightly clamped, hoping if I said nothing, not one word, no one would notice how stupid I was.

But with Becca, it didn't matter. With Becca, I knew exactly what I wanted—to remove any obstacle between us, class, age, experience, and most of all clothing, to strip all that away and find her softest places. I knew it was my one true purpose, that in fact God had created me specifically to do this. I understand now that this was a biological imperative, but at the time it seemed like a spiritual calling of the highest order.

It never occurred to me that it was sin.

Three times a week, I sat in Poetry of the Romantics and listened to her read aloud in her measured, cool, sweet Southern voice. At night, she was mine in boy's dreams that sent me to sleep hopeful, woke me gasping, arching. I prayed like a mad man that she would be mine.

Some prayers do get answered.

Becca turned twenty that October. I stayed sixteen. She didn't know this because I didn't tell her. I didn't tell anyone, not her, not any of our friends, no one. I knew this was a lie of omission, I knew exactly what I was doing. I kept it up until she scared me to death by bringing up marriage. Becca came from a good family with a lot of money and she was twenty years old. I was nameless, penniless and so young that what we were doing was against the law, and she wanted to get married. In a stroke of brilliant adolescent reasoning, I avoided her, hoping she would never find out why. But she found out.

She found out from my roommate, Daniel Shaw.

They married, eventually. They had a little baby girl with red hair, Ariel Rossetti. They had each other. But I had Becca first. Oh Becca, with her wavy red hair and fair freckled skin. I couldn't think about it for too long. Becca with a baby at her breast.

Gentle, rolling and humid.

∽

I'd never visited the Shaws in Atlanta because of some unfortunate behavior on my part on the night before their wedding, three years before. When I say unfortunate, I mean unforgivable.

We gather for weddings because we all believe in church weddings, but I was surprised to get the invitation to Becca and Daniel's. This invitation held an envelope within an envelope, with a liner and some tissue and a pre-stamped card to RSVP ("Gentry and Guest"), simply worded and printed with the kind of raised lettering I associated with diplomas.

The whole thing seemed important.

I went through all the pieces and extracted the actual invitation, which I laid down on the floor of my apartment. I sat down and stared at it for a few minutes, picking it up to hold under my nose. It even *smelled* important. I laid it down to stare at it some more.

I finally called Paige and asked her if she thought I should go. Paige said she would personally kill me if I didn't go. "My mother is going to meet us there and watch the kids so we can actually enjoy the ceremony and go to the reception like grown-ups, so you *have* to come." I reminded her that I didn't have a guest, I hadn't had any guests so to speak since my last week of graduate school. Could I possibly bring Bosco? Paige said, "No, your dog cannot be your date, Gentry. I don't care if you come alone, you still have to come to this wedding."

I mailed away the little card and when the summer came, I drove Bosco to North Dakota, where he remained with Mel, then drove south.

I was going to the wedding because I wanted to be forgiven. I hoped the invitation meant I was. It was my second visit to Becca's little Georgia hometown. My first was over spring break of my freshman year when she brought me home to meet her family. I'm not known for making dynamic first impressions and that visit was no exception. I was surprised to be asked back under any circumstances.

I had one other small objective in attending. I'd had some long and lonely years in Detroit, only Bosco keeping me company. I hoped somehow to convince Becca to forget the wedding and leave with me. If I couldn't convince her, I planned to kidnap her and take her away. That was my one small objective.

Becca was wise to my objective, I think. She refused to talk alone with me. I decided to carry her off. The night before the wedding I sat in the motel room I shared with Kevin, conquering cowardice with alcohol. I got drunk. Very drunk.

Sandy dropped by. Sandy was the man who encouraged me to go get Becca in college ("Don't be a coward, Grasshopper!"), and the man who encouraged me not to go get Becca on the night before her wedding ("Don't be an idiot, Grasshopper!").

I was a coward. I was an idiot.

I told Sandy what I planned to do and he listened, nodding, gradually adding alcohol until I was immobilized. Daniel dropped by, then. I only wish Sandy had been able to immobilize my mouth before I said those things to Daniel. I apologized to him for depriving him of the gift of her virginity. I said that. He didn't even hit me. He was that forgiving. At that point I would have preferred being hit to being forgiven, but he just looked at me with tears in his eyes because he was the forgiving type.

I would never forgive him.

I was sick at the ceremony, but at least I was quietly sick. I'm sure I looked a little haggard, there, maybe even deranged with mourning. Becca's mother kept looking at me like I was going to erupt or something. I was only trying to live through the organ music.

My Dear God.

I sat on the groom's side next to Sandy. Paige came down the aisle and stood with a sweep of bridesmaids. And then came the most beautiful children.

First, a solemn little dark-haired boy in a grey suit walked down. He carried a pillow. He counted so he would walk the right way, and he had a Band-aid on each of his thumbs. He was followed by a troop of blonde and red-haired girls in white dresses who kept pushing at each other and shedding flowers, shoes, hair bows, and gloves.

I'd never seen anything as beautiful as those children.

Certainly it was paranoia, but I felt like all Becca's relatives were looking at me. Right at me, like I was an itinerant who had dropped by the church looking for odd jobs and found myself shoved into a pew. I endured the stares of all the people on Becca's side, the cousins and aunts and uncles and grandparents, all those tall, beautiful people with their ocean-colored eyes and shining hair in every shade of red and gold. Staring at me.

Daniel's side, where I sat with Sandy, was just as full, though not quite as splendid. Daniel came from dun-colored stock, blue and green eyes, light hair. They didn't shine, but both sides of the church brimmed with all the golden families, all the friends, all the noise, all the happy tears. The joyful noise.

I looked at all of them and I wondered, who would sit on my side of the church if I got married? Mel would perform the ceremony. God, please, who would be there for me? Five friends from college?

The music changed. We stood. Becca appeared on the arm of her dad in a long white dress that bared her shoulders and fell like foam around her ankles.

Sandy caught me and held me up and kept me standing. I lived through it.

It was thought best to bodily remove me from the reception.

After we left the motel we'd taken over and trashed in an elitist and literary fashion, I went home with Sandy and Paige to Norman. I spent time there drowning in self-pity. I drank myself through it. The oblivion system. This lasted for a week. I lived through it. I went back to North Dakota and Mel and Bosco.

In the fall, Bosco and I returned to Detroit.

~

I carried in my shirt pocket the birth announcement. I dug it out and reread the return address. Hadn't she asked to see me? Hadn't she? Having babies seemed to put people in a forgiving mood. I prayed for it to be so.

Amen.

I drove through Buckhead Forest, a winding, tree-filled neighborhood every bit as enchanted as the name would imply, looking for their house number. It didn't help that every street was named Buckhead. Buckhead Way, Buckhead Place, Buckhead Drive, Buckhead Lane, Buckhead Avenue, Buckhead Loop, Buckhead Loop East, Buckhead Loop West, and so on.

I finally found the Shaw home through sheer luck, or maybe it was repetitive circling. I parked and stared at the front door. Their house was small. Nice, but small. For some reason that made me feel better. The thought of hauling myself up the walk to a place like Daniel's family home was too defeating.

I got out of the Jeep because I'd attract police attention if I sat staring at the house for too long. I was skinny and tired and filthy and my jaw was wired shut and there I was, and if Becca ever thought it was a shame we didn't last, she wouldn't think that anymore.

I knocked.

Oh, Dear God, there she was, and she was still so beautiful, even more beautiful, and when she looked at me, she wasn't angry anymore. She was horrified.

God, if it took this to get the betrayal out of her face, then it was almost worth it. Almost, but not quite.

"*Gentry*? Is it really *you*? What *happened* to you?" I tried to say something, and she put a hand over her mouth. "Oh my God. Oh my dear God. Oh *Gentry*." She fell against me and I buried my face in her hair, the sweet scent of night flowers. My hands remembered where every pin would be, I pulled them out and her curls fell down like the sunset over her white shoulders, and she hugged me and cried. Oh Dear God, I gave thanks to You, for Your mercy, and for hers, Oh Dear Lord.

Amen.

She stood up straight, wiped tears from the corners of her eyes, recovered her composure. As if a decision had been made, she took my hand and swiftly led me through a living room, a hall, a bedroom, into a bathroom where she started the shower. "You need to give it a minute to warm up." She withdrew and closed the bedroom door behind her.

I peeled away my clothes and threw them out into the bedroom so I didn't have to smell them. I could still smell myself. I unwound my ribs, then removed the rubber bands to exercise my jaw's connective tissue. That was the high point of any day, those small repetitive movements that were safe to make with my jaw. Also, I could carefully brush my teeth. I'd left my last toothbrush in a gas station after it fell on the floor, so I used someone else's. It was probably Daniel's. I decided he might want to boil that toothbrush.

I inspected the stitches that were such a torment that I'd caught myself scratching my privates in public. A nail clipper worked to snip the threads, and I yanked them out. Four times ouch. It looked like someone tried to castrate me with a dull knife and missed.

Thank You, God, for that miss.

The shower ran hot and strong. I stepped in and leaned back to wet my hair, awestruck that I could raise my arms without feeling like I was being run through with a knife. I could even lift them over my head, a miracle, God, to be able to raise my arms. I held them up and out and let that hot water wash over my armpits, thinking of Whitman and almost crying with joy.

I had a small orgy with soap, shampoo, and a rough sponge. I removed an entire layer of skin. I shaved twice. The water was tepid and I was pink and raw and shining by the time I got out. But to be clean, really clean, it takes more than the kinds of soap you find in a beautiful woman's shower. I didn't get clean that day and I may never be truly clean again.

But I tried.

When I emerged from the bathroom, Ace bandages in hand, I saw a crucifix on the wall, my empty duffel bag on the floor and a clean pair of shorts on the bed. I stared at one, then the other, then the other. Underwear, bag, cross. These three things seemed to be profoundly interconnected, symbolic portents of something greater to come. My whole body trembled.

"Gentry? Are you dressed?" The door opened and she put her head in. I was embarrassed, not by my nakedness, she'd seen all that, but by the bruises all over my ribs. She leaned against the doorframe, a tall, barefoot woman with full lips and curling red hair and a dress the same color as her eyes, all of her perfect and framed by the dark wood trim like the work of art she was. "You're skinnier than you were as a freshman."

I held out my filthy bandages like a cured leper offering them up to his savior.

"Do you want me to wash those?"

I shook my head.

"Get rid of them?"

I nodded.

She took them away. I gave thanks for women. Amen.

One side of the bedroom floor lifted up and tried to tip me over while I was putting on my shorts. I sat down hard on the bed, shivering, and studied the polished plank flooring, wondering how it did that, thinking about fulcrums and leverage and hinges and the fact that I was tired enough to hallucinate. I needed to orient myself. I pressed my palms into the bed. Above me the ceiling, beside me the wall with the cross, below me the bed. The bed where Becca and Daniel slept together every night under a cross as man and wife. I imagined him asleep on his side, her behind him, her warm belly fitted into the hollow of his back.

I burned with a sick, shaking jealousy.

She came to sit beside me. Put a hand on my back. "I heated up some red beans and rice. That's my specialty, if you remember."

Saliva poured so heavily into my mouth, I was afraid I would choke. But I needed to explain, and I had to keep my teeth clamped tightly as if the bands were still in there, lacing it shut. "My jaw is broken. If I eat I might wreck it. The doctor will have to re-break it and rewire it and I'll have ten more weeks in this instead of four if I don't do everything right."

"But you can drink, right?"

I nodded.

"Okay. I'll get the blender going. You can have a beans and rice smoothie." She kept stroking my back. "How did this happen?"

"I don't know. I can't remember."

Our eyes met, held. Hers were full of tears and history. I'm sure mine were full of shame.

"Look at those eyes. You need sleep more than you need food." She pulled back the sheets and laid me down. The pillow smelled like her hair. I rolled over and buried my face in her soft scent. When I'm lucky, I sleep without dreams. I slept fast and hard that day in her bed because I felt safe.

Amen.

~

And here was a beautiful dream.

Someone rubbed my shoulders, soft, but strong, my shoulders that had been like iron for the last three months, and I felt no pain. And then someone rolled me over, gently, and kissed me, gently, and I knew it was real, because I wouldn't feel these braces in my mouth, I wouldn't smell her hair if this were a dream.

I opened my eyes. Becca sat on the bed next to me, looking down. "You've been asleep for about two hours. Ariel woke up and had her lunch and played, and then she went back to sleep. You missed her."

"Hm. You picked such a nice name." I wanted to go back to sleep, to dream some more, that's what I wanted. More of that dream. I felt my eyelids slipping shut. "Becca? Did you love me?"

"I almost died of it, I loved you so much."

"Me too, Becca. Me too."

Oh, I wanted to sleep. But something happened, because something always happens. I did what I was not allowed to do. I closed my eyes and put my hand on the back of her head, I wove my fingers into her hair until they were part of it, until they were rooted in her. I drew her down for another kiss.

She pulled away.

The bed shook. I opened my eyes to see as wonderful a sight as there could be in this world, Becca drawing her dress over her head, Becca removing everything else, Becca in all her freckled, golden red glory. The softness of her, the perfection. And she did the same for me.

Oh Becca, please tell me this is not a dream, please tell me I'm awake and you're here, naked, and kissing me like this, please. I must be dreaming because, oh, onto me, please, into you, oh Becca, this is better, so much better, because I don't hurt you any more, do I.

You're beautiful and golden, your breasts are astonishing, larger and full and the nipples are darker, now, and is it all right if I touch you? Tell me, tell me. Tell me what you want.

There, is that what you want? You like this and I do too, I can feel myself move in and out of you when I touch you here. You're doing all the work, but I like that. You like this, you do.

Then, touch me here, please, softly, barely, because we both know what we want, now, don't we, and it should always be this way, two people who know what they want.

Oh, yes, please come, come for me, Becca, I never knew how to make you come while I was in you all those years ago, and now I know what you need, oh, how you sound, your eyes, this is Paradise, and when you come, the beautiful white milk, it pours out of you, your breasts are weeping milk, it runs over your stomach, down you, into your red, beautiful hair, into my hair next to yours, and I cry too, I can't wait, mine too, oh here I am . . .

That was too beautiful to be a dream.

∽

I woke to Ariel Rossetti between us.

"Gentry, this is Ariel. Ariel, this is your Uncle Gentry."

"Hey, Ariel." Ariel was a peach. She was full of creases and dimples, and covered with golden fuzz, just like Becca said. Her feet. She had miraculously fat little feet. "Look what you did, Becca. How did you do this? This is . . . *amazing*."

"This is just a *baby*." She smiled, bemused. "I thought you might have even found your own by now, Gentry." Tears filled Becca's green eyes. "Were you even looking?" I nodded, but couldn't speak. I thought, Becca, maybe someday I'll tell you about Oregon, what I looked for and what I found, what I left behind, but for now let me look at your sweet baby girl.

Ariel smiled at me, dazzling, just like her mother, but without teeth. And then she changed her mind, she screwed up her face and complained in a restrained and ladylike fashion like I was supposed to fix it. "Well, what do you want, Ariel?"

"She's hungry."

"What does she eat?"

Becca laughed. "Me, of course."

Hm. I could be in trouble, here.

She fastened her mouth on, it was more of a clamping-on procedure than I'd have imagined, if I were sick enough to have imagined something like this. She sucked on her mother, something I'd avoided because how could I do that with all this metal in my mouth, and besides I'd probably fall into a chasm of fixation if I did. But Ariel wasn't a grown man, she was a tiny round peach. She got to work on there. And then I saw it, I actually saw it, filling up the breasts the way Kathryn described it, I could see it.

"Does it hurt?"

"At first, when the milk comes down. But it's a beautiful pain." Becca smiled that sacred, secret smile women make for the painful things they love. To see that smile. Ariel made the softest singing noises. She was happy, and Becca was happy, and I felt honored to see it.

Ariel's little pink starfish hand played absently over her mother's other breast. I saw it then, the white drops, the white milk Becca wept when we, oh God, she wet her tiny fingers in the drops. I took the baby's hand and kissed it. It was sweet. Sweet. I waited for the gag from sweet liquid in my mouth. It didn't come.

I lay back and put a pillow over my face.

She pulled it away, shook her head, smiled. "Every man in the world wants to do that, Gentry." Becca was amused. "That's what they told me in my lactation support group. I don't know why, but you all want to see what it tastes like." I had to kiss her, then, kiss her with my mouth full of sweet milk and metal, because Becca you were my salvation. I'd have kissed you so much more sweetly if the inside of my mouth weren't in shreds, I would have.

And then Ariel reached up and got a good purchase on my hair, my hair that fell all over her while I kissed her mother, and she yanked, hard.

Ouch.

"Ariel, I hate to ask you this, but when does your dad get home?" Because we were all in there together and we were naked, except for Ariel, who, being a modest young lady, wore a diaper.

"Nine. Dan has a night class on Mondays."

We lay there for a while longer while Ariel sucked away and then pulled back to look at me on the other side of her, and she stretched out the nipple like a rubber band . . . I had to get trussed up, I needed to deal with my rubber bands or I'd be in trouble.

I was in trouble.

But this was nice, this being naked in a bed with a woman and a baby. This was so nice it hurt my heart. This wasn't my woman or my bed or my baby. I needed to get out of the bed.

Becca looked at me and her face shone with grief. She studied my eyes. Did she hate herself for this? "Gentry, take another shower before dinner. Your hair always carries the smell of sex, you know."

And I thought, Yes, I know, Becca. You always said so. But I was so happy to remember being with you. I let my hair get long in college so I could have it fall in my face, smelling of you. I'll take a shower right now, though.

Right now.

When I came out, dressed this time, I could hear her in the kitchen singing. I had forgotten that about Becca. Her low voice, the way she made every song sad. Sandy heard her sing at a party and said, *"Your woman can sing, Grasshopper. It's a sad and beautiful thing, her voice."*

I took a moment, then. A moment to pretend I was walking into my kitchen, finding my wife there at the table, robe open, our baby at her breast. I wanted that moment.

She looked up and smiled. Yes, a beautiful moment.

"I'd better get dressed before Daniel gets home."

The moment was over.

Becca had a blender. She served me in courses, an illustration of the type of kind and gracious woman she was. I prayed over each glass, I gave thanks to God, to Becca, to the blender. Amen.

I craved an apple, but what I'd started with was a glass of liquefied celery. "I bet you need fiber." I needed everything. I had liquefied celery and then a glass of milk and then I drank down a full glass of liquefied beans and rice through a straw.

The belch was magnificent.

She laughed softly, and sat down at the table across from me. She had on that ocean colored dress, and her hair was a darker red at the end of each long curl, where it was wet from her shower.

I had to say it. "You go to a lactation support group."

"Don't you tease me." We were both laughing when we heard the car pull in, the car door slam. We looked at each other. The kitchen door opened. Daniel walked in and saw me seated at his table, holding his daughter, talking to his wife. His jaw fell open.

"Gentry? My *God*. Is it really *you*?"

Something scalding and terrible exploded behind every square inch of my skin.

This was shame.

"Why didn't you *tell* us you were coming? Beck, did *you* know he was coming?" She shook her head no. There were tears in Daniel's eyes. He grabbed me, it hurt my ribs and I slopped my dinner all over us but we didn't care. "Three years, I can't believe it, three years, can you believe it's been *three years*?" He was crying hard, did I look that bad? He whispered in my ear, "Tell me who it was. I'll hunt him down and kill him, all right?"

I thought, Daniel, if you knew about this afternoon, you would pay him to finish me off.

Oh God, why didn't You let him finish me off?

God, how can You ever forgive me? I can't forgive myself.

Daniel was the forgiving type. He was the kind of young man who took the younger and more vulnerable under his wing. I was a special admission. By some lucky miracle, or maybe it was careful planning on the part of the dean of student affairs, I ended up with Daniel as my roommate. When I had a question, he answered it. When I had nightmares, he woke me and sat with me until I could sleep again. He watched out for me. He took care of me. And he did it even though he loved Becca.

I had no idea. I was too young and stupid to know what it meant, how he watched her face, listened to every word she spoke when we were in class, in the dining hall, at coffee shops after class. Sometimes I brought her into our room when he was asleep. The torture it must have been for him, trying to sleep, waking up to her red hair on my pillow. But Daniel forgave me.

And when I stopped seeing her, frozen by fear of her knowing anything about my life, he helped me hide. He forgave my cowardice. We sat up and drank and I confessed everything to him. I told him how old I was. I told him my uncle wasn't my uncle. I even told him my name. I trusted him.

I spent that summer in North Dakota driving combines and plotting, planning, rehearsing my apologies, figuring out how to get her back. When I returned to school, Daniel sat me down and explained that she would never take me back. When she came back she wanted nothing to do with me. I waited it out, sure I could change her mind.

When she returned, it was to him, not to me.

I moved in with my friend Kevin and moved on. I moved on with a vengeance. She gave me cold, pained looks while she finished school. She never forgave me. I never forgave myself. But Daniel had Becca, so he could forgive anything, even my having her first. I doubted, however, that he would forgive what I'd done that day.

And all the days that followed.

Daniel would get up in the morning and I'd stay asleep on the couch because of the time difference, cocooned in the sleeping bag that Becca washed for me, my face in a pillow she loaned to me, one that smelled like her, and I pretended to be asleep until he left. I didn't want to look at him in the morning.

Once he left, I'd sit at his table and watch his wife move around the kitchen in her robe the color of celery. I craved a stick of celery. I'd listen to her hum, and she'd watch me with a hurt smile while I drank coffee through a straw. I didn't want him to know about his wife's smile.

While he was gone, I spooned food into the mouth of his smiling baby daughter. We shared, you see. Becca laughed. "She's too young!" I cooed to her and encouraged her and congratulated her for her cleverness and her appetite and her sticky perfection. I made her laugh, a husky little gurgle. I didn't want him to know about his daughter's laugh.

I rose from that table, full of food and the laughter of a baby. And Becca laid Ariel down for a nap, and then I laid Becca down, and we did all the things only Daniel was morally entitled to do with her. Wonderful, wonderful things. I didn't want him to know about those wonderful things.

God, forgive me those wonderful things.

And then I'd sleep more, to rest up for lunch and the afternoon nap. And the afternoon nap, being longer, was even more wonderful. When the afternoon nap was over, I'd stand in the shower, the water as hot as I could stand it, scalding my skin. I swore to stop.

I would dress. He would come home. We'd all eat dinner (actually I drank my dinner) and then I'd do the dishes. Then we'd sit and drink iced tea, relaxed and happy and calm. Every time I looked at her I'd remember her eyes rolling back in pleasure, the roses blushing across her cheeks and chest, her scent like cedar, the sounds she made, her wetness, that milk, her hair down all over me. How strong she was, the miracle of her sheer physical stamina, what she could do, what she could take. I'd look at her and it would all wash over me.

I'd look at him and feel that searing eruption of shame.

I couldn't stop. Dear God, I couldn't stay away from her, I couldn't leave her alone. I spent the hours I wasn't in her bed thinking about what I'd do when I got there, what I would try next, anticipating just exactly how it would feel, what she would sound like. The blushing, yielding girl of my youth was gone. She met my desire with an athlete's strength, rearing back so hard she almost bucked me out of the bed. I took her to the place where she lost her composure, her dignity, sobbing, pleading. It was the most beautiful sound of my life. I would think, remember this, Gentry, remember this because it might be the last time and you were too stupid to understand that the first time around.

I kept waiting for her to turn me away. She didn't. We cried in that bed, and she swore at me, and I begged her, I begged her for what I knew she couldn't give me, to bring the baby and come away and make a life with me. We could go to Texas, my bad Vietnamese would get me a teaching job there in five minutes. We could live on the Gulf and raise Ariel and have our own, finally, together. Oh please, Becca, please. I begged her.

"Why *now*, Gentry?" She cried and cried.

And little Ariel would wake up and come in with us and I knew that it wouldn't change. Becca could never take Ariel away from her dad, it would be wrong, all of it was so wrong, God, but I had to do it, I had to ask, because I was crazy with need and want and Becca was what I needed and wanted. Dear God, forgive me the wrong of everything I do, all wrong. Always, what I want is so wrong.

Amen.

On the morning of the fifth day, I sat in the Jeep and she stood there with the baby. I was leaving before the morning nap. She wouldn't stop me, so I had to stop myself. Even I have limits. She put her pillow in the back of my Jeep. I looked at her. "Tell Daniel goodbye for me."

She nodded, crying. Ariel reached out to me, Dear God, why do you do this to my heart? "Tell him goodbye, please, please come with me . . ." Oh I had to ask one more time, forgive me, God. "It's one word. One word is all it would take, Becca." She shook her head, cried. "Say yes to me."

She clamped her lips shut.

We were even. When she wanted to get married, I couldn't. Now that I wanted to, she couldn't. It seemed like there had to be something to give her, something I could offer to show her what I was ready to do. "Becca? Do you want to know my name?"

She looked at me, pained. "I know your name."

I kissed her lips, I opened them up, this wasn't the kiss I wanted to give you, Becca. I had a different kiss in mind.

I kissed her good-bye.

∽

Before I was eleven, I sought out company when I could. Trips next door to see the neighbors, the community of church, the easy, violent companionship of other kids who played in the streets because no one cared if we ever came home. We called each other by our last names because there was a challenge in it. That was fine by me. But that was childhood.

When I was eleven, the only human companionship I trusted was Mel's. Everyone else was encouraged by whatever means necessary to leave me alone.

The boys I went to high school with seemed anxious that classmates would know who they were. It was "bad form" (they used phrases like that) to allude directly to your family origins, but if a boy had a ridiculous first name and a formidable last name, he was probably someone. I had the ridiculous first name, but no last name of note. I was no one. Again, that was fine by me. I only wanted to be left alone.

In college, we were all striking out, giving the slip to our pasts. Within days of arriving, I no longer wanted to be left alone. I wanted friends and I found them. As I drove away from Becca, I wondered why I'd moved to a part of the country where none of them would ever visit, let alone live. I chose Detroit. I asked to go that far away from my friends.

Why had I ever left them?

∽

Paige and Sandy Sanderson lived in Norman, Oklahoma. Sandy was close to finally getting his Ph.D. at the university. Paige decided to delay getting her own until their kids were in school. The only problem with this plan, as far as I could see, was that the kids kept coming, each bumping back her doctorate another few years.

I'd visited the Sandersons three years before, to drink myself into a stupor and then return to sobriety. And like a dog crawling somewhere safe to heal, I'd returned. The Sandersons were right where I'd left them, on McCullough Street in a sort of a Grapes of Wrath, Okie Dust bowl, Uncle Tom Joad's cabin. It looked tumbledown and picturesque, squatting next to a creek and near these other shantytown structures, all inexplicably appealing to me.

Paige ran out the door, smiling. She was so pretty and short and pregnant and happy to see me, but she took one look and started to cry. "Oh, Gentry, Becca said it was bad, but I didn't realize it would be as bad as all this." I was tired of pity, yet I craved comfort. "You look like a famine victim." She pressed me against her round baby stomach. It hurt, but it felt so good. Too good. I felt myself panic. I thought Oh, Dear God, am I going to do something stupid here, too?

I let go of Paige.

She took me into the hot kitchen. I smelled something spicy and unidentifiable on the summer air in Oklahoma. Paige was always cooking for us in college, and I never knew what any of it was because the recipes were her mother's and she got tired of explaining what was what. So we came up with a system whereby she cooked and we ate in perfect ignorance. All her recipes took a lot of ingredients and a lot of preparation, and she had to stop chopping in order to properly gesticulate, as if every conversation held within it a game of charades.

"Where are the kids?"

"I have them enrolled at the U preschool over the summer. Sandy brings them home." She sent a sweet and piercing look my way. My longing had to show. "They'll be home around four."

I could wait until four.

She distracted me with tales of far-flung friends. Dexter, first. I remember Dexter for many things, but will never forget his passionate master's thesis on Blake's erotic imagery, a work so moving that after I read it, I had to lock myself in my room for an hour to commit phantom acts. "Dex slings drinks in a place called the White Swallow." Hm. This was new for Dexter. He was living in Baton

Rouge, dating someone who was either a drag queen or an ugly woman. "I hope for Dexter's sake it's a drag queen, as he'll never hear the end of an ugly woman from Sandy." She told me that Kevin was teaching high school English and attempting to marry some Presbyterian money in Kentucky, which I hadn't known from his letters.

"Hey Paige? You say he's marrying money?"

"Just a big pillar of Protestant cash," she told me.

"I thought he was marrying a woman named Parker."

"He's marrying into Mammon. But at least it isn't Baptist money. Drink this." She handed me a glass of her concoction and a straw. "Becca warned me that I'd need straws." Paige didn't look at me funny for praying over my glass. Paige was Catholic, Sandy was Catholic, Daniel was Catholic, Becca was Catholic. So were Dexter and Kevin. I had all Catholic friends down there, and they were a tight unit, bound as they were by a deep fear of Baptists. They let me, a northerner, into the club because I was Catholic, too. Nobody made fun of me for that, nobody was embarrassed, we all knew the secret handshake, we knew the drill, we were all in this one together, we all mistrusted Baptists and we all prayed over our food.

She looked at my wasted body. "Gentry, if you'd drink malts, you'd be as fat as me." She said this with affection. Paige was pregnant, not fat, and Paige knew I couldn't drink anything like that. All of my friends knew about my food troubles. All of them knew, none of them cared. "I can't believe you took that job. That's one shabby little school, Gentry. Wait until you meet my neighbor. She teaches there. I think she's representative."

"Hey Paige? I don't plan to work there for long. I just need . . ." And I couldn't say the rest, but I didn't have to. She hugged me again.

"I know. I know. At least it isn't the esteemed Hillsdale Free Will Baptist College. Sandy talked about checking there, but I told him forget it. All these years we've lived here, I've never seen one person go in or out of that building." And then she sat down across from me and looked at me, and took my hand. "What happened, honey?" She waited. "How did you get like this?"

"My jaw's wired shut."

She shook her head. "I'm not talking about your being skinny. I'm talking about your being so beat up." I slurped away at the straw, relishing the taste of onions. Even though they tasted sweet and that was sort of a chunky liquid, those onions tasted good.

"Becca said you wouldn't tell her. But won't you tell me?"

I would never talk with my mouth full.

"Don't sit there and fill up your mouth to avoid talking to me. What happened to you?" Oh, I forgot, she knew all my tricks. How many cafeteria conversations about parents and hometowns did I chew my way through, to avoid talking about what I didn't want to remember? "Please, tell me. I'm asking how you got hurt." A direct question. I tried to answer those.

I swallowed. "I don't remember."

"You're telling me you don't remember this happening to you?"

"The last thing I remember, I was walking into my landlady's kitchen."

"And then?"

"I woke up in the hospital."

"All of a sudden you were in the hospital?"

All of a sudden. That was a game we'd played with each other in college, but I was too tired to play it. I drank my soup. Paige waited, watching my face.

I finished the soup and set the glass on the table very carefully. I decided to tell her, because Paige would get it out of me if I didn't. "I had a box of stuff in my arms. I told Bosco to stay, I'd be right back. Everything after that is gone, until someone shining a light in my eyes and saying my name. I tried to move and couldn't. I couldn't make any noise. It hurt too much to breathe. Someone said something like, 'he's coming out of it, put him under' and that was it."

She shook her head. "Honey, who would want to *hurt* you?"

My stomach rolled. I reached for my scissors. Where were my scissors?

I stood up so fast the kitchen chair flew back and hit the floor. I knocked the screen door off the hinges and ran to the Jeep. They were on the passenger seat. I shoved the blades in my mouth and cut my mouth open and held onto the Jeep and heaved and heaved and heaved until I thought my stomach would come out.

And that, so help me, was the moment it happened.

Because I lifted my head and looked down into an inquisitive little face. I stood there with snot running out of my nose and vomit in my hair, retching up spit with rubber bands in it, and she smiled. She smiled at me. I thought, Dear God, how could any human being smile at someone who just threw up in a driveway?

I should have known that anyone who could smile at misery was someone who would devote her life to creating it. I should have climbed in the Jeep and driven away as fast as it could go. I should have used the scissors in my hand to slit my own throat, right then and there.

"You must be *Gentry*!" For a tiny woman, she had a huge voice. "I'm *Miriam*!" She said this to me like it should mean something to me. "You know. Didn't they *tell* you about me?" My knees started to go out from under me. "Oops! *Steady*!"

Miriam took my arm and grabbed my duffel bag and steered me back into Paige's kitchen and sat me down. The two of them fixed me up. Paige put a cold cloth on the back of my neck and brought me water and a toothbrush so I could brush my teeth. Miriam laced the new rubber bands in a business-like and proficient manner. I wanted to say, are you a dentist? But I was too tired to ask.

I apologized about the screen door and Paige said I could fix it later and she brought in my sleeping bag and Becca's pillow and put me to bed on a cot in the utility porch right next to the dryer. I didn't mind, wherever, so long as I didn't have to sleep in the Jeep.

I slept.

~

Sandy's voice came booming into my dreams. "Great God in Heaven, Grasshopper, what the hell *happened* to you?" I opened my eyes to his face above me and he hugged me so tight it hurt my ribs and I cried out. He let go. I lay back down and he studied my face, oh don't look, I wanted to say, don't see me like this. "By God, look at this face. This face is fucked up. If you looked in the dictionary under 'fucked up,' there would be a picture of this face."

The visceral pleasure of a lame joke told by a smart friend in an accent that blended Georgia, Arkansas and Oklahoma. I'd never heard anyone else, anywhere, who sounded like him. He shook his head. "Daniel told me, but I didn't believe it. Let me see the hardware." I bared my teeth. He whistled. "Shit, Grasshopper, look at you." He pulled up my shirt and studied my ribs like a map. "Who did it? Tell me, Gentry."

"Nobodaddy."

He smiled. "Ah, you liberal artist, you." In years past, Sandy would have picked me up and carried me around a little. He had a tendency to do that. But I was too tender for it.

People said Sandy and I looked like brothers, but I always felt like his smaller, darker shadow. We called Sandy "The Poetry Stud." He would get into fistfights over verse. Sandy was almost a Poetry Priest instead of a Poetry Stud. He had wanted to be a missionary. *It was a close call. They almost got me.* He was concerned that I, too, would be snatched up by the Call, even though I told him I hadn't seriously considered the priesthood. He took one look at me and said, *Bullshit. I hear God calling your name, and I'll be damned if I let you go to God without tasting the Devil first.*

Oh Sandy, I tasted the Devil, and he tasted like Hell. I pulled down my shirt.

"Did you at least hurt him back? I know you must have kicked his ass. Tell me you kicked his ass." Sandy pulled me out of the cot and hugged me again, but gently. "Grasshopper, your hair smells like puke."

"Thank you."

He laughed, lifted me up and carried me into the hot little kitchen full of the smell of something delicious, where he gently set me on my feet. Paige handed me a screwdriver and a drill, and I got busy fixing the screen door. "Hey Paige? Can you put tandoori chicken in a blender?"

"I can blend up whatever you want."

A voice cut the air. "I have some GREAT recipes you could use." I hadn't even seen her over there, watching everything with her large eyes.

Sandy snorted. "Recipes? Your recipes?" Paige made a little sound of warning, but he continued. "I've been your neighbor for a year, Miriam. I've taken potluck with you. You may have noticed that Grasshopper here is a little on the emaciated side. Paige plans to fatten him up. And I'd never want to insult a lady, but I'm afraid that those productions you refer to as 'recipes' might put him off his feed forever."

Miriam's face darkened. I ignored her because it was time to remember the good old days. The days when I could still drink, oh I could never drink, but we remembered the days before I knew that. All those nights on the town in Buckhead with our fake IDs, Sandy and Daniel and Dexter and Kevin reminding every bouncer at every door, every bartender to card me for every drink. "What was your drinking name? We bought his ID off a Cherokee guy from Oklahoma. What was it?"

"Billy Ward."

"Billy Ward was a legend at darts. We would all be roaming around the smoky depths of some dive, trying to get laid, and Grasshopper would go off to the boards. He'd end up with a hundred dollars." That was how I got my spending money. "And *then* he'd get laid. All Gentry ever had to do to get laid was hold still for a minute." Miriam made a small noise like the hiss of a nocturnal animal. "Miriam, I sense your disbelief. I speak the gospel truth. Grasshopper had to fight the women off with his great big stick."

"Shut UP, Sandy." Paige frowned.

He shrugged. "Wife, I remember the trail of girls who showed up on campus looking for Billy Ward. The Trail of Tears, I called it."

"Sandy, you're racist, sexist, and culturally insensitive."

He raised his arms. "As a white male, it's my cultural legacy to be an ethnocentric asshole. And I'd appreciate it if you'd respect that." Paige looked like she might be ready to throw something, so Sandy turned his attention to me. "Do you remember when I carried you to the nude bar? You were an ungrateful young apprentice. I was broadening your horizons, Grasshopper. It was my duty as your mentor, and you wouldn't even take a little peek." I was sixteen and just getting used to girls with clothing on. The possibility of them with it off sent me into a nosedive of panic. "You punched me, you altar boy."

I did. I knocked him across the street. The only way Sandy would forgive me for hitting him was if I either got a tattoo or pierced my ear. "We must cut our bodies, Grasshopper. We must practice the art of self-mutilation." He said it was my punching penance. I chose the piercing penance, because I thought I could let that grow shut. But I didn't. The farmers in North Dakota laughed at me, the brothers laughed at me, Mel laughed at me. But I liked my earring.

Sandy still practiced the art, I saw. He had so many holes in his ears, I expected to see a little line of print that said, "Tear at perforation." He must have been doing a piercing penance of his own. Other than that he hadn't changed. His hair was long, but his hair was always long.

"Hey Sandy? What else have you pierced?"

"NOTHING! Don't you give him any ideas!" Paige looked upset. I got up and lowered my face into the dark blanket of her hair, which smelled, as always, like warm milk and some perfect spice. Bliss. I went over to where Sandy sat at the table and put my hands on his shoulders and lowered my face to his hair. It had taken me weeks to work up the courage to do it in college. I'd never in my life wanted to smell another man's hair and wasn't sure what this meant for my future. But I got drunk and did it one night, buried my face in all that hair because if I hadn't I'd have ended up hitting him out of sheer frustration. He smelled dusty and wild, like a pheasant feather warmed by the Dakota sun. The smell made my heart burst.

I'd hit him anyway, knocked him down outside that strip bar.

I remembered the day after. The night had gone on, we'd pierced our ears, sworn our fealty, drank ourselves sick. That next morning, I woke groaning with the pain of a hangover on the floor of his dorm room, his boot nudging me in the ribs, his gigantic hand like the hand of God extending a cup of coffee down from Heaven towards my suffering body. *Drink it.* I registered that his left eye was swollen shut. I was too miserable to speak.

He made me sit on his bed and sip until I qualified as awake. *Are you awake now?* I nodded. He sat down beside me, put his arm around my shoulder. *Grasshopper, you hit me last night.* His arm around my shoulders was strong, not heavy. No menace. *Gentry, I want you to understand something. No matter how many times you hit me, I am never going to hit you back.*

I cracked wide open.

Ten years later it was his turn, sitting at his kitchen table, cracking open. He stood up and pulled me in. "By God, I've missed you. You little hair sniffer, I love you so much, I swear." He was crying. Paige was crying. I would have cried but Miriam's eyes were on me, wide and dark and almost orange, glowing like coals. I didn't want her to see this, to know how all of us were broken by our love.

I had to bring this moment to a close.

I looked Sandy in the eye. "No one could shoot himself in the heart three times."

He dashed his tears away with the side of his hand, drew himself up to accept the challenge. "Are you saying a WOMAN could bring him down? A mere WOMAN?"

"How could you shoot yourself three times in the heart?"

"SACRILEGE! HERESY!" He chased me out the kitchen door, and I knew he would catch me, and I knew he would hold me down while I struggled. He would make me repent. But gently.

I could do it all, but only gently.

"Daddy? Daddy?" A small voice rose from the kitchen door. "Why are you killing Uncle Grasshopper?"

The Sanderson children stood, hand-in-hand, on the wooden steps.

∽

The Sanderson children were Heaven, and they were Hell.

I found this out as the weeks progressed.

Lucy Rose was five years old. Her desire for lace gloves and plastic shoes was, I was told, typical. But I was unsure how my earnestly feminist friend Paige managed to produce this girl. Sandy blamed his mother. "These things skip a generation." Paige rolled her eyes and didn't make a fuss about it.

Lucy Rose insisted that I play with her. "Uncle Gentry, it's time for you to *play* with me." This meant that I had to play with toys. I told her I didn't know how. Lucy Rose didn't believe me. "Of *course* you do. Now sit down *here*. We're having a *tea* party." I learned the tea party social rules, which involved holding the tiniest cup imaginable in one of my huge hands ("Hold out your pinkie, Uncle Gentry! Like this!"). In the palm of the other I had to balance a tiny plate of whatever was served to me. Paperclips, pebbles, broken crayons, little yellow Legos, cockleburs. The food had interesting names, like "jelly butter pie" and "mix-a-cola cherry tacos." I was instructed in how to thank her for it ("Miss Lucy Rose, thank you ever so much for inviting me to this beautiful tea party today.") and how to pretend it was something delicious as I mimed eating ("Mmmm. This is the best popcorn soup I ever tasted."). Sandy took a series of photos ("I'll call it Grasshopper Takes Tea.") because he found the whole thing so amusing.

So, that was tea parties, and we had quite a few.

We also played Barbies. I usually got to be Ken, unless we had a Barbie shopping trip emergency, in which case I had to be another, less affluent Barbie who stood around and wished she could afford all the great clothing that Lucy Rose's Barbie got to buy. As with the tea parties, Lucy had the thing tightly scripted. As long as I learned my lines she was happy.

Lucy Rose was Lucy Rose. She was coy and flirtatious and demanding, and nothing at all like Gretchen. She had her mother's brown eyes and streaky blonde hair like her father. But when she was silent, or walking away from me, the thinness of her arms, the swing of her hair, I felt a giant roar threaten to break out of my head.

God, there was nothing to take away how much I missed Gretchen.

So that was Hell.

∽

Byron was easier. He took after his mother, so he was a dark boy, but generally sunny, not really Byronic, not passionate and heroic, but how Byronic could a child his age be? There were times when looking at him hurt, and I had no idea why. He expected me to play, so we played with various injection-molded people, threw balls around outside, looked at the creek, caught bugs. Byron was fascinated with bugs. This reminded me of Gretchen, too.

Hell.

One day, I took him to the duck pond. We picked our way around dog piles, holding hands. He liked to hold my hand. We braved the edges of the green, sluggish water to look at the turtles. "Those snappers will take your EN-tire finger off, Uncle Grasshopper." We kept our EN-tire fingers away from the snappers.

Everywhere I looked that day, there were dogs, romping and rolling and shaking and sniffing and barking, chasing balls and catching Frisbees. Byron liked the dogs, the bigger the better. We petted a few of the friendlier ones and threw a few sticks. I thought of Bosco and the beach. I wondered who was throwing his sticks, who his playmates were that day, what breed my big shaggy bear of a dog was rolling around with on the sand, gentle and huge and smelling so bad.

Hell.

I took Byron home and cleaned his shoes.

Byron had great toys. My favorite was this system of plastic channels that we could hook together to drop marbles through. I thought this was such a neat toy that I went to the toy store and bought three more, so we could expand our structure into an enormous one that dominated the tiny living room. Paige was tolerant. Sandy walked in and said, "Grasshopper, you should have been a plumber!"

I tried to use the marbles to explain the concept of gravity to Byron. "Hey Byron? Things fall down. Have you ever noticed that?"

"Not if they fall up."

Hm. Falling up. We tried it out, the falling up thing. We decided that things did fall down, after all. "That's the law of gravity. The marbles fall down because of the law of gravity." Byron repeated "the law of gravity" several times, and he was quite serious, grave in his own right about this idea. We played awhile more, we chased marbles. We lost a few. I invited Lucy to join us, but she voiced disdain for what she called "boy toys." I decided to review. "Hey Byron? Now what was the law about the marbles?"

He thought, hard. He looked at me, his face stony from the effort, the concentration. And then he smiled. "Never put them in your mouth."

"That's absolutely correct. I'm proud of you, Byron." The kid was young, after all. I decided I didn't understand the preschool educational process, yet. Maybe when I had my own.

If I ever were lucky enough.

The hell was children. But what a beautiful hell they were, even if they made me miss her so much that I wanted to get in the Jeep and drive back, every hour of every day. I knew it was wrong to be away from her, wrong in a way that was fundamental to everything.

I knew I had no right to go back there. None at all.

~

Miriam returned every day. She tolerated our stupid jokes, our repetitive stories, our endless arguments about our fallen favorite. She sat through one long session of "all of a sudden" that made us all laugh so hard we had to stop because it hurt my ribs. She listened to stories about professors and places and people she'd never known. She barely said a word.

"How about when Gentry was talking about Melville?"

"Yes, and he said, 'Um, you know. That, um, whale thing.'"

It was hard to laugh with my mouth wired shut.

"Remember when he had to read that poem aloud in class, and he got sick? Just ran out of the room and barfed in the hall? Why did that poem make you sick?"

"Remember when he almost killed himself on the stairs?"

Miriam's ears pricked up. "He almost killed himself?"

"My protégé here used to sit and eat grapefruits when he studied. He just sucked them down like I eat oranges, getting a good dose of vitamin C. And one time, being such a tidy young man, he was carrying some peels down to the trash in the middle of the night."

"They smell funny when they dry out."

"We'll get to your extraordinary sense of smell in a minute. Anyway, he was making his way down the outside steps. His belt was off, I assume so he could reach into his drawers and scratch those king-sized huevos of his, and his goddamn pants were so big they fell down around his knees. Well, Grasshopper was laid low. He fell down two flights of stairs, and he got to the bottom, and he lay there for a minute. I was down there working on my bike, and I saw him come rolling down, and I thought he might be dead. But he got up and hobbled over, and he *threw away those grapefruit peels*. He never even *dropped* them!"

"I finish what I start."

"Heroic, you were. You almost died in the name of tidiness."

"That's right." Ah, but I was just a wild, tidy daredevil, living on the edge with my trips to the trash.

"I always worried that some grief-struck girl would kill you." Sandy shook his head. "Or some pissed-off father. Remember when Jillian's father almost blew him away?" Paige saw my face and hushed Sandy. I couldn't laugh about another time when my own stupidity had almost gotten me killed.

This talk of the past kept my mind on Becca, and kept my mind off Gretchen, and my mind wrestled with my soul, which got into the Jeep and drove to Georgia or Oregon on a daily basis.

God help me, here.

I went through their entire kitchen, tightening every screw, oiling every hinge, checking every bend in every pipe. I hated having to talk, the sound of my voice with that metal in there, but occasionally I'd have to correct some fine point in a story. Mostly, I laughed. I laughed until my stomach hurt. No one could listen to Sandy and Paige without laughing. Even the fights were funny. Sandy and Paige had English major fights.

Sandy was a Dead White Male specialist. Paige collected and quoted the modern woman's canon. She also defended it. She liked all the poems about women locked in these frondy, kelpy, oysterish embraces, all of the goddess poetry. Sandy despised it, so the two of them would come nearly to blows over poets like Muriel Rukeyser, because, you see, they cared, passionately, whether or not Muriel Rukeyser was recognized or dismissed. "It's crap!" Sandy would fume. "Rukeyser is crap! It's some sort of Saturday Evening Post tripe with pussies!"

"I HATE it when you use that word! And your gender-centrism is APPALLING!" They raged, quoted, tore each other up.

Once in a while I'd ignite Sandy's anger with a well-placed comment, like, "I don't believe he was mixed. Why do you always say he was mixed?"

Sandy would be inspired to rage and shouting. "OF COURSE HE WAS MIXED! LOOK AT HIS PHOTOS, GRASSHOPPER! THE MAN HAD TO BE BLACK!"

I would be forced to repent, so mostly I stayed quiet.

I was the scarecrow who slept on the porch and drank huge amounts of food through a straw after bouts of compulsive home maintenance. Miriam was the neighbor who complained about work to Paige every day, then settled down to listen. Sandy and Paige were our entertaining friends.

I listened to them while I got better.

∽

The doctor said that all was well, but he was concerned about my weight. Actually, my weight was up, I could tell by the way my belt fit. He said I was still down about fifteen pounds from where I'd been when I got to the hospital in Astoria.

I thought, Well, Doctor, I'm trying to eke out whatever digestible body mass I have until you get this crap out of my mouth. Free the mandibles, and I promise you I'll put on twenty. Do you think I'm excited about the Ichabod Crane thing? Open the jaw and I can promise you, I'll eat like a pig.

He said three weeks, that was all. Three more weeks of Hell.

∽

I tried to talk to Paige about the Shelley name. "Percy Bysshe Shelley was a brilliant, miserable man, and for all we know it could have all been due to that name."

"Well, maybe we can name him Percy."

Sandy arrived home in the middle of this conversation. "Shelley was a miserable man because of his wife."

"WHAT?" demanded Paige, swatting at him.

"Which wife?" I wanted to know.

He defended himself from Paige's mock blows. "Grasshopper, tell me your name, and you can name this baby."

"No deal."

"I can't believe your name is any worse than mine."

"Believe it."

"Worse than Wilton Lilbourne Sanderson. Willy, Lilly, or Sandy. Your name is worse?"

"Yes."

Miriam was in on this conversation. She seemed to be in on every conversation, listening to me talk through clenched teeth like a hostage with a gun in my back. "You don't know his name?"

Paige shrugged. "Gentry's first name is one of life's great mysteries."

"I can get him to tell me." Miriam sounded surprisingly sure of herself. "I have ways."

Ways? I let my eyes slip over her firm little frame, wondering about those ways. All her clothing seemed to be made out of T-shirts. When she walked into the air-conditioned house, her nipples rose as dark and hard as blueberries behind her shirt. When she stood, the fabric of her short skirt caught up in the back in a way that, well. It intrigued me. She emitted a constant level of heat that had nothing to do with the weather.

She'd sit at the table, complaining about work, disengaging a lock of her dark hair from a tangle of hoops and chains hanging from her ear. I stared at the damp hair lifting away from her face in waves. I wondered what it smelled like.

Not a good idea, idiot.

Usually, listening to her talk was enough to settle me down. She was always complaining about her job. I'd been under the impression that a vo-tech school was an educational institution, but according to Miriam, it was Hell, plain and simple, Hell. I was supposed to run the computer lab at this school in the fall. "You'll *hate* it, Gentry. I can't believe I let them treat me the way they do, but where else can I go?"

"Aren't you a nurse?" asked Paige, but the phone rang and she answered it before Miriam answered the question. "Oh hey Rebecca. I'm sorry, he got here fine. No, he's fine. Everyone here is fine. I'm sorry I haven't called. How's the little Georgia Peach?" Paige talked while Sandy waited for his turn. Miriam eavesdropped. I went and lay down on the cot in the utility porch and felt pathetic.

Paige brought the phone to me.

"Hey."

"Hey, Gentry." Jin-tree.

"Are you okay?"

"Don't. Don't even ask me something like that." I could hear her trying not to cry. "Dan keeps talking about driving over there to visit. And I don't want to see you. Do you understand?"

Hopelessness and shame. "I have nowhere to go, Becca. Nowhere but here."

"Then we'll stay away. And you stay away from here. Dan wants to have you back, but you stay away. Do you understand?"

"Yes."

"You'll stay away?"

"Yes."

"Swear it to God."

"No. I'll always hold you."

"Don't you *ever* say that to me again."

I lay there, listening to the dead air.

Paige took the phone and pushed the button to end the call. "Bad?" I rolled away from her. She rubbed my back. "It's probably time to get your own, Gentry."

My own. Becca was supposed to be mine. She was meant to be mine and I'd messed it up because I was too young when I met her, but God meant her for me. I knew it and she knew it and somewhere in there, even Daniel knew it. But it was all messed up.

Paige sat with me until I fell asleep.

∽

The next morning, I woke to the sound of Paige arguing on the phone. "Yes, Mother, she is very excited about the pony. No, Mother, I won't enter Lucy in that pageant, and that's the end of it. No, we can't discuss it. If you take her to see one of those, she'll want to do it, and I forbid it. Because those pageants are one step away from kiddy porn." This conversation was repeated at least every other day, as was the other one I overheard. "I don't owe you one word of explanation about why I'm pregnant again, Mother. We're happy about this baby." Apparently, Genevieve wasn't too happy about this tribe of kids, especially since Paige wasn't interested in giving birth to any pageant winners.

Paige hung up. "I've had it. I'm done, Sandy. Finished."

Sandy took it with a deep sigh, a roll of his eyes, and a shake of his lion head. "We're supposed to carry the kids out there for a visit this weekend."

"I refuse to go. Tell her I'm too pregnant. I won't fit in the door."

He raised his hands to quiet her. "I'll do it. I'll drive over on Sunday after church and stay the night."

"Just one night?"

"I have classes on Tuesday."

Paige crossed her arms. "If Lucy Rose ends up made up like a five-year-old harlot with teased hair walking down some runway in a swimsuit to be judged by a panel of child molesters, I'll never forgive you, Wilton."

He drew himself up and crossed his arms. "Come along, then. Make sure yourself."

I decided to leave the room.

Lucy Rose was packing. "I'm going to visit my pony."

"That sounds nice."

"Her name is Buttercup. She bites." She held out two dolls. "Uncle Gentry, should I bring the white Barbie or the black Barbie?"

"Hey Lucy? Why don't you take the white Barbie and the black Ken?"

"Okay. I need to find them some clothes."

"No, it's too hot for clothes. Pack them naked. Right next to each other. That way they won't be lonely during the trip."

"You're smart, Uncle Gentry. And very sweet." She packed her Barbie markers that smelled like chemical fruit, Barbie coloring books, plastic Barbie jewelry and, of course, her Barbie makeup. Lucy was only five but she had quite a bit of makeup.

I suggested that she might put some clothes for herself, naked Barbie miscegenation was one thing, but surely Lucy needed some clothes? She packed a hat, a jacket and a swimsuit.

They left after Mass. Paige stayed home.

∽

If anyone deserved in-law problems, it wouldn't have been Paige. Aside from all the intellectual attributes that I admired, she was a good mother and a wonderful wife to Sandy.

All this was lost on her mother-in-law. Genevieve Sanderson.

I was a graduate student when I met her at Sandy and Paige's wedding, which was held at the Sanderson horse farm of his youth. Sandy's parents were having it there and paying for everything because Paige's parents (who were both professors at our college) had no money for the kind of wedding that Genevieve Sanderson wanted for her fair-haired son.

Sandy explained this to me. *Mother has a "vision," Grasshopper.*

On the morning of the wedding, the groom and his groomsmen showed up, unwashed, hungover and reeking of the bachelor party we'd improvised in the car on the drive from Georgia. Somehow we'd managed to avoid death or arrest, but not for lack of trying. We'd had to listen to Sandy's music, which is the kind of music I can't believe anyone listens to on purpose, for the entire trip. I needed to find a bathroom.

The house was enormous and smelled like fresh paint. A crew of men swarmed through the banks of tents and rows of chairs and expanses of white-clothed tables, carrying food and cakes and flowers and various large pieces of silver. They were all shouting at each other. Every available surface was hung with magnificent swags of flowers and ribbon. Even some of the horses were decorated.

Dexter looked around and smiled. *Look, a homosexual circus wedding.*

Is there any other kind?

We milled around Sandy, confused and suffering from alcohol-induced vertigo.

His mother stared us with distaste. *I guess they'll do.*

Sandy gritted his teeth into an approximation of a smile. *Hello my beautiful mother.* I peered over at her, not trusting the evidence of my own eyes. Yes, she appeared to be beautiful in that middle-aged way. But with that kind of beauty, it could all fall apart up close. I didn't intend to get near enough to find out.

She frowned. *Which one is which?*

Let me sober up my tribe before I introduce them, all right? He herded the lot of us to one side of his horrified mother.

She called out, *Your FATHER will be up to see you SOON.*

Of course. Good old Papa Hondo. I'd actually heard about his father. Mr. Sanderson was a ghost of a man who spent the majority of his life hiding in a family room, drinking scotch and watching John Wayne movies. He never went near the barn, didn't even know the name of a single horse in the cantering herd that was his wife's pride and joy. He just wrote the checks. As Sandy had put it, *Mother wouldn't board a horse, but she couldn't wait to board her only son. When she shipped me off to Subiaco, Papa Hondo never said a word. He just wrote the checks.*

Sandy led us up to his boyhood room. We were young enough that whatever we'd done to our bodies the night before could be remedied with hot water, soap and razors, so those were applied. Sandy split open packages of new underwear, undershirts and socks, passing them to those of us who had lacked the foresight to bring anything clean (which was every single one of us).

We suited up, or at least tried to. My hangover was really kicking in and I couldn't figure out how all the pieces of my formalwear went together. I remember standing with something hanging from each hand, mumbling, *Everything has a buckle. Why does everything have a buckle?*

Mrs. Sanderson's voice floated up and into the open windows of the room as we sorted out the buckles. *The carafes are supposed to be PREHEATED, so I want them PREHEATED! My husband isn't paying you to screw up my son's wedding! Remember, he wrote a CHECK for this, and he can STOP PAYMENT!*

Sandy smiled a slightly bitter smile as he blinded me with eye drops. *Blink, Grasshopper.*

We passed around the Visine, we passed around a bottle, dusted each other's shoulders, combed our hair. We finally stumbled down the stairs and out on the lawn, where various important and powerful men came over to grasp Sandy's forearm, wish him well and quietly suggest a haircut.

Sandy took it well. *Mother told you to tell me that, didn't she?* The powerful man would chortle or guffaw, some manly expression of mirth, and clap him on the back. He would call me over for introductions. *Senator Stevens, this is my friend Gentry. I suggest you ignore every word he says, sir, because he'll never vote for you. Judge Gibson, this is my young protégé, Gentry. I singlehandedly rescued him from the priesthood. Governor, I'd like to present to you my friend Gentry. He has a brilliant mind and the largest dick I've ever seen on a white man.*

I nodded, shook hands, smiled. I didn't care how he introduced me because I wouldn't see any of them unless I was sent to court in Oklahoma. And no matter what he said, it was taken as the finest joke ever told by these substantial, satisfied men. I realized that with a few small adjustments (less hair, more belly, thirty years) Sandy could be one of them.

Mrs. Sanderson stormed over, pressed flowers to our lapels and jabbed them violently with pins. I averted my eyes during the process. Once adorned, we were sent to our ceremonial places under a canopy in front of a temporarily relocated china cabinet (*Be CAREFUL! Do you idiots have ANY IDEA how much that BREAKFRONT is WORTH?!*) meant, I assume, to serve as an altar. Sandy, then me, Dex, Kevin, and last of all a pale-faced Daniel, who had spent most of the morning bent over the toilet. But we fanned out and tugged at cuffs and shifted cummerbunds and buffed our toes on the backs of our pant legs. We straightened up.

I had to admit we looked very fine, though we were getting warm.

I looked out over the sea of people waiting in their white folding chairs, fanning themselves in the rising heat of an Oklahoma morning. *Please, God, bring an end to this agony before everyone dies of heatstroke,* Sandy prayed.

Amen, we breathed in unison.

Just remember, Sandy muttered softly enough that only I could hear him. *In three days, we do this right*. I nodded. In three days, we would have do-overs in the campus chapel with Father Ned. Besides God, there would only be four of us present, and we had all agreed to wear jeans.

But first, the circus.

Papa Hondo finally came outside, blinking and pale. *Let's hope he doesn't see his shadow*, I heard Mrs. Sanderson say. I remember thinking how bitterly, unfairly hilarious that remark was as I watched him move uncertainly to sit beside his wife, who ignored him while gesticulating wildly at the musicians.

More music, more waiting. More sweating.

Finally, Paige's sisters appeared, six young women who varied greatly in age, complexion, hair color and height, each wearing a brilliantly colored sari. As different as they were, they all had the white smile and dark eyes of their mother.

Sandy spoke softly so that only I could hear him. *I wish I could marry all of them. I'd marry her mom, too*. I turned my laugh into a cough. I looked to find her, a short woman in a gold sari who was internationally respected in the area of Post-Colonial crit. She sat alone, waiting and strangely small outside her classroom, somehow diminished in this crowded setting.

This bothered me. The heat bothered me. The breakfront bothered me.

Don't get weird, I told myself. Hang on.

And then, finally, the moment I'd been craving and dreading. Becca walking down the aisle. Not in a sari, sadly. I would have liked to see her pale, unfreckled torso in a sari, but she had on a dress of the clear blue I associated with chlorinated water. Becca moving towards me with flowers in her hands, flowers in her red hair, as stately and calm as the first day I saw her. Becca taking her position as maid of honor at the breakfront, my counterpoint in this ceremony. Becca with the stoic eyes of a Renaissance Magdalene.

I thought I would die of grief.

That didn't quite kill me, standing up with Becca. Not quite. Watching her marry Daniel, that killed me, but when Sandy and Paige got married we stood up together, Becca in a blue dress and me in the largest, shiniest shoes I'd ever seen in my life, at least on my feet. I looked at the freckles on her bare shoulders and knew with painful clarity that we were supposed to be married, and we weren't.

What a horrible mistake.

I was so sick at heart that I barely saw Paige in her pink sari, walking down the aisle on the arm of her father, an older man of Irish extraction with red, wild, curling hair and brows who gave brilliant lectures on Western Civ. I hardly heard what the priest said as he did God's handiwork. The rings were exchanged. I made my way without umming through a poem I'd written at Sandy's request (*Grasshopper! We must have an epithalamion!*). That poem made Sandy cry, which almost made me cry, so I spent the rest of the ceremony staring at my shiny shoes and brooding over Becca.

Papa Hondo seemed greatly relieved when it was time to drink.

The tents were miraculously cooled. I sat down at a flower-filled table on Sandy's left and loosened anything with a buckle. Genevieve Sanderson sat across from me with her flashing blue eyes and sharp tongue, barking out questions. Why didn't I tell anyone my first name? Did I know what an unusual name that was, Gentry? Did I have relatives in California? There were Gentrys in Texas. Or was I any relation to the Charlotte Gentrys?

Sandy said, *Is that your name? Charlotte Gentry?*

Uncomfortably close. I looked around for poison.

She turned to her husband. *That boy wants to be a teacher? How does he ever expect to stand up in front of a classroom and teach if he can't even speak out loud?*

I guess she thought I was deaf. I was certainly mute after that.

She demanded to know, how did I feel about horses? She could tell so much about a person from how he treated horses. I shook my head, shrugged, I'd never in my life been around any horses. She persisted. Well? Was I a horse person?

Yes, Mother. He's a centaur. It was hell finding him a tux.

She wouldn't quit. Where was I from? *Well, what is your father's first name, Gentry?*

I stared at her, wondering if I had ever in my life said that name out loud.

I began to shake.

Sandy put his arm around me. *Don't pay any attention to Mother. She learned her social graces in California.*

Papa Hondo looked at me and opened his mouth. His voice sounded creaky from disuse, but he smiled when he spoke. *Say, Gentry. I'm heading to the bar.*

Can I bring you something? It was the nicest thing anyone said to me all day. And it was the only thing I heard him say to anyone. He spent the reception drinking more scotch and absorbing his wife's insults. He never said another word. He just endured.

I responded to the general tension by getting drunk. I did have a date, though not officially, as I didn't have official dates. I would find myself spending time with someone and Paige would ask if we were dating. I'd say, *Well, more or less.*

Virginia was a more-or-less. She'd come to the wedding with a few people from our college and fastened herself to my side. Genevieve mocked her, of course. *You hang on that boy. I should just call you Virginia Creeper.* I don't remember Virginia's last name, but I remember her blonde hair, her nervous laugh, and having her hard against the patterned wallpaper of an upstairs bathroom. It helped to relieve my general tension.

When we opened the door to find our way back to the reception, Genevieve stood in the hall with her arms crossed. We were in trouble. She was a grim and furious Sibyl who had intuited (or maybe overheard) the despoiling of her guest bath.

Virginia wisely slipped away. I found myself hobbled by the accoutrements of my tuxedo, a piece of which had fallen around my ankles. Genevieve pointed to Sandy's childhood bedroom. *Get in there and remove everything rented, right now. If I put a deposit down on it, I want it off you.* I quickly disrobed and re-dressed with my back to her. When I turned around, she was still staring at me. *You're not from North Dakota, are you.*

I finally made myself speak to her. *No. Not originally.*

I knew it. Well, it's a neighbor. And I know exactly where you're from. She stepped up and tapped me in the chest, her face full of stony, hateful conviction. *My son might have married some half-caste feminist,* she hissed, *but at least he didn't turn out like you.*

Those might be the cruelest words ever spoken to me.

~

So, that was the woman Paige had to contend with as a mother-in-law. The children were with her, and I was alone with Paige.

We settled ourselves in front of the air conditioner with books. "I want to read all afternoon," Paige told me, fanning herself. "I don't want to talk or cook or move. I just want to read."

When Miriam inevitably hove into view, Paige lied to her and said we had the flu. Miriam left, fearing contagion. I watched her retreat through the window, the fall of curls down her neck, the muscular movement of her backside. I vaguely imagined what might have happened if Paige had gone to her in-laws and I'd been there alone. I would have worked her like a piston.

"What are you thinking about?" Paige's voice was bright, forced.

"Um, nothing?"

"Liar."

We spent a nice Sunday together, Paige and I. She read poetry to me, and argued with me even when I agreed with her, and called me an idiot, and liquefied food and pushed it on me, and I liked all of this.

"He better not have let his mother enter Lucy Rose in that pageant."

I alliterated for Paige. "Paige protested, protecting her precious progeny from predation, parading, painted, procured for a panel of pedophiliac perverts."

She beamed. "That was beautiful."

The evening came. She watched television and I read more. Paige had to watch television, I understood this, because she was a pop culture repository and she needed to keep up. She knew of everyone in the entire world, and almost all of it was wasted on me because I paid no attention to anything. But Paige was the woman to go to for jokes about anyone famous, she filed them away and then she sort of scrolled through them on request. She knew all the celebrity scandal jokes, the serial killer jokes, the white trash jokes. She knew all the one-syllable men's names jokes, she knew knock-knock jokes, she had an impressive array of Ken and Barbie jokes.

The only problem was that at times I felt like we were back in college, me and the Japanese student chuckling politely at jokes we didn't understand. I didn't know about most of those things. But I liked to watch her decimate English majors with this humor because it was so different than the usual array of puns, alliteration and obscure references.

She turned off the television in the middle of some artificial laughter. She looked sad. "I wish I could drink." She sounded sad, too. "Then we could play Synonym Wars."

"It is a drinking game," I agreed. Players had to accumulate the silver tabs from beer cans for wagering. Those were the stakes. So, a person would have to be pretty drunk before we ever started, so as to have a bank of tabs. And then, we would all try to exhaust the possibilities for shared meaning.

When I remember how fun this was I'm baffled, but we would hoot and holler, blood would run hot, the dictionary would fly through the air, fists raised over whether "ribald" was truly an adequate synonym for "humorous." All for silver beer tabs. I won because I went for the obvious. They would be out there in the realm of the arcane, and I'd say "funny." I had piles of silver tabs. What was the point? The point was to win.

Paige was best at obscene synonyms. She studied Middle English, and she had great dictionaries. She put a hand on mine. "You're not drinking, are you."

I shook my head.

"Oh well. No one plays Synonym Wars anymore. Our hollering would wake up the kids. Though that wouldn't be a problem tonight." She looked over at me and smiled. I looked away. I tried to keep my thoughts away from the contemplation of her small, rounded form, moving through the house, her hair down, those beautiful breasts she had, her smart eyes and the way she stopped and put her hand on the small of her back and sighed, so softly . . .

Stop it, Gentry. Don't listen to her sighs, don't think about it, why are you thinking about her hair, her breasts, why does it matter that you're alone together in this house all night, just go lie down next to the clothes dryer and try to think about something safe. Think of something safe.

And that's what I tried to do. There was a thunderstorm. I fell asleep on my cot in the porch trying to be a good man. Rain-filled dreams reminded me I wasn't.

Gentry. Look at me.

Open your eyes.

Look at me.

I prayed.

God, these are not nightmares but they are. Why do You send me dreams that make me hate myself? Oh, God, these dreams, I want them out of me, I do. I ache and I throb and if I do this, I'll put this in my head, God. I won't put this in my head.

I lay there and tried to forget. The sound of the rain was more than I could stand. I listened to it for all the months of Oregon's fall, drumming on my roof, tapping at the windows. Maddening. I thought it would send me over. And then, hardly noticing when or how it happened, I got used to the steady sound of rain on my roof. I liked it.

But I'd forgotten about this southern weather, the wind and the thunder and the sheet lightning and the brilliant forks that touched the trees, exhilarating and terrifying. And I had to go. Lightning does that to me. But I had to get to the bathroom through the big bedroom. Why didn't those little houses ever have hallways?

Paige was in that bedroom.

I thought about going off the back steps. I imagined getting struck by lightning, a graphic mental image of urine as the conducting element that burned off my equipment. Like a Tesla wire. That was the kind of thing I should have prayed for, incineration of the offending organ, but what a terrible way to lose it. Not that there could have been a decent way.

I could see no light under her closed bedroom door. I decided to risk it. I crept through her room into the bathroom. Several lightning flashes during my time there assured me that I'd made the right choice.

I washed my hands, of course. I was so compulsive about it that I even washed my hands after I went in the shower. And I didn't even touch myself when I went in the shower, I just let it fly. If I did something as filthy as going in the shower, why did I bother to wash my hands?

I looked in the mirror. Along one side of my jaw was a thin purplish line of pooled blood waiting to be carried away. All that was left of that night with no memories.

Except one. Her in my robe.

Open your eyes.

How could I even look myself in the eye? Why did I think about the things I thought about? Why did I want the things I wanted? I was sick of myself, I was sick of my ways.

I prayed.

I don't want to be me, anymore, God. I want You to take this person away and send someone normal, that's all. Please. Amen.

I came out of the bathroom.

"Gentry?"

I wanted to say, I'm sorry, Paige, I should have gone outside and let the lightning reduce my private parts to briquettes and washed my hands in the rainwater afterwards. But I came in here, and I woke you up. But all that came out was, "Sorry."

She rolled over and turned on the light. Her face was perplexed. "Sorry for what, honey?"

For wanting her. For wanting anyone, at that point. "For waking you."

"I think the thunder woke me. Not everything in this world is your fault." She patted the bed beside her. "Come here. I want you to feel something." Because I was worthless, I sat down on the bed. "Lie down." Because I was scum, I did. She took my hands and put them on her belly.

Oh.

I felt a little person in there jumping, pushing, making himself known. I closed my eyes and felt him push and roll. Ah, this was wonderful.

"If you had a baby boy, what would you name him?"

No question. "Max."

"Max? That's all?"

"With a name like Max, he wouldn't need anything else."

When she laughed, the little acrobat within her quieted. I imagined he was listening. Then he began again. Amazing. I'd never, ever felt this before, the life before a life. I couldn't ask my pregnant students in Detroit to let me touch their bellies, could I?

I thought about Tiffany. God, why is life so sad?

We lay there, my hands on the little boy with the funny name. He jumped around. "Why don't you name him Francis?"

"And call him Frank?"

I nodded.

"Sandy says he'll never do that, because then that would be his favorite son. It wouldn't be fair to name anyone after Frank."

A favorite son. Trying to imagine that.

"So are you going to tell me? What happened?" I wouldn't because Oregon wasn't something I could stand to talk about. "Because, she called me. She was a wreck, an absolute mess over you." She was talking about Becca. "I want to know what you think you're doing." Had I ever had any idea what I was doing? "Well, Gentry? What do you have to say for yourself?" I had nothing to say for myself. "Do you still love her?" I didn't answer. "Gentry, you're so damn quiet about anything important."

I was quiet because I was falling asleep. I was falling fast in that bed with her, and if she were as kind as I thought she was, she'd let me sleep next to her and ignore what pressed into her hip, and she wouldn't feel the need to do anything about it and neither would I.

Paige was as kind as I believed her to be.

~

I woke up alone in her bed. I gave a swift but heartfelt thanks to God for what hadn't happened the night before, and went out to find her at the stove.

"Hey."

"Good morning." I sat down at the table. She poured me a cup of coffee and kissed the top of my head. "I've been meaning to ask you. Is Bosco with Mel?"

"No. I left him with a friend in Oregon."

"Until you get settled?"

"I don't think so, Paige. He's old, and he loves the beach more than anything."

"More than you?"

I pressed my hands to my eyes, then stood up and pushed through the screen door. I was going to find the paper, that's all. I just wanted the paper.

If Bosco had been with me, he'd have wanted to carry it.

I hid behind the paper until Paige served me grits with white cheese and green chilies. Trying to get it off the braces would take a good hour but I decided, slurping it down, that it was worth it.

She was at the sink, her back to me. "I meant what I said last night."

"About what?"

She stood there carefully rinsing a pan. "About how quiet you are. I think you need to talk more, so you don't have those nightmares."

"I'm having nightmares?"

"You have them almost every night." She nodded. "Sometimes you're crying, yelling. I could really hear you last night. Stuff about the teeth? You talk about the teeth. And you always say you're sorry." She turned around. "Oh Gentry, oh honey, I'm sorry, don't . . ." She came to me, put her arms around my head. I buried my face in her belly and the baby was still and I thought, Gentry, you're such a mess that you frighten the unborn.

"It's happening all the time? Do I wake up the kids?"

"Oh no. Never. Just Sandy. He goes in there and takes care of you."

"I don't remember, Paige, I'm sorry."

"Oh, honey. Don't be sorry. I'm just sorry you have them. I wish you'd let some of this out in the daytime, when it's not so scary." She rubbed my hair. And she was so close, and I thought, she's right here, all I have to do . . . I pulled away, I hated myself and everything I ever wanted and everything I'd ever done.

"I shouldn't stay here."

"You're not going anywhere." She spoke so softly. Like she was making sure not to scare me away. "Don't you have a doctor's appointment? You'd better get ready. It's the big day, Gentry." I looked in her eyes and saw it. I knew I'd better keep moving.

Most of all, I knew I'd better find my own.

~

It was time. Six weeks, and I was healed.

I was ready. I had my brand new soft bristle toothbrush and some peroxide toothpaste. I'm weird about this even when I don't have orthodontia, so the fixation on it with wiring was mighty. I'd revealed the urgent nature of my oral hygiene requirements to my doctor, and he was amused but understanding. He began to free my jaw. The young assistant helped him.

I was asleep when the hardware was installed, but not that lucky during removal. I was awake for every pulling, twanging, yanking moment of it. The assistant held my hand. She watched, wincing when I winced, soothing me when I twisted. My pain was her pain. I felt like he was going to pull out my teeth.

When it was over, I moved my jaw with great caution. It worked.

I gave thanks. Amen.

She showed me to a bathroom in the office. I brushed for about thirty minutes, and then I rinsed with cold water until my gums stopped bleeding. And then I smiled, oh I smiled, I showed myself what a great smile I have. My smile is the nicest thing on me.

Oh God, this is to give You thanks, Thanks, for clean teeth. Amen.

A knock on the door, which opened. The assistant peeked in. "Are you all right in there? We're getting worried."

I smiled, and she smiled back.

"Come here."

She stepped in and I put my hands up behind her neck and pulled her to me and kissed her, and she kissed me back. I kissed her with my clean teeth and wireless jaw, my newborn mouth felt naked and innocent, just my lips and her lips, our urgent tongues and the sweet, shared breath of it.

Finally, she put two hands on my chest and pushed herself away. She was whimpering. I was panting. She smoothed things down and I straightened things out.

"We have to book your follow-up appointment."

"Um, oh. Okay."

We left the bathroom and went out to reception, where I got the card that told me when to return and she gave me some instruction sheets and six new toothbrushes.

I looked at her sweet, trembling mouth. "Thank you." My voice was hoarse.

She blushed. "I've never done that before."

"I know. If you had, I would have remembered. But it was very nice."

"It was, but . . ." She shook her head. "I'm married."

I nodded. "Everyone is married."

The receptionist gave us both a strange look.

I left.

~

It was time to eat.

No restaurant phobias, no ordering pathology could keep me away from food that required chewing. I even knew what I wanted. "A cheeseburger and iced tea." There, that wasn't so hard.

"What kind of cheese?"

"The orange kind."

"Cheddar or American?"

"American."

"Do you want onion on that?"

"No."

"And how do you want that cooked?"

I ordered a hamburger, not a steak. "Just cook it medium?"

"Steak fries or crinkle?"

"There are fries made out of steak?" What a great idea.

She shook her head. "What kind of dressing on your salad?"

"What?"

"The cheeseburger comes with fries and a side salad. What kind of dressing? We have ranch, blue cheese, Thousand Island and oil and vinegar. Which would you like on your salad?"

"Ranch."

"On the side or on the salad?"

"Put it on the lettuce."

"Would you like to add a cup of soup for a dollar?"

"Yes."

"Which soup? We have beef barley and turkey noodle today."

"The first one."

"Beef barley?"

"Yes."

"Crackers?"

"Yes."

"Sweetener for your tea?"

"NO." I felt like the top of my head was going to explode, and if I hadn't been starving, I'd have walked out.

But then the food came, all at once. I gave thanks, I gave thanks in a big way for that food. Oh I can't even think about how awful I must have looked, shoveling the food in with my hands, moaning. I should have eaten in the Jeep. All around me, patrons were probably losing their appetites, asking for different tables. It was a wonder the restaurant manager didn't call the police.

I had to stop several times because I was so overwhelmed. Pacing myself. But I ate it all. I paid and went to the bathroom and brushed my teeth.

When I got back to the house, I couldn't stop smiling. I showed my teeth to Sandy, who had returned home in my absence and was in the yard hacking at a piece of stunted vegetation that should have been left alone. He threw down the clippers. "I should use your incredible teeth to prune this bush!"

I wanted to show my teeth to Lucy Rose. "Where are the kids?"

"I left them at Mother's. Paige is going to divorce me, I think." He shook his head.

"She won't."

"She might."

"She won't. We're Catholic." This seemed to cheer him up a little.

To celebrate my magnificent teeth, I decided to write the letter I needed to write. How could I write this letter? Should I even write this letter? I had better write this letter.

Paige was in the kitchen talking about divorcing Sandy with Miriam. I sat at Paige's small desk where she paid the bills and wrote her own letters, and borrowed some stationery and a pen.

Hey Gretchen,

I got the wires out of my mouth today. I went right to a restaurant and ordered a cheeseburger. You would have been proud. I was worried I would get sick but my stomach is already asking for more.

I'm sorry I didn't write sooner. I had to get used to being away. It has been a month. It has been a long, long month. I'm sorry. I spent the first part of it driving to Georgia, where I stayed for less than a week. Now I am in Norman, Oklahoma. I have a job here but it hasn't started yet. I am staying with friends.

Summer here is so hot and humid that you have to come inside to sweat. I am not exaggerating. I am sorry that I never experienced summer with you. You said September was the prettiest month. I remember every word you ever said, I think.

I hope you are fine. How is Bosco doing? Does he sleep with you? Is he sad? Does Bosco miss me at all? I miss him but I know he wouldn't like it here. It's too hot and there is no water to walk along. There was a bad storm the other night and he would have been frightened by the thunder and lightning.

Bosco would feel too lonely for you. His hair would get matted without you to comb it out for him, and he would be hungry all the time without you to feed him. Imagine if Bosco couldn't ever have any of your fried chicken. Imagine how miserable life would be for Bosco without your fried chicken.

Hey to all.

Always yours,
Gentry

And I folded up the letter and put it in an envelope and stamped it. I walked to the corner to mail it, because if I didn't mail this letter and figure out how to get some fried chicken on my own, I'd go get in my Jeep and drive the thousands of miles and find her. I missed her that much.

I opened the front door. "Hey Paige?" There was silence. I guess this did sound odd after a month of near muteness, my calling out in my normal, unbruised-larynx, unwelded-teeth, liberated-tongue kind of a way. "I want to take you and Sandy out for fried chicken, okay? Miriam, you're invited."

∽

It was a diner in a trailer. Mel took me to these when he could, knowing how much I liked a diner in a trailer. This one had a counter with big chrome stools and two booths with little jukeboxes on each table that reminded me of the pushbutton Philco radio in Lorrie's truck. A gum-chewing waitress with tall, unmoving hair and thick lipstick in a color not found in nature presided over the place, stepping lightly in her white nurse shoes.

I remembered the pretty assistant and sighed.

When we sat down, Sandy and I sat together, and Paige and Miriam sat together. The waitress took our order in a no-nonsense fashion. She didn't brook any English major guff, no quaffing or imbibing or ingesting, just southern style eatin.'

Miriam said the food sounded greasy. "I don't do greasy."

"I live for greasy," stated Sandy.

The waitress smiled. "Well then, y'all have come to the right place."

Everyone else ordered, Miriam had a salad, and then it was my turn. The waitress looked at me expectantly. Paige said, "Gentry will have the half bird, mashed potatoes, green beans instead of slaw, an extra biscuit, and a large milk."

"Jelly for the biscuits?"

"Yes, grape if you have it. And bring the milk with the meal, not before, or he'll drink it all before the food gets here."

"Got it."

Sandy asked, "Can he get two hind quarters with that? He likes dark meat better." She nodded. "Extra gravy on the potatoes, too."

"You bet." The waitress wrote it all down, and she left.

Miriam looked from me to Paige to Sandy, back again. "Just what is all that about?"

Paige took a sip of water and blinked. "What's all what about?"

"Can't he order for himself?"

"He can. But Gentry has a hard time ordering."

"So you order for him? Like a kid?" Paige nodded. I flipped through the songs on the jukebox. Roy Orbison. Mel liked Roy Orbison and could sing just like him. "That is just too weird."

Sandy laid an arm across my shoulders. "Grasshopper is our Sensitive Plant." His arm tightened into a hug. I don't like men to touch me, but Sandy could put an arm around me any time he wanted to. A good old boy passed the table, what Sandy called a Bubba, and he gave us a sideways look. Sandy leaned over and kissed me on the cheek. I patted his hand.

Miriam's voice cut the air. "Are you all queer?"

Paige erupted in laughter, Sandy and I were laughing, but Miriam sat there. She didn't understand the joke, even though she was the person who made it. She had never heard of the Sensitive Plant, she thought we were gay, she had heard enough of the Grasshopper thing, what was the deal, anyway, it was just too weird, none of this was funny to her, she was stone, that Miriam.

Paige left the table because she couldn't laugh or sneeze or cough without a run to the bathroom in those days. This had something to do with being pregnant, but I didn't ask for details. While she was gone, Miriam suggested that we trade places to avoid getting lynched, and Sandy agreed, but not because he was afraid of the Bubba. "It's just because I can't keep my hands off this gorgeous man, here." Miriam brought herself over next to me.

This was the closest I'd been to Miriam since the first day I met her when she put the rubber bands back on my teeth. I smiled, I let her see my nice, clean teeth.

Are these some wonderful teeth, Miriam?

She smiled back. She had nice teeth, too. I noticed the same thing I noticed that other day, that Miriam had a soft little mustache that rivaled mine. Not that mine was anything spectacular. When I tried to let my patches of facial hair grow, I looked unwashed, not bearded.

Paige returned, noted the change in seating arrangements. She didn't look pleased.

The food arrived, and I almost but not quite forgot to give thanks. Sandy and Paige gave thanks with me. Miriam looked happy, then. She was sitting at a table full of longhaired, publicly praying, Catholic, possibly bisexual, greasy food eating, visibly pregnant English majors. I bet she was having the time of her life.

Miriam nibbled her skimpy salad. She kept watching me eat. I couldn't help it, this was only my second meal in six weeks and I was starving again. I ran aground on my lust for that mountain of dark meat. My manners deserted me. I ate in pre-Jesuit school fashion. I popped and snapped and sucked and bit and chewed. I licked my fingers, I rolled my eyes. God, it was so good. Thanks be to You.

And then, I froze. Covered with chicken grease, groaning while I chewed, hair in my plate and all, I felt it. And I made a sound that had nothing to with the chicken, though it sort of blended in with the previous sounds.

Miriam's eyes were a light orange brown, amber, really, and large, but determination made them small and tight, like her hand around me. That rush of blood, that release of chemicals. She wanted me, and I wanted her.

But first I wanted to finish my chicken.

I wiped my hands and tried to remove her hand. I tried, and the best I could do was to get her to put it on my leg, my leg that kept twitching and thumping and bumping the tabletop as we wrestled over how much of what I had she could handle while I ate.

This woman was persistent.

My upper half was engaged in dinner, conversation. My lower half was locked in a vise grip of want. I didn't long for the leisurely acts of mercy and desperation I shared with Kathryn, with Becca. I longed for swift acts, fierce acts.

We finished, we were laughing, we were all having a good time, but I knew I would be having a better one before I slept. I would be having a ferocious good time, the kind I hadn't had in years because it would be with someone I didn't care about. It was lust, pure and simple. But lust was never pure, never simple, not for me.

We played the jukebox, we alliterated, we drank iced tea. I paid the check and left a huge tip for Louetta Mae, that was our waitress's name, Louetta Mae. Sandy asked her. When we got to their car, I got in the back and Miriam hurtled in after me. She was in my lap, her body hard and hot to the touch. I pressed my face to her hair and breathed in the sharp, sweaty scent of her hunger.

Not safe, not safe, my mind told my body.

Don't care, don't care, my body replied.

We parked, got out. Miriam tugged me toward her house by my belt loops. I turned back to say goodnight to my confused friends. The best I could manage was an apologetic shrug. Sandy started laughing.

There was no laughter from Paige as I was led into the house of Miriam.

∽

Talking was not the only thing Miriam did relentlessly.

There were a few activities at which I excelled as a kid, activities that didn't require my brain. At least, my brain wasn't required in any way that I understood. Running, soccer, basketball; there was always a point where the brain faded back and the body moved ahead. The body knew what to do, how to do it, and the mind could recede.

It was like that. Like sport.

When I finally rolled away for the last time, spent and sated, her eyes shone in the streetlight filtering through the window. Her voice was soft. "Wow."

I wanted to say something, too, like "Yeah," or maybe "Whoa."

I was asleep before I could speak.

∽

I woke and for a moment, had no idea where I was. I saw a dark head on a pillow. Morning. Oklahoma. Miriam. I put my arm around her.

She shrugged it off. "It's too hot. Go."

"What?"

"This beds sags. I can't sleep with you here."

"I'm, um, sorry."

"Don't bother being sorry. Just go."

Well.

I sat up, swung my feet to the floor. Parts of me ached. I started for the bathroom. "Don't." I stopped. Most of her face was hidden in the pillow. "Don't use my bathroom. Go next door."

I found my clothes by following a trail to the front door. I put on my jeans and went back into her room. "Hey Miriam? I'm, um, leaving now." She didn't open her eye. "Bye." Nothing.

I walked out into the summer sun, carrying my boots and shirt, shaking my head. I was embarrassed. Why had I done this? I'd sworn off sex that meant nothing when a man shoved a shotgun against my forehead and made me pray to him like a god.

I wanted a shower and a priest.

∽

When I let myself into the little Joad shack I could hear slamming, thumping in the laundry room. Paige, folding up the cot. My duffel next to the washer, packed and ready to go.

"Hey Paige?" She wouldn't look at me. "Paige, please. Paige, I'll be right back." I turned toward their bedroom.

"Don't you dare use my bathroom."

"But, I . . ." My voice choked off.

"You infuriate me, Gentry. Get out of my way." She picked up my bag and attempted to shove past me.

Sandy stepped out and relieved her of my bag. "Wife, what is this?"

"Will you help him with the shit in the shed?"

"Is this because he got his dick wet? Hell, woman."

She went into the bedroom and slammed the door. Sandy and I looked at each other in bafflement.

He helped me carry my stuff out to the Jeep. My computer boxes had been in the utility room, and Sandy had already loaded those. Those were *heavy*. I stood staring at the cartons that held my computer and peripherals, two boxes of books and a duffel bag. My earthly goods.

"There's no talking to her when she's gone Kali, but I'll reason with her later."

"Why is she so mad?"

He shook his head. "Grasshopper, the ways of women confound me."

I shifted from foot to foot. "I'm afraid I'm going to have to go to the bathroom in your back yard, Sandy."

"Be my guest."

"GENTRY?" It was Miriam. I looked away from my Jeep to her, waiting on her own front steps, wearing a tiny robe. She opened her front door. She sent me to the shower and then took me back to her sagging bed. The bedsprings complained but I did not.

I tried to be gentler, but she didn't like gentle.

∽

I found a place that would be available mid-September. Miriam said I could stay with her for the remaining weeks, and she let me help her with the rent. I could sleep in her bed, use her bathroom. But there was a rule that I had to follow, a rule that rang a deep bell of warning and remorse.

Miriam wouldn't let me kiss her.

I was in no position to make demands, but I had a problem with it, and she wouldn't relent unless I told her what the "issue" was. I couldn't tell her how I did that once, I followed that no-kissing rule, and it almost killed me. "I like to kiss, Miriam. A lot."

"Kissing is unsanitary."

"Pardon?"

"The mouth-to-mouth microbial exchange is just *staggering*." Miriam was scientifically oriented. She had been a nurse for years before she started teaching. The most obvious manifestation of her scientific orientation was an obsession with clean hands that rivaled my own. Handwashing I understood, but she also flushed the toilet with her foot. I didn't understand that, and I didn't understand her hatred of the smell of her own body. She doused herself with a chemical substance that smelled like a hospital bathroom. I had to take a shower immediately after sex so I wouldn't smell like her.

Was this normal? How would I know, anyway?

And then there were the other activities that were off limits. Touching up here, back there, around that, no. No mouths on anything, anywhere. Anywhere? Anywhere. Well, I didn't like that. But I did like the relentless velocity of everything else we did, the almost machine-like working of our bodies together in sin. Our sin.

I knew better. I knew sin.

I kept trying to figure out what I was doing there, what we were doing in that bed. I considered begging my way back into the utility porch. I thought about it, and thought about Paige gently swelling.

I'd moved from woman to woman for five years, then kept it under control for five years. I'd contained myself until the afternoon I carried my beautiful landlady up the kitchen stairs to her bed, where I made careful love to the dry white flower of her body for fourteen hours straight. The back seat with Darlene, that catastrophic kiss with Marci in my bed. I should have recognized that I was out of control. I should have foreseen the desperation that shot me out of Oregon like an arrow that landed in Becca. My mind had receded and my body had taken over. And my body was no longer capable of celibacy.

I decided to stay where I was.

∽

Paige wouldn't acknowledge me, but Sandy and I went fishing. I went to church with him on Sundays because he took Byron to one Mass and Paige took Lucy to another. "We divide and conquer these little heathens," he said.

Miriam was teaching summer quarter. I had to do something to stay busy, and mouth-to-mouth microbial exchange was out. So I worked on the yard, if you could call that a yard. It was more fun than cleaning gutters. And far easier than putting up storm windows. And when I was outside, the kids and Sandy would pass time with me.

One day I was outside weeding and talking to Lucy Rose. She had on what was, according to Lucy, a "twirly dress." She showed me how that worked. She gave all the credit to the dress but I was impressed by the precision of how she turned on her heel.

We were talking, and she was twirling. She was excited about kindergarten. "But I can already read," she told me. "Mommy says I'll be bored because I can already read."

"I could too, when I started kindergarten."

She smiled, her brown eyes flashing. "Who taught you to read? Daddy taught me."

I answered without thinking. "My mother taught me." Sitting at the table in a tiny kitchen with a stack of library books, her hair in a thick rope of braid, her tiny feet hooked in the legs of a wooden chair, laughing as her finger moved under the word "house." *I wonder how you're supposed to sound this one out, little man.*

I felt my head spin, my throat close.

Where did that *come* from?

Paige came out and gave me a look of such searing hatred, I almost doubled up. "Lucy Rose! Come in and wash your hands for dinner right now!" Lucy ran away, her hair whipping out behind her.

I couldn't eat that night. And it wasn't just Miriam's cooking. I wanted to forget, to bury, to lose myself in the oblivion of her bed, and I did. I knew it was a sin, what I was doing. But it was temporary, I thought. Back with my college friends for less than two months, and I'd come up with a new category, temporary sin.

And then, after two weeks of doing whatever it was that we were doing, I finally figured it out. Because one morning she got up and went into the bathroom to get ready for work. When she came out she was crying.

Emotion. She'd never expressed much emotion. My current emotions ran the gamut from lust to loneliness to self-loathing. But she was crying, and I felt something else. Maybe remorse, because it was probably my fault, or maybe it was concern, or even affection that I felt. I wasn't sure, but it was something.

I put my arms around her. We sat down on the bed. Her head against my chest, I put my face in her hair and breathed in her sweat and sorrow. I said something about what was it, was she okay, sh, I was there, hush now, could I help, that general litany of useless, ineffective things men say when women are in tears.

"You won't underSTAND."

"Well, maybe if you told me, I would."

She blurted it out. "I'm not PREGNANT."

"Pardon?"

"I said I'm NOT pregnant."

"*What*?"

"Are you DEAF? I was hoping, but I got my period. I'm not pregnant."

I had the feeling that the floor had tilted up and I was slowly sliding down the incline, down into oblivion. I let go of her. "Hey Miriam? Were you *trying* to get pregnant?"

"Of COURSE I was trying to get pregnant. That's just LIKE you, not to KNOW that. You're a total IDIOT." And she dissolved, and I was stunned. She collapsed on the bed, and she told me that she was thirty-five and tired of waiting, and according to Paige, I was a man who wanted to be a father, and clean, and heterosexual. I seemed intelligent. "And you don't smoke, either. And it's just a genetic fact that kids look more like their fathers than their mothers, and I want a baby that looks like you. You wouldn't have asked me to abort because you're Catholic."

Well, she had things planned out well.

"WHY DIDN'T YOU ASK ME?"

That felt good. I hadn't yelled in a while.

And I thought, I've had it with women. All the way around, every way there is, I've had it. I can't figure out any of them, and I can't stand it any more. I've been used and refused and ruined in every way I thought there was, but this?

I started to throw my paltry possessions in my bag, because this was it, I have limits, I do, and I'd reached them.

"What are you doing?"

"Leaving."

"I'm sorry. I'm sorry, I'm sorry, there is just nothing else I can say except that I'M SORRY!"

I looked at her, there on the bed, weeping.

And I thought, Gentry, you righteous Catholic idiot. What's the difference if she did it on purpose or accidentally? You were there, you know the risk, you take it in every bed you climb into. You get all worked up and think this is immoral and unfair but what have you done, ever, once, to make sure it doesn't happen? You're too Catholic, remember, you're a good Catholic who exposes himself and every partner he has to God knows what and making children that people don't want, because you're a good Catholic.

You're a hypocrite, Gentry, because what she's done isn't something she could do alone.

I stopped my packing. I looked out the window. It was the beginning of September. And as I looked out the window, Lucy Rose climbed on the school bus for her first day of school.

She saw me. She waved at me through the window, a little wave. I waved back, a little wave. She climbed on happily, wearing the dress she showed me and her plastic sandals. There was nothing in her of the girl I saw over her like a scrim of memory, but it still stopped my breathing with how much I missed Gretchen.

God, why was I here? Why was I away from her?

Because she wasn't mine. God, I wanted my own.

And God, I understand that this was where the simple sin became something complicated. We didn't love each other. We didn't even really want each other. She wanted a baby and I wanted refuge. But we were in pain and we were in need.

I looked over at Miriam. "Come here." She carried her grief to me, and I met her with mine. She let me kiss her.

She tasted sad.

∽

The new apartment was on Biloxi Drive, nearer to the university. Not as close to the Sandersons. They came out and stood on their front steps and watched me parking the U-Haul, standing side-by-side with sober faces. Sandy needed to be holding a farm implement.

I walked over. "Hey. Will you help me carry the television?"

"Grasshopper. You do not own a television."

"Miriam does. It's too heavy to move on my own."

The disbelief in his eyes. "This is a mistake."

I looked at this couple, this pair of the finest friends a man could have asked for, and I thought, Idiot, listen to your friend. He explained everything to you, from Roland Barthes to the exact way to make a woman happy in bed. He knows what he's talking about, so listen. Apologize to Paige, let her forgive you, she'll take you back.

I studied the pain in Paige's face, and the heat. I remembered what I'd done with Becca.

And I knew, don't risk it, move on, move away. Get your own.

~

It wasn't bad with us, really it wasn't. It was nice at first.

Every morning, we got up and ate breakfast together. She hated peanut butter, too. I guess a mutual hatred of peanut butter wasn't a huge patch of common ground, but it felt significant at the time. We usually ate cereal. She didn't use sugar on hers, either.

Some mornings she made me fried eggs. I liked that, even if she said eggs were unsafe unless cooked well. I ate overcooked eggs and drank coffee. We divided the paper. I read the sports and did the crossword. On Saturdays I read the automotive section, out loud if she would let me. Usually she let me. She read me the current events.

Every day we drove to work together in her little Toyota, even though it was orange. It got excellent mileage. We did our jobs. At lunch, we convened in the cafeteria to complain to each other about the morning. She complained more than I did, but she was a teacher. I only administrated. We finished our workdays and met in the parking lot. And then, because she didn't really enjoy cooking (and what she did cook was hard to eat), we ate dinner out. I always suggested Vietnamese because there were some good places in town. She always said no and suggested somewhere else.

When we got to wherever it was she wanted to go, I asked her, please, would she order for me. At first she did. She didn't spend much time on it, she just looked for red meat and said I'd have that. We'd eat, I'd pay. I always drove, so I'd drive back to the apartment. Fortified by beef, I'd encourage her into bed. After, I'd have to go take a shower, fine, whatever, I took a shower. It woke me up, so I'd lie in bed and read library books while she sat cross-legged beside me, working. I felt her hard little body next to me, and I wasn't alone.

We washed our hands a lot.

And she let me kiss her. I explained that it was my only rule. She didn't mind the mouth-to-mouth microbial exchange, once we started. I would kiss her mouth, her cheekbones, her eyes, her ears, her neck. I kissed her with all the hunger and the frustration of the last six years. I kissed her until she was panting, sweating, until her hips moved and small, helpless sounds escaped her throat.

I thought she liked it.

In fact, she visited the lab several times a day for some of it. It never mattered what I was doing, I was more than happy to take her in my office and get her all fixed up, as far as the kissing. I was working hard towards my objective. I was going to kiss her like that until she wanted me to kiss her everywhere. But first I had to get her to stop using that Lysol stuff.

One step at a time.

That was our arrangement. It was a nice arrangement. We were a couple. I liked it, being part of a couple. I'd never lived with a woman before. Near women, but never with one. I thought it was working. And I appreciated Miriam. She was a good teacher and a terrible cook, and I thought the former was more important than the latter. I liked the way she looked, I liked the way she moved. I liked the way she felt when I reached for her. And I was always reaching.

God, I never meant to sin. I never meant to. But the ease of it, the calm of it, because I wanted her without loving her.

The lack of fire meant no burning.

∽

One evening we sat down at the restaurant and she pushed a menu my way. "Order for yourself."

"I can't."

"Of course you can."

"Hey Miriam? I guess I like it when people order for me."

"Too bad. I'm sick of ordering for you."

It was our first 'issue.'

She wanted to talk about the "roots" of this "issue". So I explained. I knew I was weird. I knew it was probably annoying, this inability to decide on anything, except it had never annoyed anyone I'd explained it to before. Amused, yes. Annoyed, no.

She pestered me to figure it out, and I responded to the pressure by becoming unable to order at all. My specials systems no longer worked for me. The waiter would ask for my order and my mouth would open and a torrent of "ums" would pour out. I could tell that Miriam hated that. Well, I hated it too.

So, she started to deliberately order things for me that she knew I'd hate. She laughed at my distaste when these inedible dishes were set before me. I was humiliated, the concerned waiter asking me if I wanted a box, having to pay for something I couldn't eat, a lump in my throat.

"Pick out something you like, then. Order what you like, or I'll order something you hate." I had to hand it to her, it worked. I developed a preemptive ordering strategy to head off any fruit and meat combination dinners. I actually forced myself to look, choose, order and live with my choice, rather than calling the poor harried waiter back six times to change my mind. I finally learned to order in a restaurant.

But I never understood why she was so mean about it.

~

Not long after we moved to the new apartment, I was summoned to the hospital. He had arrived, Percy Shelley Sanderson, the new baby boy with the terrible old name. Babies put women in a forgiving mood and I hoped Percy would earn me Paige's.

I held the wonder of the baby man. "His hair smells great."

Paige smiled. "What does it smell like?"

I gave it another whiff. "Baby-cleaning products and milk. And . . ." There was something under, something rare. I moved my nose around his head until it reached the back of his neck. Ah. There. I felt it flood me, a deep satisfaction, a desire to protect. "What is that?"

"It's the newborn baby drug." She smiled. "It only works on you if you're meant to be a parent."

I had to smile.

I inspected him a little more, doing baby math. He had one of what he was supposed to have one of, two of what he was supposed to have two of, and ten of what he was supposed to have ten of. "His eyes are navy blue."

"They'll turn brown. My mom's eyes seem to be dominant."

I was concerned about his ears, which curled like small red sea shells. "Will his ears unfurl?"

"Yes, Gentry. His ears will unfurl. They all look like this when they're born."

"Oh. Did Lucy Rose's ears look like this when she was born?"

"No. She was always perfect." And we had a talk about Lucy and Byron, and Sandy, and Paige's ever-receding return to school. She asked after my job, which I said was fine, everything was fine, just fine.

We were quiet for a moment.

"You decided to do it, I see."

"Do what?"

"Play sperm donor for Miriam." She sighed. "If you have a child with her, I'll feel guilty for the rest of my days."

"You're not responsible for what I do."

"Of course I am." Her brown eyes were soft and teary. "Gentry, I love you so much. Sandy and I, we want you to be happy."

Hey, Percy, you look a little squished but I'd bet you're going to be beautiful in spite of this rolled-up ear thing. Are you going to be small and dark like Mom, or long and light like Dad? I'm going to put my money on long and dark.

I smelled Percy a little more. "I think this would make me happy."

"She's a more-or-less, Gentry. You can't have a child with a more-or-less."

Outside confession, I never tell anyone anything. That has always been my way. I only tell God, and He holds it for me and forgives me for it and lets me move on. This is my system.

But that day, I told Paige.

I told her what I could stand to about Oregon, about loving a woman who had decided to spend her life belonging to a man who didn't want her. I told her how that nearly killed me, but loving Gretchen was worse because she was that same man's daughter. "Everything I want seems to belong to someone else and I'm tired of wanting what I can't have." I told her about Becca, asking her to leave with me. I even told Paige about those weeks I spent watching her and wishing, and wanting.

"You wanted me?"

"Of course."

"You mean our lust was *mutual*?" And she started to laugh, but she kept wiping at the edges of her eyes with her hand. "Oh honey, it's a lucky thing I didn't know.

We could have been in all kinds of trouble. Why do you think I was so damn mad when you went to Miriam?"

We forgave each other. We were still friends. And she understood, then, that I needed someone to belong to me.

That someone, it seemed, was Miriam.

III. RECKONING

God, thank you for making me fat. It helps, sleeping on the floor, to be fat.

I wake up early and go upstairs to make coffee and start some bacon. Mike comes up looking wretched. It's about four AM his time. He sleeps in sweats, too. His hair sticks up all over the place. This surprises me for some reason. I guess I thought he always had precise and groomed hair. He looks more like a fellow human being in the morning.

"Nice apron."

"Thank you. I found it in a drawer when we moved in."

"It goes with the kitchen." He sits down on a barstool at the counter. I pour him a cup of coffee. He takes it, makes a noise of thanks, blows a little foul breath my way.

Mike, you should always brush your teeth first thing. I do.

"Do you want some milk for your coffee?"

"No." He looks at the pan on the burner. "I thought you couldn't cook."

"Miriam refused to feed me. So I learned how to feed myself."

"Oh, she decided to make you more self-sufficient."

"No. She just hated me."

"Well, Gentry, most wives hate their husbands."

He would know, I guess. He's had twice the wives I have.

I have a system for flipping eggs. I never break the yolks. I make Mike butter the toast. He flattens it. "You're even worse at buttering toast than I am."

"I try, Gentry, I try." He digs into the greasy plate I put before him. "You eat like this every morning? No wonder you're getting a gut on you."

"I hate you Mike, you know that?"

"Yes, I know that, Gentry. Just like my wife." He watches me give thanks, amused. Well, that's my job, to amuse the world with my prayer. I fill up my gut. Then it's time to drink more coffee. "Can I ask you a few questions about your financial situation?"

Questions. Great. "Yes."

"Do you have any savings?"

"I try, but then I have to pay something."

"Any retirement?"

"I borrowed against my teacher's retirement."

"How about where you work now?"

"I have nothing like that at my job." How can I explain my benefit package to Mike? It's a complicated arrangement of smoke and mirrors, designed to give the illusion of benefits. I have health leave as long as I never get sick. I lose all accrued personal time off if I ever take any. I'm paid by the hour if I work less than forty hours a week, switching immediately to salary the moment I put in an hour over that. "Mike, I'm told that I have benefits, but I have no retirement, no life insurance, no dental, no vision, and my health insurance covers no prescriptions, no physicals and no illnesses."

He rolls his eyes and makes that drain clearing sound. "Is there any money anywhere that you have access to? Anything at all?"

"No. Nothing."

Having verified my lack of financial resources, Mike's ready to look at the mess. I kick it over from the side of the kitchen to the barstools. I have two boxes of mess for Mike. He looks a little surprised. "This is it? Is it organized by any sort of system?"

"Of course. I have a system for everything. If it had to do with money, I threw it in here. When this one got full, I put it in there."

"Very organized."

"Thanks."

"I guess I thought you'd have all this on your computer."

"I'd never put anything like this on my computer. I like my computer." He goes downstairs and comes up with his vintage legal briefcase. I like that briefcase. Miriam bought me a new, ugly leather briefcase and I told her to take it back. She threw it at me, hard. It hit my thigh and made the most extraordinary bruise in the shape of . . . but that's over. Miriam and her bruises are dead.

Mike takes out a printing calculator, which seems quaint to me. He puts on some glasses. I might have a fat gut on me, but I don't have glasses.

Mike keeps shaking his head. I do the dishes, I watch him, I sweep, I watch him, I mop, I watch him. I don't know what I expect him to do, a type of secret banking voodoo, some sort of high finance magical money-handling dance, or something. But he does what I used to do back in the days when I had money. He makes piles. I used to make a "pay" pile and a "throw" pile. When he's done, there are seven piles. "Is the mortgage current?"

"Yes." The only thing that is, though.

"Was this the other car?" He waves a coupon book at me. "Ford Motor Credit?"

"Yes."

"A Bronco, right?"

"No."

"Was it an Explorer?"

"No."

"Tell me it was a truck."

"That would be a lie."

"What was it, then?" Don't make me say it, Mike, don't humiliate me. "Gentry, was it . . . a Taurus?"

I give him this, this humiliation, as a gift. "Yes." I drove a Taurus. At least it wasn't a Tempo. "She liked it, Mike, it made her happy." Great, blame it on the dead wife, coward. But she did buy it. It says "Miriam Hirsch" right there on the coupon book.

"A Taurus." He shudders. "Well, it's history. Credit history, unfortunately." He sweeps the entire pile off the table and into a box. And he looks through the utilities, and I can tell he's shocked. All the envelopes have those red rectangles that say "Final Notice" on them. I'm the next Grand Prize Winner in the Final Notice Sweepstakes. "Is anything turned off?"

"The phone was supposed to be shut off yesterday."

"And was it?"

"I haven't checked."

"I'll take care of it." He keeps looking at my monetary shame. Eventually he opens up all the charge account envelopes, and he reads off the things she charged, one after another.

"Mike, don't. She went kind of crazy there at the end. There was something wrong."

"She sure did go crazy." He looks at me. "Did you get rid of her things?"

"Um. Not yet."

"Are there bags anywhere?"

"Bags?"

"Of what she bought."

"In the closet maybe."

"Let's take a look." He goes into the bedroom. I'm not going in there. "Gentry, bring that stack of statements in here." He's probably in the big closet.

"I, um . . ."

"Get in here and bring those statements." I don't go in there. I never went in there. My clothes were in the other bedroom closet until I moved them downstairs. I never went near her closet, even before the end. "Gentry? Are you there?" I'm not going in her room. I haven't been in there since the day I stormed out of the office, ready to kill her, and got home and ran up here and found . . .

"GET IN HERE."

I go in. Chills run up and down my arms. I need a drink.

I won't drink after breakfast in front of Mike.

The closet door stands open. He's in there talking to me. "Jackpot. Tags on. Receipts in the bags. We're in business." He brings out some bags, dumps them on the floor. "I want you to try to match some of this up. We have the credit statements and most of this shit's still tagged, so we can take it back."

"I never thought about taking it back."

"Eve always asks me to take stuff back. She gets embarrassed."

I see. Mike is also a Taking Back Expert.

We go through the crammed closet, matching clothing to receipts and statements. It's all "better ladies sportswear" to me, but Mike understands what's what. He holds up some tiny embellished thing. "What the hell? Did she just buy whatever was ugliest?"

"No. It had to be ugly and expensive, both. But she never wore any of that." That was the strange thing. She just bought and bought and bought.

I find that after my throat opens and I can breathe, I like sorting this stuff out, preparatory to getting rid of it. "Mike, we need a system. Pack it store by store. I'll put the bags in order."

Mike and I pack the bags and we pack it all into the Toyota. We fill up the trunk with shoeboxes. I wish I had a trailer. We tie bags on top, looping twine through the car windows and over the top. He smiles. "Like a Christmas tree."

"What?"

"It's like tying a Christmas tree on top of the car. You know."

"I've never done that."

He changes the subject. "Go get dressed. Wear a suit."

"A *suit*?"

"Sure. We'll be treated with more respect." I trust Mike, he knows these things.

I hardly ever buy anything but food, but clearly, Mike shops for actual consumer merchandise.

I iron our shirts. Mike watches me. "You need to get laid."

"Hey Mike? Shut up."

~

Miriam had a shopping system. I went with her a few times early on. She made me hold her purse, but the point is I know where to go.

Quail Springs Mall is closest. We keep returning to the car and getting more shopping bags. My fingers are numb from the handles, but we empty one after another after another. Then we move on to Penn Square, and we hit Penn Square hard. The looks on those clerks' faces when we carry in all those bags, it's awful, it's terrible.

They protest because the merchandise is so old. The tags read $250.00, but under their scanners, the clothes ring up at $2.99. Mike draws himself up to be a little more imposing, a little more impressive. He smiles and charms and waves around receipts and statements. If that doesn't work, he bullies. He demands a manager, and then he lies. "My client's wife has cancer, and is too thin to wear these things." They appear to believe him. I think he likes thinking up a new lie for each store. "My cousin's wife had a nervous collapse. She can't wear these things in the institution, and he needs the money to pay for therapy." His stories are absurd, especially when he claims to be related to me. "My brother's wife died in a car accident." When he refers to me as his brother the clerks don't even pretend to believe him. He's too old and tall and well dressed to be my brother.

The amount of money Mike manages to get credited to all the accounts astonishes me. It astonishes him. He keeps looking at me, shaking his head, patting my back in manly commiseration.

Don't touch me, please. "Mike, these people are upset."

"They deserve it for selling her this ugly shit in the first place." Hm. I never thought of it that way. Miriam's accomplices.

We take a break to get huge piles of Chinese food that's supposed to be healthy at the food court. Mike watches me say my grace. "You sure are Catholic, aren't you?" He watches me chew. Is this necessary? I shovel in a little more. "You understand that she did this on purpose, don't you?"

I swallow, wipe my mouth. "What do you mean, on purpose?"

"Women do this on purpose, run up this kind of debt. She never wore it, right? She probably hid most of it. It's a calculated financial revenge. Are you sure she wasn't going to divorce you?"

"She had no plans to divorce me."

"Are you sure?" I nod. "She hated you, though, right?" I nod again. He nods, too. "I figured. Women do this when they hate you."

"Did Kathryn ever do anything like this?"

"No. Kathy had too much pride to do something like this. Her lawyer did, though." Oh, shut up, Mike. And knock it off with the patting.

He eats next to nothing. He's too busy watching me make a pig of myself.

~

It takes all Tuesday to get it returned.

There's one item I handle personally. Mike insists I try. We walk into the store and the smell of leather is enough to make me sneeze, but I control myself. I have a mission. I put my item on the counter. "I'd like to return this, please."

The clerk sniffs a little. He has a severe haircut, worse than the one I used to have. "We don't stock that one anymore." He starts to turn his back on me.

"I, um, have the receipt." Mike says they have to take it back if I have the actual receipt.

The clerk snatches it from my hand, scans it, frowns. "This was purchased well over a year ago." He gives me a withering look. "Could I ask you why you wish to return this?"

"Because I don't want it?" That is clearly no reason to return anything by the expression on this clerk's face. Mike squeezes my shoulder. I wrestle an urge to hit him in the face. He smiles at the clerk, who smiles back. And there is a subtle shift as the man behind the counter begins to toady.

"Would you like store credit or cash?"

Mike pushes me. "Cash." I'll receive cash for the thing.

While I do the paperwork, Mike keeps a hand on my shoulder. His voice is intimate and remorseful. "I'm sorry you didn't like it."

The clerk admonishes Mike. "You bought this gaudy thing for him? For shame. I thought you'd have much better taste than this."

"It was a gift from my parents." Mike sighs. "This man is so patient with the whole thing." He gives my shoulder another meaningful squeeze.

There is a limit.

"Well take a look at his *hands*. Who would buy him a case with such a small *handle*?"

Mike raises his eyebrows. "Yes. His hands are . . . enormous." They trade a look. Mike pats me. I control the urge to hit them both.

Let's see, so far today I've been Mike Mumford's brother, his cousin, his client, and his wife. God, get me through this, all right?

"Hey Mike? Could you stop talking about me like I'm not here?"

The clerk smiles and says, "Feisty." He counts out four hundred dollars. I put it in my wallet before he changes his mind. He swings an attaché up on the counter. "You should make him buy you a nice case. Have a look." I run my hands along the smooth sides, use my thumbs to snap the latches. They open with the smooth click of exceptional hardware. I lift the top and study the fittings of the interior.

Perfect.

"It's been here too long, waiting for the right customer." The clerk's eyes flutter. "Tell you what. I can let you have it for a thousand."

Mike breaks out in a laugh so loud and strong that for one moment, I almost love him.

He buys it for himself.

∽

Our last stop of the day is a shoe store where as his brother, I have so much credited to a card that I could charge something if I needed to. I immediately break the card into pieces. The clerk is so angry she starts to cry.

The Toyota is purged of Miriam merchandise.

We collapse on a bench outside the shoe store. The banners that hang overhead remind me of the special banners in church for Easter. I remember the men on the ladders, hanging them, getting it right while the altar society ladies supervised. Mel and I watched. I haven't been to church for so many years. The mall was Miriam's place of worship.

I'm tired.

He reaches down and grips his ankle with a wince. "We closed down the mall."

"I wish that were possible. Closing it down."

He sits up and pats me. I'm tired of being patted. I'm not a dog.

The mall begins to lock itself down for the night. Every store has a huge metal gate that rattles down, the noise of those gates, the shriek, the clang, the jingle of keys. It sounds like prison, not church. Like a jail.

This is not jail. This is a mall.

Dear God, I'm so tired.

Amen.

∽

I jump, cringe, when I wake. "Sorry."

"Don't worry about it." He wipes at the shoulder of his suit with a hanky.

"I, um, I didn't sleep much last night." I seem to be able to sleep everywhere but where I'm supposed to. I check my stupid watch. I was asleep for forty-five minutes on this bench, drooling on Mike. The stores closed almost an hour ago. He let me sleep.

"I noticed. Do you want me to drive?"

"Please." I give him the keys and we go out to where I've parked my terrible car. His disgust at taking the wheel of the Toyota is palpable. "Mike, lots of people drive crappy cars, all right?"

"All right." His voice is soft.

"Not everyone's life is like yours."

"Whatever you say, Gentry." He sounds patient.

My eyes keep sinking shut. Oh, God, I want to sleep.

Amen.

∽

I wake up in my crappy driveway, at my crappy house. "You remembered how to get back."

"It's so flat, I could sight my way home."

That was Chinese food, so I decide I can eat again. I go upstairs and make us a light snack of cheeseburgers. Mike eats part of one. I eat two. "You sure can put it away."

"Yes. I can."

"But it's catching up with you."

"Thanks. Do we always have to talk about how fat I am?"

"Okay. Let's talk about cars instead." He punches himself in the chest. "Do you have any antacid?"

"I might be fat, but I'm too young to get heartburn." I give him some milk.

We go downstairs. He strips away in front of me but I close the door to my study. I have no modesty because I lived in a dorm from the age of twelve on and that will cure you of it, but I would kill myself if Mike saw this belly.

I emerge to iron a clean shirt.

"What are you doing?"

"Brain surgery."

"No, seriously."

"Ironing a shirt."

"Why do you keep doing that?"

"So it won't be wrinkled."

He's disbelieving. "Don't you send them out?"

"They starch them too much."

"You should order them 'folded no starch.'"

"Hm." I iron my own shirts because I'm taking no chances. I won't tell Mr. Folded No Starch that Miriam handled the cleaners, and that as a result I always had shirts with cuffs and collars as starched and swooping as nun's wimples. My shirts were rigid enough to crack when I put them on. I won't reveal this particular brand of sadism on the part of Miriam.

She's dead, after all.

I hang up the shirt. I go behind my incomparably ugly wet bar and pour us each a drink, ice in Mike's, mine neat.

Hey, Poison.

We sit on the couch. We drink. We sigh in unison. "Gentry, I need to stretch out. My ankle hurts from those damn marble floors." I move to the floor. He groans and straightens his leg, rubs his ankle. "I tore it up pretty badly playing racquetball." I nod, hoping not to laugh. "A bad back and a bum ankle. I hate being old."

Well, Mike, you are old. I don't care how good you look, I think you're old. Especially for racquetball. Sandy and I used to watch racquetball at college just to laugh. We called it "human pinball." Of course, my jaw aches sometimes in the winter.

"Hey Mike? Do you want a heating pad?"

"No. I usually ice it." I go upstairs and hunt through Miriam's copious medical supplies, make an ice bag, bring it down to him. I can see that he's truly in pain, and grateful. "Thanks. Why don't you bring your sleeping bag out here?"

"Pardon?"

"Put your sleeping bag out here so you don't have to sit on that carpet."

"Hey Mike? Do you mind if I, um, watch the news?"

"Watch whatever you want. I'll be out like a light in a minute. But don't sleep in that creepy little room." I go into the creepy little room. I look around. He's right. It is a creepy little room, but I always felt safe in here. I bring out my sleeping bag and sit on it, leaning against the end of the couch where Mike has his feet.

I feel like a dog.

"What was that room supposed to be, anyway?"

"I think it's a bedroom. It has a closet."

"I don't think so. Not without any windows. Maybe it was supposed to be a bomb shelter."

"Who would carpet a bomb shelter?"

"This is Oklahoma, Gentry. Whatever it is, it's creepy." His voice is thick with imminent sleep. "That's such a creepy little room." He starts to snore.

I'm tired, very, very tired. Oh God, are You going to let me sleep? Please? Thank You. Amen.

~

"Gentry, wake up. Wake up, now." He puts a hand on me and I hit at him. "Settle down." He backs off, and we sit there while I do what it is I do after these nightmares. "It's okay. It's all right."

"I'm sorry."

"That's what you keep saying in your sleep. Don't worry about it. Graham had night terrors for years. I'm used to it." He gets up to turn off the television.

"Hey Mike? Could you, um, leave it on?"

"Sure. Can I turn it down a little?"

"Yes." He lies back down. He reaches down and tries to pat me. "If you touch me again I'll rip off your hand."

"Gentry . . ."

"I'm sorry."

"Just try to sleep." Oh, the last thing I want to do, ever, is sleep. I listen until he snores. I get up, take his melted ice bag upstairs, put the dishes away, eat some cereal. I think about coffee but go back downstairs for a little more poison instead.

I could iron another shirt.

Mike is still snoring. I think maybe if I listen to him breathe, I could sleep. I try.

Not a happening thing.

I lie there, look at the television. Lunatics on parade. I never had a television, and look at me now. I wouldn't be able to live without this late night stupidity, these idiots who shout at each other about their private lives. These people make me feel normal, almost. But I could be on a number of panels.

Oh, God, why did I have to do that in front of him, of all the people in the world? You might have spared me that.

"Gentry? Are you asleep?"

"No."

He gets up and goes over to his suitcase. Maybe he has a shot of barbiturates in there for me, or maybe a gun. Maybe he'll shoot me and put me out of my misery. I sit up to face my fate.

Letters. That's what he has. All the letters I ever wrote her, I think.

"Gretchen wanted you to look at these." Oh God, she saved hers the way I saved mine, and she sent them out here? For me? "She wants them back, but she had this idea that if you put them all in order with hers, and read them, that you could, I don't know, understand? Make it right?"

She wants to make it right.

I take the letters out to my Jeep, where I have hers hidden. I sit there and I put them all in order. The few I wrote to Kathryn are in with hers, too. I didn't save any letter that Kathryn sent me, I only saved Gretchen's. Oh Gretchen I love you, you know that, don't you?

I don't have to read the first one I wrote to her. I remember every word. But her reply, I'll read that. I used to sit out here and read them, but it's been two years, I haven't read any of them since before that honeymoon.

I'll read them all, and see if we can make it right.

Dear Gentry,

I'm mad at you. I'm mad at you for leaving and I'm mad at you for not writing. But I forgive you, because you finally wrote.

Bosco misses you very much. I have to make sure he doesn't run away and try to find you, that's how much he misses you. He sits in my window seat and he looks out the window, thinking about how maybe you will come back. Sometimes he cries about it, but I tell him not to cry because he is too old to cry about stuff like this. Sometimes we go in the little house and we lay on the bed together.

Yes, he sleeps with me. I comb his hair a lot. I tell him secrets. He never tells secrets, did you know that about Bosco? I bet you knew that. I will never tell secrets, again, either.

Mom is very nice to Bosco. She pets him and she lets him eat off her dishes. Mom and I have made a bunch of jam, strawberry and raspberry, and we did broccoli, corn, and peas.

Coach Gilroy came over. He brought a yearbook up here, he wanted to send it to you. I looked through it and there were a lot of pictures of you, so he said to forget it, he could get you another one, I could keep it. I thought that was nice.

I'm yours, too,
Gretchen

Hey Gretchen,

Lorrie does not have to get a yearbook for me. I remember everything.

Do you like the middle school? Things change between grade school and middle school, don't they? I hope you like school a little more, and that school starts to like you.

This letter is going to be mostly about two friends of mine, Miriam and Sandy. Sandy is a friend from college, the friend I was staying with until two weeks ago. We went fishing last weekend at Thunderbird Lake. I caught some bass and a whole "mess" of catfish, great big ugly ones with whiskers. Catfish slide along the bottoms of the creeks and suck up all the offal but they are fatty and very tasty. I gave the bass to Paige, Sandy's wife, because she likes them, and I came home with the rest. I didn't cook them all, there were too many, so I froze some and when Miriam opens the freezer, she screams because they're so ugly.

I'll cook the rest this weekend.

I wish I could taste that jam.

Do you know something stupid? I don't have a picture of Bosco. I tried to tell Miriam what Bosco looks like, but I am no good at describing things. I guess I would really like a photo. Could you please maybe do that for me?

Here is another address. I moved right next door to where I was, but you need to send my mail c/o Miriam Hirsch, because the mailman is picky and he won't put any mail in the box that doesn't have her name on it, and the landlord won't put my name on there because my name isn't on the lease. Petty tyrants, the both of them.

Yours,
Gentry

Dear Gentry,

Who is this Miriam? You live with her? Is she nice? Is she as pretty as my mother? My mom is really pretty, now, really pretty. She takes walks with me and Bosco on the beach, and she quit smoking. If you saw my mom, you wouldn't believe how pretty she is. She is the prettiest person in the whole entire world, my mom.

I would eat anything you cooked, even scum sucking catfish.

Do you like your new job? Are there any interesting kids in your classes? School is okay, I guess. Yes, it's better. Here are some Bosco pictures and also my school picture from last year. Stupid, huh?

Gretchen

Hey Gretchen,

To answer your question about Miriam, she is my girlfriend I guess. And to answer your other question, not everyone in the world gets to be as beautiful as your mother.

Thank you very much for the school picture. For a school picture that is really nice. I think one of the worst things about being a teacher is having your picture taken by those school photographers every year, and knowing that this ugly picture will be in the yearbook. I don't change that much from year to year. Why can't they run the same one? The students change, it isn't like they would know, or care, even. Of course, this is not a problem where I work, now. My job is not a teaching job.

And here is another new address. My last name is on this mailbox.

Do you need another computer? Did your sister take hers? Because I finally set up my computer, and we could chat.

I remain, yours,
Gentry

Dear Gentry,

Is Miriam's name also on your new mailbox?

Do you like Biloxi Drive?

Why aren't you teaching?

Marci visited for Thanksgiving. She asked if I had heard from you. I told her about Miriam. As much as I know. Marci was weird. She wouldn't pet Bosco. I think she maybe even kicked him. I bet she did. But she took a picture of all of us, and here it is. Of course, she is not in it, because she was taking it.

Can you see how beautiful my mother looks?

Did you have a nice Thanksgiving? Do you remember last Thanksgiving, when you lived here? You ate with Coach Gilroy. And you were sick that weekend.

Yours,
Gretchen

PS. Gentry, I'm adding this on the way to the post office. Marci took the computer with her when she left. Mom says no Internet. Mom says no email. I have to show her all your letters, Gentry, and all the letters I send, unless I sneak them, I wanted to tell you that. I don't know exactly how I feel about your having a girlfriend but I love you so much, Gentry, and I miss you, and so does Bosco.

Hey Gretchen,

Thank you for the picture. You're right. Your mother looks beautiful. I think you look just like her. And Bosco looks very good, very fine, healthy and happy. Thank you for taking such good care of my dog. But of the three, you, your mother, and Bosco, you're the prettiest. Even Miriam says so. She called you a "Shiksa goddess." She says I'm no good at describing anything.

Miriam is very nice, but she does not know my name.

Do you really think your sister kicked Bosco? It takes a mean person to kick a dog, and I don't think she would do that. If someone kicked Bosco, I'm absolutely sure it wasn't her.

I would like to send you a present at Christmas. I need to know if that would be all right. Can you find out? Please ask both parents.

Yours, always,
Gentry

Dear Gentry,

This is a letter I'm writing at school and sending from here. For starters, I'm not now, nor have I ever been, a goddess. Gross. Please don't ever call me a goddess.

Also, it's okay. You can send me a present. Mom and Dad talked about it, and they say okay even though Mom had the kind of reservations that don't involve a restaurant.

Gentry, I think you are good at everything. Except ordering in restaurants and cooking. But what exactly do you do if you don't teach?

We have to go to my dad's the day after Christmas. Bosco will stay home and keep Mom company. Do you remember last Christmas? You got a new coat from Mel.

He was here while you were in the hospital, did you know he came up to the house one day and introduced himself to us? Well, to me and Mom, Marci wouldn't come out of her room, she was packing. He came up to see all of us, but I think he was trying to find out what happened to you. I wonder, too. I want to know what happened to you.

He was very nice. He has little hands, and I was surprised at how tall he is. I like his accent. He was nice to me. But when he and Mom went outside, he yelled at her. I listened. I heard what he said, he demanded in the name of God that she stop hiding the truth, and things like that. He left, and Mom cried. Mom doesn't know the truth, either.

I hope you have a nice holiday, I will try to write to you from Dad's. If I can't, Merry Christmas.

Always, yours, love,
Gretchen

Hey Gretchen,

Mel was born in Australia. That is the accent. But I think he sounds more Irish. I wish I could hear his voice. This is the first Christmas I won't be with Mel in seventeen years. I miss him. He yelled at me, sometimes, and I always called it "the voice of God." I miss him enough to die.

I don't know what happened to me that night either, so if you were trying to ask me, the answer is still, I can't remember.

This is not a very cheerful letter. I think I'll go and write another time.

Yours,
Gentry

Hey Kathryn,

I asked if I could give her a present, you and Mike talked about it, I got permission, and I don't recall any parameters as far as what would be a permissible amount to spend on Gretchen.

The model I had sent out to her is not expensive. There is reference software on there I picked out. I really thought about this, Kathryn, I can afford it, I want her to have a computer and I don't want her to have some piece of junk. I wanted to build one for her, but I don't have the time to do it. Gretchen needs her own computer and access to the Internet for research. If you don't want me to email her, I won't email her. This is about her having the educational tools she needs. What can I say to make you see that this is important?

To answer your question, yes, Bosco was on heartworm medication before we came to Oregon. He took the once a month kind. There is a lot of heartworm in the Midwest but I didn't know you had it out there or I would have left him on it.

If you decide not to let Gretchen have the computer, please donate it to the lab at the high school.

Sincerely,
Gentry

Dear Gentry,

Thank You, Thank You, Thank You. It only took a minute to set it up. I love everything on there, it is perfect. I have star charts, lunar charts, and where did you find a tide pool simulation? It is interesting to see what tide pools are like by other oceans. Tide pools are interesting, aren't they? I love all the games, and I love it that there is no stupid "Hello Kitty" stuff on there.

But. No Ruin?

Yours, forever,
Gretchen

Hey Gretchen,

No Ruin. You're welcome.

Please put your arms around Bosco's neck and give him a good hug and pull him around for me. Pull him around until he makes that funny sound, and then wrestle him. Can you do that for me or is he too big? I am worried that no one wrestles him anymore.

I hope you had a good Christmas. I got my usual avalanche of cards. I sent another change of address form to Darren over at your post office and everything found me. Will you tell him thank you when you're in there? I'll spend January writing back to everyone.

Here is another address. Please write.

Mel sent me smoked salmon from Oregon. He found it in a catalog. Can you believe that? I miss the food, I miss the apples, the strawberries, the peaches, I thought Georgia had the best peaches but you had wonderful peaches in Oregon. I miss the seafood, I miss the fish. Catfish doesn't compare with brook trout and salmon and clams.

Enough.

On Christmas Day, I went to church with the Sandersons. I got to hold their new baby. It was beautiful. Crowded, but beautiful. It was an earlier Mass. I wanted to go to midnight Mass, I usually do. Of course at the monastery I go to quite a few Masses over the holidays. But I was happy to go at all this year.

Happy New Year. I'll write more when we're settled.

Yours,
Gentry

Dear Gentry,

You sure move a lot. This is the fourth address. I thought you hated to move. Do you like Brooks Street better than Biloxi Street? Are you going to stay put?

School is good. Gentry, I kind of like it, now.

I tried to wrestle Bosco and he was very careful with me, but I think he had some fun. He's sad right now. He keeps looking for you. He goes into the little house and looks through it, every corner, under the sink and in the big closet and behind that bathtub. He's happy when he's looking, like it's a game, but then he gets sad and lays down in front of the fridge and he won't move. He just lays there. I'm not sure how to make him feel better.

Who is it that you will write to, who do you get all the cards from?

Yours, forever,
Gretchen

Hey Gretchen,

I think it's a draw, as far as Biloxi Street and Brooks Street. I liked McCullough Street the best. We will be moving soon. We haven't given notice, but it's only a matter of time. It seems to only ever be a matter of time. We stayed at one apartment for three weeks. I never even sent you that address.

You asked about my Christmas cards. I get cards from my former students. These kids, Gretchen, you wouldn't believe these kids. Some of my students write me from prison. Some are as successful as your dad. I always write back, always. And I must cut this short, and finish.

I miss you, Gretchen, so much sometimes I think I'll die. So much. And of course I think of Bosco every day. I never meant to make him sad.

Yours, forever, too,
Gentry

Dear Gentry,

Have you caught any more catfish?

Speaking of scum sucking bottom feeders, I saw Marci at Christmas. If you thought she knew everything before, you should see her now. She knows EVERYTHING, now that she is at school. No one else can even talk about anything, because she has to run every conversation. Dad got mad at her. She even dresses stupid.

She goes into New York on the weekends and she has seen where ex President Bush has a summer house. BIG DEAL.

She wrote short stories for us for Christmas gifts. Mine was about a woman with breast cancer. What a nice present.

Yours, always,
Gretchen

Hey Gretchen,

You should have seen what an idiot I was the first year I was home from college. We only had enough money for a bus ticket home for one of the holidays. I came home for Christmas. I rode the bus back to the monastery to see Mel and to tell him all about how smart I was and stupid he was, I guess. Mel was a patient, patient man. He didn't even yell. After I started teaching, I had to call him all the time to tell him how amazing and fantastic and mind-blowing that was, because I guess no one had ever been a teacher before.

But as insufferable as I was, I never gave anyone a short story about cancer. I haven't laughed so hard in a year. I miss all of you so much.

I couldn't always go see Mel on my breaks. Sometimes I'd go on a mission, which was interesting. When I was a freshman, my roommate Daniel took me home for Thanksgiving. His family home makes your dad's look like my little house at the beach. It was like a cathedral. I felt like a wandering altar boy and was made to mow the lawn by the gardener. And once I went with a girlfriend to her grandparents' farm, where I made a bad impression and spent a lot of time with the tractor. It was better to go home to Mel.

I was always home for Christmas. In the summers, I was too busy cultivating corn, haying, combining to bother Mel with all my newfound knowledge. I think he was probably grateful not to have to listen to me.

Maybe Mel can find a summer job for your sister in North Dakota. I can ask him. Would you like that? Has she ever done haying? Does she have much custom combining experience?

Yours, I remain,
Gentry

Dear Gentry,

Happy New Year! Do you have any resolutions? I don't believe in them. Please send me a list of yours so I can make fun of them.

Mom said she didn't have any, either. She doesn't smoke, and she doesn't drink, and she walks one or two miles every morning. She is doing really well, Gentry. Bosco has a New Year's resolution about you.

I will let you guess what it is.

I miss you so much. What is a mission? Is it a God thing?

Yours, for the whole entire New Year,
Gretchen

Hey Gretchen,

The Short List of Gentry's New Year's Resolutions:

1. Make none. Wait . . .

Miriam thinks I should make some, but I don't believe in New Year's resolutions. Like Valentines, I don't believe in those, either. I explained to Miriam that I don't believe in giving Valentines and she took it very well. She knows that it's a Catholic day, and Miriam is not so excited about anything Catholic. So Valentine's Day is not an issue.

My job is very dull. If I were to have any New Year's resolutions, they would involve finding a better job.

A mission is a trip organized through a church or a nonprofit where you pay your own way to go do some kind of work for the betterment of a community. I went all over the south because I had to be able to take the bus. This was pre-Jeep. The God parts of it were subsidiary to whatever project we were taking on. I mostly helped build things. Shelters, clinics, schools. Even when it was a church, it felt like a building project more than anything else. Have you heard of the medical missions?

I need to find a place around here to volunteer for something. I don't know what needs doing around here. By the looks of certain neighborhoods, everything.

Miriam's dad called me a "pisher" last Sunday. I had to look that up. I'm not now, nor have I ever been, a pisher. He called Miriam's brother-in-law a "mensch." I looked that up, too, and I don't understand why he gets to be a mensch, and I have to be a pisher. Is that fair? Since we're both goyim and all.

If a Valentine shows up at your house, just ignore it, throw it away, rip it up. Please pet my dog for me. Tell him I miss him.

Yours, truly, always,
Gentry

Dear Gentry,

I bet you are a mensch, Gentry, whatever that is. I know you are not a pisher. That is one mean thing to call someone. Especially a guy, because so many of you are. I read an article about it and it said that something like eighty percent of bedwetters are male. I wonder why. There is no satisfactory physiological explanation.

Mom said at least you are not a putz.

Thank you for the Valentine. It isn't Valentine's day yet, but it came two weeks early, so I opened it. I like funny Valentines, I just hate mushy ones. Bosco is saving it. I thought you might send one to my mother, but I guess that's pretty stupid of me, huh. Thinking that.

You said, in your letter, that Miriam is not so excited about anything Catholic. You are Catholic?

I've heard of the medical missions but I never thought they had anything to do with God. The one that worries me is the cleft palate mission in South America. Listen, Gentry, these communities are very isolated so they have a big problem with recessive genetic traits like cleft palate. The missions come in and fix up the kids so they can live normal lives. That sounds like a really good idea but then they get married and have kids with even worse palates. I tried to talk about this with Mom and she said I'm Darwinian. That means survival of the fittest, which is a terrible idea. I'm not sure what the answer is but it makes me upset to think about so I am going to write about something else, now. Except to say that I don't understand how you can believe in God when I think about it.

Don't be mad.

Yours, forever,
Gretchen

Hey Gretchen,

I would never be mad at you for talking about anything. And I am not very adept at talking about God. I am religious, not spiritual. I am not sure if that distinction makes any sense to you. I know and trust that God loves me, but I have no idea why. I owe Him everything. All I manage to give in return is one tenth of my income and a constant stream of apologies for my behavior.

But that is God on the personal, and you are asking about a much larger thing. You are asking how anyone can maintain belief in a benevolent God when there is injustice and suffering and cruelty in this world. If you want to know how I manage it, I believe God's plan is so much larger than we could possibly comprehend. We see less than a speck of it. I can't judge the whole by the mote I perceive. Like the blind men and the elephant story, except if the elephant was the size of the cosmos, and the blind men were the size of atoms. This doesn't make me feel insignificant, it makes me feel part of something incomprehensibly vast and eternal. So I find comfort in the fact that I don't understand. So I cling to the rote. I go to Mass, say my prayers, sing the hymns, take communion. I light the candle and go on. This works for me.

Always, yours,
Gentry

Hey Kathryn,

As you know, Gretchen's birthday is coming, and I want to get her something. Being who I am, I'd like to get her something electrical. Tell me what to get her, tell me what not to get her, I'll abide by what you suggest, I promise.

Sincerely,
Gentry

Dear Gentry,

Here is a picture of me on my twelfth birthday. Am I cute? As you can see, Bosco looks very cute in a party hat. Mom took this. The boy in the picture is named Chris. He likes computer games and science. He also likes Japanese animation, which I don't.

You were the first friend I ever had. Chris is the second.

Gentry, you give me the best presents, ever. I have never seen a phone this neat. Incredibly neat. But how did you know I finally have a friend to talk to on the phone? Did Mom tell you?

Have you learned to cook anything else besides fish, marshmallows and coffee? I would like a photo, please. Maybe one with you and Miriam? How is your job? Do you like it? Are you ever going to be a teacher again?

That last letter was very interesting. It made me think. I like getting a letter from you that is about more than what you do, and about what you think. I have a different name for what you call God, Gentry. I believe in it too, but I call it "physics."

Your letters are sometimes too short. I wish all your letters were longer.

Yours, forever, always,
Gretchen

Hey Gretchen,

It's hard to write long letters when you're the nomad I have been in the last few months. Miriam seems to like this place so I'm hoping we can stay put for a while.

I had to answer all the cards. I'm trying to write. Please be patient.

How is my dog? I miss him.

Toast and scrambled eggs, how about that. I'm working on fried, but flipping is tricky. So is buttering the toast. It's about the thickness of a potato chip when I'm done. I've mastered everything in the category of breakfast pork. I heat up a mean can of soup. I make huge sandwiches and they are all good because I've learned that the secret to making a good sandwich is to set a pickle beside it. As you may remember, I open a pickle jar with remarkable ease.

So you see, I can do nothing complex, I think that will have to wait.

Yes, you are cute. Let's see. Chris? Just friends, right? You are not allowed to grow up, Gretchen, please don't get any older. You can keep having birthdays but keep turning twelve from now on. I'll put Bosco on it, make it one of his jobs, to keep you from getting older.

Yes, I wrote to your mother and she suggested the phone. Please don't give me any credit for the idea. I only found the incredibly neat phone and mailed it out there. I'm as bad as your dad, now, I no longer know what you like.

My job is kind of fun, actually. It's not a teaching job, but I find it gives me some chances to teach, you know, the students who work here for me, the students who use the lab. Of course, if I were mistaken for a student at the high school, you can imagine that happens here, too.

Have I told you that Miriam teaches here in the nursing program? She was a nurse, previously. She is an excellent teacher.

You asked for a picture. I looked through the pictures taken of me over at Miriam's parents' house and I seem to be eating in most of them. Her dad says that no one can eat like the goyim. In the rest, I look like I'm trying not to burp. Anyway, no one takes pictures of me that I like, so I don't have a recent one. I finally got an Oklahoma driver's license. So I'm sending you my Oregon one. Weird, I know, I'm weird. But it's a better picture than the one in the yearbook, I'd bet money on it.

I'm smiling right now. I'm remembering your bringing out jars to the little house for me to open. I'm wondering what your mother does, now. Her hands are so small.

Could I ask you a question? How tall is your mother?

Yours,
Gentry

Dear Gentry,

You will never be as bad as my dad, ever, in a million years, never say that. Don't worry, he didn't get me another bike, the blue one is the right size now and I told him so he wouldn't get me a third bike, probably a pink one. With a Hello Kitty seat, or something. He got me riding lessons. Mom told him I wanted those, too.

Thank you for the driver's license. I will use it to go buy beer in bars, I think, since I'm in such a hurry to grow up.

Actually, Gentry, that's a cute picture of you. But the one in the yearbook is cute, too. There are some funny ones of you in the yearbook. There is one of you on the blue bike, popping a wheelie. There is the one of you teaching PE, you are blowing a whistle and your cheeks are puffing out. There is one of you helping Tiffany Green in the lab. There is one of you dancing with Miss Lazarre at prom, that one is really cute, really, you can't even tell that your shirt cuffs were stapled shut.

There are more. There are about fifty of you in there, I think. And Marci put them all in there, you know. She says she doesn't want her copy of the yearbook, so if you decide you want one, tell me and I will send it out.

Bosco is excited about the spring. He is barking at all the birds that come around this time of year, and he is busy digging for moles. Mom got him some doggie vitamins and they make his breath smell even worse if you can imagine that. But he looks very shiny and happy.

When Mom needs a jar opened, she bangs the lid with the edge of a butter knife, and she swears a little, and then I get it off for her. My hands are way bigger than hers, now. I'm going to be too tall. Mom is 5'2." Why?

I read your letters all the time. Even the weird God one.

Bosco misses you, but he is doing fine.

Yours, Forever,
Gretchen

Hey Gretchen,

Why is baking so hard? I mean, there are too many ingredients, and you have to combine them in certain ways or it won't work, and it all seems to be contingent on certain oven conditions. It's worse than chemistry, and I hated chemistry. At least when I messed up in chemistry, no one had to try to eat it. I don't like baking, not at all. I like frying. Or heating. I may never progress beyond this level.

My job is dull, dull, dull.

I'm not in a very good mood. I think if Bosco were here, he would cheer me up. He always believed in good days and good moods. He was always happy.

Yours, grumpy.
Gentry

Dear Gentry,

Why? Why are you in a bad mood? Are you going to get all sad, again, like you were this time last year? Maybe it is a seasonal cycle, or a lunar pull, that pulls you all out of your normal orbit.

Or maybe you should avoid baking. I read Mom your letter and she suggested that you use mixes, you know, like Betty Crocker or Jiffy, and she said baking is really hard, and not to get discouraged.

I'm impressed. I guess I should have started you out at the beginning, like toast and soup, instead of trying to teach you how to make complicated things like lasagna. I guess that Miriam is a better teacher than me.

Also, I can't wait to take chemistry.

The beach is beautiful. Everyone is flying kites, and it makes me think of you. We never got to do that.

Bosco is fine. He is kind of restless, though, he runs on the beach a lot and he keeps running up to every man in a blue coat. I think he thinks you have been gone long enough, and it is time for you to come back.

Yours, Hoping,
Gretchen

Hey Gretchen,

I miss Bosco. I miss you. I miss Oregon. I miss teaching.

You are a fine teacher. You taught me many, many things. I imagine you could have even made chemistry understandable.

I'm sorry about the kite thing. I always meant to fly a kite with you. We would have had to learn how to do it together, and I would have looked foolish but I have always wanted to learn. I've been sitting here wondering why we never did that.

Miriam wants to buy a house. We spend the weekends looking at houses. I hate every house we look at, and Miriam is getting a little upset with me. But I can't help it. The houses here are awful.

Something interesting about sharing a mailbox with another person. You find out all the things that are wrong with you. I had no idea how many things were wrong with me.

I have nightmares, my clothing is too big, I can't order in restaurants, my hair is too long, I spend too much time on the computer, I fish too much, I go to church too much, my ear is pierced, I read too much, I volunteer, I sing in the shower, I don't make enough money, and all my friends are English majors. I'm no good, I guess.

How is school? How is your mother? Do you ever see Lorrie Gilroy, did you know he married Vicki Lazarre? I miss them. I miss you, more.

Yours, such as I am,
Gentry

Dear Gentry,

I would just like to point out that you shared our mailbox for almost a year, and I never thought anything was wrong with you. I want you to know that Mom just about died laughing when she read that letter.

There are lots and lots of nice things about you. You are very clean, and you always have nice breath because you brush your teeth all the time. You have pretty hair. Mom says you are the tidiest man she ever met. And you are smart, and also funny, not to mention interesting.

But I never knew you had nightmares all the time. Is this something new? What kinds of nightmares do you have?

Yes, of course I knew Coach Gilroy got married. This is a little town, remember? I see them at the store. Mom takes me now, she helps with the shopping, again. When we see them, we all talk about you. They are having a baby, you know.

I think you are great,
Gretchen

Hey Gretchen,

I'm sorry that I haven't written. I know that Lorrie and Vicki are having a baby. They both write to me. I do write back. I'm happy, and I'm envious.

The bad dreams. You may have noticed that I am, shall we say, weird? And there are years in my life that I don't remember. I think the nightmares are about all of that.

Here is a new address, we bought a stupid house, I don't know why, but here we are. If you could see this house. But thankfully, you never will.

Did you have a nice Easter? I sat at Miriam's parents and wished for my church. I don't go to church every Sunday, anymore. Miriam likes to visit her family on Sundays, Sundays for her are like my Saturdays, and I get tired of discussing it. So, we go over to her parents on quite a few Sundays. And Easter is a Sunday, you see.

Gretchen, have you ever been to church, ever? What is the most beautiful thing you know? That is my church on Easter.

Forgive me, I sound ridiculous. You must be tired of letters like this one.

Love, Yours, Always,
Gentry

Dear Gentry,

I'm not tired of your crabby letters. I just worry about you. Gentry, you need to go to church. But to answer your question, no, I never have been to church, ever.

Marci was here at Easter, unfortunately, I mean here at the beach, not here at

Dad's. She spent one whole entire day talking about how terrible it is here, how economically underprivileged everyone is. I think she meant poor.

Vu came by to see her and he left, calling her a pseudo intellectual dilettante. Does this mean they are in an argument? Bosco kept breathing his vitamin breath on her, and leaning on her. She ignored him. He just wanted a pat.

I think Mom was ready to start drinking again by the time she left. But Mom didn't. Mom hasn't had a drink for over a year, now. They had some kind of a party for her at AA in March. I know that it is supposed to be embarrassing to have a parent that goes to AA, but Gentry, I'm so proud of my mom.

Your house couldn't be that ugly, because you live in it. But does that mean you are staying there?

I have been thinking about your nightmares. I don't think you should try to remember too much unless you are ready for it. Because sometimes it's easier to forget the things that scare you, I know. But will you promise me something? When you do remember, will you tell me about it, will you tell me what you remember? And will you please remember that I'm not a baby, and that I will never make fun, or laugh, or be mean? Because I love you, Gentry.

What is the most beautiful thing I know?

You.

Always,
Gretchen

Hey Gretchen,

I'm not now, nor have I ever been, beautiful.

I'm proud of your mother, too. I think what she is doing is strong.

I don't plan to remember anything. But if I ever do, I will talk about whatever I remember with you. This is a promise.

I was looking forward to this summer. A friend of mine, Kevin, is getting married in Kentucky. Kevin was my roommate for years. He always had more clothes than I did, and he always had more friends than I did. Luckily, he shared both.

He is marrying is someone I haven't met. Her name is Parker. This will be a very large wedding. Many people I haven't seen since I graduated from college will be there. I was looking forward to it. But I won't be going.

Other friends are moving, leaving for Colorado right after Kevin's wedding. I was thinking of going along to help with the driving. But it looks like I'll stay here and work, instead, for reasons I won't go into.

The moving friends are Paige and Sandy Sanderson, and they have three kids. The kids are named as follows: Lucy Rose, Byron Branwell, and Percy Shelley. Since you liked my name, I thought you might have mercy on these, as well. I'll miss these friends. I'm so sad.

Please pet Bosco for me.

Yours,
Gentry

Dear Gentry,

It is very, very hard to have your best friends move away from you. Believe me, I know. If you are lucky, the friend will leave something for you to hold on to when you miss him, something like his dog, or his beautiful name. I think if your friends would just leave you one of the kids with the weird names, you would feel much better.

I'm almost done with sixth grade. Bosco has been here a year, now, and I think it will be all right if I leave him with Mom and visit my dad this summer, just for six weeks. Mom promises to take him down on the beach, and brush him, and throw sticks, and let him sleep in her room. But if he gets too lonely, she promises I can come home and see him. She says he is the "priority." Dad agrees.

I take riding lessons every two weeks when I'm at Dad's, and I'm going to be at the stables every day while I'm there. Graham is still terrible, he is mean and gross, but Spencer takes riding lessons at the same stable I do. We have fun there. He is younger than I am, but we get along. He's very funny. He feels like my brother and he feels safe. Marci says that Graham feels like a big gall bladder that's going to explode all over the house. As you would say, "Not kind." I like how you use the word "kind." Marci is actually kind to Graham, and I'm not. Spencer and I play this game where we ignore him for one, two, three days at a time. It's one of those extremely funny things to do that leaves you feeling ashamed. But he's so awful, Gentry.

Gentry, why are my brothers so different? It's like a normal person got divided in two, and Spencer got everything sweet, and Graham got the rest. Marci calls them Cain and Abel, and I don't understand what that means. But it's a Bible thing, so I thought you might.

It has been almost a year, Gentry. Isn't that long enough?

Always yours,
Gretchen

Hey Gretchen,

No, a year is not enough. But I wish it were.

Cain and Abel were the sons of Adam and Eve. Cain killed Abel. It is possibly not a very nice nickname for those boys, even if it seems apt. Not that Graham would kill anyone.

I only saw Spencer twice. He carried your bag, and he seemed polite. You know that manners score points with me, correct? Spencer scored high. Graham made a different sort of impression on me. There is a brother at the monastery named Brother Victor. He has classifications for people, and he would call Spencer an "altar boy." Brother Victor would call Graham a "nose picker."

What you're describing is the hardest part of teaching for me. Teachers are supposed to find something to like about every student. Occasionally you have a student you can't stand in any way. You keep studying the kid, hoping to find the redeemable characteristic that will make him tolerable. And the more you look, the more you loathe. It's a terrible thing to feel as a teacher. It must be even more difficult as a sister.

But one thing I learned from teaching was that people, kids especially, change. Sometimes for the worse, but sometimes for the better. I don't seem to be able to change at all.

Yours,
Gentry

Dear Gentry,

What is wrong? What is it? Oh Gentry, please write and tell me what is wrong? You need to write me, and let me know if Miriam is taking good care of you, and that you're all right.

Gentry, you have to be all right. Because something scary is happening out here. And I need you to be okay. My mom has a spot on her lung. And the doctors are going to operate on her next week. By the time you get this letter, we'll know if it is cancer. My mom is only forty-eight. So it can't be cancer, right?

I keep thinking about that stupid story Marci gave me at Christmas and I want to kill her. That stupid story did it, and I'm going to tell her that when I see her. This is all her fault. She is coming home for the surgery, why doesn't she just stay away, she doesn't care.

Gentry, I'm so scared. Please come back.

Gretchen

Dear Gentry,

Mom is going to be fine. There is a little treatment to do but she is going to be fine, but all I can do is cry. My stomach hurts all the time, all the time. Gentry, what if my mother died? Anyone can die, do you know that, Gentry? Anyone. And all I could think about, once we knew Mom was okay, was what if you died. What if you die, Gentry. And not here. Please please please please please please please please come back.

Yours, Always, Forever,
Gretchen

Hey Gretchen,

I can't come back to Oregon.

I think I spent this week on my knees.

Your mother will be fine? Will you hug her for me? She is so fragile, so carefully hug her from me, and kiss her? Please, kiss her? And don't tell her it's from me? She would never accept a kiss from me, never, but kiss her. Because that's what I would do if I were there.

Stories are only stories, you know that. Please don't always blame everything on your sister, everything can't be her fault. She is not to blame for any of this. Or the other, not that either. Stop blaming it on her.

Your mother is truly all right?

I don't have any plans to die any time soon. I think about dying. But I promise, that if I die, it won't be from my own sadness or stupidity.

Gretchen, everyone dies. I'm not afraid of dying, because of Heaven. But I don't have all the answers, I don't have any of the answers, only what I believe and what helps me personally. So, as usual, I don't have anything helpful to say.

But your mother is all right? Please let her be all right. I don't have any idea what to say.

Except that I'm still here, and I plan to stay,

Yours, forever,
Gentry

Hey Gretchen,

I know I sounded stupid in that letter. I don't even remember what I wrote, just that it was stupid. I know I said everything wrong, I'm sorry and I don't know what else to say about it. I got my feelings all mixed up with your feelings and I said everything wrong, weird, I shouldn't have talked about your sister, I'm SORRY. It was worse than writing to you about God.

Please write to me,
Gentry

Hey Gretchen,

Fall is here. My friends are gone.

I wonder how my dog is, I wonder if he enjoyed his second summer at the beach. I didn't enjoy a second summer here in Oklahoma. It was too hot for words here, worse than North Dakota.

I worked all summer, because I'm not a teacher, you know. Miriam teaches, but I don't. I run cable and wire things up, and I argue about money with the school administrators.

You must be mad. That's okay, you go ahead and be mad at me. Not one day passes that I don't think of you, and your family, and all the people there and especially Bosco. I wonder if you and your mother put up things, again, this summer, if you made jam.

Is your mother all right? The last time I heard from you was back in July. I hope your mother is doing fine, and that you are, as well. Gretchen, I miss you terribly, and whether you like it or not, I remain, Yours,

Gentry

Hey Gretchen,

It will be winter, soon. You turn thirteen this February. No, I forgot. You have to turn twelve again. Remind Bosco of that for me. I'm sorry. I was upset, forgive me? Please?

Yours,
Gentry

Hey Gretchen,

It has been quite a while since you wrote. I need to hear that you're all right, and how about Bosco? Please let me know that you're okay.

Gentry

Hey Gretchen,

I don't know what to say to you, I'm at a loss. I'll stop writing, I guess. Is that what you want? Do you want me to leave you alone? I will.

Gentry

Hey Gretchen,

I said I would stop writing, and I will. But I had to tell you one last thing. The only thing stronger than how much I miss you is how much I love you. I'll never forget you, and if you ever change your mind, please write to me.

Always,
Gentry

There's one more, one more from Gretchen, one that came later, one I can't stand to read.

Oh, this hurts, God. I want to die all over again. How does this make it right, how can this help, to do this, to rip it open like this? She hated me, the Sandersons moved, I was alone, so alone, Mel wouldn't even talk to me. God, you were all I had, and I couldn't even get to my church.

The door opens.

"Are you going to live?" Mike heard me, how could he help but hear me in this overgrown tarpaper shack of a house.

"I have allergies."

"Sure you do." Of course he comes out and sits in the Jeep with me. He hands me a bottle. "Bad?" I hand him my awful letter, my terrible, sick, craven, sniveling letter about his ex-wife and her illness by way of explanation. He reads it. "No wonder she got so angry." I have no pride, I take off my T-shirt and bury my face in it. Let him see my belly hanging over my sweats, I don't care. At least I don't have glasses. "Gentry, I don't think you understand."

She asked me to come back, and instead I wrote that mess to her.

"Stop crying, and listen to me. She was mad at you because you wouldn't come back, but she was more angry at her mother because she thought Kathryn sent you away."

What stupid lie is this? Why is he lying, why is he doing this? "I don't believe you. You're making this up."

"What?"

"You're making this all up."

"Why? Why would I make something like this up?"

"To get me to stop crying."

"I'm not making this up, but I do wish you'd stop crying." I wish I would, too. I swab my face with my shirt and get a hold of myself. "Was it Kathy who ended it? Is that why you left?"

Why I left. I feel it for one moment, the angry lust when I pinned her to the bed and put my mouth on hers.

Oh God, I need to confess this.

I set it aside.

He shakes his head. "She was such a hard woman to love."

"Stop."

"I'm sorry. Look. I'm just trying to explain to you that Gretchen was an angry little girl for a while, there. I took her to see somebody but it didn't help. She was furious at both of you for getting married."

"Both of us?"

"Both you and Kathy. She was furious when you got married, but she was worse when her mother remarried."

"She *remarried*?"

And now I know, God, that I'm the biggest joke of all. I put my hands on the steering wheel of my useless Jeep and sit there. Useless.

"I thought you knew."

Oh, whatever you thought, about anything, ever, Mike, you were wrong.

"She had the surgery in the summer, and she got married that next spring, right before you did. She married her surgeon. And they live up by us, now. Well, near us. More like right above the old neighborhood, in Northwest."

I'm the punch line of all the great cosmic jokes.

"Will you be all right?"

I'll never be all right.

"Maybe it would help if you cried some more."

I'm past crying. Kill me, God. Just kill me. I know, I'll tell Mike what no one obviously ever has, about me and his other daughter, and Mike will kill me.

"Would you stop PATTING me?"

"I'm sorry." He stops. "Do you want me to stay out here? I won't mind, this is a nice garage. This is nicer than my garage." He takes a good look. "You know what? You should move out here."

"Hey Mike? Go in."

"Are you sure?"

"Yes." I don't need Mike. I have what I need. "Hit the light, please." He turns out the light on his way in. I'm afraid in the dark, but I need to think. I'll think on this to understand, God, why things are the way they are.

I think I'll stay out here forever. I'll stay out here, in my broken Jeep, with my brown poison, in this horrible house, in this ugly town, and I'll drink until I die. But I'm not alone. I have my dead Jeep, my dead wife to keep me company. And You.

God? Are You here? Are You dead, too?

Am I truly alone, now?

IV. REMEMBERING

She said I had to meet her parents. I told her I never made a good first impression. Ever. She said I still had to meet her parents.

I told her they would hate me. I knew from past experience that something would be unacceptable. "Something," meaning "me."

She told me not to worry. Even though she was Jewish, she explained to me that the religious difference was, and I quote, "not an issue." She also acknowledged the fact that I was younger than her. Again, not an issue. The fact that I owned nothing? Not an issue. But height? "I come from a very short family. Whatever you do, don't make my father feel short. Height is a very sensitive issue in my home."

I spent a week trying not to think about my height. I was short for so many of my formative years that I never got used to the idea of being tall. Maybe this explained why even after I hit six feet, I invited the head-patting of a much shorter person. Men called me names like Sport and Kiddo and Pal, not to mention Little Buddy, so maybe that was part of the problem.

What was I supposed to do? Shrink a few inches out of respect before I went over there?

~

Her parents lived in a very nice neighborhood. "That's, um, a huge house." I didn't have such great associations with huge houses.

She sighed. "They live in about three rooms of it. The rest they close off so it stays tidy. Remember. Try not to come across as too tall." I got out of the car and tried to stoop, but stooping ran contrary to four years of Jesuit indoctrination to stand up straight.

I made myself go up the walk to face my fate.

The front door appeared to be regulation height.

"Hey Miriam? Isn't it kind of early for dinner?" We'd gone there right after work, and I was hoping for a last-minute delay.

She rolled her eyes. "Not for MY parents. You'll see." She gave me a good once-over before she opened the door and led me into an entry. "We're HERE!" The air smelled wonderful. I raised my nose like a hound to take it in. Had Bosco been along, he'd have howled.

Miriam elbowed me in the ribs. I hunched a little.

Her parents rushed us, smiling. I had a nice view of the tops of their heads, looming as I did like a grain elevator on the Dakota horizon.

Miriam made the introductions. I shook the outstretched hand of Mr. Hirsch. "My daughter, she drags home another one," he said.

"DAD."

Mrs. Hirsch was a few inches shorter than Miriam, even in her little brown high heels, which were so small and cunning, the elves must have made them. She wore an apron over her elegant little dress, and pressed her hands into it rather than shaking mine. Her voice was loud. "Miriam, such a TALL one! Tall, like your father."

"He's a tall one, all right." His diminutive hand packed a surprising wallop when he clapped me on the back. "Let's not stand around here all night. Dinner will get cold."

I had to agree. Any dinner that smelled this good should not be allowed to get cold.

Mr. Hirsch ushered us to the table, which held enough food for twenty people. I was relieved to sit because I was getting a pain at the base of my neck from all the stooping.

Mrs. Hirsch scooped, ladled and served me a plate. I looked down at a mound of tender brown meat, mashed potatoes and vegetables invested with enough butter and salt to stop a human heart. All of it was running with gravy.

This was my kind of dinner.

"I can't eat ANY of this." Miriam's face folded up. "NONE of it."

"Have the salad, then."

"Are there CAPERS?"

While they grumbled over the roughage specifics, I surreptitiously bowed my head and gave profound thanks.

Amen.

When I looked up, her father was staring at me and her mother was staring at Miriam. But no one said anything. My stomach twisted and thrashed like a small child demanding attention, but I knew it was a bad idea to take the first bite. I waited.

"I'm taking it you're a Catholic?"

"I am."

He tilted his head to one side. "It's not great to be a Jew or a Catholic down here in Oklahoma. I think it might be worse to be a Catholic, to tell you the truth."

"DAD."

He glanced at his daughter and let out a gust of a sigh. "So tell me, young man. What do you think . . ."

Mrs. Hirsch shook her head. "Ira. Can't you see the boy is hungry?"

"I just want to know where he stands on a few things, Ruth."

"DAD."

They finally picked up their forks, the universal signal that it was all right for me to begin. I wanted to bury my face in the plate, but I politely gathered up a little of everything on my fork and took a bite. The flavor of the gravy was so intense that something blissful gathered up and exploded behind my nose.

I closed my eyes and swallowed and gave another round of thanks.

I looked up and saw Mrs. Hirsch smiling at me. I smiled back. "Hey, um, Mrs. Hirsch? This is *fantastic*."

She waved away the compliment, but her eyes were shining. "Oh, it's just pot roast."

"This is the very finest pot roast I have ever tasted in my life."

From that moment on, no matter how much I ate, my plate was refilled. It was like a fairytale, the magical plate that would never be empty.

Between my mouthfuls, we did manage a little conversation about careers. Mr. Hirsch was not retired, though he looked like he could be. He owned a "finer men's store." "Perhaps you've heard of it," he said with the unmistakable pride of a man who thought I certainly should have. "Forty years, one location." I nodded and kept my mouth full. It was probably clear by looking at me that I wasn't one of the finer men.

I took a reluctant break from my enthusiastic chewing to explain that I was a teacher.

"So you'll be going back to that?"

"Um, I, um . . ."

Mrs. Hirsch smiled brightly. "I was a teacher, Gentry, for thirty-five years. Home Economics."

"I made her come home and take care of me for a change." Mr. Hirsch said this with the satisfaction of a man who has been taken care of every day of his married life.

She smiled at her husband, then turned to me. "Oh, the students I've taught. It's a hard job. But I miss it." She had the same amber eyes as her daughter, and they filled with the quiet joy and hopefulness of what we did for a living. "There are schools here where you could teach without a credential, you know."

"What?" Mr. Hirsch was sputtering. "Like a Catholic school? Why would anyone let their children near those priests? It's rotten, I tell you, rotten through and through."

And he was off. It was a discourse, not a conversation, with commentary on the corruption of the office of the Pope, catamite choirboys, mandatory tithing, the wealth of the Vatican, Mary as an appropriated pagan goddess, and the price of birth control ignorance in the Third World. He finished with a succinct summation of the current far-reaching and stomach-wrenching situation that made it difficult for me to unfold the paper each morning. "These men need to stop having sex with children and calling it God's love."

I set down my fork.

I wanted to explain the difference between the Holy Roman Church and the flawed human beings who populate it. I wanted to explain how the church saved my life, to offer the shining example of Mel. But I didn't.

I politely reminded him that he'd forgotten to mention the role of the Church in the destruction of Native American culture and society.

He winked. "Who cares?"

"Ira, you are IMPOSSIBLE." Her mother stood up, pressing the heels of her small hands into that apron. "Are you done?" I nodded. I was completely done. "Would you like a cup of coffee, Gentry?"

"We have to GO," Miriam announced.

But Mr. Hirsch produced an antiquated camera, which he waved earnestly to attract attention. "Wait! Let me take a photo before you leave!" I looked at Miriam, who rolled her eyes and hopped over to sit in my lap. I felt heat rising in my face. "Look at the blushing rose," her father chuckled, which only made it worse.

"Oh for GOD'S sake." Miriam stood up beside me. "Stop blushing."

"A beautiful man," her mother said softly as the shutter clicked.

We all rose to our feet. I, of course, rose much higher than everyone else. I thanked them and offered to help with the dishes. It seemed like the least I could do, being Catholic and all. Plus I'd eaten more than the rest of them combined.

"Dishes? A joker, this one!" her father said, slapping me a little harder on the back than necessary to convey his amusement.

I still had blue rectangles in my eyes as Miriam pulled me by the arm to the door.

∽

Miriam kept silent as I drove us back to Norman. She scowled out at the horizon, her eyes as dark as the night sky blanketing us.

"Hey Miriam? I told you they would hate me."

"They didn't hate you. In fact they ADORED you."

"All that stuff about my church? Your father . . ."

"That's his version of a joke. My father liked you just FINE. And Mom LOVED you. They liked you better than anyone ELSE I've brought home."

I've never known why, but I have pinpointed that exact instant as the moment in time when Miriam began to hate me.

∽

We went on with life. In some ways it was easy. In others, well. Not so much.

I had lived near but never with women. Each day offered more exposure of just how ignorant I was. To state the obvious, men and women are fundamentally different. I had maintained a willful innocence of certain specifics. I won't go into it, but my lack of knowledge in these matters astonished Miriam.

My ignorance was an issue.

Fine, show me an area where I don't know anything and I'll make the effort to learn. I headed off to the library to escape her derisive laughter when I asked too many questions. But nothing in the library explained the toilet paper thing. Women use so much toilet paper. You really have to be aware, or you will run out. I laid in a toilet paper stockpile. Miriam said I was "anal" about it, and I thought, well.

The library was no help with the issue of scratching.

I thought of scratching as something to do when you itch. But women don't seem to share the male urge to give all the hairy parts a thorough scratching once in a while. Didn't women itch? Miriam not only didn't do it, she expressed a fair amount of disgust when I did.

Also, any kind of air coming out anywhere was unforgivable. I had good manners, I did that when alone when I was able and excused myself for it when someone else was present. Even when that someone was Bosco, who was usually interested rather than offended. I even excused myself when no one else was present, just to be on the safe side. But I grew up in a dorm full of boys and summered in a monastery full of men. This wasn't something I spent time worrying about. Did every quiet belch have to be a cause for outcry? And why didn't it ever happen to her? Ever?

The library had no answers.

She kept categorizing me according to a post-Freudian model. She watched me get dressed in the morning, do the dishes and work on the Jeep, and she called that "anal." Edging the lawn was "anal." Alphabetizing my books was "anal." Basically, all of my systems were "anal." My food troubles, my hunger, those were "oral." My desire to put my mouth on her anywhere or have hers on me, also "oral." Singing in the shower was "oral," too. Brushing my teeth was both "oral" and "anal," a combination that had never appealed to me. "You're right back there at the oral/anal stages of psychosexual development, Gentry." I told her that this all made me kind of sick.

She laughed. "Haven't you ever read Freud?" I told her, only as far as he applied to literary criticism. She asked, "What does Freud have to do with literature?" I told her, quite a bit, actually, but did she really want to have a discussion on language as a mediating force in the gratification of frustrated infantile desires? No. She wasn't interested in having a discussion about that. She was interested in discussing something else entirely. "Gentry? Don't you want to find out what's wrong with you?"

"Most of my life has been an earnest attempt to never find out what's wrong with me."

She didn't understand that. She was alert to life. Always paying attention. She always had an opinion. It was true that she didn't read what I read, she hadn't studied what I had studied. She had no formal training in education, and no background in literature, and no interest in computers, none at all. But she was smart. She was a very good instructor. She always had a snappy story to tell. She had an intensity about her, a focus.

She turned that focus on me.

For me, that was an issue.

In Oregon, I'd learned that women were cued in to the specifics of my appearance. This came as a shock to me, as Bosco didn't express any opinions about what I wore unless I'd spilled something interesting on it. I'd wanted to believe that the Mumford women were strange, that no one else really cared what I wore or how long I went between haircuts (usually a year, which, since my hair grew an inch a month, meant a full foot would be cut off). But Miriam cared. My appearance was an issue.

I liked the way she looked. I liked it a lot. Her hair was a big mass of dark curls, and her skin was beautiful, tawny and smooth except for some lines between her eyebrows. Her large eyes were a strange color, the amber iris surrounded by pure, clean white, framed by the dark fringe of her lashes. She wore a color spectrum that started at yellow and moved into oranges and browns. In the summer she wore small dresses, short skirts, small shirts, everything snug, and sandals. When Oklahoma plummeted from unbearably hot to painfully cold, she wore the same things with big sweaters over and thick tights under, and boots. In winter, she looked like she should have a quiver and bow slung over her shoulder.

Since she was so specific about her own clothes, I thought she would understand that I, too, liked to dress a certain way. But she didn't.

What she wore was good. What I wore was an issue.

She let me know that her clothes cost a fortune, as did her shoes and her jewelry. She liked earrings that tangled in her hair. She'd start to pull a lock out of something gold and complicated and dangling, swearing and fussing, finally asking me for help. I'd work her curls out of the complicated arrangement of whatever hung at her ears, carefully unclasp what hung around her neck, unshackle her wrists. In the process I became so inexplicably worked up that I'd have to bump her into a corner, smell her hair and remove some garments as well.

Thankfully, this was not an issue.

The Sunday afternoon dinners with her parents continued. I met the sister, a younger version of Miriam named Evelyn. She had the same muscular little body, amber eyes, dark hair and perpetual scowl. Her husband, a balding man named Ben, was present in body if not spirit at these dinners. I would fill my stomach until I was almost unable to move, then discreetly thump my chest to let out a little air so I'd have room for more. Mr. Hirsch would watch me, pleased by the compliment to his wife's cooking. "This one can certainly put it away."

"This one" certainly could. The "other one" put it away, too. He was financially successful, and only a few inches taller than Mr. Hirsch. Obviously, an all-around better deal than me. But my eating was noteworthy and admirable. While Mr. Hirsch delivered his comparative theology seminars, I concentrated on the food. I never defended my church or my faith, knowing it was pointless. I did quote Saint Augustine on the subject, Sandy's favorite words, and that made Mr. Hirsch roar with laughter, tears running down his carved cheeks.

Mostly, I ate.

Sometimes we were joined by out-of-town relatives, small men with impeccable clothing and bemused expressions, dark-eyed women with loud voices, nice manicures and some of the most beautiful hair I'd ever seen in my life. They regarded me with amusement and discussed me in the language I didn't know. I knew they were talking about me because they would gesture in my direction to illustrate some point. Miriam's voice would rise up defensively. What was she explaining? What was she defending?

I ate.

Mrs. Hirsch made dishes I'd never heard of on special occasions, dishes full of salt and chicken fat. These dishes had tremendous cultural importance, and luckily, they tasted incredible. I found myself looking forward to all the Jewish holidays. But we were never invited on Friday nights. Miriam was welcome to complain about the menu during any other meal of the week, but not their Sabbath meal. "My mother won't let me come over. She says I'm not in ruach shabbat."

When they were speaking English, I listened to what everyone had to say. I had no choice but to listen. The volume. They all had opinions, the changing cast of relatives, Miriam, her parents, her sister and her sister's husband, who was almost as bad as me but not quite, because though he was a Baptist, at least he wasn't "my kind." That's what Mr. Hirsch called us, "your kind." I found it uplifting to sit there on the Lord's day, hearing about "your kind and my kind." As if we were of different species. But I was an appreciative and voracious eater, and that counted for something.

Miriam's mother was an expert at Southern standards, smothered pork chops, baked spaghetti, macaroni and cheese, coleslaw, fritters, sweet potato pie, peach cobbler. I'd had this food in Georgia and Detroit, and hers was the best. Her jalapeño coleslaw brought tears of gratitude to my eyes. Or maybe it was the jalapeños, but whichever, it was great.

Miriam hated her mother's cooking. "Mother, I can't eat ANY of this."

"Of COURSE you can eat this. Chicken is HEALTHY. Have a fliegel." She turned her attention to my empty plate. "Gentry, do you want both of the pulkas?" I certainly did.

Miriam would glare. "Fried chicken is TERRIBLE for you. Especially the DARK meat. Are you all trying to KILL him?"

"Stop your NOISE, Miss Vegetarian. Have some GREENS." I loaded up on those greens, sour, vinegary, pork-filled greens.

"Mother, that has HAM in it."

"Not HAM, Miriam, SALT PORK."

"MOTHER!" Miriam's distaste for pork wasn't shared by the rest of her family. They all liked it. So did I. Miriam would often refuse to eat at her mother's table but that was all right because I ate enough for the both of us. Mrs. Hirsch kept my plate heaped full. Maybe it was out of pity, a penance for her failure to instruct Miriam in the culinary arts.

When I'd pushed myself, my mouth, my stomach to the absolute limits of capacity, I'd offer to clear the table and be sent off with clucking and huffing, what an idea, my being helpful. I'd lurch into the living room and collapse on a couch. I tried not to groan. Usually I fell asleep.

At some point, they would wake me up to have my picture taken. Mr. Hirsch had several complicated cameras, and he was forever fiddling with shutter speeds and F stops, frowning and muttering and making us all stand or sit, faces frozen into unnatural grins, waiting.

"Get over there by that one!"

And then, this day immortalized, we could leave.

On the way home, Miriam would gently let me know what she thought of my eating habits. She would tell me, in her kind and loving way, that I was a disgusting hog. "I just can't BELIEVE the way you eat over there. You're just such a disgusting HOG. I'm just EMBARRASSED by you. You'll get FAT, Gentry. That would be JUST LIKE YOU, to get FAT. And let me tell you RIGHT NOW, you'd BETTER NOT GET FAT."

I wanted to tell her that there was precious little danger of my getting fat on her cooking, but I bit my tongue. I lived like a snake, digesting around the lump of her mother's cooking until the next time I could fill up. It almost made it worth it, having to personally apologize to Mr. Hirsch for the Blood Libel and Pius XII.

Almost, but not quite.

Miriam got a look at my bank statement. "You need to buy a house."

"I like to rent."

"No, you need to BUY."

"Why?"

"Because you can and the tax breaks are worth it. You don't have anything else to write off."

"I don't care about paying taxes."

"What do you mean, you don't CARE?"

"I mean I like roads and schools and hospitals and libraries."

She narrowed her eyes and pursed her mouth. "This money shouldn't just sit here. We need to buy a house." Meaning, me. I needed to buy a house. Because her credit, she informed me, was shot, and she didn't have any money for a down payment.

"Miriam, I prefer to rent." I liked renting because I knew I could pack up my Jeep and leave if I wanted to. But in the year I'd lived with Miriam, we'd moved like tribal nomads, breaking camp because there was some run-in with the neighbors or the landlord, some feud. Miriam was always up in arms about something. I found it exhausting, moving all the time. But still, I didn't want to buy a house.

Even though I *had* always wanted a garage.

~

Miriam had only started at the vo-tech a year before I did. That surprised me. I'd have thought she worked there for years because she had such a grasp on all the administrative conflict. She was aware of and involved with every dispute. She took sides, and she did it fiercely. I'd nod, say "hm," whatever you do when people tell you about things that are none of your business. My standard disclaimers, "That doesn't involve me," or, "That's not my department," or, "I try to stay out of it," those didn't fly with Miriam. She wanted to draw me in. The problem was that eventually, she ended up on the wrong side of everyone on the staff. Except Ardis.

Ardis Fillard was student teaching in Miriam's classroom that year. I'd heard about him, he came around the lab now and then and kind of . . . stared at me. I eventually introduced myself because I knew who he was. He blushed and wandered away.

I asked Miriam about him at lunch. "What's wrong with that Ardis kid?"

She stared at me, eyes wide. "What do you mean, what's WRONG with him?"

"He keeps coming around the lab but he won't say anything."

"He's socially retarded. We need to have him over for dinner."

Fine, this was new to me, this entertaining thing, but we had him over to dinner. He spent the evening staring at Miriam, hanging on her every word, his brown eyes wet with hope. After, he drove off in his Beetle.

"Okay," I said over the dishwater. "I understand what's wrong with him now. I think Ardis likes you."

She shook her head. "He is just such a drip. Pathetic."

"Hey, be nice. I think he really likes you."

She frowned. "Please. He looks like an extra from *Yentl*."

I wasn't sure what that was, but I knew it was Jewish. "He's Catholic, Miriam."

"How do YOU know?"

"Because he wears a crucifix."

"He could be a BAPTIST for all you know. Just because he wears a CROSS doesn't mean he's CATHOLIC."

"I didn't say he wore a cross. I said he wore a crucifix."

She looked at me, her eyes narrow. "Oh. You mean the cross with the dead Jew hanging on it."

"Hey Miriam?"

"Don't you HEY MIRIAM me. Jesus isn't GOD. He's just a DEAD JEW. That's JUST LIKE YOU, to worship a DEAD JEW."

I shook the water off my hands and left the room. Therefore creating another "issue." The religious issue. I didn't think it was my religion, so much as my determination never to argue about my religion that created the issue.

~

"You never tell me ANYTHING about your childhood."

"I don't remember it."

"How can you not REMEMBER it?"

I thought very carefully how to explain it. "Mel took me in when I was eleven. I don't remember most of what came before that."

"Like amnesia?"

"Something like that." If you can have amnesia on purpose. But I didn't tell her that part.

"You remember your name, right?"

"Of course I remember my name."

"Are you ever going to tell me what it IS?"

"I never tell anyone my name."

The name thing became another "issue."

I did try to talk about where I came from, to tell her a little about how I'd lived, the things I'd done. The parts of my life that seemed to interest her were not the parts I wanted to talk about. She didn't want to hear about, say, church, or Mel, or college, or the school where I taught in Detroit, or anything general about Oregon. She wanted to know about my sexual history. "Don't you want to SHARE?"

"I'm, um, not so much on the sharing thing, Miriam."

"Well, I've NOTICED THAT." Then she would proceed to tell me about the men in her past. And this I never, ever wanted to hear. But she told me anyway. Every man she was ever with came complete with a set of genitalia and a set of idiosyncrasies, and she told me about both.

"Could we talk about something else?"

"Why? You're such a PRUDE."

A prude? She wouldn't partake of about half the possible offerings, and I was a prude? I tried to explain that my sexual curiosity about other men was right around zero, but she'd slip in some anecdote, some oddity of construction or coloration, some secret need. There was one who jumped out of her bed and said, "God can see what we're doing, God's watching us." Actually, I could kind of understand that guy, but most of the things she told me were too private or too sad to be shared. A baby talker. A man who put on her underwear. I liked Miriam's underwear, I arranged key parts of my morning schedule to see her in it. But only her. I didn't want this in my head.

I wondered what tales were told by the women of my past. The thought of some woman saying, "There was this guy I knew in college, and he liked it when . . ." The *idea* of it.

I knew only one way to make a woman be quiet. "Come here," I'd say, slipping my hand up the back of her neck and into her hair, pulling her close. I made her be quiet. I liked to make her be quiet. I liked to bury myself in her and forget my failures, my losses, my fears, my sins.

I walled them all up inside her.

~

She found a very patient realtor. I let her make appointments. I showed up and walked through one pit after another without saying a word. It was ridiculous. I hated those houses.

We were driving back from Oklahoma City one night after looking at a house.

"I LIKED it!"

"It had four bedrooms and no hallway. A house with four bedrooms should have a hallway."

"We could FIX that!"

"We could. Or we could just not buy that house. It didn't have a garage. The only reason I'd ever buy a house is to have a garage."

"You're not REALISTIC! That's what you can AFFORD!"

"I'd rather live in the Jeep than one of these houses."

"IF YOU DON'T LIKE WHAT YOU CAN AFFORD, THEN WHY DON'T YOU GET ANOTHER JOB THAT PAYS BETTER!"

"Please stop yelling."

"I AM NOT YELLING, I JUST TOLD YOU THAT!"

"Hey Miriam? Why can't we at least look in Norman? Why do we have to look in Oklahoma City?"

"I'm sick of NORMAN."

"We both work there. My church is there. The houses are cheaper. The Sandersons . . ."

"I want to get OUT of NORMAN."

"Why?"

She stared out the window. "My parents are getting older. I want to be closer to my family. I guess you wouldn't understand that, would you. What it's like to be part of a family."

I held on too tight to the steering wheel, thinking about Oregon. That was as close as I'd come to being part of a family. Kathryn and her daughters had welcomed me to their table and some part of me had climbed out and hurt them. The same part of me that watched Paige with an aching fascination, and craved revenge on Daniel for having what I wanted. It was part of me and it hurt families. I was unfit.

I pulled the car over to the side of the road.

Miriam reached over and touched my arm. "Are you crying?"

I pulled her onto my lap and buried my face in the salty heat of her hair. She was there, God. She was there and I had not hurt her.

Sometimes, that can feel like enough.

~

It was a fantastic garage. An oversized double with electric doors, a workbench, a wall of pegboard, 220 outlets, shelving, shop lighting, a floor drain, and best of all, an old fridge with conservative bumper stickers all over it. It was the most conservative refrigerator I'd ever seen. That garage was first class. The house attached to it? Not so much.

We stood in the front entry. I had my hand on the ornate hammered metal door pull. Miriam had her hand on my arm, trying to prevent me from walking out. The realtor who had patiently shown us twenty-two houses stood there waiting for us to argue. She looked from face to face.

"It's PERFECT!"

"Perfect? What about this house is perfect?"

"What's WRONG with it?"

Where to start. "Miriam, I really like the garage, okay? But even I understand the garage should not be the best part of the house."

"It's a STARTER HOUSE. Look at all the POTENTIAL!"

"*Where*?"

The realtor said, "It's in a great neighborhood." It wasn't in a great neighborhood, it was near a great neighborhood. Her parents' neighborhood. "And she's right, it has potential."

They were ganging up on me. I felt panic. "Maybe, I don't know, can Miriam and I, um, maybe take a walk by ourselves?"

The realtor smiled. "I can listen to my voice mail. You two take another look around. You didn't take much time downstairs, why don't you check it out again? Have another look at that garage. I'll be outside." She stepped out a front door that looked like it had been made by the same company that manufactured the zodiac shield hanging over Lorrie Gilroy's television.

Miriam pulled me down a short flight of steps. "Isn't this family room COZY?"

Cozy. It had warped pressboard paneling and multicolored high-low shag carpet in green, orange and gold. A cloud of musty odor rose with each step we took. The room looked and smelled like the decomposing floor of an artificial forest.

There were two windows that let in no light, and though I looked, I didn't see any handles to open them. A door, but I refused to open it because it led directly into temptation. That door led to the garage. It was a wonderful garage. But this was a terrible house.

She opened a narrow door towards the back and put her head in wherever it led. "You can put your COMPUTER in here!" She came out and stared at me. "Look, Gentry, it has everything on your LIST."

My list? All I'd asked for was a garage and a hallway. Was that a list?

I pointed at something crammed into the space below the stairs to the main floor. It was made of paneling, with a spotty brass top and a padded vinyl edge. There was a sink the size of a cigar box in a counter, and behind that whole arrangement, a wall of mirror tiles veined with gold paint. "Hey Miriam? What *is* that?"

"A WET bar! For ENTERTAINING!"

"Entertaining?"

Miriam crossed her arms and glared at me. I stared back. Then she walked over and opened the door to the garage and turned on the lights. She hit the switch for a state-of-the-art garage door opener. I heard it smoothly opening to a nice wide concrete driveway, free of oil stains. A small breeze blew through, carrying with it the scent of pegboard, motor oil, and the dust collecting on a built-in air compressor installed by the previous owners.

She walked back and put her arms around my waist and looked up at me, her eyes glowing gold with reflected shop lighting. "My parents aren't getting any younger. They want us closer by. It would make me happy to live by my parents, Gentry."

I could see the small fridge just inside the garage. It was curved and old and covered with bumper stickers. One of the stickers said, "I will surrender my gun when they pry my cold dead fingers from around it's barrel." Sandy would love that sticker. Especially the apostrophe.

I dropped my face into her hair, breathed in her anxious, angry scent. Her arms were around me tight.

This would make her happy.

∽

I made her sit in the car during closing because I had to sign my full name. And even though I hated the house, I thought, well, at least I won't have to beg some neighbor to help me carry that deep-freeze sized television out of another apartment. When I wanted to move, I could sell the house, right? I was stupid enough to buy it, so someone else would be, yes? I could get out of it, couldn't I?

She seemed happy. "Just think of all the things we can do to IMPROVE it!" The house offered nothing but opportunity for improvement. The best method I could think of would have involved a bulldozer, but Miriam was busy imagining all the hypothetical improvements we couldn't afford to make. She spoke without yelling, she made lists, she had phone conversations with her mother about "redoing" rooms. And she charged a bunch of furniture for the living room and dining room. All the tables had glass tops.

"Do you LIKE IT?"

"Hm." I didn't like the furniture. But I liked it when Miriam was happy.

I wanted to make her happy.

∽

She stood behind me and watched over my shoulder as I wrote out the check for the first payment. My checks bore only my initials, so I didn't care. Let her watch. "Why is it SO MUCH?" she wanted to know. "It wasn't supposed to BE that much."

I sealed the envelope and put on a stamp. She found some papers, stuck them in my face, pointing at a figure on a worksheet. "THIS is what it's supposed to be. HERE."

I looked at the figure to avoid looking at her finger, which struck me as wizened. Her hands and feet didn't go with the rest of her. "That's the principal and interest. There are taxes on top of it, and I had to get mortgage insurance because I'm a first-time buyer. And this neighborhood has a homeowners association fee. It all adds up."

"What are you SAYING?"

"I'm saying we're going to be broke."

I actually thought we were broke back then. God, did You laugh when I thought that? I had no idea what broke looked like.

∽

The immediate neighbors invited us over, household by household. But I had long hair, and Miriam suntanned in the front yard, and we were not married, and this was Oklahoma. We spent polite evenings with polite people who studied us like aliens. Those evenings were enlivened by edible food, so I did try to make conversation.

"You all are from Ory-gone?"

"Um, yes." Sort of.

"Well, Larry Mahan's from Ory-gone. Have you all been to the Cowboy Hall of Fame yet?" They all asked me that at some point.

"Um, no."

"They have Larry Mahan's saddle over there. We'll have to take you all over there." They all said that. Did I look like someone who would especially enjoy the Cowboy Hall of Fame? And who was Larry Mahan?

I liked the Cooks, the neighbors who lived directly across from us. They had us over for dinner once, but Miriam announced when we got home that we wouldn't be reciprocating. "I didn't like the way that woman looked at you." That woman was Bonnie Cook. She was a single mom, and her son, Derek, was seventeen. He came with the usual teenaged accompaniments, visiting friends who roared through the neighborhood, loud radios, rumbling engines, late night tire squealing.

Derek had a '69 GTO, white. The car had no engine, but Derek didn't mind because he bought the car for the interior. He invited me to sit in it, so of course, I did. What an interior. Tuck and roll leather in internal-organ red, a gleaming mahogany steering wheel, plush black shag carpeting on the floor *and* overhead, black and white snakeskin accents. He sat beside me, his hands cradling the wheel, his eyes heavy with automotive lust. "It's just like a Tijuana whorehouse in here, isn't it?"

"Hm." I'd never been inside a Tijuana whorehouse, myself.

Eventually, he located an engine. I offered the use of my fantastic garage. We awaited the arrival of the 389 with all the anxiety of expectant parents. I rented an engine winch, I checked the Chilton out of the library, we made trips to Schuck's to lay in the necessary supplies. After the delivery, we rebuilt it. And finally, after weeks of waiting, work, and worry, we dropped it in.

Hey God? I've never seen anything like the smile on that boy's face when that engine turned over. Thanks be to You. Amen.

Miriam was relieved when he got the car out of the garage. "What a MESS." I missed the mess. I'd hear the rumble of the engine and smile. Miriam did not smile. "It sounds like a TRAIN going by!" Every few days, Derek observed the holy rites of automotive worship by changing his oil. Miriam didn't approve. "HE'S CHANGING HIS OIL IN THE STREET!"

"He uses a pan."

"THERE'S A NEIGHBORHOOD COVENANT ABOUT THAT!"

"Hey Miriam? It's his first car."

She wrote to the neighborhood association and signed it with my name, since technically, not being a homeowner, she didn't belong. Derek no longer changed his oil in the street. He no longer spoke to me, either.

Then, there were the newspapers. We all had ornate but hollow plastic-covered front doors, and the thwack of the morning paper delivery against all that faux medievalism was pretty loud. Miriam hated that. She called the newspaper office and made enough noise that the carriers left the papers at the ends of the driveways.

It was quiet, then. Quiet, until a little later each morning, when every single neighbor cursed and grumbled as they left the ease and comfort of their front steps and picked their way to the end of their drives to retrieve their papers while wearing their pajamas. When they called the newspaper office to complain, they were told exactly what had happened, and who was to blame.

The social invitations dried up.

Not long after Derek was banned from changing his oil in the street and our neighbors started having their papers dropped in the street, someone knocked down our mailbox. I fixed it. It happened again. I put it back up again. On the third day I came out and saw it on the ground, I stood there with that hot wind blowing my hair around, and I felt everyone peering through their windows at me. I felt their eyes watching me make my repairs. I felt like a character in a Shirley Jackson story.

The mailbox was knocked down over and over again. Some bumper had to show the dents, but I could never pinpoint the car. I poured a concrete footing. I mounted the box on a 4 X 4, then a 6 X 6. I considered a railroad tie. One day in disgust, I dug up the old footing. I poured twenty cubic feet of concrete, and used that to anchor an eight-inch hollow steel pole. I filled the pole with concrete. The pole stayed up, then.

Nothing could save the box.

Oh, it stayed on the pole because I'd selected brackets of such strength, nuts and bolts of a diameter capable of ending the random beheadings, but the mailbox was battered, defaced, looted. It seemed cruel, leaving it out there to take its medicine like that. What did it ever do to anyone? I straightened it out. I painted it black again. And again. And again. And again. I gave up on the little flag.

Some days, we arrived home to find our mail scattered. On one of those days, she stood in the front yard and gave voice to her frustration. "I CAN'T BELIEVE THIS IS HAPPENING AGAIN!"

Again. It had never happened to me before. I scratched my head, trying to think of how to put it. "Hey Miriam? Maybe, I don't know, the thing with the papers, or the oil?"

"Why don't you STICK UP for me? That's JUST LIKE YOU!" She started to cry, I'd made her cry.

"I'm sorry." I put my arm around her. She shoved me away and went into the house where we'd lived for just over three months.

Miriam, it seemed, was no longer happy.

~

The objects in my life often carry mysterious emotional connotations. I work around them. I know I'm weird, I know no one else understands. I accept that.

Miriam had the same problem. But she expected me to somehow intuit the connotations she assigned everything and adopt them as my own.

As an example, the toilet seat.

For me, the toilet seat carried no emotional freight whatsoever. It was, simply, a thing I put down once a day and scrubbed on Saturday mornings. If the toilet seat had any larger implications, I was ignorant of them. But I left the seat up and Miriam took a dip in the early hours of the morning. Her howl of rage sent me scrambling out of bed.

She found me in the back yard. "What the HELL are you doing out HERE?" I had no idea. It seemed like I should get out of the house as fast as I could, so that's what I'd done. I followed her back to the bed, but I was unable to close my eyes, veering from fear to rage, heart hammering, mouth dry, shaking so hard the bed trembled.

The next morning at breakfast, no amount of sincere apology on my part would placate her. "I'm sorry, Miriam, but I've never lived with a woman before. I only put the seat down when I have to."

"That's gross."

"No, it's male." I could see that she wouldn't want it up all the time, I could understand that. "I could leave the seat down all the time."

"NO! You'll just SPLASH. You'll just get it all over the SEAT."

I have great aim, but Miriam had a point, I had to admit. Splashing was a concern, because I poured out such powerful, manly streams. "I'll wipe it off if I splash."

"That's not sanitary."

"What if I use cleaning products?"

"You might miss a spot."

I thought about designating a tree in the back yard, since I was too filthy to use the indoor facilities. But this was Oklahoma. There were no trees in our new back yard, just sharp, parched grass.

"I just think you should SIT DOWN when you go."

"Excuse me? You want me to *sit*?"

"That way you wouldn't SPLASH, and you sure as HELL would remember to put the SEAT down."

"I think if I try to sit down, I might get my chin wet."

Miriam was not amused. She kept on the subject. I fought laughter. I wanted to tell her that I liked to go. I have always liked to go. I like everything about the whole act, the proper stance, the directional challenge, the blissful sensation of release, the roar of my thundering cataract, the shaking and stashing of my equipment. I liked it.

"Hey Miriam? I won't sit down."

Miriam didn't speak to me for three days. If I was in the room with her, she acted like my presence was an insult. Clearly, I was not the only person capable of loading up an object with a heavy dose of meaning. The toilet seat was the first, but not the last object to become invested with immense symbolic power. Everything started to represent something negative.

A wallet chain was no longer a means by which I assured myself that my wallet would remain on my person. It was an illustration of my desire to be a dangerous bad boy outsider, a desire that would probably doom our relationship. This meant that my wallet chain was a visual expression of my desire to move out.

"But I don't want to move out."

"That's not what your WALLET CHAIN tells me."

"I can't follow your logic, Miriam."

"That's such a SEXIST THING TO SAY, that because I'm a WOMAN that I don't have any LOGIC!"

"I'm saying it's a fallacy, like when you say that only racists like grits."

"STOP TALKING DOWN TO ME!"

My Bibles were a slap in the face, those were her words, "a slap in the face" to her older, wiser, and infinitely more persecuted religion. I'd never felt like a Nazi for owning a Bible before, especially since part of it was, as I understood, one of her sacred texts. But her reaction to my pointing this out was nothing compared to her reaction to the idea of my hanging up the crucifix under which I had slept since I was eleven years old. My ears rang for an hour.

And the Jeep? She opened her mouth and started, but I wouldn't hear it. Because the Jeep was loaded with all kinds of connotations, and all of them were great as far as I was concerned. She needed to be quiet about the Jeep.

The objects of my daily life became the means by which I could be indicted for my thoughtlessness, carelessness and privilege. I found myself living in a post-colonial or feminist crit text, always on guard for intersectionality.

The minefield extended into what I did. I dried the dishes with a towel. She thought I should air-dry them. I tried to explain that I dried dishes with a towel because then I could put them away faster. But it was explained to me at length and top volume that no, my drying them with a towel meant that I had no respect whatsoever for her education and superior knowledge in the area of sanitation. "YOU THINK I DON'T KNOW ANYTHING, DON'T YOU!"

I was left openmouthed, unable to reply.

A CD I liked to listen to was no longer just a CD I liked to listen to. If it was new music, it was a musical illustration of my previously noted desire to be too young to be with Miriam. If it was older, it was an assertion of my belief in my superiority to her when it came to everything aesthetic.

"You just think you're so much BETTER than me."

She started listening to classical records, not to enjoy them, but to get mad if I recognized what was playing. She gave me far more credit than I deserved, with her shock that I recognized Vivaldi, Mozart. She even asked me if I recognized Pachelbel's Canon. Was that one a stumper? She'd stare at me and demand, "Do you know what THIS is? How did you KNOW that?" That wasn't any special talent, it was a year of required music history courses at a private college. I tried to explain. "Stop throwing your EDUCATION in my FACE."

Is that what I was doing?

I didn't know where any of this was coming from, and I didn't know how to calm her down. Everything I ever said just made her more angry. I only made it worse.

I gave up what I could. I unchained my wallet and stopped drying the dishes with a dishtowel. Whenever she asked me what was playing, I said I didn't have any idea. I wasn't trying to compromise. I simply thought some arguments were too stupid to have.

But I still kept my Jeep. I still listened to my music. I still read my Bibles. I still stood up at the toilet.

Maybe that was compromise, after all.

~

We were at work, in my office.

The door was closed. I was sitting in my chair, Miriam on my lap, facing me, her legs around my waist. I had a hand behind her head, a hand on the small of her back. I'd kissed her into silent submission, her eyes half-closed, her hips moving in slow but urgent circles against me. Her body was hot to the touch and damp with sweat. I moved a hand to her ribs, then cupped a breast. I sighed in her ear, and she moaned and reached down between her own legs.

The door opened.

Ardis walked in, then backed out.

She scrambled off my lap. "Goddamnit. GODDAMNIT." She was gone, then.

And I remembered.

I was nine years old. At the swings. A girl stood next to me. All the swings but one were occupied. We had reached it at the exact same moment, both shouting "Dibs!" My hand on one chain and hers on the other.

I was turning to leave, to let her have it, but she stopped me. "We could make a spider. You sit down first." I sat down. She settled herself facing me with her legs around my waist.

It was astonishing.

We worked in rhythm, higher and higher, legs pumping in counterpoint, up and up and up. I'd always thought you had to stand up to have fun on a swing. But with this girl, I was having more fun on a swing than ever before in my nine-year-old life. Her hair blew away from her freckled face, her skirt fluttered up. I made a little sound. She smiled again, and pressed a dry, sweet kiss on me.

The swing stopped with a jerk that sent us both tumbling to the pavement.

A teacher had hold of the chain. She yanked us up by our arms, saying "You're *filthy*," dragging us up to the office. The fury in her face. The little girl was crying, docile, but I was twisting, fighting. "I'm calling your *house*," she yelled. "We'll see what your *parents* have to say about this."

I broke free and ran.

I ran all the way there. I let myself in the back door with the hidden key and broke my fingernails prying the phone I was not supposed to answer off the wall and took it in the garage I was not supposed to enter and used the tools I was not supposed to touch to smash it to wires and plastic shards and bent metal.

The garage door opened. He stood there, he saw.

I sat in my office and tried to empty my mind. Please God, take it away, hold it for me. I don't want it.

Amen.

∽

Miriam didn't speak to me on the ride home. She didn't make any dinner. She worked out until it was time to go to bed, stomping and sweating and pushing herself while the video blared. I went to bed early and tried to read, but all her noises kept me jumping. I kept rereading the same page over and over again, twitching and spooked.

When she finally came to bed, she turned off the light and went to sleep without a word. I lay in the dark, praying to not remember.

Amen.

∽

I woke myself up, my throat full of yelling.

"Do you know how many times a week you have dreams like that?" Her voice was exhausted. Too exhausted to yell. "What is it?"

"I don't remember."

"You just woke up. You have to remember. What was it?"

"I'll go sleep on the couch."

She sighed again. "You don't have to go sleep on the couch." She stroked my back. "Sh. Just go back to sleep, now." I put my hands in her hair, and she didn't push them away. We lay there for a minute. I felt my heart slow down and leave my throat. I started to relax, feeling the softness of her hair. I dozed.

I woke up when she took hold of me.

I grabbed her wrist hard and pushed it away. She pressed her hand to her breastbone. "That HURT. What's WRONG with you? Jesus, you FREAK."

~

She hated me in the morning. I knew this when she announced, "Eggs are just BAD for you."

"They are?"

"Yes, and I'm not cooking you any more. I'm not here to WAIT on you."

Fine. I could pour my own bowl of Cheerios.

I saw her again when we ate lunch at the school. The food was excellent there because of the culinary students. They also only served one entrée a day. I ordered my own lunch, feeling unjustifiably competent. That left dinner. She wouldn't still be mad at dinner, would she?

She came home and announced, "I'm NOT cooking dinner for you."

"We don't have the money to eat out tonight." Which was true. After I bought the house, we had less money for eating out. Unless I'd been fishing with Sandy, in which case I fried the fish she wouldn't touch, Miriam was in charge of the evening meal. Her menus were healthful and meatless and flavorless. It was like dining on damp packing peanuts every night. I always had bread with my meal, bread she selected that tasted vaguely fermented with bits of something hard and sharp in there that made me think that someone had added a handful of toenail clippings to it before baking.

I looked in the freezer. No fish. What were we supposed to eat? Well, I knew what I'd be eating. I opened the cabinet, got down a bowl.

"You're not having CEREAL!"

"Hey Miriam? I don't know how to make anything else besides fish."

She was dead set. "I'm just TIRED of doing all the cooking. Why don't you ever COOK?"

"I can't."

"How can a grown, single man not COOK?"

Oh, I didn't know. I was too embarrassed to try to explain this to Miriam. Could I tell her about my childhood neighbors who encouraged me to eat with my hands? Could I tell her about my Sunday dinners in Detroit, the different homes I went to weekly, adopted by a congregation that felt sorry for the solitary white man who brought his dog to church? "It wasn't something I learned."

"Well, you're learning. Starting TONIGHT."

I shut up and learned how to make a grilled cheese sandwich.

And so, finally, I learned the rudiments of cooking, the absolute basics. The stuff that turned out to be so embarrassingly easy that even I had to admit that it was odd that I'd never learned to do it. During the actual instruction, Miriam was a good teacher. She was patient and thorough. But after, she never said, nice job, Gentry. She never said, thank you, this tastes good. She said things like, "It's about time you learned this." "I told you it was EASY." "You should be GRATEFUL to me. I'm FIXING you. You should be GLAD."

I was glad, I was grateful, but her teaching style made me feel like an idiot.

∽

I'd had a plan, of course. The inspector said the house was structurally sound. It needed a new kitchen and bathroom because they were so ugly, but the rest could be fixed with wallboard and flooring and paint. I didn't have enough for the kitchen, but I'd saved back some money by putting part of the down on a balloon payment so we could use the cash to paint everything, fix the flooring and put in a new bathroom.

Ah, plans.

The first thing to give out was the air conditioning. The cost of having that replaced in the middle of the summer wiped out a large part of what I'd saved back. As soon as winter came, the furnace went dead. The shower developed a serious leak and threatened to take down the popcorn ceiling in the family room.

The house stayed ugly, her mood became uglier.

I oiled every hinge, tightened every knob, made every door and drawer open and close smoothly. "Why are you DOING this?"

"Because I want to."

"WHY?"

I didn't know. Did I have to explain everything I did? I liked things to work right.

I took the toilet apart three times until I gave up and let it run, a low, comforting gurgle that made the water bills high. When I could no longer avoid it, I went downstairs and tackled that family room. I figured out that the windows were installed backwards, with the handles removed so they couldn't be cranked open from the outside. What moron did this? I found the handles in a box of junk in the garage and spent a weekend putting the windows in the right way. Then I opened them and left them open. The room immediately began to smell better.

She followed me around complaining as I reattached the paneling.

"Why don't we just REPLACE it?"

"We can't afford to."

I found some spare sheets of paneling in the shed and tacked them up over the mirrored tile behind the wet bar. Pressboard paneling was bad but those tiles were worse and I had limits as to what I'd walk through on my way to my computer.

The computer room was small, dark, clean and bare. I kept it that way.

∽

Miriam kept talking about how different I was from the men in her past. "You do everything DIFFERENT," she told me.

Hm. Different. I'd been doing this on and off for more than ten years, and I'd never had a complaint before. I'd labored under some delusion of basic sexual aptitude. I considered telling her this, but I didn't want to start some kind of a vicious sharing cycle.

In college, one of my girlfriends decided that my nickname was "Mr. Tell Me What You Want And I'll Do It Till I Die." I liked that nickname. I earned that nickname. But not with Miriam. After the first year, we'd settled into a sexual routine. There was the way we did things when she was fertile, and the way we did things when she was not. When she was trying to get pregnant, Miriam would make it clear in her way that she expected a procreative attempt. She approached me like it was a medical procedure, like she was prepping me for something. I expected her to swab me down with rubbing alcohol, that was how clinical she was. Sometimes I rolled away, and that angered her. "Just what the hell's WRONG with you?" When we did continue, she was on the bottom. Nothing much seemed to happen for Miriam on the bottom. "What's TAKING you so long?"

I was confused. That wasn't a question I'd been asked before. Was I supposed to hurry? When the sight of her grim, impatient little face below me became too much, I closed my eyes and thought about whatever it took to get it over with. The only thing that worked for me was thinking of Becca, and I felt like I was committing a sinful betrayal. But it wasn't Miriam I betrayed. No, it was Becca.

Miriam would narrow her ginger eyes at me. "You always close your eyes."

"Hm." What could I say? "Isn't that involuntary?"

"I mean before. What do you think about when you close your eyes?"

"You, of course." God forgive me the lie.

After, I wanted closeness and sleep. That wasn't what Miriam wanted. Miriam wanted me to go take a shower. "Did you wash your hair? I swear I can still smell it."

"Maybe if you didn't use that stuff, it . . ."

"Just shut up. Just drop it." I dropped it. "I'm hot. Move over." I moved over. "Farther. Move farther away." I did. And I fell asleep. So I got half of what I wanted. The sleep.

When Miriam wasn't fertile, she preferred to be on top. All she needed was friction. That seemed to be her favorite part of sex, the friction. My job was to hold still. But when she finished, she hopped off, leaving me with a problem that was hard to miss.

"Hey Miriam?"

"I'm not FERTILE today and you TAKE too long."

Okay, fine. I would take a shower, my post-coital decontamination procedure. In the shower I could take care of myself, but it seemed like a waste to send this down the drain if she still wanted to get pregnant. Which, it turned out, she did.

It had been a year, and nothing had happened. She began to consult books and to visit a certain aisle in the drugstore. I protested. "There you go again, Gentry, getting Catholic on me."

"Well, I am Catholic, Miriam. You counted on that, didn't you?"

That remark didn't make her happy. Again, my ears. And I did want kids, I always had, and I still did. But I wanted them to come from God.

Soon, we had manuals, thermometers, various kits. There were positions, there were pre- and post-coital precautions. She had cups to go in and sticks to go on, she monitored something that involved her tongue. I had to eat certain foods and refrain from others in order to maximize my potency. One morning at breakfast she looked at me. "You can't beat off anymore, Gentry."

What? What was she talking about? The Church's position on that had changed, even Mel said it was okay. I didn't even have to confess it.

I looked at her like she was crazy.

"I know you do it, so don't look at me like that." How did she know? "All men do it. You can't do it anymore because it wastes sperm."

I cleared my throat. "I have plenty of that."

"DO YOU WANT A BABY OR NOT?"

I sat there, thinking about it. It took me a moment. "Yes," I told her. "I do."

But I still abused myself.

I never had any privacy when I was away at school. The attempt to carve out five minutes alone took up mental energy, and made it oh so sweet when I could. In college I was so, ah, well, what can I say, I was busy. I did it every day, though, to keep in practice.

I had trouble in Detroit because my neighbors kept up a bloody battle for mutual annihilation. They were so loud, so relentless, that I could even hear them when I was in the shower. There was no way to relax when the people next door were screaming about killing each other. And the lack of a lock in Oregon. No wonder I was pent up.

In Oklahoma, Miriam was a diligent watcher of my time in the shower. I think she timed me. If I skipped a shampoo and maybe got in a few clandestine strokes, I felt guilty because according to Miriam, this would inhibit conception.

What was the problem?

Everyone else seemed to be clipping right along. Sandy and Paige had three kids, and I expected news of number four any day. Becca and Daniel had Ariel, and they might have waited a while on purpose, but I refused to speculate on any aspect of their private life because part of me couldn't admit that they had one. Kevin and Parker had only recently married. I could have watched their union and wondered whether or not they were using family planning, but I didn't.

My own union was unproductive.

~

One day, Miriam confessed to me that she'd had a nose job. Her real nose had a hook in it. Would I still want kids with her if they had big noses? She looked afraid when she said that, but truth is I wanted my own kids and I wanted them badly. I told her that I'd love our kids, big noses, little noses, whatever. And she smiled.

But I still abused myself.

I like to shut bathroom doors, I like bathroom doors that close, that lock even, so laugh at me, sue me. I like to be alone in the bathroom. Maybe this is the result of years of never having any privacy. I don't know. Miriam didn't believe in privacy. Nothing made her more irritated than to try a door and not be able to enter. She might NEED something.

She left the door open while she was in there. If I walked over and shut it, she laughed at me. "It's just a normal bodily function, Gentry." I thought that attitude was contradictory in a woman who used something akin to Lysol on her female equipment. But far be it from me, the king of weird, to point out something weird about someone else, especially a woman who flushed the toilet with her foot.

One day, she walked in the bathroom while I was in the shower. I'd left the door unlocked to avoid a diatribe, but she was in a panic over some work she hadn't finished correcting. I thought I was safe for, oh, I don't know, at least a half hour. But I was wrong. She walked in on me. Yes, that was what I was doing, yes, she saw me, yes, I was caught.

I started to shiver even though the room was steamy.

"Just what the HELL are you doing, don't you listen to ANYTHING I tell you, you STUPID ASSHOLE? I just can't BELIEVE this, I just can't BELIEVE you, this is JUST LIKE YOU, to come in here and BEAT OFF like a stupid TEENAGER! We'll NEVER get a baby if you keep THIS up, you SELFISH ASSHOLE!"

I threw up.

She stopped, shocked. She thought I was sick. I wasn't sick, I was scared out of my mind. And there was no way to explain because I had no idea what was wrong with me. She turned the shower hotter to help me stop shivering, she didn't yell, she cleaned it up, I was so afraid she would make me clean it up and I can't, I just can't, what's wrong with me.

"You need to go to bed. You're sick." She called in for both of us. "You're so sick." She sat beside me. I was covered in a clammy sweat, shaking. She made herself stroke my hair. When I slept I had nightmares. The worst ever.

Please, God, not these again, Please. I won't remember, I won't.

I was only sick for a day. I got better, I went to work. Within a week or two,

I stopped shivering for no reason. But after that day I stopped abusing myself. It wasn't because of Miriam, or wanting a baby. It was something else.

I didn't want to know what it was.

~

I woke up. She was shaking my shoulder. I have always been able to tell exactly what time it is without a clock, so I knew it was the middle of the night, maybe 2 AM. I looked around, a little panicked but more confused than anything else. For once I wasn't having a nightmare, so why had she shaken me awake? Had she heard something?

I sat up, rubbed my eyes. "What's wrong?"

"We have to talk."

"What?"

"I said we have to talk."

"Now?"

"Yes, NOW." She turned on the light.

I covered my eyes. "Hey Miriam? I'm not going to talk. I don't like to talk."

"No, we're going to TALK."

"I want to *sleep*." I lay there, my throat closing with anger. "Do you want me to leave?"

"No, of course not. I want us to see a therapist."

"For what?"

"For COUNSELING."

"I'm not going to counseling. I hate counseling."

"Have you ever *been*?"

"Yes."

She stared at me. "*When*?"

"In high school." Counseling had consisted of sitting in the counselor's office, staring at his diplomas while he gently tried to get me to talk by saying things like, "You're an internal processor, Gentry. I know that's comfortable for you, but feelings find a way to come out. Yours are coming out in violence." I wanted to tell him if people would just leave me alone, there would be no fighting, but I was determined not to speak. And I didn't.

Twice a week, every week for the entire first year I was at school. Once a week for the second year, even though I'd stopped fighting because I'd systematically beaten my way through the list of kids who bothered me. But I still had to go to counseling.

I'd arrive and he'd have a board game set out. He'd hand me the lid of the box so I could read the rules, and we'd play in complete silence for the hour. One day he looked me in the eye and said, "Well, Gentry, you win." And I never had to go back.

"Miriam, is this really necessary?"

"Yes. My parents will pay for it. You can choose not to go, and that would be just like you to refuse to go, but I just hope you're prepared to live with the consequences. Because there will be consequences if you won't go."

Consequences.

We went to see a therapist.

~

We went in, introduced ourselves, sat down. I looked around hopefully for a board game. The therapist had on expensive-looking shoes that seemed to be missing their soles, and patterned dress socks. That was all I could focus on, the man's shoes and socks.

"Now, you're not married, is this correct?"

Miriam nodded. "We're very committed, we want to have a family together, but we're not going to get married. For religious reasons."

What? I was confused.

"So we want to stay together, but we have issues. I mean, Gentry does. Gentry has ALL these issues."

He looked at me. "Would you like to talk about them?"

I shook my head. I was an old hand at remaining mute in a counselor's office.

Miriam took over. She tried out her "oral" and "anal" theories on the therapist. He looked at her and smiled. "I'm not a psychoanalyst, Miriam. How about we set that Freudian stuff aside and talk about what's going on. Why don't you folks tell me about some of your issues?"

Miriam piped up immediately. "I can't believe Gentry won't even tell me his first name."

He looked confused. "Is your name not Gentry?"

"That's his LAST name. NO ONE knows his first name."

I looked at my boots, blew some air out of my mouth, scratched my head.

Miriam scowled at me. "You're supposed to TALK now."

"About my name?"

"YES." She crossed her arms, rolled her eyes. And waited.

I considered my options. I wasn't in high school. I wasn't a terrified twelve-year-old kid, I was an adult. Lots of people went to counseling. It might help.

I cleared my throat. "I hate my first name. I stopped using it when I was eleven. I don't have it on my ID or my bank account, and I sign my name with my initials."

"Could you use your middle name?"

"My middle name is just as bad as my first name. Maybe worse."

"Why don't you change it?"

"Because I don't want to."

"Why?"

"I don't really know."

"Do you want to work on that?"

"No."

The therapist smiled. For someone who practiced such a high level of grooming, he seemed to be pretty sincere. He leaned toward me. "Why won't you at least share your name with the woman you love? Gentry? What are you afraid of?"

They both looked at me, expectant.

"I don't want to talk about my name anymore."

They went to work on me for a few minutes, together. Breaking down walls and building intimacy and trust while releasing shame and achieving self-acceptance. When that didn't work, we moved on to something else Miriam hated about me. "Gentry could DOUBLE his income if he would just take a job in private industry, and he REFUSES." The therapist looked at me expectantly.

"That's right. As soon as I get my Oklahoma credentials I'll go back to teaching."

"But WHY? You could make SO much more money!"

"I want to do something that matters." Defensive, again. But pious enough that they decided to attack on another front.

"Gentry has all these oral aversions."

Oral aversions? The sound of that. What a horrible phrase. "I hate peanut butter. Lots of people hate peanut butter."

"What about the ICE CREAM?"

"It hurts my teeth."

"And the SODA issue? He can't STAND soda in his mouth. It just makes him GAG."

The "soda issue"?

The therapist stared at me for a moment. "Do you have any trouble with, say, mayonnaise?"

I felt myself shudder. "No, but I *will* if you ask me this type of *question.*"

He nodded. "Perhaps we'd better move on to something else."

Miriam actually raised her hand to get his attention. "Gentry has some THING going on with this little girl in Oregon. This weird THING. And I totally do not understand it. It's weird."

The therapist looked at me. "A thing?"

"We write letters." We still wrote back then, and I let Miriam see the letters. Well, most of them.

"I just think it's kind of STRANGE. She's ELEVEN."

"She's twelve. Gretchen's twelve, now."

"And what exactly is your relationship with her?"

"She was my neighbor. I left my dog with her when I moved. He's an old dog." I thought about his blunt muzzle, his wet, sweet eyes, going from dark brown to dark blue with cataracts. But he still ran, I told myself, he still played. He wasn't that old.

"Does she send you news about him?"

"Of course."

He looked at Miriam, then, as if to say, well . . .

She tried something else. "Gentry's hair, that stupid earring, that wallet chain, the way he DRESSES, it all just makes him look so stupidly YOUNG." He looked at me again.

I crossed my arms. What was I supposed to say? I wore jeans, I wore shirts. Sometimes I tucked in the shirts, sometimes I didn't. What about this was so youthful? "I've always looked young. It doesn't matter what I wear."

"But if I have an ISSUE with it, you don't even CARE?"

I chose my clothes by a personal system that was probably based on enough paranoia and aversion to keep this man busy for an entire year. But that was not the point. The point was, these were *my* clothes. "Hey Miriam? Why would it *matter* to you?"

"Because I have to be SEEN with you."

"I get to decide what I wear and you get to decide if you want to be seen with me. This is all about choice, isn't it?"

The therapist looked from one of us to the other.

Miriam had more, of course. "He has these terrible nightmares. He yells and screams and looks at me like a CRAZY MAN when I wake him up." The therapist sat up straight, listened. "He won't let me touch him, he just sits there and SHAKES, and he won't say what he was dreaming about. Sometimes he CRIES."

"You cry?" The therapist leaned forward, expectantly, hopefully.

"I don't remember."

"You don't remember crying?" He studied me. "It sounds like PTSD."

Miriam shook her head. "He's not a VETERAN."

"It's not only veterans."

My heart hammered so hard I felt it in my teeth. "I won't talk about this."

"Gentry, why are you so DEFENSIVE?"

"Beats me. I need to go for a walk." I stood up.

The therapist lifted his hands. "No, no, no. No walks, Gentry."

I felt like I was choking. "I can leave if I want to. You can't make me stay here."

He looked at me. "I can't and I won't. But I hope you'll stay. Because now it's your turn to decide what we talk about."

"I don't want to talk."

"Are you sure?" He looked at me, his face kind, not demanding. "Are you sure that you don't have anything you want to bring up, Gentry?"

I sat down. I thought about it. "I might want to talk."

"Well, if you do, we'll just listen. No one will say anything."

"Really?"

"Absolutely."

"I might start umming."

"Um all you want."

"Miriam hates it when I um."

"Miriam will be quiet." Miriam was never quiet.

"I, um, can't talk if she isn't, um, quiet." I guess that was a little umming trial run, and her face darkened.

"I promise you. She'll be quiet."

I'd never actually known Miriam to be quiet.

I thought, and then I spoke. "I feel like Miriam's trying to change me into someone else."

And the sincere therapist looked at me, and he said, quite kindly, "I'm not sure that I understand you. Can you give me a specific example?"

"The way I look, the way I dress, what I do for a living. How I talk. She objects to everything." Miriam shifted, she squirmed. But the therapist looked at her in a specific way that made her be still. I didn't know what he did.

I wished I had a look like that.

I continued. "I had this food thing. And it got in the way, I knew that, I mean, I knew it was strange that I wasn't able to feed myself, but with her help I'm able to cook a little now, and order in restaurants. She helped me and I'm thankful. But it's never enough. She just moves on to the next thing. Now, she says I have a 'soda issue.' She wants me to 'come to terms' with pop. Why? Do I *have* to drink pop? Is this a requirement?" Miriam shifted, fumed. The therapist looked at her. She kept quiet.

Amazing. Absolutely amazing.

He made a little steeple with his fingers. "When two people are in a relationship, each expects that the other partner will try to address the things that make staying in that relationship difficult. It's a reasonable expectation, within the context of a relationship."

"Why would anyone care that someone else didn't drink pop? Why would that be an issue that required addressing?"

"I think it's part of a larger issue."

"Right, and the larger issue is that she expects me to change everything about who I am."

"Do you feel that Miriam expects you to change *everything* about yourself?"

"It feels like it."

"I don't think so, Gentry. I think she only hopes for change in certain areas."

"Just certain areas. Like, how I act, how I talk, what I read, what I listen to, how I live, how I drive, what I drive, who my friends are, when I was born, what I believe, what my name is, where I live, how I live, what I do for a living, every aspect of my food intake, and every part of my appearance that wouldn't require plastic surgery. What's left?"

Everyone was quiet for a minute.

"So, what I hear you saying is that you're tired of being the only part of the couple who is confronted about what he needs to work on."

"I didn't say that. I don't think I need to work on any of those things."

"Even if they make Miriam unhappy?"

"Don't you understand? Everything about me makes her unhappy. I make her unhappy. Wouldn't it be easier for her to find someone she liked, instead of trying to change me?"

He took a deep breath, let out a huge sigh. "As far as I can see, you two are at an impasse."

Great. We had issues and an impasse.

"Do I get a chance to TALK, here?"

He looked at her. "This is Gentry's turn, Miriam." She was quiet. How did he do it? I decided I would pay money to find out the secret. "Gentry, are there any other issues, things about Miriam, say, or specifically about the relationship, that bother you?"

"Yes."

"Do you want to talk about them?"

Did I want to talk about my issues? Mine? Besides wanting to be fed some meat now and then and wanting to have my hair brushed, which made me feel like Bosco, and besides my anger at having to take a defensive posture about my basic existence, I had another issue. A big one. But I couldn't talk about it. "I, um, well, um, it . . . I . . . um, no."

He stared at me, waiting.

I shook my head. "Don't take it personally. I don't like to talk very much."

He smiled. "I don't expect you to come in here and go against your basic nature. But I would hope that you'd try to talk as much as you're comfortable with. Only say what you're comfortable saying. Stop any time you need to. It's my job to help you, but I'll try not to push you."

"I don't like all her rules."

His eyebrows popped up. "What kind of rules?"

Miriam gave me a look. I shut up.

There was a long moment, then. He looked at me. I looked at her. She glared at me. The therapist looked at her. I looked at him. A three-way stare down, and I wasn't going to be the one that blinked.

She blew. "Those aren't RULES, those are BOUNDARIES. I'm ALLOWED to have SEXUAL BOUNDARIES, aren't I?" Well, those were pretty high boundaries. Some basic areas were fenced off. But I said nothing.

"I see. Rules about sex?" He looked at me. "Is there one in particular you don't like?"

"One? I don't like any of them."

"Could you start with one?"

"I, um, wish, I could, uh, I, um, wish she would let me, um . . ." I lost him, there, lost him in a sea of babble. He had no idea what I was trying to say. I was red, stupid, stupid, I could talk about this in bed but not in an office in front of a man wearing expensive shoes.

"He means oral sex. He's talking about oral sex. That's JUST LIKE HIM, to bring up oral sex." The therapist looked at me. I looked down at my boots. Miriam crossed her arms. "I just HATE oral sex. It's UNSANITARY."

The therapist nodded. "How do you feel about it, Gentry?"

"I love it."

"OH PLEASE. It's totally NASTY."

I was ready to get up and walk out. "You know, she's never let me try. Not once."

He spoke so calmly. "Would you be willing to let him try, Miriam?"

"No. I don't like chomping."

Chomping? What did she mean, chomping? Did she think I'd go down there and crop grass? "Hey Miriam? I don't chomp."

She made a contemptuous hissing sound. "Just FORGET it."

Everyone sat there quietly. Finally, I spoke up. "So, are we at another impasse?" The therapist looked irritated. At both of us. We sat there at the oral sex impasse, surveying our boundaries and aversions through a forest of issues. It was quite a view.

"Is that all, Gentry?"

I thought, Oh, forget it, what's the point of all this. I threw up my hands and shook my head. "You know, we don't have to work on this. On the sex thing. We don't have to bother with it. Because I'm losing desire for any of it."

Miriam's mouth fell open. She looked like she might cry.

His eyebrows shot way up. "Can you explain?"

I thought. They waited. "Lately, when Miriam wants to . . . I feel this kind of, um, airlessness. Suffocation."

"Do you have any idea why?"

"Because she immediately grabs for my, um . . ."

"His DICK!"

"And that bothers you?"

"Yes. I can't breathe."

It was quiet, then. But not for long.

"JUST what kind of a man doesn't want to have his DICK touched? In my entire LIFE, I have NEVER been with a man who objected to having his DICK touched! Can't you see that something is totally WRONG with him? Something SERIOUS?"

We sat for a moment. Pondering the insurmountable impasse.

"Gentry, did you have something you wanted to say about this?"

Let's see, what did I want to say? "Look, Miriam, could you maybe try something *else* for a change?"

She sat there scowling. Ready to blow. She looked at me like she wanted to kill me. "You're a PERVERT."

The therapist sat back. I looked at him. "I think you should handle this on your own, Gentry. You need to be specific. I want you to think about it, and I want you to look at Miriam, and tell her exactly what you want."

"I can't do that in front of you."

"Try. Just try. You want her to try, don't you? Then you need to try."

What did he think I was doing? What did anyone think I was doing, I was trying, I was there, I was trying, I'd been trying for over a year, what did these people want from me? A list, a map? Is this what people had to do in counseling? And I was the pervert? I looked at both of them and I was furious.

Okay, fine. "Why don't you let your hands run over the hairy place at the base of my spine?"

"Just what the FUCK are you TALKING ABOUT?! WHAT HAIRY PLACE?"

"Back here. I don't see how you could miss it, it's the hairiest spot on me. When a woman touches me there, my legs start to shake." I sat back and crossed my arms.

She looked at me with hatred and disgust. "Gentry, you are just a total queer. You're a QUEER."

We were quiet for a moment. A long moment.

And she started. It was better than Mel's divinely inspired tirades. "I just

REFUSE to sit here and listen to this QUEER who doesn't like to have his DICK touched, because obviously he has some kind of HAIR fetish, and an ORAL SEX FIXATION, this so-called MAN who doesn't want to have sex with ME, who wants to fuck SANDY, I always KNEW that SANDY was QUEER," and on and on. "YOU listen to ME, Gentry," like I had a choice, here, "I will not just SIT here and take all the blame for what are obviously YOUR problems, YOUR hang-ups, all the things that are WRONG with YOU, there is NOTHING wrong with ME, it's ALL YOU, and it's JUST LIKE YOU to blame the fact that you're a HOMO and a QUEER on ME . . ."

"Enough, Miriam. This is enough." Oh, now he shut her up, now that she'd said things like that to me. Forget it. I didn't see any point to it.

Enough.

We left that office, not speaking, and we went home, not speaking, and we ate dinner, not speaking, and then we lay down in the bed beside each other. Not speaking.

I lay in the dark thinking about the things I said. The things she said. I talked about that hairy spot in front of a stranger.

I couldn't help myself. I started to laugh.

She turned on the light and looked at me. My eyes watered, I couldn't stop. I finally wound down. And then I said, "So, Miriam. Is this relationship growing?" And I started to laugh again.

She watched me. And she didn't laugh. "It would. I think it could. But you're just so fucked up. You're in denial about so many things."

I stopped laughing, then. "If you try to make me go back there, I'll leave."

"That's just like you, to threaten me like that. Well, don't worry. I'm too embarrassed to go back there."

We never went back.

∽

"I'm fine, just fine, Paige."

"Are you sure?"

"I'm sure."

She sighed, not believing me. "We miss you at church. Why aren't you going to church?"

"Hey Paige? It's, um, complicated." It wasn't complicated, it was embarrassing.

Sunday mornings I woke with Miriam straddling me, moving with piston-like determination. We wore ourselves out. I fell back asleep until it was time to get up and get ready to go to her parents' house.

Besides, I hadn't confessed since I left Oregon.

"Gentry, I love you. And if you're ever not fine, you tell me, all right?"

"I will, Paige. I'll tell you." I had a suspicion that I was no longer fine. But I couldn't make myself tell her. "Hey Paige? Do you want to come over and see the house?"

I could hear the smile in her voice. "We thought you'd never ask."

~

Sandy walked in and burst out laughing. "Gentry, you BOUGHT this place?"

"Well, I'm told it has potential."

Sandy shook his head. "Potential for disaster, among other things. Maybe you can pray for a tornado. Are you maybe in a flood plain?"

"Hey Sandy? Come see the garage. It's a fantastic garage."

He looked around the living room. "I thought this *was* the garage."

My turn to laugh. "Come on. Come see the garage."

"Don't go downstairs YET. Who cares about the GARAGE? Aren't you going to SIT DOWN?" No one sat down but Lucy Rose, who sat herself at the coffee table. Lucy Rose took a coloring book and one crayon out of her bag. Forest green. She was silent as she colored in a face with it. The rest of us remained standing.

Percy shifted on his mother's hip and butted his face into her shoulder. Paige let go of Byron's hand. He ran over and took mine. "Hey Uncle Grasshopper!" He pulled at me, smiling, jumping, tugging. A little slingshot of a boy. Then he let go too fast and fell back into the shelf. Something tumbled off and hit the hearth. "Hey Byron, are you all right?" He wouldn't look at me, he ran to Paige and buried his face in her hip. "Hey. It's okay."

Miriam frowned. "Something's BROKEN." She picked up the pieces of a ceramic figurine, part of a pair of something knick-knacky.

Paige shifted baby and bag and gently scolded her son. "Byron, settle down, look what you did."

"Hey Byron, don't worry. It was an accident. Come here." But he still wouldn't look at me. Neither would Lucy Rose. She just kept coloring that face a darker and darker green.

Miriam's voice was plaintive. "It was part of a PAIR. The two figurines go TOGETHER. They were a HOUSEWARMING present from my MOTHER."

"Hey Miriam? It was an accident."

"WELL, I wonder what is the BOY supposed to do, without the GIRL?"

We all stared at the ceramic young man in question.

Sandy finally broke the silence. "Maybe if you're lucky, he'll break that, too."

"Well! We'll just be going. Come on, kids," Paige announced, shifting Percy on her hip and taking Byron by the hand. "I think the kids are tired."

"WHAT? What about DINNER?"

Lucy stuffed her book and her singular green crayon in her bag and went down the stairs to wait by the door, still not looking at me. Paige kept hold of Byron's hand. Sandy followed, shrugging apologetically, but possibly relieved at being spared Miriam's cooking.

I followed them to the front door and dropped to my knees. "Lucy Rose? You didn't say hey to me."

She frowned down at her plastic shoes. "You never come see us. Daddy says you never go fishing with him. You never ever come to church anymore."

"I'm sorry. I've been really busy."

She lifted her head, tossed her blonde curls. "I guess you like her a lot better than us." She turned and faced the door.

Byron threw himself at me in a hug. "I'm sorry, Uncle Grasshopper."

"It's okay, Byron. I'm not mad. Please don't worry."

Paige pulled him away and out. Paige hadn't spoken to me, either. Sandy gave me a hug and a shrug and followed his family out to their van.

I didn't get to show him the garage.

"If that isn't just the rudest thing I ever SAW," Miriam said into the silence. "Well, come ON. Let's EAT." I walked upstairs to face my fate. We sat down at a table set for six, and she lifted the lid on a casserole. I stared at my plate, realizing that unfortunately, there was now plenty for me. She ladled me a serving of something that looked like it was made of grapes and shoelaces.

I took a bite, chewed. Swallowed.

"Paige is so moody." Miriam poked at her plate. "She's probably pregnant again. They have three kids and no money. Why don't they use birth control?"

"Maybe they do." I took another bite, chewed that into submission. Luckily, it had no flavor whatsoever. I swallowed. Fought a shudder.

"Why do you CHEW like that?"

I set down my fork. "Am I supposed to eat my food without chewing it?"

"Don't SNAP at me." She scowled down, used her fork to play with a shoelace. "There's a SOLUTION to the whole problem, a PERMANENT one."

"A solution to *chewing*?"

"No, to having so many KIDS. You're all just so damn CATHOLIC. Why have more than three kids when they're so totally BROKE?"

For as long as I'd known them, Paige and Sandy had been broke. Broke was the condition of life, as far as my college friends went. We all had our ways to make money back then. Dexter gave haircuts. I hustled at darts. Sandy wrote term papers for foreign students. Kevin dated rich girls as part of a long-range plan for the acquisition of money. Daniel came from money so he was never broke, just pretending to be so as not to appear too fortunate. After he turned twenty-one, he was a notary public. He would sit down in Legal Services and get paid to watch people sign their names. We were all envious of that particular endeavor. But we were all, always, all of us, broke.

That never stopped any of us from being happy.

I thought about that during what turned out to be our last visit to the Sandersons' tumbledown house. The Poetry Stud had finally delivered and defended his dissertation. We were celebrating. Paige was making something wonderful and unnamed, and because her recipes were just as easily made with meat as without, Miriam would probably eat. Percy had pulled up on my legs asking to be lifted and I held him tight, sneaking in some cheek kissing, some hair sniffing. It was so noisy and hot that he quickly fell asleep.

The other kids ran laughing out the back door when Sandy entered, growling, "Run for your beggarly lives! It's Doctor Stud!" He began lambasting me about something. Paige bumped him out of the way, told him to shut up and set the table. "I'm too damn educated to be setting any damn table, Woman! I'm a damn DOCTOR!"

Miriam had been in the bathroom for a while. She walked back in and looked around. The windows were steamy. The walls dripped with condensation. Percy's dark curls lifted around his ears, and his upper lip beaded.

"Could you turn up the AIR?"

Paige tasted from her cooking spoon. "It broke." Miriam looked at her, and I knew by her expression that she wouldn't eat a single bite of whatever Paige had made because of the spoon tasting.

"I'll, um, look at it after dinner, if you want."

"Would you, Grasshopper? I'm too damn intelligent to be mechanical." The kids ran in, attacked their dad, ran out, hoping to tempt him to follow. "I'm too damn hot to give chase, progeny. And too damn *intelligent*."

Miriam's eyes narrowed. "I don't see how you STAND it. You're just packed in here like a bunch of SARDINES."

Paige smiled. "What an original simile, Miriam. 'Packed like sardines.' Let me write that one down."

I couldn't help it. I laughed. Miriam looked at me. I stopped laughing.

"Well, I'm not original. I'm no fucking ENGLISH major. But at least I don't live HERE anymore."

"Thanks to Grasshopper."

I knew I'd better make a joke. "Hey Sandy? Do you want my house? I'd trade you."

And his voice boomed. "Forget it, Grasshopper. Your house is just too damn ugly. If you looked in the dictionary under 'ugly' . . ." Paige and I groaned. He tilted his head back, raised his arms to emote. "I ask the great gods of Poetry, how could a man with such a beautiful soul buy such a hideous house?"

Miriam scowled. "Our house is NOT UGLY."

Paige laughed. "Gentry's house is the Platonic *ideal* of ugly."

Miriam didn't appreciate that joke on any level. "I can't BELIEVE you two. You two are SO RUDE. I swear, I never KNEW anyone could be so RUDE. Like when you WALKED OUT on DINNER the other night. That was SO RUDE."

Paige held up the spoon. "Miriam, I'm sorry if we offended you. But why don't you bring it down a notch or two. You're shouting."

"I AM NOT SHOUTING!"

Paige shook her head. "You're rattling the windows."

"WHY DOES EVERYONE ALWAYS SAY I'M SHOUTING? I'M JUST TIRED OF YOU INSULTING GENTRY!"

The baby stirred. Paige took Percy from me and carried him away, why? He wanted to sleep in my arms, he chose me, Percy chose me. But she took him away. No one spoke while she was out of the room. Miriam had her arms crossed.

Paige returned. And when she spoke, she was firm and motherly and quiet.

"Miriam, I know we sound like we're making fun of him, but Gentry's been my friend for twelve years, now, and . . ."

"SOME FRIEND, you all are just the BEST FRIENDS, sitting there, just making FUN of his HOUSE! Like this SHITTY LITTLE HOUSE is so BEAUTIFUL? I just don't understand how you all can STAND to live here. I HATED living here. And you all have KIDS in this DUMP, KIDS, with all these BUGS and LEAD PAINT and that muddy CREEK back there. I just don't see how you all can STAND to bring up a FAMILY in a HOLE like this."

There was silence.

Sandy stood there. I waited for him to fire back, to laugh. He couldn't.

I'd never once seen that happen.

Paige's dignity served her when her humor was exhausted. "Sandy's flying to Colorado for an interview next week." She looked around, shook her head. "I'll miss this little house when we go. I've loved living here." She looked to her husband.

He reached down and hugged her. "Good God, I love you, Woman."

I felt a cracking inside. "Colorado?" My voice cracked, too.

Sandy saw my face. "Grasshopper. Hey, now. They have high schools in Colorado. They have high schools and computers and poor kids. How long are you going to stay away from teaching?"

Miriam let loose. "Well, GOOD. I'm GLAD. I hope you GET that job, and I hope you find a HOUSE out there that isn't a HEALTH HAZARD for your CHILDREN. This must be the WORST street in TOWN. And this is the WORST house on the STREET."

Paige gave Miriam a look of equal parts patience and ice. "I disagree. The only house worse than this is right next door, and as I recall you were living there when Gentry met you."

"Well, that house was SHITTY, but at least I had some decent FURNITURE in there."

"What, the orange couch?" Sandy sounded bemused. "What is it with you and orange, anyway? Your couch is orange, your car is orange . . ."

Miriam stomped her small foot. "You SHUT UP. You all can STUFF THIS HOUSE with all your BEAUTIFUL Catholic BRATS until it EXPLODES. That won't make this house any more BEAUTIFUL, that won't CHANGE the fact that THIS house is SHITTY, THIS house is UGLY, THIS HOUSE IS DOWNRIGHT UGLY!" She was almost screaming.

Paige's voice was low and calm and reasonable. "It's a funny thing about ugliness, Miriam. I've been making a study of it lately. And I'll tell you something. The beautiful doesn't always end up with the beautiful. Sometimes the beautiful ends up with the downright ugly."

I looked at Sandy, and he looked at me, and we headed for our respective women but it was too late. Paige didn't require physical restraint. Miriam did. I plucked her up like a bag of groceries and carried her out the door.

That was the last time we went over there.

Oh, we did see them one last time. Sandy called. He had the Colorado job, a position in a department committed to literature, exactly what he'd wanted, worked for and earned.

I felt orphaned, and he knew it. "Come with us, Grasshopper. I mean it." I considered it. Considered ending this thing with Miriam and selling my mistake of a house, packing up and following them back West, where I would live as the perpetual bachelor uncle in their home full of children. The loneliness in that, and the joy.

Was it wrong, God, to want my own? To try for that, rather than to live on the edges of what other people had?

The day of departure was fast approaching. They wanted to see us to say goodbye. Daniel and Becca were coming out, Paige said she wanted Miriam there, too, everyone together one last time.

"I'm not GOING," Miriam announced.

"Okay. I'll go alone, then."

She frowned. "I'll ONLY go if I can pick the restaurant."

"We decided on Othello's."

"I HATE Italian." Miriam hated any food that had a flavor.

"Hey Miriam? Pick any place you like."

"ANY place?"

"Any place."

∽

We met in the lounge. Daniel had tears in his eyes when he saw me. Why did he always cry when he saw me? Becca wore her hair up. I hugged her hello, hard enough to hurt, and my hands ached to find the pins. "Hey, Gentry." The sound of that. "And this must be Miriam." Becca held out one of her long, freckled hands. "I'm so glad to meet you, finally. I've just heard so much about you."

Miriam gave me a glare. "That's funny. I haven't heard ANYTHING about YOU. Not one WORD."

Becca graced me with one of her small, mysterious smiles and dropped her eyelids to half-mast. "Well. I must not be that important, then."

Okay, this was already awful.

She smiled at Miriam. "You know, that melon color is just beautiful on you. I've always wished I could wear it, but I can't."

Miriam brightened. She'd asked me before we left how she looked. What was worse, she expected an answer. The answer was never supposed to be "fine." No other answer was correct, but for some reason, "fine" was the most offensive, even worse than "okay" or "nice." I had learned to stick with "great," but even "great" sometimes triggered an explosion of disgust and a return to the bedroom, where she would stare into the closet with hostility and mistrust. It was the same way she stared into the refrigerator. Eventually, it was the way she stared at me, too.

But when she asked me how she looked that night, I answered in all honesty that she looked perfect. I'd always liked the dress she wore. There wasn't a lot to it. Her jewelry was more substantial. Daniel kept looking at her and smiling, looking back at me and smiling. I had the feeling he was right on the verge of offering me a congratulatory fist-bump. I put my arm around her. She shrugged it away.

Paige whispered, "Honey, this is going just fine."

It was one of those places where the waiter pulls out the table, and you all sit, and then he puts the table back. "What do I do if I have to go to the bathroom?" asked Paige.

"*Pregnant*," Miriam hissed in my ear.

I had an uncomfortable spot. Miriam's rock-hard thigh pressed against one leg. Becca pressed against the other side, foot to hip. Oh Dear God, the splendor of those hips. I prayed. Please, Dear God, let Miriam keep her hand out of my lap. Please?

Amen.

We opened the menus. Daniel frowned. "Who chose this place?"

Miriam smiled. "The food here is TERRIFIC."

He lifted one eyebrow. "It had better be."

Paige looked at the menu, and she looked at Sandy, and they smiled. They ordered what they wanted. They even ordered wine. I loved them so much.

Miriam ordered a salad. Everyone was impressed when I ordered for myself. "Good JOB, Grasshopper!" I felt like an idiot, I felt proud. I know I smiled.

"If you all hadn't played his game, he would have learned how to order for himself a LONG TIME ago." Miriam said that, and Paige and Becca traded looks.

They talked kids for a while. I was caught up on the progress of Ariel in the areas of vocabulary and gross motor development. I admired Paige's ability to name to the month just when her kids rolled, sat, crawled, stood and took steps. She'd stored away this knowledge for the purposes of reassuring another mother that whenever her kid did what kids do, it was fine.

Miriam said, "We'll have some of these stories, ourselves. You all just give us some time. I think Gentry will be a GREAT father."

Daniel stared at his wine glass. Paige and Sandy looked at each other, frowning. Becca sat with a white hand pressed to her mouth.

I cleared my throat. "It's nice of you all to agree so . . . wholeheartedly."

Sandy burst out laughing. Everyone joined in. The moment passed, moments always pass, all was well. The small plates arrived and the food was outstanding.

Paige was correct, it did go well once we all began to eat. Everything continued along without any outright disaster. Miriam seemed happy to sit at a table with my college friends and be part of the conversation and hear the old stories and laugh.

Maybe there was hope.

Miriam was actually fun. Snappy, complaining, but still, fun. She talked about work and made the Poetry Stud laugh out loud. They swapped faculty stories. I was envious, not being faculty anywhere, but I enjoyed the stories.

The wine and the food kept coming. I didn't have any of the former, but I liked the effect it had on everyone else. They all relaxed, even Miriam. She ordered bottle after bottle, she told stories, she laughed when we told ours. She tolerated the verse quoting, the alliteration.

She even put up with the part of the conversation that inevitably devolved into an argument, one we'd been having since college that started with "I swear he was mixed" and went on to "No one can shoot himself in the heart three times" to "He didn't even have powder burns on his hands" to "No one could do that to a man of that brilliance" to "I don't care how brilliant a man is, if I were pregnant and he came home to me from another woman's bed, you can bet I'd shoot him three times in the heart" to "Was she really pregnant? Why do you always say she was pregnant? She wasn't pregnant and he wasn't mixed" and so on from fact to speculation to myth to apocrypha. "He had to have been murdered. He wouldn't have killed himself. He was Catholic." "Do you think Catholics are immune to despair?" Which made us all laugh out loud, sad as it was.

"He had no integrity," announced Becca.

Sandy's jaw dropped. "No *integrity*? He might have been a tomcat, but the man had impeccable artistic integrity."

Daniel scoffed. "He wrote *drunk*."

Paige tsk'd. "Becca's right, he lacked moral integrity. All those women."

Sandy agreed. "You're right. He was almost as bad as Grasshopper."

"No, he was worse. Gentry never overlapped his women."

Sandy gave a smile that was more of a leer. "That's true, isn't it. You worked on one woman at a time. But so *many* of them, Grasshopper. You were legendary."

I raised my eyebrows. "Next subject, please."

Sandy laughed his hurricane laugh and another bottle came. Miriam was working on that wine. She filled her glass too high, then poured some off into my empty glass. Sandy spoke out. "My God, woman, don't waste that on Grasshopper. He doesn't drink wine."

Miriam stared at me. "You don't, do you. The entire time I've known you, you've never had a drink."

"*Really*. Well, that's *good*." Becca said that in a kind, supportive voice.

I decided that would be the most awkward moment of the evening.

"Dessert, folks?" The waiter was there with a cart, and I wanted to fall on my knees with gratitude for the distraction.

Miriam wanted a poached persimmon and she wanted me to share it. Paige tsk'd. "Gentry *hates* persimmons, Miriam. They are far too sweet." Paige pointed to a breadish thing. "Can you make this without the sauce? You'll like this, honey." I did.

When the bill arrived, Sandy, Daniel and I squared off to fight for the check. I was successful in relieving the waiter of his folder because I was closest to the edge. I drew my wallet and won.

I loved winning.

"We just can't AFFORD this, Gentry."

The table went silent.

"Um, pardon me?"

"I said, we can't AFFORD this." She shrugged. "Well, that's ridiculous, to expect us to pay for EVERYTHING at a place like this."

"Hey Miriam? Why did you choose this place, then?"

She scowled at me. "I didn't realize we'd have to pay for EVERYTHING. All I had was a SALAD."

I tried to speak softly. "You ordered at least a hundred and fifty dollars' worth of wine."

She looked around the table, frowning. "Well, I mean, JESUS FUCKING CHRIST!"

Five Catholics winced.

Daniel recovered first. "Let me split it with you."

"No, I'm paying it."

"Just let me pay half." His voice was low and tactful. "Let's divvy it up, Gentry."

"GOOD. SPLIT it." Miriam turned to Sandy and Paige. She said, "I know you two are always BROKE, but couldn't you at LEAST afford to leave the TIP?"

Becca's hand went to her throat.

Sandy gave the table a mighty shove that nearly upended it. The Sandersons left the restaurant without speaking. Daniel calmly removed the check from my hand and handed it to the waiter with his platinum credit card. His lips were white. "I'll get the tip, too."

I stood there unable to speak.

I didn't want to look at Becca, but I did. There was something worse than anger in her eyes, something worse than betrayal. There was pity. She put her arms around my neck. "Bye, Gentry." She breathed that in my ear with her soft, honeyed voice. She let her beautiful hips linger against mine, but there was nothing left to show her how I felt about her. I reached into her hair and found one pin, loosened it, knowing it would send the whole river of it down around her shoulders when she was in the car, a glorious spill of red and gold.

My throat ached like I'd swallowed a knife.

She pulled away and gave Miriam a look of distaste. Daniel shook my hand. As usual, there were tears in his eyes. I watched them leave.

Everyone was gone but us.

I don't understand etiquette, but I have good manners. As a matter of fact, I have flawless manners. There were no girls in my high school, but those Jesuit brothers drilled us as if we were preparing for careers as chivalric knights. I don't take off my coat and lay it over puddles but I do everything else. I rise when women enter, I take off my cap, I hold doors for women, I let women precede me, I help them with their coats and carry their packages and push in their chairs.

I pushed out the door, letting it fly back in Miriam's face. I heard her heels trotting behind me as we approached that stupid Toyota.

I let myself in. She stood by the passenger side, her arms crossed, waiting.

I started the car.

She got in. "What's WRONG with you?"

"Hey Miriam? I hope you made your point."

"I wasn't making a fucking POINT."

"Well, you made one." We drove home in silence.

I pulled into the garage and turned off the car. I sat there waiting for her to get out. My plan was to sit in the car by myself and privately reevaluate this whole not-drinking thing. But she wouldn't get out.

"I'M the one who should be UPSET, them talking about your old GIRLFRIENDS."

"Is that why you did it?"

"Did WHAT?"

"What you did to the Sandersons."

She shifted, crossed and uncrossed her arms. "Okay, I'm sorry, all RIGHT? I'm SORRY. I just wanted a decent DINNER. It's not my fault your friends are so fucking POOR, and they keep cranking out those KIDS, I . . ."

"Shut up."

She sank her nails in my arm. "Don't you DARE tell me to shut UP."

I pried her hand away.

"OH, so now I can't TOUCH you? What's WRONG with you? You and your fucking FRIENDS, all so PERFECT, I guess they're not so perfect NOW, they're BROKE now and even with that new job he's STILL going to be BROKE unless they stop with those fucking KIDS, all those fucking KIDS . . ."

Enough.

I clamped my hand over that yelling mouth and she bit me hard. I pulled my hand back, trying to shake away the pain.

"Oh my GOD. It's BLEEDING. Oh my GOD. It's getting all OVER."

I got out of the car and she followed me through the family room and up the stairs, her voice echoing behind me. "It's getting on the CARPET. Oh my GOD, it's really BLEEDING. Just let me FIX it. Gentry, I'm SORRY, just let me look at your HAND." I shut the bathroom door in her face and ran cold water over my hand, watching it run red down the drain.

It washes away. The water the blood the drain. *A shower is all you need, my boy. A good, hot shower. Let's get you clean.*

My knees buckled. I held on to the edge of the sink and pressed my palm into a towel. I would not remember.

The door resonated with her pounding. "Do you think you need STITCHES?"

I pulled open the bathroom door and took her by the shoulders.

She opened her mouth.

"Shut up." I heard blood in my ears, the thud of my heart, the high, hard moan of excitement escaping her mouth. I shoved her into the bedroom and down on the mattress and yanked away whatever clothes were between us.

God, forgive me.

∽

The fall brought a dry wind that made my cheeks burn, my lips crack. My stomach hurt all the time. What was wrong with me?

Gretchen had stopped writing to me.

I thought about looking for a different job, but it was so easy, commuting together like that. I drove the car. She didn't argue about my choice of radio station as long as I kept the volume low. I kept it low. She, in turn, concentrated on work. I'd look over at her, her legs crossed, her lap full of paper, her dark head bowed, quietly going over her lecture notes. Her silence was a mercy.

I'd increase the speed, open it up, go too fast. I don't know why I was speeding. I liked that time in the car. I almost hated to get there. What was this pain in me?

It was loss. The Sandersons were gone and Gretchen no longer wrote to me.

∽

We ate together at lunch. Usually Ardis joined us, because he was working there that fall. She would give me the latest information on whatever departmental intrigue I was doing my best to ignore. Ardis chimed right in, agreeing with her, defending her. I found that I had very little to say. But I listened to their spirited talks.

I hated listening to the classes taught in my lab. It made my stomach hurt, listening to the way teachers broke things down. Sometimes, to avoid listening to some idiot skip something crucial, I sat in my gloomy office and played games with some of the students. I set up a little three-machine gaming network. This was a gross violation of policy, and fun.

Ardis ventured down once in a while, having socially advanced to the point of speaking to me. He prefaced his remarks by saying, "Do you want to hear about something really fascinating? Listen, this is really fascinating." And then he would talk about the least fascinating topics. "Have you been to the Pennzoil website? That's really fascinating." "That weather this weekend was really fascinating." "This laundromat I go to is really fascinating." He was inadvertently entertaining, as well as a real game geek. He could kick my backside at Ruin.

I thought about playing games with Gretchen and my stomach ached and ached.

When I wasn't hurting, I was bored. I had things under control in the lab. I had nothing to do. I went to her classroom sometimes to watch her teach. She had an approach, a combination of expectation and explanation, that worked. She knew her stuff.

When we drove home, I listened as she "vented." "I just need to VENT." Venting was a geothermal process, I wanted to tell her, but that would have brought on Old Faithful and I was trying to stay calm, to keep her calm, to calm it all down. Venting helped.

Sometimes she complained about Ardis. I told her I thought he was a good kid. She told me he was no kid, he was twenty-four. I tried to remember being twenty-four.

I remembered less and less every day.

"What's wrong with you? Is it because that girl's not writing to you?"

"Her name is Gretchen."

"What's the big DEAL?"

"I don't want to talk about it." And I didn't.

We would get home to our ugly house. Sometimes we went out for dinner but usually Miriam would prepare a dinner I'd try to eat. Then she would go do her workout, and I'd leave. Some nights I'd go to a restaurant and order for myself like a functional adult. Sometimes I was too broke to get a burger. I'd go hungry.

I hated being hungry.

Usually I took a drive. Those flat, straight Oklahoma highways. All the stars. It was like the Dakotas, even though I was nothing like the boy I was in the Dakotas. The boy who thought he'd made the break, run down the last city street, escaped to a place that was flat and empty and clean and free. Bosco with me. He loved it there so much. His big face, the weight of him against my legs, his joy whenever I got home to him.

He went with me. He left the prairie and came back to the city. I thought about how we'd walk down the street in Detroit and something would catch my eye in a window, and I'd turn to look and so would he, turning to inspect the shop window as if it would be of interest to him because it was of interest to me.

Was he all right? Did he miss me? Did Gretchen still love Bosco? Would she ever forgive me? Would she ever write?

I would turn up the stereo and sing. I'd sing until my throat closed so tightly that I couldn't make a sound.

Eventually, I would drive home. I usually went to my study because the rest of the house felt too full. She'd left the second bedroom alone, some superstition about waiting to fill that room with the needed items. Aside from that empty space waiting for a baby, my study was the only room that Miriam didn't fill with "homey touches." Every wall, every surface was cluttering up with homey touches, but I was allowed to have that dark little room as uncluttered as I liked. I spent time on the computer in there. I played games, I wrote letters I didn't send. Mostly, I just hurt.

I would go up and lay beside Miriam, and ache. And sometimes I'd turn to her and erase the ache with the determination of a hurting, mute animal. "What is UP with you?" she'd ask afterwards, her chest pumping, her eyes shining. She'd insist I go shower, and I hated that. But I didn't want to argue, to make my blood rise again. I wanted to stay calm. So I would take a hot shower and fall asleep after with my hands in her soft, dark hair.

I longed to sleep. I wanted to dream about the salt smell of the ocean, rain on a roof, and the icy blue eyes of a quiet girl, the shine of her hair and length of her neck, the sweet flight of her hands as she stood by the water, throwing sticks for a dog as big as a bear.

I was falling apart.

∽

About this time, Miriam embarked on a self-improvement drive. "All I'm trying to do is just look BETTER for you! You're never SUPPORTIVE of me!"

"I like the way you look."

I did. The strange hue of her eyes, her face as pointed and sharp as a fox. Her hair was thick and soft and sweaty, and my face was in it whenever she'd allow me to worry her into a corner and let me smell her. I admired the tanned resilience of her body. Her firm little breasts sat surprisingly near her collarbones. I could span her waist with my hands, but preferred to gently cup the perfect bisected glory of her backside. She complained about her underwear's tendency to disappear up there. I didn't mind it a bit.

But Miriam was on a mission to change. She bought more tapes and equipment. Her workouts went from regular to obsessive. She started to bulge with musculature. Her breasts completely disappeared, only her dark nipples to mark where they'd been. A man who liked breasts was an oral suspect in the Freudian model, so I kept my mouth shut. But I didn't like it.

Maybe it was my fault, because I was younger than her. "We walk around that school, and every stupid twenty-year-old girl just starts DROOLING over you!"

"I don't drool back."

"That's not the POINT!"

"Men look at you."

"Don't be POSSESSIVE. That's JUST LIKE YOU, to be POSSESSIVE."

I wasn't possessive, but men did look at her. All the time. It was the brevity of her clothing, how it showed what was beneath. But she put those clothes away. "It's not PROFESSIONAL. It's not STRUCTURED." She invested in a new type of wardrobe for her thicker body. All of a sudden her clothing had buttons, snaps, zippers and shoulder padding. She called these "career pieces" and spoke of "investment dressing." She stopped wearing her complicated, entangling jewelry and bought pearl earrings that she had no trouble removing on her own.

She asked me what I thought. I lied. I told her it was fine, just fine.

She had longer nails put over her real nails. I feared those fingernails. She went to a department store and spent a fortune on makeup, which she wore like a mask over her true face. One afternoon, she brought home a little electrical wand and took it in the bathroom. She left the door open, so I stood in the hall, watching her removing the dark down from her upper lip. "Hey Miriam? Doesn't that hurt?"

She turned an enraged look on me. One side of her lip was bare and oddly white. "DON'T MOCK ME!! All I want to do is look NICE for you, and you make fun of how HAIRY I am! That is JUST LIKE YOU, to make FUN OF ME FOR THAT!"

"Stop yelling."

"I AM NOT YELLING!"

My ears rang. How did such a little woman make such a big noise?

~

I said nothing. Nothing, until the day she walked in, smiling, with all her beautiful hair cut off.

"You don't like it."

"No. I don't."

She started to cry.

I will admit, God, to liking her softer, with breasts and longer hair, without all that makeup and nails like Jeannie Green and clothes that made her look like she worked in a bank processing car loans.

What was she doing?

~

I was talking with a student. A tall girl named Phaedra. What a name, Phaedra. We leaned against the wall, speaking softly so we wouldn't disturb anyone while she told me about computer shopping the weekend before. And it was nice, I have to admit this, it was nice to have a woman speaking softly to me, making me laugh with the absurdity of a long story about trying to buy a computer. It felt so good to laugh.

"WELL." We looked up. Miriam stood there with her overloaded briefcase and furious face. "Isn't THIS cozy."

Phaedra faded away in a hurry.

I steered Miriam into my dingy office and closed the door. "Don't yell here."

"I WORK HERE!"

"I work here too."

"WELL THAT IS JUST LIKE YOU, TO HANG ALL OVER SOMEONE WHERE I WORK!"

"We were talking computers."

"Oh RIGHT! COMPUTERS!" Like computers were an inconceivable topic of discussion in a computer lab.

I sat down on the corner of my desk, not looking at her. I didn't want to look at her, this angry short-haired stranger. "Hey Miriam? Just don't yell, all right?"

"I AM NOT YELLING!"

"Calm *down*." That was not the right thing to say. That was never the right thing to say. She turned, I thought to leave, but she kept turning in a complicated little movement that I didn't fully understand, a winding, turning movement that ended with her briefcase full of books slamming into me.

I landed on my tailbone. My ears rang. My head spun. My first thought was that if I'd understood that she was going to hit me, I could have blocked it with my arms. My second thought was that if she didn't leave, I might tear her into pieces.

"Get out of here."

"I . . ."

"GET OUT OF HERE." I didn't recognize my own voice. That would pass, I knew that. If I sat there and waited, the coursing of rage and blood would stop, the shaking and hammering inside me would die down. My own voice would be returned to me.

If I just sat there and waited.

~

Another teacher gave me a ride home that night. A woman named Kim Barnes, who taught in the culinary department. I had to direct her because she didn't know where we lived, no one there knew, besides Ardis, I realized.

No one at the school talked to Miriam besides Ardis.

When we pulled up to my house, Kim opened her mouth to say something. But there was nothing to say, because no matter what she said, what I said, I still had to get out of that car.

I went up to my ugly front door and used the ugly doorknob to enter my ugly house. I went down the ugly stairs, through the ugly family room, into my ugly study, to find the only thing in the house that wasn't ugly to me, my computer.

Welcome home.

I sat in my chair trying to decide what to do.

"I'm sorry, Gentry. I'm just so sorry." The only light came from the monitor. She was a shadow before me, a shadow with dark hair and crossed arms, a sorry shadow. She came close and touched my hair. "It's just that . . . it's you. You make me so *mad*. I'm sorry but I wish you wouldn't make me so mad." I turned toward her. Her touch was soft. So gentle.

Mine wasn't.

God, I should have left her then.

~

I couldn't hold on to anything, remember anything. I'd start off for the store and be halfway to Norman before I knew it. "What took you so fucking long?" Miriam would ask. I was embarrassed to say.

In the morning, I drove without seeing. "WAKE UP! You missed the EXIT!" I'd turn around. "What's WRONG with you?"

She thought it was the sleeplessness. She suggested pills. I declined.

"I'm tired of how BORING you are," she told me one day. "You never TALK anymore."

I was always late. She bought me a watch. I wore it. She bought me a Day Planner. I put that in a drawer. She suggested vitamins. I declined, again.

What was wrong with me?

~

There was something wrong between Evelyn and Miriam. They would spar with each other in covert womanly ways. They always smiled when they did it.

"Is that a new blouse?"

"Yes. I just got it yesterday."

"Really. It reminds me of one I threw out six years ago. That's quite the color."

"I had my colors done, and this was supposed to be a good one."

"It WAS? Really. Hm. That color?"

"It wouldn't hurt you to have yours done. It might help."

They had things "done" all the time. They complained about how much having things "done" and "redone" cost. A "doing" contest.

Evelyn and her husband had recently moved into Nichols Hill, and they saw a lot of the senior Hirsches. Evelyn was "redoing" the house, and she consulted her mother for decorating advice. Miriam took the fact that she wasn't consulted as an insult, but Evelyn had been to our house, so no one could really blame her for seeking advice elsewhere.

We were there for dinner and Miriam was offering a suggestion about "homey touches." "A house isn't a home without homey touches."

"What the hell's a homey touch?"

"A homey touch is like, pillows and knickknacks and baskets. And things for the walls." I looked around at the home of the Hirsches Senior. It abounded in homey touches, and had an entire hallway wall devoted to framed pictures of their girls growing up in matching outfits sewn by their mother, captured by the lens of their father's camera. I hadn't ever seen a photo of myself younger than eleven.

"Like that big paper fan you have up over your couch? And those ostrich plumes?" Evelyn rolled her eyes. "You decorate like you cook."

"I cook healthy!"

"Healthy? That's what you call it?" Mr. Hirsch looked at Ben, the "other one," his satisfied corpulence, looked at me, getting a little stringy in those days. He shook his head, as if to say, this is what they dragged home? "A woman needs to cook well to keep her man."

"That's true," chimed in Mrs. Hirsch. "You win a man with his heart, but you keep a man with his stomach." Everyone looked at me. I didn't move a muscle other than those required for chewing. Mrs. Hirsch loaded my plate. Miriam glared.

"My little Evelyn got her mother's touch in the kitchen. My poor little Miriam didn't." He kept looking at me. Did he want me to agree? To complain? I knew better. He watched my immobility in the middle of this minefield, as did Miriam, alert for any sign of betrayal.

Miriam let out a blistering volley in the tongue I didn't understand. She scolded her mother, scolded her dad. They scolded her back. Evelyn joined in. Finally she let out a sentence in English. "It doesn't matter if he's great in the BED! It doesn't matter if he's a TIGER in the BED! Eventually, Miriam, you have to get OUT OF THE BED!"

I looked at Evelyn's husband. He looked at me. He lifted his fork. I lifted mine. We ate.

~

Miriam fumed on the short drive home. "Ben just looks like a heart attack waiting to happen. Have you ever noticed that vein in his head?"

"Hm." It was hard to miss, that vein.

"Something in that man is going to give. He'll probably die of an aneurysm or a stroke. He'll just explode one day. His head will pop."

A head exploding. Please, God, let her talk about something else.

"He used to smoke, did I ever tell you that?"

"Yes."

"I just hate smoking. Have you ever kissed a smoker? It's just like kissing an ashtray."

"Hey Miriam? Have you ever actually kissed an ashtray?"

She ignored me. "He smoked until his blood pressure went up to 160 over 120. He has to take medication, even though he quit smoking. The first one they put him on made him totally impotent, so they switched him to something else." Fascinating. Just fascinating. "Evelyn says his dick is so little that it hardly matters if he's hard or not." She put her hand in my lap.

"Hey. I'm driving."

She withdrew her hand. Thank You, God, You do listen sometimes.

"He's just a disgusting hog. He should lose weight, he's so damn FAT. I'm so glad you're not FAT." She put a hand on my leg. Checking. I was unaccountably reminded of Hansel extending the little stick through the bars of his cage. "I just wonder how she can stand to have him sweat over her every night."

Please, God. The genital reference was bad enough, but the thought of Ben Hogan laboring in bed was enough to make me lose all the fine food that Mrs. Hirsch had pushed on me. Was there nothing else to talk about?

God? A divine conversational transition, please?

"Evelyn just thinks she's so PERFECT. Evelyn has just always been so fucking PERFECT. Who do you think looks older, Evelyn or me?"

Sometimes God punishes us by answering our prayers.

I needed to think. Evelyn was younger than Miriam. She looked younger. Think, Gentry. Don't be an idiot. Lie. But I hated to lie. "Um . . ."

"Evelyn is getting fat, don't you think?" Evelyn was as trim and tidy as Miriam. They looked like two halves of a tumbling act, that was how taut and toned they were. "Don't you think Evelyn is fat?"

"Maybe she's pregnant."

Miriam sank even further into her gloom. "You always stare at her. You just watch her, all the time."

I wondered if that were true. I drove along. I watched Miriam and her sister because the resemblance mystified me. It was eerie. Their hands moved in the same way. They shook their heads and pushed at their hair and drummed their fingertips on the table. They spoke with the same intonation and the same inflection. They would effortlessly break into their other tongue, impatiently finishing each other's sentences in two languages. They shifted in their chairs and reached over each other's plates and frowned in exactly the same way. And judging by the photos that lined that hallway, it had always been like that.

I set aside my automatic slide into guilt, and considered the two sisters I knew in Oregon. They were the only other set of siblings I'd observed at close range in my life. One was tall, pale, sweetly diffident. Her hands floated through the air as gently as her hair. The other was compact and tanned and self-aware, and went through her life with the physical self-assuredness of a professional athlete. I didn't remember them as being any more alike than, for example, myself and Ben, my partner in "putting it away."

"Gentry?"

"Hm?"

Miriam's voice was uncharacteristically gentle. "Why do you watch my sister?"

I thought about it. How would that feel, to look into eyes that were exactly like your own? What would it be like to have what you were, how you looked, moved, spoke, acted, mirrored back to you?

My throat was tightening, so I spat it out.

"I guess watching her makes me wonder what it would be like? To see someone so . . . like you."

Silence.

I felt her nails in my arm. "You DISGUSTING PERVERT! I would NEVER do anything like that, NEVER!"

"*What*?"

Her eyes were on fire. "That is JUST LIKE A MAN, to want to do it with SISTERS."

"That's not what I meant."

"Don't LIE. I know how you MEN are."

"Hey Miriam? You know nothing about me."

She pulled at her door handle. "PULL OVER. LET ME OUT OF HERE." The door started to open and I grabbed her arm and yanked the car to the curb, braking hard, skidding and smoking, panic inspiring every nerve in my body to sing and hurt. We sat there for a moment. I could feel the panic crawling over my skin, the sweat funneling down my back to the seat of my jeans. Doom, wherever I looked.

I turned to her. "Don't *ever* touch the door handle when a car is moving."

She struck me across the face.

It was as if I'd been born to do it, yanking her up and shoving her between the seats into the back. There was a beauty to it, a smooth and practiced ease, as if I had always known how to take a small woman by the arms, shove her into the backseat.

God, forgive me what I did in the backseat.

∽

Oh, she was making a sacrifice, staying. I knew that. Miriam was not happy with me. That second year, when she wasn't complaining about work, she was complaining about me.

She made me tired.

I'd find myself in the Jeep. I always visited the Jeep, but it didn't run. I was only visiting it. The battery was disconnected, the hoses cut. The keys were in the ignition, my hands turning the keys. Why?

I'd pick up the phone at my office, and forget who it was I was supposed to be calling. I'd sit there and look at the receiver, feeling afraid. Who would I have needed to call? Was it important?

Miriam would refer to something. I'd look at her, confused, and she would say, "I TOLD you that, I just TOLD you that in the car yesterday on the way home from WORK. WHAT is WRONG with you?"

"I forgot." I forgot more and more every day. I tried to put how I felt into words. I only came up with one.

Inconsolable.

Neither of us had ever used the family room. It was the home of the orange couch and some rickety old tables, a furniture graveyard I walked through on my way to the study. Miriam had put her ancient television in there. She bought two more, one for the living room and one for the bedroom. I'd never lived with a television. There wasn't one in the rectory and the Jesuits had no use for that foolishness. I avoided the television lounge in college because who had time to sit and stare like that? But somehow, I had three televisions in my home.

She was angry when I slept with the light on, but she liked the television. She liked the noise. I liked the pale, impersonal light it gave off. Miriam watched the one type of show I wouldn't, I couldn't. Cops, murder, stalking, beating. Anything like that made my nightmares worse. I tried to explain that to her.

"That's RIDICULOUS. You're just so FUCKED UP inside your head. Stop BLAMING the TV for it. That's JUST LIKE YOU, to blame TV for what's wrong with YOU. Something's WRONG, Gentry."

Something was wrong.

She would fall asleep next to me, that blue light on her dark hair. Since I'd given up sleeping, I lay there and watched television for the first time ever in my life. I found out what I'd been missing. Great stuff. Canned laughter and car wrecks.

I was lying next to her in bed, watching some talk show, a host I didn't know asking questions of a person I didn't recognize concerning a movie I'd never see. As I said, great stuff.

She rolled over and looked at me. "What's WRONG with you?"

"Nothing."

"NOTHING? You're like a ZOMBIE."

"I don't know what you mean."

"Yes you do. You don't TALK, you don't answer the PHONE when people call, you just sit down at your computer and play GAMES. There's something going ON."

"There's nothing going on."

"I think you're upset because that little girl won't WRITE to you anymore. Why don't you just CALL that little girl?"

"I've never called her."

"Well, you really shouldn't put up with that kind of TREATMENT. It just isn't FAIR for people to just totally cut you out of their lives like that. People just don't have any RIGHT to do that."

"I need to respect her."

"She's just a little GIRL! What do you MEAN, RESPECT?"

"It wasn't like she was a little girl."

And the air iced up.

"Just what the hell HAPPENED between you and her? Just what IS IT that you won't TELL me? There's something WEIRD about this whole thing, Gentry."

I lay beside her, too stunned to speak. If she had those suspicions about me, why would she have me in her bed? Dear God, why would she talk about having children with me, why?

She reached for me. I batted away her hand away and got out of bed.

That was the first night I slept on the couch.

~

The last time was about money.

I paid all the bills and there was nothing left. I told her that. There was no money in our account. "What the HELL happened to it?"

"I guess we spent it."

"Well, we're out of FOOD. What are we supposed to EAT?"

"Furniture, I guess. One of the televisions. Shoes. This ugly house."

That earned me a poisonous look before she left, to return with a carload of food, the ingredients for those wonderful recipes of hers. I thought her parents had given her money.

About a week later, we got the notice from the bank. "You wrote a bad check?"

"We had to EAT!"

"I've *never* bounced a check."

"What were we supposed to DO? What's the big DEAL, they PAID it, it only cost us twenty-five DOLLARS!"

"Hey Miriam? Why did we buy this house? Why did we buy all this furniture, that car, this television? Why do we need all of this? I don't want it if it means we have to write bad checks to EAT."

"All I want is for us to just have a NORMAL LIFE! What is wrong with having NICE things, with getting AHEAD? You were NOTHING when I met you, you didn't have SHIT!"

"And what do I have now, Miriam?"

She was all over me, then. I grabbed her wrists. She fought, kicked, struggled, but that didn't matter, that was all part of it, what she loved. That I was stronger than her.

I pushed her back against the counter and held her there. I saw the strange orange glow of her eyes, the way her mouth swelled, how her chest rose and fell. Waiting for what she wanted. I remembered holding a sobbing girl against the blackboard, tears sliding down her cheek, the way I ached to taste just one of those tears.

I let go of Miriam's wrists and stepped back before I caught fire.

She moved toward me. I will always remember how she stood there staring at me, trembling with anger, blinking away the humiliated tears in her amber eyes.

"You fucking *bastard*."

She left the kitchen before I . . .

Before it happened.

I don't pray on my knees unless I'm in church, but I fell on my knees that day.

God, forgive me, God, save me from it. Save me from myself. Don't let me be like those people in Detroit. God, I'd rather be useless, have You take it out of me, than to have it be like that. Most of all, please don't let a baby come from that.

Amen.

V. RECKONING

Ah. A night in the Jeep. I haven't slept in the Jeep since the funeral. And I have a hangover and I'm cold out here. I'm always cold. I don't even have on a shirt. I find one to cover up this gut. I go upstairs to brush my teeth, because I won't blow dog breath on anyone.

I smell coffee.

Mike's wearing my apron and cooking omelets. I wouldn't put in that many mushrooms, but it looks good. He finishes the cooking while I flatten the toast. "I, um, have to go into work for a while." There was a shouting message concerning this on my machine when we got home from the mall.

"You sound excited."

"Hah." He can be funny, I guess. I say my grace and we begin. "This is very good, Mike. Thank you."

"Glad you like it." We eat, and then I get to work on my cleaning system. Mike does the financial thing, and I do the cleaning thing. To each his own. "I need to ask you something. Don't get insulted, Gentry, and don't get pious. It's something you need to think about, and knowing you, you probably haven't. Have you ever considered declaring bankruptcy?"

"Of course."

He looks shocked. "You have?"

"I called some lawyer on the television. And he said I can't. Miriam declared bankruptcy the year before I met her."

"Oh." Mike looks embarrassed. "That's out for a few more years. Well, then, I need more information about the balloon payment and I want to know if there's a payoff penalty, so I need to see your mortgage agreement. I looked for it in that creepy little room where you have your computer, but I couldn't find it."

"I, um, well, um . . ." I rinse the dishes. The dishes are pretty well sterilized before I put them in the dishwasher.

"The mortgage agreement?"

"Hm?"

"I need to see it, Gentry."

As soon as I get the sweeping done.

"Gentry?" Mike takes off his glasses, looks at me. "Could you get that for me? Now?"

I think I need to mop again, today.

"Gentry, look at me. Could you please go to wherever it is that you keep your important papers, and find your mortgage agreement, and take it in your hand, and bring it here to me so that I can look at it? Right now? Please?"

"No."

"What?"

"I don't want to."

"What?"

"I don't want you to look at my mortgage papers."

"Why the hell not?"

Shut up, Mike. I go and I get them. I know where they're hidden, with my marriage certificate and a few other things that are legal enough to require a full signature. I take them to the kitchen but I don't hand them over. He looks at me like I'm crazy. I am, I'm crazy. "Your name? Is that it?" I nod. "For one thing, your full name is right here on this judgment, you dip. And for another, I knew your name before I met you. Do you think I'd let anybody live next door to my girls without knowing his name?"

I'm dumbfounded. "How did you find out?"

"I called the school, got your name and had you checked out."

"Checked out?"

"By a private detective."

"You know my name?"

"Before you ever drove into town, I knew your name, your date and place of birth, your parents' names, your grandparents' names, your guardian's name, your school records, the adoption, everything. Party affiliations, speeding tickets, landlords, credit rating. Your doctors, your vets. That business in Detroit. I have a list of every food bank and soup kitchen you've served at. I even have the names of the farmers you drove tractors for in North Dakota."

"You never told anyone?"

"I wouldn't do that. It was a bum deal."

Is he talking about my name? Detroit? Or my life in general?

I hand over the papers and sit down. I need a drink but have some coffee, instead. He looks at the papers and I look at my coffee.

"Hey Mike? I think you know more about me than I know about myself."

He gives me a long look. "I think you might be right."

~

Mike calls a realtor on his cell phone. He says the magic words, "We want to price it to sell." We do. The realtor tells Mike some numbers, and he gets busy on his calculator and he starts to add things up and take things away, and he looks happy. He looks at the mortgage information and the tax bill and grumbles. He does some sort of whiz bang grand mumbo jumbo, and he shows me a tape, and he points to a number. "If you get what he says you can get, this is what you'll have left."

Unbelievable. A fairytale. "I need to pay her parents back for the funeral."

"They billed you for that."

"They billed me?"

"I found a letter in here in the box. Unopened. 'You ruined the funeral, so you can pay for it.' And they'd written out an invoice."

"Hey Mike? I did ruin the funeral."

"Fine. I already included it in what you owe."

"I need to pay for the stone."

"Christ." He shakes his head.

"You included the doctor?" The stupid hack, witch doctor charlatan.

"Gentry, I included everything. Every penny. And you can clear it. You hate this house, but from what the realtors say, you got it for a song and the market has changed and you could sell it tomorrow."

"Then we'll sell it tomorrow."

I go to shower, because I'm not nearly as clean as my house.

Even on the hottest of days, I like my shower hot. I miss the smell of the soap Mel used to send me. It's tied up with what I used to do in the shower, the hot water, the clean smell of that rough soap. I used to have fun in the shower. I have none, now, so I get out of this shower before I use up all the hot water and Mike is left with none. I dress in the bathroom.

When I emerge, clean, clothed, and only slightly hung over, I hear Mike on the phone in the kitchen. He's talking about something important, I can tell, something worthwhile that he's neglected by coming here. His voice is painfully harsh. "No, you listen. Listen to me. Give it a try, listening. You might learn something. Because I'm *concerned*, that's why. I mean, really concerned. And underneath your pride or ego or whatever that is, you are too. We can't let this continue. We have to do something fast. Because *someone* has to. Well, I don't know. I thought you might have an idea. We're pretty far outside my area of expertise."

If he talked to me like that, I'd have to hit him in the mouth. "Hey Mike?"

He looks embarrassed. "Yes?"

"I, um, have to go. Bye." I hope he pays his employees a lot of money, to put up with being talked to like that.

~

Ah, the office.

"Good morning, Gentry."

"Good morning, Fanny."

"Did you have a good breakfast?"

"Hm."

"Jesus loves you, Gentry."

He has a funny way of showing it, making me work with Fanny. I catch a whiff of her heavenly perfume and nicotine odor on my way to get a cup of coffee and I am incapacitated by four violent sneezes in a row. She says "Blessyoublessyoublessyoublessyou!" And strains out one of her maniacal giggles.

I hate this job.

I enter the little room of purgatory that belongs to me, my office with my battered desk and my bookshelves of fantastic Formica, and I sit. Because I have some work to do.

Important work.

There's the Daily Crossword, the Word Find, and the Jumble. I bring my paper, and Phyllis brings hers. She calls almost immediately for thoughtful crossword puzzle advice and heartfelt Jumble encouragement. "Who was 'unbound,' Gentry, who was that? I keep thinking Sisyphus."

"Prometheus."

"Perfect. Bye, hon."

"Bye." And so begins the Daily Crossword. I have a system, of course. I get everything all set up and ready to go. I have my coffee, my mechanical pencil, my *PC Magazine* in my lap, my paper folded into the correct shape, and I'm about to fill in 1.a., "Easton of musical fame," someone who I have recently seen on a talk show, when my boss barges in, rudely, to show me that HE IS THE BOSS.

"WHERE THE HELL WERE YOU YESTERDAY?"

"I called in to say I wouldn't be here."

"WHY THE HELL NOT! WHY THE HELL WEREN'T YOU HERE!"

It's been almost a year since I missed a day of work. There is a limit. "Hey Ben? Will you be there on Sunday?" He stops, blinks. He forgets, sometimes, just as I do. We're related, Ben Hogan and I. We're brothers-in-law. I was married to Miriam, and he's married to Evelyn, her sister. I'm related by marriage to this man. Or I was, because Miriam is dead.

"I'll see you on Sunday, won't I?"

"Yes, of course. I'm sorry, Gentry. Of course we'll be there. You can meet Miranda."

"Great."

He leaves, embarrassed. I'm far more embarrassed than Ben will ever be. I've used my wife's death as a currency of manipulation, and I despise myself for it. But I can't stand the yelling today.

I hate this job.

I get my work done in the time it takes to drink three cups of coffee. I only have to call Phyllis twice, and she calls me once. And then I have nothing else to do. I could clean my desk, but my desk is immaculate. Every employee in this office has an immaculate desk. I think this is a direct reaction to our feelings of helplessness. We maintain our workspaces in a precise and military fashion in order to demonstrate that even though we might be subject to the whims and tantrums of an angry boss, at least we control our desks.

I decide to organize my desk drawers, which are full of supplies I don't use because everything I do is on the computer. I don't need any of this stuff. But I have it. I like it. All of it organized. Ah, the feelings of mastery and accomplishment I gain from making sure that my yellow Post-it notes are in the one little space that fits them best, that my pens have caps, my pencils are sharp, my stapler full, my paper clips separated by size.

Hey, wait a minute. My stapler is gone. I rarely staple anything, but I keep my stapler filled and poised for its occasional duty. And someone has come into my office and stolen my stapler. I find that I'm angry about my stapler.

This is ridiculous.

I go out to find Phyllis. She sits at her desk. Phyllis has toys on her desk, and candy. People walk past, they stop and eat a piece of candy, play with a ball. And then they walk on, and she picks the wrapper out of the candy dish, and she lines up the toys. Even Phyllis has the immaculate desk disease. "Someone took my stapler." I say this in a low, urgent voice.

Phyllis compresses her lips into a tight line. Her eyes flash. "You had the blue retro Swingline, right?"

"Yes. It was there a couple of days ago, and it's gone. I just filled it."

"I can't believe it." She rises and wraps her sweater around her as if girding for battle.

We do a smooth circuit of the office. I have the only stapler like that in here, and if the thief is stupid enough to have left it on his desk, we'll find it. We stop and chat with the other workers, trying to act casual. Phyllis is better at acting casual than I am. I'm too angry.

No luck. "Gentry, I'll keep my eye out for it."

"Thank you." I feel better knowing she's on the case. I pass Fanny, dodge a Jesus grenade or two, curse my life. I return to my office to brood over my stapler and wonder just how my universe shrank to this point, anyway.

My phone rings. "This is Gentry."

"Gentry, can you get in here?"

"Sure, Ben." He must need to yell at me for something. Usually he yells at me in my office, because more people can hear through my office walls than through his, and the humiliation is amplified by an audience, of course. He must have a chart, the humiliation factor chart, to help him factor in all the variables for maximum employee humiliation.

His pretty assistant waves me through. I step into his office. He's on the phone, of course. He's always on the phone when I have to come in here. I sort of stand there and bob and sway, doing a little dance of obsequiousness. Should I stay? Should I go? Hm? I feel like a waiter. And he stops me, freezes me with a glance and an upraised hand, and motions for me to sit. Because I tower over Ben, it's always best to sit in his presence. I wouldn't want him to think I was challenging him to a height war.

I sit and listen to him talk to someone else. "YOU GET IT UNDER CONTROL! I MEAN IT!" Maybe I'm in here to listen to someone else be anonymously humiliated. "I PAY YOU TO HANDLE THESE THINGS!"

Ben Hogan is the only person in this office who doesn't suffer from the immaculate workspace disease. His office looks like a flood washed through, lifted everything up on a huge wave, and then receded, leaving the contents in a state of chaos. I fight an urge to tidy up.

Why am I in here? Finally, he gets off the phone. He looks at me expectantly. I look at him expectantly. "How are things with you, Gentry?"

"Pardon?"

"Are you doing all right?"

"I'm fine, Ben. Just fine."

"Well, things are running smoothly. Good job. Just wanted to tell you that."

In the entire time I have worked here, I don't think he's ever praised my work. I don't know how to handle this. I'm much more comfortable with being yelled at, I'm used to that. I think this "good job" is a reference to the fact that the entire network no longer freezes up due to the ineptitude of the last LAN person. But I fixed all that the first year I was here. I went through every cable connection personally in a Puritanical state of righteous, prurient glee at what a sinful, lazy job my predecessor had done. I was the Cotton Mather of wiring. I fixed it and fixed it right. It's been a year since I had anything much to do, truthfully.

He stares at me. I stare back. What does he want?

"You're coming up on the anniversary of your second year here."

Was it necessary to remind me of that?

"I wanted to tell you that we're upgrading our benefit coverage. We're adding dental and vision."

"Hm." I can probably have dental work done, as long as it doesn't involve my teeth.

"I just wanted you to know that I see a future here, for you. A future for a man with your qualifications."

"Hm." When I think of a future here, I think of Sartre.

"You're a company man. You know how to keep your pie hole shut."

At the mention of pie, my stomach makes an embarrassing noise.

We look at each other for a minute more. Tick, tick.

"I, um, have to go. Reports."

"I wanted to ask you about something." About this so-called future? About dental benefits? About pie? I wait. "Are you planning to do something about your hair?"

"My hair?"

"I noticed that it's past your shoulders, now. Have you noticed that?" I try to feign surprise, but I'm not much of an actor. "Well, I understand. Without a woman around, we men tend to forget things like haircuts."

"I have my hair cut all the time."

"I don't mean trimmed. I mean cut. Do you plan to get it cut?"

"Short?"

"Yes."

"Um, no, I hadn't planned to."

"You should cut it."

"It was two feet longer than this when you hired me."

"Miriam said you would get it cut. And you got it cut, and you kept it cut. You need to cut it again. And you should do it before Sunday, Gentry. Out of respect. It would be disrespectful to show up with it like that. It's a slap in the face."

I stand to leave. "Is that it?"

"That's all I can think of."

"I will, um, talk to you later, then." And then I see it. Right there on his desk, shamelessly exhibited for anyone to see.

My stapler.

I stand, frozen. I want that stapler more than anything right now. I may not have a use for it at the current time, but just as with all my equipment, I like to know it's there if things should change. And at least that stapler works.

He follows my gaze. "Oh. I borrowed that because mine broke." I look at him, and I know he can read my contempt for his stapler-thieving ways in my eyes. He hands me the stapler without another word, and I leave.

On my way past Phyllis, I flash it to her, triumphant. I have tracked down the rare and coveted blue retro Swingline, and she laughs out loud, she crows for me, the mighty one, the returning hunter, with his steaming fresh stapler kill. I ignore Fanny. I return to my office and put the stapler under the tick sheets in one of my drawers. My phone rings. "This is Gentry."

"Are you busy?"

"No, Mike, I'm just hiding my stapler."

"What?"

"Never mind."

"Look, there's a realtor on his way over there with an agreement for you to sign. He already has a couple in mind for the house so just sign the agreement, all right?" He gives me the number for his cell phone in case I need to call him. I guess he thinks he might need to talk me through the signing of my own name.

"I, um, have to go."

"Important work, hm?"

"Very important." We hang up. I play a little solitaire. I make the cards dance. I call Fanny and tell her to expect the realtor. I call Phyllis and we talk about sandwiches.

Fanny shows in the realtor. He's a happy man, a glad-handed, mustached, dapper, chipper little fellow of indeterminate age. He has on a red bowtie. He looks like he knows how to whistle. "Hey there, I'm Hank Proffer." He extends a chapped red hand.

"Gentry." We shake.

"Dandy, just dandy to meet you, Mr. Gentry." I nod. I motion for him to sit, but he sort of swoops and buzzes around, instead. "I met with your father over at the house."

"My what?"

"Your father. Dandy man. He says you're anxious to sell because of a balloon payment?" I nod. "That's dandy, just dandy." I nod. No laughing. "Well, your father had a look at this, and he said you should sign it." I look at it, I sign it, I hand it back to him. He looks at the paper. His bowtie bobs up and down. He looks embarrassed. "Er, Mr. Gentry, I needed *your* signature."

"I just signed it." He just watched me sign it. What kind of an idiot did Mike find to sell my house?

He looks more embarrassed, now. "No, er, I believe you accidentally signed your wife's name."

"That's my name."

"Seriously?" He looks again, squints, looks at me. "Okay, then, that's dandy. Tell your father I'll call him. I'll have those folks by real soon to see the house." He buzzes on out of my office.

I dial Mike's number.

"Michael Mumford here."

"Hey. Um, Mike? That dandy realtor just left." He makes a noise like a drain clearing. "He told me to call you. He wants me to tell you that he has some dandy folks to bring by."

"Great."

"No, not great, Mike. Dandy."

"Okay, then. Dandy." We both make the drain clearing noise.

"Is the house clean? Because he sounded like he'd have them over there soon."

"The house is dandy."

"Dandy. He'll call you. Actually, his words were, 'tell your father I'll call him.'"

"Your who?"

"My father. He thinks you're my dad."

"You lie."

"I never lie." Well, that was a lie. "How old do I look now?"

"Fifteen."

"Thank you. Hey Mike? There will be people coming in and, um, looking at the house."

"Yes, that's usually how it works. People like to see the house before they buy it."

"Oh." I knew that, I bought the thing, and as ashamed as I am to admit it, I looked at it before I bought it. "There isn't any furniture in there."

"I noticed."

"Well, isn't that, um, weird?"

"Let's see . . . I'll say that you're relocating, and that the wife went on ahead with all the furniture, all right?"

"Well, um, could you, I mean, just, um . . ." Spit it out, oh get it out. "Could you make sure no one touches my computer?"

"Yes, I can do that."

"I, um, have to go. Bye."

People in my house. I'll never survive this.

∽

I'm trying to hide and there's nowhere to hide.

I bolt out of each room just before the realtor enters with this tidy young couple. I should leave. But I'm fighting a paranoia so intense about my computer that I can't leave.

I escape to the family room where Mike sits, watching television. He's watching COPS. He looks at my panicked face. "Gentry, come watch TV."

"I HATE that show."

"Gentry, could you sit down here, no, get over here, and sit down, no, sit here, and at least TRY to act normal for a few minutes?" I sit. He takes my hand, he actually takes my hand, and I actually let him, that's how desperate I am. He says gruff, inane, comforting things, and I hold on for dear life. I'm desperate.

They've come downstairs. The husband shoots his wife a look. I pull my hand away like it's been scalded. Hank Dandy says, "This is the owner, Mr. Gentry, and his father." They look placated, then. They wouldn't want to buy any homo house, that's for sure. Idiots.

"This is the family room." No, this is the bathroom, Hank. We don't have any fixtures, but feel free to go anywhere in this ugly room. It could only improve it. "There's a den in here." A den? No, Hank, we call that the creepy little room.

They go look at my study, the strange room with no windows. My vault. "Why are all these locks on the door?" I hear the woman ask. I look at Mike, panicking.

Mike calls out, "It used to be a wine cellar! But my son doesn't drink, so he converted it to a study!"

Good save, Mike. The room shows no sign of conversion, but you tried.

I hear the husband say, "That's a nice computer, a nice set-up."

This is killing me. "Don't TOUCH that!" Mike grabs my arm. "Don't TOUCH me!" He shakes his head, makes me stay seated.

They come back in and look at me and Mike grappling on the couch.

"You've got to see the garage," says my bobolink of a realtor. "It's the best part of this house. You're a mechanic?" he's saying as he walks them out, and Mike has me in a hold and up and on my way upstairs.

"That's MY GARAGE! I have TOOLS out there! The JEEP!"

"Shut up, Gentry." He takes me in the kitchen, makes me drink some water and calm down. "This is almost over. Just hold on."

This has to be over.

But no, they have to troop up the stairs, again. They go back through the bedrooms. I hear the wife say, "Relocating, right. The wife took the furniture but she left all her clothes. Like he doesn't drink and did you see all the scotch in the wet bar? And that's his *dad. Right.*"

I hide in the kitchen, but they come in here, they look at me. Don't worry, folks, the idiot doesn't come with the house.

The husband asks, "There's a garbage disposal?"

Of course there's a garbage disposal. I tell him yes, and then I tell him the horsepower. Mike makes the drain clearing noise and gives me a look like, just exactly what kind of idiot knows the horsepower of his garbage disposal? This kind of idiot, I'm *exactly* the kind of idiot who knows the horsepower of his garbage disposal. But he's a mechanic, Mike, so he actually wants to know.

He rejoins his wife. They amble, wander, meander, dawdle, lollygag. Will they ever leave? When they finally do, Mike says, "Let's get you a drink."

I almost fall down the stairs in relief.

Oh, Poison, I'm so glad to see you. I haven't had a drink all day. I have some time to make up for. I knock it back as quickly as I can. It hits immediately and hard.

I will live.

"You sure put that stuff away, don't you."

"I do."

"Kathy said you couldn't drink."

"Well, Mike, practice makes perfect. I've been practicing, and I think I've developed a system, now."

He laughs. "You have a system for drinking?"

"I have a system for everything. It was one of the things my wife hated most about me." I excuse myself to get out of the stupid suit. Mike has on jeans. I hate him. I come back out in my sweats and sit next to him on the couch but I don't hold his hand. He tops off my drink with the reassuring clink of glass to glass.

Mike is a little toasted. He started during COPS. I'd bet that Mike is not much of a liquor drinker. He probably has a small glass of red wine and an aspirin every night, and that's all. But he's had a few, now, and he's extremely relaxed. "Tell me about these *systems*, Gentry. Why do you have all these *systems*?"

"I like to figure it out once and operate from there."

"Well, no one makes life up as they go along every day. I mean, it's like sock, sock, shoe, shoe, like that, right?"

"I think you have it wrong, there, Mike. It's sock, shoe, sock, shoe." He doesn't even know how to get dressed correctly. Sock, sock, what kind of idiocy is that. He probably puts his pants on with the left leg first. "Mike, you're an idiot."

He considers this. I consider this. Just who is the idiot, here? We drink a little more.

"Gentry, do you have a system for sex?"

"Sex. Hm. I remember that."

"Has it been awhile?" He looks at me with a blend of curiosity and condescension masked with false sympathy. It's a complicated look. "How long?"

I try to remember. But most of the sex I had with Miriam wasn't memorable. "Hey Mike? Do you want to know how long since I had sex, or how long since I had sex I enjoyed?"

He laughs. "Sex you enjoyed."

"Two years ago, then. I had sex I enjoyed on my honeymoon, and that was right around two years ago."

"That's a long time. Two years."

"Well, not so long that I can't remember what it was like." I wish I could forget what came after. I have another drink.

"So, do you have a system for that?"

"For what?"

"For sex. I'll bet you have a sex system."

"I'm sure I don't."

"You don't do the same thing every time, like smooch, tit, snatch, hump, like that, do you?"

"Nice language."

"Well you know what I mean."

"I do. But women are all different. A system would never, ever work for women."

"You're sure." He's too interested in this topic. I'm not going to talk about this with him. He'll bring up Kathryn and I'll have to hit him in the mouth.

We each have another drink.

"Hey Mike? I think I had an approach to sex, not a system."

"An approach?" He looks amused.

"Yes. I had an approach. I had to get the woman to tell me what she wanted, that was my approach."

"And they would do that. They'd tell you what they wanted."

"Yes. You just have to ask. Most women are more than happy to tell you."

"So, you'd get them to tell you what they wanted, and . . ." He waves his hands around, signaling me to continue. He's dense, I think.

"And go from there."

"You'd go from there?"

"Full steam. Whatever she wanted, I'd do it. I had a girlfriend in college who called me Mister Tell Me What You Want And I'll Do It Till I Die."

"Mister Tell Me What You Want And I'll Do It Till I Die?"

"You have it right. That was her nickname for me."

"That's a hell of a nickname."

"Well, that was my approach, to achieving the objective."

"The objective?"

"Yes."

"You mean, getting her off?"

"Yes." Though I wouldn't say it like that. Oh, what I'd do to see a woman come, but how would I explain myself? I wish I could find a nice, kind, understanding woman, and say, look, this one part of me died, but the rest of me works and I want to see your face when you come.

"Did it work?"

"Pardon? I was elsewhere, Mike."

"Your approach. Did it work as far as making the objective happen?"

"Every time." Over and over and over . . .

"Was that your only objective?"

"Well, no. I had my own agenda."

"Your own *agenda*."

"Of course."

"You wanted to get off, too."

"Yes, eventually, of course."

"So, you had an approach, an objective, and an agenda. It sounds like a system to me." Is he laughing at me? I think Mike's laughing at me. We drink a little more. "Gentry, do you ever swear?"

"I hate swearing."

"Say a bad word for me, Gentry. Just one. Please?" He must be drunk.

"I say crap. That's vulgar."

"No, no, no. Something dirty."

"What? Like, come? I say that." I say that word because it seems harmless, inane. I always mentally distinguish it from its three-letter variant.

"No, no, not like that. Not cum." He says the three-letter variant, I can somehow tell. "Say something really nasty." He's laughing. What a jerk.

"I don't do that, Mike. I consider that a violation of my personal moral code."

I think I said that very well, considering that I'm about to go look around the wet bar for another bottle. I find one. I return, and he's elevated his ankle again, so I sit on my bag on the floor.

"So, tell me about this personal moral code, Gentry."

"What's to tell? I'm Catholic."

"Confession?"

"Yes."

"So, you pretty much do whatever you want, and then you go see the priest and say you're sorry, and then you go do it again, right?"

"It's a SYSTEM, Mike!" And we howl.

"Sounds pretty good to me. Just say you're sorry, and then go do it again. Sort of how I handle marriage, actually."

"No, you don't understand."

"What?"

"You have to do more than just SAY you're sorry. You have to BE sorry."

"Or what?"

"Or you aren't forgiven."

"So, you have to work yourself into a sorry frame of mind."

"Yes, at least temporarily. You have to be repentant, that's the word you're looking for, there, Mike. Contrition. You must detest the sin."

"Detest it? How the hell do you detest it?"

Mike is not an idiot. Mike has hit the proverbial nail on the head. "This has been my problem for four years."

"And you haven't confessed?"

"Not for four years." I may have lived in a state of forced attrition, but I haven't been repentant. "I haven't taken communion since before I left Oregon."

"Do you still go to church?"

"No. My church is mad at me, I think." I didn't say that right, but he understands. "Hey Mike? Do you go to church?'

"No, never."

"Good." I would be envious. "Do you have a personal moral code, Mike? I've always wondered. Because it doesn't seem like it."

"Well, I'm sure I do. I mean, everyone has one, right? I haven't thought about it very much, to tell you the truth. Maybe I don't." He sounds wistful.

"Would you like to have one?"

"Sure, I think it might be nice to have a moral code."

"Well, Mike, that's easy enough to fix. Let's codify one for you."

"Let's get a morality system for me, Gentry."

"Okay!" Mike has everything else, why not one of those? I go into the study and locate paper, a pen.

"What's that for?"

"We need to write it down. Because we're drunk, and we'll forget."

"Good idea. Let's start." He sits up, excited, ready to get a morality system. I think this is great. He'll fix my finances, and I'll fix his morals.

"Okay. Now, I'll run through some things, Mike, and you tell me if these things are all right with you. You tell me, okay or not okay."

"Great. Shoot." He's ready to go.

"Lying."

"I'm a businessman. I have to lie. Okay."

"Stealing."

"Not okay. Especially if you get caught."

"Swearing."

"Okay."

"Masturbating."

"Oh for Christ's sake, Gentry, that's like washing your hands. Of course that's okay."

"Hey Mike? You wanted to do this."

"Sorry."

"Fornicating."

"Okay."

"Committing adultery."

"Okay."

"Hold on. You think it's okay to cheat on your wife?"

"As long as you don't get caught, sure."

I shake my head. "Mike, I don't think we have much of a moral code, here. So far, the only thing you don't do is steal, and you're so rich, you don't have to do that. We need some other ideas."

Mike thinks. "I don't beat my wife."

"Well, that's something. Wife beating, not okay."

"I don't pay for sex. I mean, I have, but not for myself. For a client. Or two."

This man has *daughters*. "That's pandering. That's just as bad."

"Well shit." He thinks again. "I've never killed anyone."

"Murdering, not okay." Kind of what Lorrie would call a "no-brainer," but, well, at this point, we're looking for anything.

"I think you're right. I don't think I have much of a moral code." He sounds sad.

"At least you never hit Eve. Or Kathryn." You cheated on them, you old slime bucket, but you never hit them. "Mike, now concentrate, we need to work on this."

But he's elsewhere, he's no longer thinking about his moral code. "I was so stupid." About what? He looks like all the air is leaking out of his face. He looks as old as he is, and I know he's in his fifties. "I was such a fool to screw things up with Kathy like that."

"You were. I have to agree." Mike is a fool.

"You should have seen her, Gentry. She was beautiful."

"She still is."

"I know. I meant, now. I went to her wedding, and . . ."

"You went to Kathryn's *wedding*?" Things have changed, things have changed, oh how things must have changed there in Oregon. I wonder if the ocean is still there, or have things changed that much, even.

"Of course. Kathy's a different woman. She looks better than she ever did."

It's more than how she looks, you jerk.

"They got married in the garden of her new house, you know how Kathy was about gardening, and she looked so damn gorgeous. I sat there next to Eve, and Eve's fifteen years younger than Kathy, and it didn't matter. I looked at Kathy and ate my heart out."

I do a little drunken math. Eve was twenty-one when he left Kathryn? Twenty-one? What happened with the teeth, think about the TEETH, Mike.

"I thought it would kill me, sitting there, watching Kathy marry that old geezer."

"A geezer? Kathryn married a geezer?"

"Yes, he's a geezer. Old. His name is Jack Fankhauser, and he's old."

"What a waste." Wait. I wasn't going to talk about that.

"Don't we know it. A waste. Kathy was . . . extraordinary. She had a gift, you know. Especially for head, she gave such good head. That woman can suck dick better than a pro. Did she ever do that trick to you where . . ."

I hit him. Hard. In the mouth.

"You little SHIT!"

Ouch. If his mouth feels anything like my hand, I'm in trouble, here.

I get in my bag and I hide because he could easily kill me, I think, and I'm not coming out until I'm sure he won't.

"You little SHIT!"

"Mike, I'm sorry."

"You little SHIT!"

"Mike, I'm drunk."

"You're lucky I am, you little SHIT."

"I'm sorry."

"I deserved it, forget it, let's just go to sleep." He gets up and turns out the light. He trips over me, hard, on his way back to the couch. Ouch. I think he did that on purpose.

Oh, her mouth. I lie there and I think about Kathryn's mouth. And I want to cry, because if that doesn't make me hard, nothing will. Ever.

"Gentry? Are you crying?"

"No. Allergies."

He snorts. He puts a hand down on my shoulder. "You're in worse shape than I am."

"I'm okay. Really. I'm sorry I hit you. And please, no more patting."

"Forget it. I should never have talked like that to you. Not you. You're a moral guy." I say nothing. "I bet you don't do any of those things, do you." I say nothing. "I bet you don't even jack off." I say nothing. "You never cheated on your wife." I say nothing. "Gentry?"

"What."

"Why did you marry that woman?"

Oh, I don't know, partly it was Kathryn and partly her daughter, and because I was alone, because the Sandersons moved and because I had to stay away from Becca and because Gretchen hated me and because Mel was mad at me and I needed Bosco and I was alone and I was sick of being alone and when I look at it, in the whole final pathetic analysis of it, with all the pain and the anger and the loneliness, I think it was because . . .

"I think it was because I'm Catholic."

"You're one moral man, Gentry."

And he sleeps. But I don't. Because I'm not.

I lie there and contemplate the fragments of my moral code.

I lie there and remember the night I asked her to marry me.

VI. REMEMBERING

She was shaking my shoulder. I sat up, confused. "What is it?" It was so early that it was still dark out. What time was it?

"We need to talk."

I pressed my hands to my eyes. "It's the middle of the night."

"I don't CARE. I want to TALK."

"I hate to talk."

"That is JUST LIKE YOU."

And I thought, what? What will it be now? Will it be my appearance, my employment, or my religion? My denial, my phobias, or maybe my aversions?

God, I had tried. I kept my hair out of her face, my opinions to myself. I kept my religion under cover, forgoing church almost entirely once we moved to Oklahoma City. I bought her a house, I never bought anyone anything and I bought her a *house*. I still had to give thanks before I ate, I was unable to eat if I didn't, but she tolerated that with a minimum of mockery.

No one else had ever complained like her. No one. But all the women who had never complained, where were they? Long gone. No one besides Becca had lasted longer than a few months. And almost two years later, two years of my weirdness and my umming, Miriam was still beside me. She stayed. And I'd stayed, too.

But staying was not enough. Nothing about this was right. I was trapped in some sin of inertia.

I looked around the bedroom in the dark, trying to find the door. It was time to find a way out. "I need to get out of here."

"I'm late, Gentry."

"You're not late. It's still dark out."

"No, I mean I'm *late*."

"It's still dark and the alarm hasn't even gone off. How could we be late?"

"I didn't say *we're* late, I said *I'm* late."

"Do you have an early meeting?"

"No, you MORON. I'm PREGNANT." She started to drone on about being very late, not wanting to get her hopes up, not wanting to get my hopes up, while I repeated variations in my mind. Miriam was pregnant. There was a baby in there. I was going to be a dad. We were having a child. This was supposed to be the most important news of my life, and it didn't seem real.

But it was.

I thought of how it had been between us this last year. I'd prayed that no child would be born of that angry sex. Every Catholic knows that prayer isn't effective birth control but we all try to use it anyway. After that was over, it didn't seem we'd done anything at all for a few months, but we must have. Because somehow, she was pregnant.

I fell back against the pillow and felt the settling of doom in every limb of my body.

"Don't you have anything to SAY?"

I said the only thing I could think of. "Should we get married?"

Women don't respond well when I propose. Miriam finished laughing in my face, and accused me of Catholicism. "There you go, getting Catholic on me. That's just . . ."

". . . like me, I know. But it's the right thing to do."

She looked at me with a strange and unfamiliar look in her eyes. "All right. I'll marry you. But only on one condition. We tell no one I'm pregnant. I don't want anyone to know."

"Why?"

"They'll think that's the only reason you're marrying me."

Oh God, please. Forgive me, because I can't forgive myself.

∽

I called Mel. "I'm, um, getting married."

"*What* did you say?"

"I said, I'm getting married."

"To whom?"

"Miriam."

"Is she pregnant?"

"I, um. No. No, she's not?"

I heard a sigh as deep as despair. "You will not be getting married in a church, I take it?"

"Hey Mel? How did you know that?"

"I have spoken with the young lady on the phone. Miriam does not seem the type to marry in a church, no matter how important that might be to a person such as yourself."

"Because she's Jewish?"

"No. Because she is spiteful. Well, then. We will think of you on that day, and pray for you. You'll need it."

"You aren't coming?"

"No, I think not."

"Because she's Jewish?"

Mel's love had no limits, but his patience did. "In the name of God, if you loved her, I wouldn't care if she were a BAPTIST. Mainly, Gentry, I will not come because I refuse to be a party to THIS KIND OF GODFORSAKEN MISTAKE!"

"Mel . . ."

"IN THE NAME OF JESUS, GENTRY, I KNOW YOU!"

"Mel, don't yell at me, please."

"GENTRY, THEN YOU TELL ME WHY YOU HAVE TO MARRY HER!"

"I don't have to."

"I WILL NOT ALLOW THIS! I SWORE TO TAKE CARE OF YOU, I SWORE IT TO GOD AND TO YOUR POOR LOST MOTHER AND TO THE COURTS OF THE UNITED STATES OF AMERICA, AND YOU OWE ME A BETTER EXPLANATION THAN THIS!"

"I no longer need your permission to do this. I don't owe you anything."

The silence.

What did I say? Oh God, what did I say to Mel?

"I didn't mean that the way it sounded, Mel, I didn't mean . . ."

"Goodbye, Gentry." And he hung up on me.

I was ashamed. And he was right. But I couldn't tell him that I had no choice.

∽

"You promise you won't laugh."

"Of course I won't laugh."

We sat at the dining room table. I felt hot sweat pricking under my arms. My stomach hurt and I knew I'd have to go to the bathroom if she laughed. "Swear it to God."

"Swear to God, I won't laugh." It was quiet. She waited.

I said it out loud.

She stared for a moment, her eyes going wide. She threw back that head of dark curls and roared with laughter.

I got up and went to the bathroom.

Once she stopped laughing, she apologized. "I'm sorry, but who would name a boy that? That's ridiculous!" She suggested that maybe I'd like to take her name. Change my first name to Gentry, my last to Hirsch. I rolled the idea around experimentally. Gentry Hirsch.

I politely declined.

She didn't want to take my name, either. "Well what will the baby be?" she wanted to know. "Gentry? Hirsch-Gentry?"

The baby. I stared at her flat stomach.

A baby.

∽

I was going to get married and become a father.

The plans picked up momentum. We set a day. Miriam wanted to get married at her parents' home. Her parents offered to cater the reception and pay for the honeymoon. My pride wanted to object, but buying the stupid house took every penny I'd ever saved and I made such crappy money, a fact Mr. Hirsch pointed out to me on the phone right before he told me to call him "Dad."

Sure, Mr. Hirsch.

I bought her a ring. She picked, I paid, the system we'd established for the house. She picked out a smart little suit for herself, and I paid for it. She made me buy a suit. I picked a cheap suit since I had to pay for that, too. She offered to get me a ring, but I told her it might be an electrical hazard.

She wrote out invitations. "Is there time for that? Why don't we just invite people by phone?" She let me know at top volume that she wanted WRITTEN invitations. Because they were IMPORTANT.

Fine.

I printed out the names and addresses for her. Since Mel refused to attend and the Mumfords no longer spoke to me and Lorrie didn't even know who Miriam was (I kept forgetting to mention her in my letters), I had eight people to invite. The Sandersons, the Shaws, Kevin and his new wife, and Dexter and Ramon. We had a moment, there, when she refused to invite them as a couple. She had an "issue" with that. I almost called it off, then. She knew I meant it. She sent one to Dexter and Guest.

I drove to the mailbox to mail those invitations. I kept telling myself, drive, just drive, keep going and drive away from here, it's not too late. But it was too late.

Because we were going to have a baby.

We went to get a license. I was in a daze, I wasn't paying attention. She kept poking me. I found my grasp of such facts as when and where I was born embarrassingly vague. "You were born WHERE? Why were you born THERE?"

What a question.

"You're just so weird," she hissed as I signed my full name.

Weird, yes. And I was going to get married and become a father.

∽

Paige called. "So, Gentry, you're truly going to do this."

"Yes."

"Does this mean that Miriam's pregnant?"

"No?"

She sighed. "You're so bad at lying. Is Mel officiating?"

"No. He won't even be there, Paige. He doesn't want anything to do with this."

"Oh, Gentry. Honey. I'm so sorry." The pain in her voice.

I wanted to talk. I didn't remember how.

∽

And the word went out that we were going to do it, and my friends gathered as they gathered for every wedding. We gathered to honor this commitment in our Catholic way, except of course, I wouldn't be getting married in a church like Becca and Daniel, Kevin and Parker, Paige and Sandy. I wouldn't be married in the house of God.

Miriam was angry. She was angry over a number of things.

She was angry because Kevin and Parker were staying with us. Kevin could afford a hotel, but I hadn't seen him since the Shaws' wedding. Their staying with us was a way to spend more time together.

I met Parker for the first time when they came to town. She was far nicer than she was ever supposed to be, considering she was the pillar of cool Presbyterian cash that he married the year before. She was nice about all this talk of the past, most of which made us laugh so hard that we never finished a sentence.

"Do you remember that, what was it, it looked like an owl?"

"Oh God, Gentry, the one next to the . . . ?"

"YES, it was that . . . what was it . . ."

"Why was it THERE?"

And so on.

We laughed until we wheezed. Miriam yawned, frowned, went to bed early. Parker lasted a little longer. She eventually went up to sleep on a pastel couch.

Kevin and I spent a night down there in the basement, remembering and laughing and talking and even crying over one or two things. Miriam came down in the morning and found us on the rented rollaway bed, sound asleep. Miriam found this suspect and disgusting. "Queer."

Speaking of queer, Dexter stayed with a friend in Oklahoma City. He wasn't able to bring Guest, unfortunately. Guest had to work. Daniel and Becca stayed with friends, too. Ariel was back in Georgia with Becca's mother. The Sandersons were staying with the elder Sandersons. Yes, Paige loved me so much that she was setting foot in Genevieve's house after two years, so she could watch me get married to someone she couldn't stand.

Genevieve was the official baby-sitter of all the children who'd been banned from the ceremony by Miriam. I made a trip over to see the kids. Genevieve let me in, demanded my name, made fun of me. I stammered. Some things never change.

Her husband apparated briefly, nodded at me and then faded from sight. I looked at the kids, the three beautiful kids. For the first time, I thought, maybe I'll have one of these wonderful and violent creatures.

Percy was a still a baby. He was not even two. He didn't remember me. He spoke in a language I couldn't decipher, but he seemed to know what he was saying and somehow we managed some conversations.

Byron talked about the marbles. "Uncle Grasshopper, do you remember those marbles?" I remembered those marbles.

Lucy Rose demanded to know about my flower girls. She was certain that I had some illicit group of flower girls, and that she'd been excluded. I reassured her that we had none whatsoever. She thought very little of the idea of a wedding without flower girls. When she heard that Miriam was wearing a suit, not a wedding sari like all her aunts, she looked at me as if we were getting married underwater. She didn't even mind her exclusion, then.

But I did. I minded.

Miriam was angry because I visited the Sanderson kids without her. Miriam was angry because Dexter threatened to wear a dress and I said I didn't care. Most of all, Miriam was angry because it was time for the bachelor party.

Not that I wanted a real bachelor party, one with strippers and the like, no, I'm too shy for that, and morally opposed to the whole idea, and all my friends knew it, but they wanted to at least take me out and get me drunk. I badly wanted to get drunk. But Miriam would have none of it.

We compromised. We would stay in and get drunk.

Miriam was angry because I'd never been drunk in these two years and she wanted to see it. No way. This was a bachelor party, and females were banned, they were out of there, because Sandy insisted and Paige backed him up. We had an unstoppable force.

Miriam was angry because All Four of My Best Friends were insisting on standing up for me. I stood up for Sandy, and Dexter and Kevin both stood up for Daniel, and Sandy stood up for Kevin, and since we weren't linear thinkers, none of us could decide whose turn it was. Sandy thought it was maybe my turn to stand up for myself. Daniel said that was impossible. We decided to let the Fates choose. We were planning some sort of a Best Man lottery. We were working out the rules. So far, we had only established that there would be drinking involved.

Miriam was angry about so many things, so many wedding "issues." Of all the things that infuriated Miriam, she was most furious at the possibility that Dexter would be the Grand Prize Winner in the Stand Up For Gentry Sweepstakes. "You're going to make my sister stand up with a GAY PERSON?"

In a dress.

The couples arrived. The women came in briefly to drop off the men, to make sure no car keys remained on the premises and look in horror at the pit I owned. "We're going to RE-DO it," Miriam announced, and then the women left. Daniel, Kevin, Sandy, and Dexter, the only bachelor left after tomorrow, and that was purely a legality because he and Guest were highly committed, we sat in the family room of the hideous box of a house I owned, and started drinking.

Dexter was our official "Wet Bartender."

We got drunk. Oh Dear Lord, and You know I'm praying here, did we ever get drunk. Nothing felt better than opening my mouth after two years and pouring down some brown poison. It felt so good. An old friend.

Hey, Poison.

And things got hopping down there in the old family room. We broke out the bottles of booze intended for the reception. Dexter made us drinks with names like "The Pink Wink" and "The Long Lick."

I don't remember everything we talked about that night, but I remember some of it. Dexter told me that I wouldn't know this, but my family room would be the perfect set for a porn movie. He said that in fact, he thought he'd seen one filmed in the very room. Kevin said it looked more like a rumpus room or a rec room than a family room. But he suggested I call it the Wreck Room. Sandy asked me if I would actually say the word "rumpus." I said no.

Sandy called out a prayer to God for the purity of my innocent vocabulary, wondering what marriage to a woman like Miriam would do to it. He asked me if I'd saved myself for marriage. He told me, don't be ashamed. Purity is a fine thing. And God loves the innocent. Daniel offered to have "the talk" with me. Did I have any questions about anything that he could address? I refrained from talking about my virginity and with whom I lost it, I wasn't going to do that again, but we did have a long conversation about technical virginity because Dexter volunteered the fact that he was still a technical virgin. Sandy said he thought a technical virgin was someone who hadn't had virtual sex over the Internet yet. Daniel asked me did I do that. I told him no, I didn't do that, what an idea. Masturbating to lines of type. And Kevin said well, he had quite a time in college with some lines of type by D.H. Lawrence and Henry Miller, among others. In order to leave this topic behind, I argued with Dexter. I told him I didn't see how he could possibly still be considered a virgin.

We turned to the dictionary. We looked up the definition of virgin, and then we looked up sexual intercourse in one of Miriam's medical compendiums, and then we broke out the Bible. Dexter was right. He was actually more innocent than every single one of us because every sexual act he participated in fell under the category of a perversion. Now, that was a novel way to maintain your purity! We congratulated him on both his virginity and his ingenuity.

Some bachelor parties have strippers. Mine had reference materials.

We drank. And drank. We geographically reminisced, covering the length and breadth of streets, alleys, and gutters with which we were intimately familiar during our college years.

Well, this house is no Buckhead, I told them that. But, I told them, we need to appreciate this house for the technological marvel that it is, we do, gentlemen. This house is a triumph of the inorganic, the man made, the cheap, the shabby, the ugly! We need to pay tribute to this combination of pressboard, Formica, and asbestos, all topped off with aluminum siding!

And I took the gentlemen on a tour of sorts, and the theme of that tour was What I Hate Most in Every Room. They got to see all of it, I showed it all to them, the crap on which I spent every penny, every paycheck. Sandy said Grasshopper, I've been meaning to talk to you about these drapes. I said I know, they remind a person of the Yellow Wallpaper, don't they? And he said yes, they were very Yellow Wallpaper. And he asked me, Grasshopper, do you think there is a sane and loving Miriam trapped behind the pattern? And I said very possibly.

We looked at the couches, we hurled ourselves upon the couches, we had an ugly couch contest and we all sat down so hard on the winner that something in it cracked.

Daniel decided we needed to settle down, so he put on some of the classical music CDs that Miriam liked. Dexter said, wait, it sounds like everyone in the orchestra changed their mind in the middle of a note and started playing something else. Did they do that on purpose? I said I believed it was just a malfunction of the stereo system over there. Sandy asked me how speakers that large could put out sound that small. I said I'd never investigated. I didn't choose this stereo, men, I was electronically usurped, I came home and this set-up had manifested itself in my home, so in general I ignored it.

Daniel said that music soothes the savage beast. The rest of us scoffed. Music soothed the savage breast, not the savage beast. As English majors, we waited for our savage breasts to be soothed, and Sandy said we should have hired a stripper, because what was a bachelor party without savage breasts. Dexter said that Guest would have done it for free, and Daniel said no offense, but that probably wasn't right up Gentry's alley, and Kevin knocked something over because he was laughing so hard, and it broke, and he said Sorry, and I said Thank You, could everyone please break something, so they did.

Tinkle, tinkle, smash, smash.

After that, we listened to a little more music. We decided we hated classical

CDs, and Sandy said they made great coasters, or miniature Frisbees. He demonstrated, and Sandy was correct. Daniel was inspecting the hearth. He was curious to know if it were really faced with Z-brick. I told him of course, what else would a house like mine have facing the hearth but Z-brick? I liked Z-brick, actually, because it was the only home building material that reminded me of Post-it notes.

And they expressed some curiosity about the things Miriam used to exercise, the weights and measures, as it were, that were strewn about the living room area. I expressed some personal astonishment at the fact that I was marrying a woman who exercised, could they believe it? I had a woman who exercised, I was actually going to marry a woman who worked out. I showed them the little box she stepped up and down on. Kevin stared at it. He was suspicious of the idea, I said I thought the stairs were perfectly fine for that, but she wanted to buy this little box. Dexter said, Oh, let me try. He stepped up, he stepped down. Wow. I feel firmer and more toned already. Guest will be thrilled.

And then they all tried it, and then they tried using the weights she lifted so her arms would be nice and hard. Daniel said that I was ungrateful, because my God look at the body Miriam had, what a body, and at least she wasn't getting soft on me. I gave him a homicidal look, because if he talked about soft, I might cross over into the unmentionable, the unforgivable, because I knew the soft, blushing roses and milk and freckles and . . .

I hollered, then. I have a rock hard woman, as soft and yielding as this Plywood box! We applauded, then, Miriam and her muscles.

We moved on to the kitchen, where we decided we were hungry so we fried eggs in the expensive cookware that I didn't know how to use properly according to Miriam. The butter snapped and popped, and the eggs snapped and popped, too. We discussed, while we ate the mess we'd made, all the small appliances that baffled me, crockpots and juicers and blenders and choppers and grinders and poachers, Poachers! Call Fish and Wildlife! We had a stupid small appliance contest. The winner would get a free trip. The electric yogurt maker won by popular acclaim. Kevin asked, what was electric yogurt, anyway? It sounded dangerous, the whole idea of electric yogurt. It sounded lethal. We agreed. So we threw that electric yogurt thing out a window and it landed on one of the neighbor's cars.

We looked through all the vegetarian cookbooks that Miriam had because we couldn't eat meat anymore. Sandy was aghast, he demanded to know whether I ate bean curd? Gentry you actually eat that stuff? Do you mean to tell me,

Grasshopper, that Homo Sapiens fought his way to the top of the food chain just so you could eat VEGETABLES? Don't you know your place on the food chain? Sandy was appalled.

But I told him I do, I'm a carnivore, hear me roar!

Sandy insisted that a man needs MEAT! There was no meat in my house. So Sandy suggested that we roast and eat Miriam, because she was so lean. He wanted to know if there were any recipes for Miriam in the cookbooks, and I said no, idiot, I'm not allowed to eat Miriam, and besides, these were vegetarian cookbooks. And he wanted to know well, wasn't she a vegetarian? What good was a vegetarian cookbook if it didn't tell you how to cook vegetarians? We agreed that the cookbooks were useless. So they followed the yogurt maker. It rained cookbooks in the driveway.

We had a ceremony. I swore, I placed my hand on top of the coffeemaker and promised to always exercise my manly carnivorous prerogative. I swore my meat fealty. Everyone cheered.

Then, fortified by the exploding eggs, we continued the tour. We fell down the hall to the second bedroom, where we had a look at all the strange clothes that she bought for me, clothing I never wore, clothing that made it look like middle-aged strangers lived in my closet. Dexter asked why my clothes couldn't live with Miriam's clothes in the big closet, and I explained that their ugliness required isolation. He said based on what he'd seen of Miriam's attire, they'd be right at home in her closet. I brought up the possibility that the male clothing might mate with the female clothing, dooming the baby to ugly clothes. Kevin said, Baby, Gentry? Sandy said Leave it be. Sandy said would you look at these *ties*? Dexter, what kind of *ties* are these? He said the ugly kind.

We decided that the ties I had were the ugliest ties ever manufactured. But I wanted them to understand that these were very expensive ugly ties. Daniel wanted to know why they were so expensive. I told him that I thought you had to pay extra to get them that ugly. Dexter thought that the only thing ties that ugly were any good for was to hide vomit. And Daniel said, No, you could hang yourself with one of these, Gentry. That might not be such a bad idea, come to think of it. Daniel, a former Eagle Scout, demonstrated some knots, even a noose or two, in case I needed one.

Hey now, I deflowered his wife, but that was no reason to encourage me to die.

But, it was time to move on. I showed them the little electrical thing Miriam used to depilate her face, I actually took them into the bathroom and I showed them that item. They were thunderstruck that I had a wife that hairy. I was proud. I had the hairiest, healthiest, hardest woman of the bunch. We decided to give it a try, the electrical hair yanker, we all tried it, and it HURT. Sandy said it wasn't an Epilady, it was an EpiDevil. Kevin decided that not only was Miriam hairier than me, she was actually stronger and more manly than me because, as he said, she can stand to pull the hair out of her face, just tear it out by the roots, whereas you, Gentry, weakling that you are, barely even shave. Dexter shared with us the interesting fact that Guest shaved his entire body. All that stubble. He shook his head. I considered this as it might apply to Miriam's abundant body hair. I shuddered. I had limits.

We moved on. We ended up down in the basement again. Some of us fell down the stairs to get there. And as we ended the tour of What I Hate Most in Every Room, Sandy turned to me and emoted. He asked me In The Name of God, what I hated the most in the whole, goddamned, son of a bitching, shit hole of a house? I told him it was a tie. It was a tie between the living room drapes, the wet bar and myself. I couldn't decide which I despised more. And then I laughed, and I laughed, and then I threw up.

Eggs and Scotch.

Sandy took me upstairs to clean me up. The other three worked on the carpet. Daniel thought they should use some of the ties to mop up the vomit, wasn't that what those ties were for, but Dexter found towels. Kevin said those towels were as ugly as the ties, so he put them to work. And they cleaned up, sort of. Sandy changed my shirt and watched me brush my teeth. This is just like college, Grasshopper. Whenever I smell puke, I think of you. And I said thank you. He gave me a hug, and took me downstairs, and we all got to drinking some more, because I had more room for poison, obviously. And there was a vote.

They decided they needed to get me out of the state. They were all in agreement. All except for Daniel, who kept saying, you're joking, right? You're all joking, right? To which Sandy replied, no, Hell no, Danny, we're not joking. We can't let this happen. We spent way too many years watching out for this boy to let this happen, and we are NOT JOKING. We're going to SAVE HIM.

I was greatly relieved until I remembered I had to get married.

My friends began to plot a rescue. They discussed the logistics of kidnapping me, putting me on a bus to Mexico or Maine. Whoa no, not Maine, anywhere but Maine, please. They wondered why I had a Maine phobia, a NEW one, but I wouldn't tell them, that was my little secret, what was in Maine. They said, Mexico, then. It was fairly close.

I was jubilant! I was headed for Mexico!

But I couldn't go to Mexico. I had to get married.

At some point we were singing, yes, I think we were singing, and I'm sure that we sounded fine, just fine, because we were all a bunch of altar boy hymn singers, although our present selection contained more of the profane than the sacred. And in walked the ladies, Paige, Becca, Parker, four of Miriam's cousins, a youngish aunt and Evelyn. And Miriam.

There was a moment. A moment that passed, as moments always do.

Miriam was inspired. "What a bunch of totally disgusting PIGS, what the HELL happened to the KITCHEN, what the HELL . . ." and on and on.

I yelled back. I yelled back, in front of my friends, me, Gentry, the man who never yelled. I yelled. "Hey MIRIAM? How about you SHUT UP?"

There was one of those awful, embarrassed palls that falls in the face of a couple who argues in public.

"How DARE YOU? You know WHAT? I don't think I'm going to MARRY you tomorrow," she said.

"That's fine with ME. Then I don't have to go to MAINE."

She started to cry.

I staggered outside, leaned against the side of the house I hated and tried to pray. And I realized that I couldn't pray, and I didn't know where my church was anymore and I didn't know if I could find it. I was a miserable man about to make the biggest mistake of his life because my church forbade me to use birth control and I didn't even remember where my church was and the truth was I was angry at my church so that was fine, just fine with me.

How? How to pray? How did it happen that I had forgotten how to pray?

I sat down and pressed my hands to my eyes.

Of course, it would have to be her that found me. I could hardly look at her because I wanted her and I felt guilty and angry over that, too. She was a little unsteady on her feet, standing over me, swaying like a tree in Oregon, tall and rooted and beautiful with her hair like the glory of sunset on treetop, blinding me.

"Hey, Gentry." Her voice was so calm, so low. Jin-tree. The sound of that. "What are you doing out here? Howling at the moon?"

"No. I'm out here being Catholic."

"Oh. That." She sighed and sat down next to me. We sat there, leaning against each other. Quiet.

"Hey Becca? How old are you?"

"Thirty-three."

"I'm sixteen."

"*Now* you tell me."

Her laughter smelled like wine. Wine made me sick but I wanted to taste her sweet, laughing wine. I put my hands in her sunset. My hands found the pins. I spoke low in her ear to keep her still as I took them out, one by one, loosening her curls, feeling the spill of her hair.

"Do you remember, Becca, our first time? You were communion." I kissed her neck, feeling her tremble. "It was so holy, taking each other's bodies. Do you remember how blessed it was, how sacred?"

She pulled back, pushed my hair away from my face. "My God, Gentry. You're still in there. My beautiful drunken poet-boy. I always loved you drunk."

"I always loved you back."

She smiled, tears in her eyes.

"Becca. Come here."

She did.

Her cool skin and scent of night-vine, her soft lips and the taste of sweet wine. There was a river in me and a river in her and they wanted to join, to flow together in thrashing, foaming glory. But I wouldn't do that to her. I would only hold her in my arms and know that she was pounding, pounding for me in her heart the way I pounded for her.

I would always hold her.

She put those white arms around my neck, pulled me back to her mouth, back where I belonged. We kissed for a few more minutes, for a few of the longest and sweetest minutes of my life. But she pulled back, she pulled away, it was only a kiss, it wasn't a question, it wasn't an answer, it didn't mean "yes," it just meant nothing.

We went back to leaning against each other, quiet.

She turned to me, and looked at me hard. "All right, Gentry, I need to ask you about something." I forced my eyes to focus on hers. She shook her head. "Actually, I'm so afraid it's something I have to *tell* you. And if this is something I need to tell you, then my entire life's been ruined."

This was making my head spin.

"It hurt so much that you'd never talk about it. You'd go silent, like a wall." She looked at me and waited. I waited, too. I had that drunken confidence that in a minute or two, understanding would hit me. I'd know what she meant.

I had no idea what she meant.

"But then I realized that you never talked about anything, so why should this be any different? And that's what I always thought it was. But then it seemed like it never even happened for you." She looked so pained. "I've never been able to figure out how it could not matter to you."

"Do you mean us?"

She looked angry. "No, I'm not talking about us. I'm talking about him."

Him? Him who? Daniel? Did she mean what we did to Daniel? Or what they did to me?

"I don't know who you're talking about." I shook my head. "Tell me what you mean."

"Are you saying you don't *know*?" And she looked at me with some kind of horrified, devastated recognition in her eyes, and she opened her mouth to tell me or ask me or whatever it was but she was so upset that she couldn't speak, she took some breaths, shook her head, and . . .

"WHAT ARE YOU DOING OUT HERE? There are CHIP CRUMBS all over the FLOOR, and someone THREW UP, they used the GOOD TOWELS to clean it up, and HALF the booze for the reception is just GONE, just what the HELL happened upstairs, just what the HELL were you doing, just what kind of LOW LIFE, ALCOHOLIC FRIENDS do you HAVE, ANYWAY?"

I rose to my feet and folded my arms. Becca stood up beside me.

"And just WHAT is the YOGURT MAKER doing out here, WHAT are these COOKBOOKS doing out here, and WHAT ARE YOU ALL DOING OUT HERE, anyway? ARE THESE MY CD's?! Just EXACTLY what are you all TALKING about out here? WHAT? WHAT THE FUCK ARE YOU TALKING ABOUT OUT HERE?"

Becca looked down on Miriam, green eyes to amber eyes, and she said, no, she *proclaimed* to Miriam, "If you must know, we were talking about the past. Gentry and I were talking about the past. We have one, you know. And someday soon, you'll be nothing but another part of it, Miriam. Just a part of the past."

"You're WRONG." Miriam put a hand on her taut stomach. "I'm having his BABY."

Becca put her hand against the house for a moment, steadied herself. She looked at me. All the forgiveness was gone. "Maybe this is a penance, I'm not sure. But don't do this, Gentry. You don't have to do this." She walked away, flaming, into the night.

"That is JUST LIKE YOU, to invite an old girlfriend to the wedding!" I looked down at Miriam. How was I supposed to know that I wasn't allowed to have any old girlfriends? I opened my mouth to protest. She hit me so hard that my head slammed back into the aluminum siding.

And I thought, those weights really work.

I slid down to a seated position. Miriam stood before me, screaming. Wrong with me. No respect. In front of her cousins. Disgusting pigs. And so on.

She had on that tiny orange dress. I stared at her stomach, tried to imagine my child growing in there. "Hold on," I whispered. "I'm going to get us out of here. We're going to Mexico."

I blacked out while planning our escape.

~

Daniel stood up for me, as his wife stood up for me the night before.

I sort of remember the ceremony, the ceremony Becca boycotted. My balance was slightly affected by the hair of the dog on the morning of the wedding. I had an impressive black eye. Daniel propped me up. He tied my tie, iced my eye, poured me a stiff drink, and got me married off. If not for Daniel, I would never have been able to do it.

Yes. We did it. No church, no priest, just a short judge and some short words in her parents' living room. I stood there and said "I will," which seemed conditional, as if my mistake would be taking place at some unspecified time in the future. She said she would, too. There was a legally sanctioned and publicly witnessed occasion for mouth-to-mouth microbial exchange, and we were pronounced husband and wife.

Her mother cried. Her dad cried. Her sister cried, as did some of the relatives with beautiful hair. Ardis was there. He cried too.

Sandy shook my hand. "You did it, Grasshopper."

I pointed at Daniel. "He made me." An old joke, but no one laughed.

I made everyone but Daniel look away while I signed my name on the marriage certificate. "I don't have to look away!" Miriam yelled. "I know his name!"

Sandy threw his hands up in disgust.

Daniel offered to notarize the document free of charge. "Let it be my wedding gift to you."

Sandy looked at my eye. "You'd better give him something better than that, Danny. He deserves some compensation."

"I said no presents, please."

We had the reception, the eating and drinking part of the procedure, and her dad made a joke about "my kind and your kind." I understood these were jokes, now, I understood that he was actually a funny old man being outrageous on purpose. I didn't care. Miriam had ordered a selection of food that cost a fortune, but I couldn't eat, her parents were paying for it.

I didn't care.

One plate was full of pink, chilled shrimp. An old woman looked at it, looked at me, curled her lip in disgust. Her lip looked like one of the shrimp. "Treif." Unclean. Did she mean the shrimp, or did she mean me?

I didn't care.

I went in to her parents' bedroom and took off that suit. Sandy followed me in, watched me change, retrieved the jacket from the floor, hung it up. I was doing up my belt, and he put his hands on my shoulders and looked at my eye. "Gentry? All bullshit aside. Is everything all right with you?"

I shook my head no. I wanted to tell him that Miriam was pregnant, and in my splendid Catholic righteousness, I'd done nothing to prevent it. I couldn't speak.

"What have I let you do?" He was crying. I had never seen him cry before. "I should have made you buy a motorcycle, Grasshopper."

"It's not your fault."

"It is. I'm supposed to watch out for you." He pulled me in and held on to me, his tears in my hair. "I could shoot myself three times in the heart over this."

The bedroom door flew open. Miriam hurtled in. The disgust on her face, like a blow. "WHAT are you DOING?"

I raised my hands in hopelessness. Sandy shook his head. "What the fuck do you *think* we were doing? I was giving my best friend a blowjob, you stupid c . . ."

"*Sandy.*"

He stopped. I watched him arrange his face and master his temper, the effort it cost him to do both. He walked out and shut the door quietly behind him.

I stared at my wife. She stared at me. "Hey Miriam? If you start yelling, your entire family will hear you." Her face twisted almost beyond where I could recognize it.

I sat down on a twin bed and put on my boots. She didn't say a word as I laced and tied.

We came out together. Paige said, "Oh look, Gentry put on his going-away clothes!" Everyone laughed. I smiled. Inside, I wanted to pray, but I couldn't. I'd lost my ability to talk to God when I got angry at my church and Mel. But I was glad I wasn't in a church when I got married, and I was glad Mel was too angry to come and watch my mistake.

In less than a year, I'd be a dad.

∽

What a strange and tragic world, Hawaii. Ruined and beautiful.

We went to this place, this tropical paradise where everyone else seemed happy. If only I hadn't had Miriam on the honeymoon with me, I would have had a good time, I think. Because, of course, we had honeymoon "issues."

First, the clothing "issue," which came up before we ever left. Miriam, being Miriam, had spent weeks shopping. She'd charged a whole new honeymoon-type wardrobe. I'd watched the parade of bags that went into the big closet, and the parade out of the strange, touristy things she expected me to wear. It wasn't anger I fought, it was laughter. There were such interesting colors and fabrics, and there was even some effort at coordination between her clothing and mine, some matching thing going on.

I knew better than to argue. I plotted.

Miriam said she would pack all the toiletries and clothes. She said all I had to pack was a "carry on." I didn't know what a "carry on" was, so I didn't pack one. The day before the wedding she started to yell about it, so I called Sandy over at his mother's house and asked him what she meant. Sandy didn't laugh at me, very much. I'd asked him much more ridiculous questions in college, including the basic mechanics of how to bring a girl to, well, anyway, as far as the carry-on, he told me the idea was simple, some hand-held luggage that was small enough to carry on the plane.

Luggage? I'd been packing my clothes in the same duffel bag since my CYO camp days. That was too big. I used the ancient Jansport backpack I'd used since college. When I say ancient, I mean that the leather was cracking and it only had one shoulder strap. Hey, it worked for me. I only ever used one strap.

I packed a toothbrush, toothpaste, floss, a hairbrush and some deodorant. My car-washing shorts. One pair used to be gray, and one pair used to be khaki. Two new packages of white T-shirts (size extra large, of course). The big, thick, indestructible brown rubber sandals we all wore in the dorm showers, so as not to have rotten toes. A pile of plaid boxers.

There. I was set. No "issues" there.

The airplane, another "issue," but this time, the issue was mine. And I didn't reveal it. I'd never flown and it terrified me.

Miriam's parents paid for first class. I asked Miriam what the difference was between first class and the other class. The serf class. "Bigger seats and free booze."

Well, now.

I followed Miriam, I did whatever she did. I sat down and strapped in. I asked Miriam if I could please hold her hand and she hated me for that. I held on for dear life, looked around at my fellow passengers, and thought, how stupid *are* we, sitting here in something that could fall right out of the sky? Are we all *idiots*?

I had considered myself a religious person, but on that plane I became exponentially more religious. I prayed as hard as I ever have on the airplane, and God sent me a nice flight attendant bearing many small bottles of scotch.

Miriam hated me drunk.

She hated me because when we landed in Los Angeles for the layover, I said "Hallelujah!" I said it loud. She hated me because I smiled at all the new passengers who walked past us on their way back to coach. She hated me because when she asked me if this was the first time I'd ever been to California, I told her I didn't think it counted if you didn't set foot on the ground of a state. And I said that pretty loud, too.

She hated me because I didn't want to hold her hand during the second take-off. She hated me because I kept dropping my mechanical pencil as I did the crossword in the flight magazine. She hated me because she came out of the bathroom and a flight attendant had fallen into my lap somehow. God is good to air travelers, you know that? He sends Scotch and turbulence and attractive flight attendants, right in the order a terrified air traveler would need them.

I made some new friends on the plane to Hawaii. I decided that it was unfair that we had free poison and the other part of the plane didn't. So, after a few hours, I talked my fellow first classmates into ordering several drinks apiece, and then I carried them back to coach and passed them out. Miriam didn't get into the spirit of the enterprise.

The falling flight attendant stopped me on my way to the bathroom, and she called me Robin Hood, and told me I had to stop doing that. And then she took me into a kitchen area and gave me a little kiss and her business card. I leaned her back against that tiny galley and kissed her like I could locate a reason to keep living between her sweet, soft lips.

I let her go. She smoothed her skirt. I found my seat.

I liked flying.

~

Neither of us had any hotel issues. Miriam said she'd been afraid there would be hotel issues, she was braced for numerous hotel issues since her parents had arranged for the hotel through their travel agent. She suspiciously prowled around the room, alert for issues, and found no issues at all to speak of.

Of course, this was the first hotel in which I had ever, in my life, stayed. I'd stayed at a dirty little motel when I went to the Shaws' wedding, one that cost something like fifteen dollars a night, and I slept in the same room as Kevin, splitting the cost because I was so broke. I didn't tell Miriam this, of course.

This hotel room was clean. The bathroom was sanitized for my protection. I liked that, and I liked the big bottle of poison that room service brought with such alacrity. One bottle, one glass.

There were two beds, each about the size of a basketball court. I wanted the bed by the window for myself, but then, I thought, well, it is our honeymoon. She can choose her bed first.

One whole wall opened onto a balcony that overlooked the pool area. The pool was full of the type of people who enjoyed swimming in bleach. The smell of that. I could see the ocean, beyond. I needed a little more scotch, then, seeing the ocean.

I liked the ice machine. The ice tasted like chemicals, but I forgave the ice. I used plenty of ice on my honeymoon. Because the issues kept coming up.

It started when we unpacked. I dumped out my backpack and Miriam raged. "I WILL NOT BE SEEN WITH YOU IN THAT SHIT!!"

"Fine with me." I changed and went to get more ice.

I thought I looked fine, just fine. My shorts had hammer loops, and I borrowed a hammer from the maintenance crew and hung it in there. Thanks to the hammer, my shorts hung even lower than usual. I looked like a day laborer. The pool guy asked me to help him, and I did. I cleaned the pool. Hey, I liked skimming the pool. I considered this as a possible escape route, becoming an itinerant pool skimmer. Going native. Just disappearing. It was still the United States, I didn't need a visa to stay. But the baby. Well, I could wait until after the baby came to make my escape, take him with me. But what would a baby do while I was working?

I went up to the room for some ice.

Of course, Miriam was determined to have the ultimate Hawaiian Honeymoon Experience. We rented a car, a Geo, a white one, no less, and driving that had to be one of the honeymoon highlights for me. Miriam asked if I had any issues with the car, but no, no, I just drove it, I didn't own it. No issues at all there. Except the fact that I was driving drunk, but hey.

Time for more ice.

We ate. Eating was a big thing in Hawaii. I ate pork at every meal, and it made her sick. But islanders like pork. I kept thinking of *Lord of the Flies*. I gave thanks that I didn't wear glasses and sucked down a few more spare ribs. Miriam had issues with how much meat I ate, but I had absolutely no issues at all with it.

Ice helped with all the issues.

Drinking was another big thing in Hawaii. Miriam, of course, was not able to drink, as she was pregnant. She kept trying to make me taste her ghastly sweet "virgin" concoctions with fruit and umbrellas in them. I tasted one to shut her up, and my gagging for five minutes reminded her why she hated me. I never resolved that issue, the sweet liquid aversion issue, we had the opportunity in counseling to address that issue, but I never would work on that issue, it was just like me to ignore that whole issue.

She didn't yell so much in front of the other Happy Hawaiian Honeymoon Couples. But she lost it one night at dinner and embarrassed herself. I was past embarrassed at that point in my life. I just had a little more ice. After that, she kept up a low-pitched hum on certain issues, the drinks I wouldn't taste, the pool I refused to swim in, what was wrong with a Geo, all that pork I ate, my hair, why was I leaving it down every day, why wouldn't I wear the clothes she bought for me, and those sandals . . . my sandals?

"Hey Miriam? All my college buddies have these, and we got them for 99 cents a pair at Wigwam. We call them our convict sandals, and we all still wear them. I refuse to hear a word against my sandals."

I wouldn't swim in the hotel pool. Miriam didn't like the beach. So we compromised. Every day we went down to the beach and I swam there. Then we lay in the sun and watched the surfers and the happy people. I lay in the sun and smelled the salt, and the salt took me back where it always took me. I remembered the Gulf of Mexico and a girl named Jillian, and I wondered why, if I were stupid enough to marry a woman I didn't love, I hadn't run off to Mexico with Jillian, a girl who I could still taste, still smell if I thought about her. I thought about her in Hawaii. A lot.

And then we went back up to the hotel and sat by the pool so Miriam could swim. I was amazed that Miriam could swim and yell at the same time. She didn't get her hair wet, so her mouth stayed out of the water and available for yelling. She swam, and she bothered me to get in the water. "GENTRY! YOU SHOULD GET IN THE WATER!" I ignored her. I napped, or I sat there and drank poison and smelled the sea air and remembered how Jillian's dark hair would wind around me in long, wet, salty strings.

"Hey Miriam? I'm going to go up to the room to shower."

Imagine this in a Speedo, Miriam, now that's a scary thought.

~

One day I took diving lessons. Miriam didn't want to dive as it would require getting "too wet." I had to agree with her, underwater can be a pretty wet place, so I went on my own.

I paired up with a woman who looked as miserable as I felt. She was tall and blonde and lovely and wretched. I wanted to make her feel better. And other things, I wanted to make her feel other things. She had soft thighs that made me ache for softness. Miriam was as hard as metal, she had a relentless exercise regime and was always threatening to devise one for me. I looked at the thighs of my diving partner and fought an urge to ask her if I could just bury my face between them, please.

I was losing it in Hawaii. Losing it in a big way, God.

Anyway, we paired up and we cheered up. We put our mouths on each other to practice rescue breathing, and that made me happy. She smiled, too.

The boat took us out. I thought about diving off and swimming away to a different island, disappearing. I had life insurance. Miriam could collect it. She'd be happy about the insurance. Maybe I could get my diving partner to swim away with me and we could make a new life together in a grass hut on the beach. I smiled at her. She smiled back. I took this as a heavenly sign. Destiny.

I remembered the baby. The baby, idiot, you put it in there one loveless Sunday morning, and then you got married. Because you're Catholic. You can't kiss flight attendants and lust over diving partners because you're married, now. Married and a dad. Even if neither one feels real.

I was losing my mind.

We dove down and I didn't drown or die because I'd paid attention to the system. My partner let me hold her hand, and I was grateful to touch a woman who didn't know me well enough to despise me. We looked at a reef, and if it were possible to dive and cry, I would have. Gretchen would have loved this so much, so very, very much.

I thought, remember it and write to her again, it's been months since you wrote your last unanswered letter of what felt like so many. Maybe things will have changed, maybe she'll forgive you for that unhinged, craven letter you wrote when Kathryn was sick. Gretchen is the smartest person you've ever known, and she's smart enough to know that people make mistakes. You're going to get her to forgive you for that letter, and for leaving, you are, and you can tell her about this reef. So remember.

I thought about everything I'd seen on the way back so I could remember. I burned it into my mind. I got off the boat and fell down on the sand. Why had I come to a beach? Because, of course, it led me to another beach, a beach I never, ever allowed myself to think about. Two years that month, God. Two long years since I left. A year since she stopped writing. A year since I let myself remember her. I couldn't bear the pain of remembrance. And I thought, maybe, possibly, I could try. I could think about it a little.

I had to.

I thought about Bosco on the beach, at first. I remembered him rolling in dead fish, the way he smelled. The meeting dance he did with other dogs, all the sniffing and posturing, and then the playing. The way he looked rolling around a little dog with his big paw, so careful and amused. His delight at finding a crab back, hopefully with some crab guts still attached. It took so little to make him happy. Throwing sticks. He loved sticks. He loved everything. Especially me.

Oh God, was Bosco still happy?

And of course, from Bosco to Gretchen. Her hair, the way it flew around in the sun and the wind, like corn tassels. Little conversations about things that were "interesting." Singing to me, her angel voice, and her laugh like bells. Showing me the tide pools. How we went to the cove, watching surfers, and both of us down on the promenade and all that caramel corn. Having fun.

Oh God, please. We never flew any kites, God. Please let me fly a kite with Gretchen. Amen.

I remember Gretchen pulling me up to the house from the beach that December. I was so disappointed and hurt and humiliated by rejection, Kathryn took a straight razor to my stupid hope and I wanted to lay down and die on that beach, but Gretchen brought me out of the rain on that cold, lonely, December day.

I thought it was Kathryn who brought me back to life, God. It wasn't. It was Gretchen. I never meant to hurt her. I never meant to hurt any of them. But I did, I hurt all of them. And then, I ran away.

Dear God, hear me, listen to me. What have I done?

God, listen. I'll do it, some way, some how, I'll remedy these errors I've made out of desperation and loneliness. I'll take the baby and leave. This is my plan. Wait for this baby, and then, with this child of my own, my own child, God, I'll get back there and make things right with the people I hurt. Babies put women in a forgiving mood, and I'll show up with mine. And I hope they'll help me do this, because, God, I have no idea how to do it, I have no idea how to be a parent. But I will. God, just get me through the next months, and I'll make it right. There must be a path out of this. Give me strength, show me the path, and I'll take my baby and follow it back to Oregon.

Amen.

I swam, let the water take my tears. The ocean was made of salt, and some of it was mine.

~

I went back to the room, sunburned and exhausted, and lay down. The sheets were cool.

"Wake up. I'm STARVING." She frowned at me. "Did you get in there without showering? Those sheets are going to be full of salt."

She brushed at them while I took myself off to shower.

I came out and ignored what she laid out for me in favor of my used-to-be-khaki shorts and a T-shirt. I was putting on my jail flip-flops when she blew.

"WHY THE HELL ARE YOU WEARING THAT TOTALLY WORN-OUT SHIT? YOU LOOK LIKE YOU'RE GOING TO GO CUT THE FUCKING GRASS! JUST WHAT IS WRONG WITH WHAT I BOUGHT FOR YOU?"

"The clothes you bought for me are ridiculous."

"RIDICULOUS?"

"Ridiculous and embarrassing, like that hat you have on your head."

Miriam looked at me as if she'd never seen me before. "So now you have a PROBLEM with HATS?" She took off hers and threw it at me. I caught it like a Frisbee.

Did she mean to hurt me with a hat?

"I don't have a problem with hats. I have a problem with THIS HAT. In fact, I HATE IT." I picked up her hat and pitched it out the door. Great spin. Miriam's ugly hat sailed out and down to the pool area, where I was sure all the other honeymooners were enjoying the Punch and Judy show through our open sliding-glass door.

I turned around and looked at her face.

Time to go find that hat.

∽

The hat sat on a chaise. I remembered chaises. Kathryn used to sit in a chaise and watch me, back in the good old days when women used to like to watch me do yard work and occasionally take me in their mouths.

I picked up the hat, turned it around in my hands.

The woman from the diving class sat nearby. It was evening, and she had on sunglasses. I could do the math on that one. Sunglasses at night meant a woman was either famous, hiding a black eye or crying. No one had asked her for an autograph, I had a black eye, so the mathematical averages were that she'd been crying.

She took off the sunglasses and looked at me with reddened, puffy eyes. "That hideous hat belongs to you?" I looked down at the hat for a moment before sending it skimming off into the swimming pool. A scattering of applause from people sitting nearby rose like the scent of unfamiliar flowers on the evening's moist air.

She held out her hand. "I'm Iris. We never formally introduced ourselves."

I shook her hand, a nice grip Iris had. "Gentry."

"Will you join me?"

I sat down. "Did you, um, enjoy it out there today?"

She nodded. "It was a nice break from crying. That's quite a shiner you have."

"Thank you. I walked into a fist."

She laughed.

I should have retrieved Miriam's hat, but a man in the pool was wearing it. I should have thought about what to eat so I didn't vacillate in the restaurant and embarrass Miriam. I should have gone back to the room and put my hair in a ponytail so Miriam didn't yell about it. My hair was down all the time in Hawaii because it was wet and I was trying to let it dry, but she couldn't figure that out, she thought I had it down to annoy her.

I decided Miriam was right.

I leaned back in the chaise and ordered six shots of tequila with limes and salt, and two beers. When they arrived, Iris and I toasted, we licked, swallowed, bit, and we made that noise everyone makes after a shot of tequila. We let out the steam. And then we laughed, and we poked our limes into our bottles, and we drank our beers.

"Are you on your honeymoon?"

"I'm on my second honeymoon. My husband and I have five kids, and we decided, well, I decided, that we needed a little getaway."

"Five kids? Are you Catholic?"

"Everyone asks me that, am I Catholic or Mormon. I'm nothing. I'm nothing at all." Something in the way she said that made me suggest another shot. We licked, swallowed, bit, knocked it back. "How about you?"

"I'm Catholic."

"No, I mean are you on your honeymoon? I saw you with your hairy little woman."

I couldn't help myself, I barked out a laugh. I tried to pretend I was coughing. "Yes, we're on our honeymoon."

"Are you enjoying it?"

"No. I'm only trying to live through it at this point."

"Me too!" She toasted, "To living through Hawaii!" and we had our third shots, and I called the waiter over again for more beer because I didn't want to get too drunk too fast.

For the first time on this honeymoon, I was enjoying myself.

She looked out at the ocean. "Do you ever feel like your life is too small?"

"I don't know what you mean."

She looked at the bleached blue of the pool. "Lately when I get out of bed in the morning and I put on my life, it feels too small. Like when you're not that pregnant, but all of a sudden nothing fits. I'm sure you can relate." She gave me a wry little smile. "I want to expand my life. Or tunnel out of it somehow." She shook her head. "I'm sorry to talk like this to someone on his honeymoon. You're just starting. You shouldn't have to listen to anyone as cynical as me."

"Can I tell you a story?"

"Sure."

"When I was twelve, I went away to school. This very nice private school run by the Jesuits. It was an adjustment. All the rules, all the time. This boy named Winston was two years ahead of me, and a lot taller. He liked to bully people. I guess he thought I'd be a good victim because I was small for my age, just this . . . short, rough kid who wanted to be left alone. And he wouldn't leave me alone, not ever."

I remember his face, the regularity of his features, the paleness of his skin, eyes and hair. He was generic in every way but his cruelty.

"We ate in a formal dining hall. It was very . . . mannered. Tablecloths, china, the whole bit. He always sat across from me and made fun of how much I ate. I always ignored him, because I did eat a lot. But one evening he started to bother me about my name."

"Gentry is an unusual first name."

"It's my last name. And he was having, you know, some sport with my first name, which is . . . unusual. I ignored him because I was eating, and that made him angry. He said, 'Go ahead and ignore me. I'm going to sit across from you every day and every single day I'm going to call you by your gay name.' And he laughed."

"What did you do?"

"I turned over the table on him." I remembered the rage and satisfaction of that moment, the dishes flying, him and his toadies hitting the floor, arms raised to fend it all off. How he cried. I took a long sip of beer, remembering. "That's what I want to do with my life, Iris. I want to turn it over like that table."

She reached over and took my hand, squeezed it. I squeezed back.

We watched the sun go down.

~

Miriam must have fallen asleep, because she didn't venture down to humiliate me.

We traded stories. Iris had some funny stories about her five kids. I told her about Gretchen, and somehow she understood who Gretchen was to me without any explanation. I told her about Bosco. She told me about her four little dogs. They had Faulkner names. We talked about my stupid job and if I should go back to teaching. We talked about her job, all her kids, that was her job, and if she should go back to school. Those were the things we talked about.

We didn't talk about where we were from, where we lived. We didn't talk about her husband or my wife. We didn't talk about my shotgun wedding, the baby I could barely imagine, or why, on the last night of her second honeymoon, we sat by the pool and drank with each other. We didn't talk about why I offered to drive her to a remote beach in a rented Geo so we could watch the sunrise. We didn't talk about why we found ourselves sitting on a blanket I borrowed from housekeeping, listening to another couple up the beach have noisy sex and trying not to laugh, waiting for the sun to rise on Hawaii.

We didn't talk about why I kissed her.

I kissed her while she was laughing. I was afraid she would push me away, but she pulled me close. She took off her clothes and chucked them into the bushes, and then she sent mine over there, too. So funny and fearless and bold, but when I touched her, she dissolved. The sounds she made, the sighs and cries. She was velvet to my touch. She lay there trembling and helpless and my heart hurt with how beautiful it was when she let go. I gathered her up like a damaged bird and held her, told her hush, it was all right. But I couldn't help myself. I had to make her tremble some more.

We could have stopped there. I had what I'd been wanting from her since I saw her at the diving lesson. But after she stopped shaking, she sat up and pushed me back on that blanket and kissed me. And then she worked her way down, that agony of soft lips and small bites and anticipation, when will she get there, will she ever get there, oh please, God, please let her get there. She got there. And it was so good, I'd missed it so much, God, You can't make a sin feel this good, You can't, it's not fair and this can't be wrong and I never wanted her to stop.

But I asked her to stop. "Ah, please, stop for a . . . I'm going to, uh, please."

She sat up and smiled. "I've been wanting to do that since I saw you skimming the pool."

"Come here." I pulled her down next to me. I kissed her until my mouth hurt. And, finally, she took me into her, so easy, so sweet, so good. Her arms around me, her legs around me, and I watched her face as she cried, and I broke down. "Don't move," I cried, "Wait," but she looked at my face and kept moving, I wanted it to last, I wanted it to go on but I couldn't oh wait, wait, oh here I am, oh . . .

When she spoke, her voice was full of wonder. "We know how to have a honeymoon, Gentry."

"We do." I kissed her again, then rolled off and lay back on the blanket, still breathing hard. I pulled her up tight to my side. Her hair was long and blonde and tangled. Stroking it made my stomach hurt. She fit her head to my shoulder and tucked her feet under mine. She was so tall, almost as tall as me. She cupped her hand over my chest and I felt the echo of my heartbeat in the palm of her hand.

Iris, gently holding my heart as we lay naked on a sandy blanket, ignoring the light radiating along the horizon. In college, I'd tried to write poems about moments like these. But the moment was the poem.

"I'm sorry I was so fast."

"That was *fast*?" And she burst out laughing. "Oh, you're funny. Fast." She didn't look sad, finally. "So what happened after you turned over the table?"

"The table?"

"At school. When you turned over the table on that boy. That can't be the end of the story."

"Hm." I thought for a moment, remembering. "It seemed like the whole dining hall exploded, but slowly, everything happening so slowly. One of the brothers came over and started, you know, interrogating everyone as to what set it all off. Brother Dmitri. Everyone pointed at me. So Brother Dmitri got a hold of me and hauled me over to this kid, who was crying. Brother Dmitri said, 'Don't you have something to say to Winston, Gentry?' I said, 'Yes.' He said, 'Go ahead and say it.' So I looked at Winston and said 'See you tomorrow.'"

She laughed, as wide and deep as that ocean, her laugh. She sat up on the blanket and started looking at me. She looked at everything, my ears, my hands, my stomach. She made a study of me, all of me, even my feet. I didn't mind, but it was, um, it appeared that . . . "Hey Iris? Are you . . . Iris, are you measuring me?"

"I need the specs for future reference. Because you're *just* right."

"Okay, Goldilocks." We laughed again. I'd forgotten that it could be like this. That it could be fun, that you could laugh. But the sun was rising. "Come here." I pulled her down. "Lie still. Hush." I closed my eyes and put my face in her hair, breathed her in. She smelled like the ocean and tequila and grief. I touched her softness all over again. Every dip, swell, hollow. She shivered.

"What are you doing?"

"I'm remembering you."

The beach was empty. We went into the ocean together. After all these years, another woman in my arms in the water, finally, her mouth on mine, tasting her salt.

The ocean was made of salt. And some of it was ours.

~

The flight home left after dark. We would fly all night and be home on Saturday morning. Back to scenic Oklahoma.

I'm no good at lying, but Miriam didn't notice. I'd stumbled in the door and she was asleep. I'd climbed into my bed and slept until she woke me up to get ready for the shuttle to the airport. We hadn't spoken much, just, do you have cash for the tips, do you have everything, leave the key here, I checked us out last night. The logistics.

I sat in first class and tried to pray, then tried to sleep. She sat beside me, scanning a magazine. "Are you going to tell me where you were?"

I thought about telling her the truth. I couldn't.

Adultery was not a new sin. It was very, very old, as far as sins go. But it was new to me. It was a sin that definitely required absolution. In order to be absolved, I needed to confess. In order to confess, I needed to be contrite. For contrition, it was necessary to despise the sin. I couldn't do that, either.

To adulterate is to contaminate or corrupt. But was it a pure bond that stretched between us? Was what held us together holy? Did I have a point, or was

I just trying to rationalize my way out of another sin? And what did it matter? I was leaving as soon as I could.

Miriam kept getting up, going into the bathroom.

I tried to think of the calendar, figuring just how quickly the baby and I would be on our way out of Oklahoma. The Jeep wasn't safe for a baby, but with the right car seat, which I had been checking out already on websites, and maybe some kind of protective headgear, maybe something like a small aviator helmet with goggles so his eyes would be safe from the wind, the baby would be safe on the ride west. But I couldn't have a baby sleeping in a Jeep. Could a baby sleep in a tent? Then there was the question of feeding the baby. The last two babies I'd been around were fed by their mothers. But there were bottles, yes?

Miriam sat down heavy in the seat next to me.

"What's wrong?"

She was crying. "Shut up."

"What is it?"

She cried harder. "I started my PERIOD."

It took me a minute. "Hey Miriam? Does this mean you're not pregnant?"

"Oh my GOD you're so stupid. I mean, I always counted on you being STUPID but this is stupid to a whole new LEVEL of stupid."

"How many hours until we land?" I looked out the window. Nothing but ocean. I felt panic rising in my chest. "We need to get you to a hospital." I'd seen this on television. "We can have them call for an ambulance, it can be there when we land."

She stopped crying, just like that. "Forget it. I'm not even cramping. I'm just bleeding."

"Well maybe it's not too late. Maybe they can, I don't know, put the baby back in there?" This was my fault, this was because of what I'd done, she'd cried all night and this was my fault, this was the cost of my night with Iris, this is what I'd done, I'd upset Miriam and now she was losing the baby and it was my fault. This was my fault and I needed to fix it. "Let me get the flight attendant. They can see if there's a doctor on the plane."

"You're such an IDIOT." She shook her head. "You're such a fucking IDIOT."

"About some things, yes, but we have to get a doctor."

She shook her head again. "It was so early." She was so calm. "Maybe something was wrong. Maybe it was for the best."

"For the best?" The sound of that, the *finality*. "So you're not pregnant anymore?" I sat there for a moment, absorbing this. My child in the small aviator helmet receded, waving good-bye to me. "So then why did we get married?"

The sound she made.

I put my arms around her. I held her all the way home, rocking her as she cried, listening to her complain about how her sister would have the first grandchild, it wasn't fair, no one loved her, what was she going to do. I held her, I rocked her. Eventually, she fell asleep.

I grieved too, because when I left, I would be traveling alone.

~

When we got back to the house, a stack of mail on the kitchen counter waited, topped with a note from Evelyn, who had been "keeping an eye on things." Miriam shared this note with me first.

Dear Miriam and Gentry,

We hope you had the time of your life on that expensive honeymoon. Here is a list of gifts, don't forget your thank-you notes. Here is a copy of the announcement Mom and Dad sent out, for you to keep. Maybe, you would like to frame it.

The honeymoon is over,

Evelyn

I looked at the announcement her parents sent. "Hey Miriam? The marriage of their daughter Miriam to 'Mr. Gentry'? This is ludicrous."

"You're so NEGATIVE."

Negative. I sat down at the counter to brood. She flipped through the mail, she handed me letters, letters? From Oregon? My heart felt so light, restrained only by the weight of my sternum. But none were from Gretchen. Who were these from, anyway?

Dear Gentry and Miriam,

Congratulations to you both! Michael and I send our warmest wishes for your happiness and success! The girls remember you so fondly, Gentry! The best to you in all you undertake in your new life together as husband and wife!

Sincerely,

Mr. and Mrs. Michael Mumford

I found the matches, and I burned that one in the sink. No. In the sink!

I recognized the handwriting on the next one from sarcastic notes about phone calls, even though it wasn't signed.

I write to congratulate you, but I can't. This burns like bile, like acid, and I can't stop crying and the truth is this all makes me want to die. Are you happy? Does that make you happy?

Burning like bile and acid. Please, I prayed, never ever let her send me a short story.

Into the sink. Up in flames.

Another one.

Dearest Gentry and Miriam,

Gretchen shared your announcement with the entire family. Congratulations to you both. I'm sure that your life together will be a happy one, full of love, laughter and children.

I have to say, however, that was an interesting way you chose to break such important news to Gretchen. I know that it has been a year since she wrote to you, but you have remained an important person in her life. There have been so many things going on here, and she was upset when I was ill. There have been changes here. I know she hasn't written, but believe me, I know from conversations, Gretchen still cares about you.

We would all love to meet Miriam, Gentry. You would only marry someone special. Perhaps you two will come to the west coast some day. Imagine, you left Oregon only two years ago, and you are married. Absolutely amazing how life changes, isn't it?

Fondly and with deep regard,

Kathryn

Burn, Kathryn. Burn fondly, and with deep regard.

Dear Gentry,

Who the hell is this woman Gretchen says you married? We ran into her at the store and she was crying like a baby. You got married, and you don't even tell me? Is she knocked up? Why the hell don't you ever write me?

Vicki is pregnant again, about to pop. Walt is kicking butt in playgroup.

What the hell place is this that you are working at now? I thought you were teaching at a college, but you are just working there? Gretchen says you aren't even teaching. What do you mean you aren't teaching? What the hell is going on with you? Gentry, how can you not be a teacher? You were the best damn teacher I ever saw, Gentry.

Sincerely,
Lawrence Gilroy

Sorry. Lorrie, but this one burned, too.

I had a question, here, an important question.

Miriam was looking at some papers, pretending not to notice that I was starting letters on fire in the kitchen sink. She always commented on everything I did, I was a source of amazement to her most of the time, there was nothing I did that didn't create an issue or at least merit a comment. And there I stood, burning letters with Oregon postmarks in the sink, and she had nothing to say about it.

She was looking at a list. "None of your friends gave us any presents."

"I told them not to."

"WHAT?"

"I said I told them not to."

"That is just the STUPIDEST thing I ever heard."

"Miriam, how did these people get those stupid announcements?"

"They weren't stupid. That's just like you, to call those announcements stupid. They were engraved, and the only stupid thing about them was that you wouldn't let my mother put your first name on them."

"How did you get one to *Gretchen*?" I was yelling. I never used to yell. But I yelled at Miriam. The Pope would have yelled at Miriam. "If my name had been on there, all your relatives would have thought you married a *woman*! And that wouldn't fit in too well with your *homophobia*, now, *would it*?"

Yes, I yelled. But I was nothing compared to Miriam. Miriam had such a gift for yelling. "Don't you DARE talk that way to ME! I let you have your HOMO friend at the wedding, I LET you have him there even though it made me SICK and he was going to wear a DRESS!"

"He doesn't even own a dress. And that still doesn't answer my question. How did Gretchen get an announcement? *How*?"

"Just WHAT is the big DEAL? I thought you would WANT her to know, I thought that was a totally NORMAL way to HANDLE things, but NOTHING about you is NORMAL! You are NOT NORMAL! Always HUGGING your friends and even SLEEPING with them and that's so SICK! And you're TOTALLY FIXATED on that girl, you're just SICK over her, that must be why her MOTHER had to read the LETTERS, right? Is THAT why you quit TEACHING?"

"Shut up."

"You want me to SHUT UP?!" She moved so that she was standing right in front of me, looking up at me, yelling as loud as she could. "You make me SICK, you make me SICK with all this. That priest probably MOLESTED you, THAT is JUST what's WRONG with you, I hear your NIGHTMARES, I HEAR what you SCREAM, ALL those priests are the SAME, and you just don't want to DEAL with it and . . ."

I shoved her so hard that she fell to the floor.

I left the house.

∽

I hated myself.

Oh, harden up, put it away, you wanted this, right, Gentry, this is what you prayed for, to be someone else, to have your own life, different from the old one, a different life in which you push a woman down for standing in your way. Is that what a wife is for, is that why you got married, so you could finally do that?

No words for how much I hated myself, none.

I went outside to check the mailbox, the poor, beat-up mailbox, because another, worse letter was out there and I wanted to get it and take it out of there and read it alone.

What was this, what were all these bills, did we even have an account there? And here was the letter.

Gentry,

And I will never call you dear again because you are not dear and I want you to know that I HATE YOU, I hate you, how could you marry that person and not even tell me that you were going to, I hate you.

My mom was in the hospital and you wouldn't even come back here and I hate you.

I hate you, Gentry and I never hated you before. I never even hated you when you kissed my sister, rolling around like that, DISGUSTING, and I didn't even hate you when I saw you and my mom that night on the couch, I SAW YOU, it was three years ago, but I remember all of it because I can't forget because it was so sick and so disgusting, I never told you but I saw what she did to you that night on the couch and I know that you liked it and that makes me sick, you make me sick, Gentry, you are DISGUSTING and I thought you might get married to my mother after you let her do that to you but you didn't and I HATE YOU and don't you EVER write to me again.

Don't you ever come back here because I hate you and I always will. Don't come back.

Gretchen

I locked the letter in the glove box of the Jeep with all the others. I got out the bottles of poison left over from the party.

Time for the oblivion system.

~

I refused to go to work. She would stand at the top of the stairs and shout down to me.

"THEY'RE RUNNING OUT OF PATIENCE!" They did, indeed, run out of patience at the school. They fired me. But the way I saw it, Miriam was always trying to get me to try something new. Getting fired was new. I thought about telling her that. But I drank, instead.

"THIS IS JUST LIKE YOU, TO GET FIRED FROM WHERE I WORK, YOU ASSHOLE!" I thought about telling Miriam that nothing could be less like me than to get fired. I'd never been fired in my life. I'd been suspended pending investigation, but never fired. I wasn't going to tell her about that. I drank a little more, instead.

"YOU'RE A FUCK-UP, GENTRY, JUST A FUCK-UP! JUST HOW THE FUCK AM I SUPPOSED TO HOLD MY HEAD UP THERE!" I thought about suggesting she use her neck to hold up her head. It was strong enough. I thought about it. But I drank, instead.

"WHAT THE HELL ARE YOU PLANNING TO DO? I'D JUST LIKE TO KNOW WHAT YOU PLAN TO DO!" Do? I thought I'd found my new occupation. I watched television. I saw some great stuff down there, on the old television, on the old couch, in the ratty family room, in the ugly house that Jack built. Miriam didn't consider watching television a worthwhile occupation, though.

"GET YOUR ASS OFF THAT COUCH! I DIDN'T GET MARRIED TO SUPPORT YOUR ASS!" Since I was busy drinking, Miriam was the sole breadwinner. I developed a deep and personal aversion to the term "sole breadwinner" at that time. "DO YOU REALIZE THAT I AM THE SOLE BREADWINNER, NOW? I AM NOT GOING TO BE THE SOLE BREADWINNER IN THIS FAMILY! I MEAN THAT, GENTRY!"

Yes, she meant that.

"IT'S SUNDAY! WE HAVE TO GO TO MY PARENTS'! YOU CAN'T STAY DOWN THERE FOREVER!" She was probably right. Two weeks of oblivion was probably as much as I could manage without dying of alcohol poisoning.

I considered my options. Death looked good, but overt self-destruction was not an option. I considered a permanent move to the family room couch. But with Miriam's sweet support, her loving help, and her gentle encouragement, I got up off that couch to go eat her mother's cooking.

As was often the case, Evelyn and her husband were there. Ben was a burly, grumpy man who wore suits and asked me questions about golf. I knew nothing of golf. He kept threatening me with golf invitations. But at this dinner, he asked me how I'd feel about taking a job in "private industry." I had a deep and personal aversion to the term "private industry." But we were out of money. I took the job.

I had to do penance. I'd stay married, that was another miserable penance. I'd do penance for the rest of my life, if necessary.

∽

According to Miriam, I needed work clothes. I told her I already had clothes I wore to work. She looked a little worried. "Gentry, I didn't tell you this, but they don't even do business casual there. You have to wear slacks and a dress shirt and a jacket and tie. Every day."

"Forget it."

"Oh, don't be such a baby. You should try it, you might like it."

"Hey Miriam? I wore that every day of high school. Every single day."

She thought. "You could wear a suit."

"Fine. I have that suit from the wedding. I can wear that."

"Every *day*? Gentry, don't be RIDICULOUS."

Even I couldn't wear the same suit every day to work.

~

I refused to go to her father's store.

"Why not? We'll get a *discount*." I flat out refused. So we went somewhere else, where we argued over the cut. "You need a sport cut!"

The salesman agreed with her. "You really are too slim-hipped for a regular cut." Slim-hipped. Just the kind of phrase I like to hear about myself. Dear God. I took myself off to the dressing room to hide in abject humiliation. He followed. I told the salesman that if he brought me a sport cut, I would kill myself in the dressing room, slit my throat and bleed all over his suits.

I got a regular cut.

I hated suits and all of a sudden I had three. Three suits. Three stupid, sickening suits. But this was a penance.

And then there was a shoe "issue." I like footwear with steel toes and Vibram soles. Miriam thought steel toes and Vibram soles were unprofessional, except for loggers, which she called "lumberjacks."

I looked carefully at all the choices. Miriam was impatient, but I took my time. I picked up the only dress shoe in there that looked like one I could possibly stand to wear. It was heavy, like a boot, and it tied. I picked it up and dropped it, and it made a good, solid thump. "I like this one." The shoe cost a fortune, but I was used to paying a lot for my boots.

The salesperson lit up. But Miriam looked at it and scowled. "That's JUST LIKE YOU, Gentry, to pick out perforated wingtips!"

I could tell that we would have another scene with another disbelieving salesperson. "Fine, Miriam, choose something."

She chose a pair like that therapist would have worn. I tried them on.

"Gentry? What do you think?"

I sat and studied my feet in disbelief. I have large feet, but they looked so dainty and graceful in those shoes, I felt like I should just jump up from the chair and start dancing ballet. I also felt like I should cut my feet off rather than have to wear shoes like that. Miriam would have found something embarrassing to put on the stumps, though.

This was a penance, the shoes.

My dainty feet went with my slim hips. But more than the suits and the shoes, I think I hated the thin, shiny, dress socks that were necessary to the whole look. I'd be climbing around under a desk, trying to get something wired right, and the pants would hike up over the tops. I'd have to stop working on whatever and adjust the entirety of it. Another penance.

I did it, though. All of it. And I listened to Fanny.

"Jesus loves you, Gentry!"

Fanny was aptly named.

I got to know my brother-in-law in a new way. At Sunday dinners, he was generally grumbling about golf and stuffing his face. I found this within the range of normal. His office demeanor verged on the deranged. He was always furious, always yelling. I couldn't take it personally, because he yelled at everything, everyone. Who was this office tyrant?

The office was in Moore, of course. I had to drive to Moore every day to go to work. When I commuted from Oklahoma City to Norman, I drove faster just to get through Moore, but I had to STOP there, and spend my DAYS there. Every single day, under the benevolently insane gaze of a water tower that should have been obliterated.

This water tower was an insult to the eyes. It was round, and painted on the side there was an actual smiley face, an enormous "Have A Nice Day" smiley face. But this smiley face was special, because one quarter of it, the upper left quadrant, was covered with a blue background and white stars. Sort of a patriotic pirate smiley face. Painted around it were the words "Moore says, Smile, America!" I was surprised it didn't say, "Moore says, Smile, Jesus Loves You!"

That water tower idiotically beckoned me to work each morning, and it leered its one-eyed smile over my shoulder each evening, laughing, because it knew I had to return. It was exactly the kind of water tower that cried out for occupation by a deranged sniper. The Smiley Face Sniper, picking off I-35 freeway commuters for Jesus. "Smile, America!" POW!

This was Oklahoma, after all.

I once asked Fanny if she lived in Norman or Oklahoma City. She said, "Oh, I live right here in Moore. I have a cute little place over by the water tower. Jesus loves you, Gentry!"

Please don't get any ideas about that water tower, Fanny.

Most of my day was spent sitting in my little office, praying for something to do or a quick death. I wanted to die so that I didn't have to go out and face Fanny. I couldn't stand her prying into what I did or didn't eat, and I couldn't take her shouting at me about God's great love for me, not at that time in my life.

"Jesus loves you, Gentry!"

I worked hard at times, and at other times I just administrated. This is the difference between teaching and any other job, I think. Teachers are always busy.

When I had nothing else to do, I played solitaire. My boss-in-law would have fired me if he had known. The boss-in-law hated games. He had the last LAN guy take all of the games off the computers, but I put them back on. Hangman and Solitaire for everyone, and if I really liked the person, I might put on Tetris. And no one said a word.

"Jesus loves you, Gentry!"

Ah, a review.

I waited for Ben to find out, I hoped someone would tip him off, someone who wanted to score some points. He would barge in and holler at me. "I DON'T PAY YOU TO SIT HERE AND PLAY GAMES!" And then he would fire me. Except that never happened.

Once, my boss-in-law came in and yelled at me because his fax machine didn't work. I ran over there and demonstrated to him that the reason his fax machine didn't work was because the brainless but attractive assistant he hired had put the pages in wrong side up. And then he yelled at me for that. "I PAY YOU TO SHOW HER HOW TO DO IT RIGHT!"

I have never heard of a LAN administrator who was in charge of training administrative assistants how to run the fax machine. But as he often reminded me, he signed my paycheck. "DON'T YOU FORGET I SIGN YOUR PAYCHECK!" So I trained her.

Sometimes my boss-in-law yelled at me because there were too many cables. People would trip on something because certain parts of the office were too small, and everybody was jammed together, and they would trip on the network cables.

"DAMMIT! THERE ARE TOO MANY CABLES OUT HERE!"

And then he would haul me out there, and I'd look at the cables, and I'd have to agree with him, yes, there certainly were a lot of cables there. I don't know if this made him feel any better, my agreeing with him. But until someone could show me a way to wire things together without wire, to make connections without connectors, to plug things in without plugs, then I guessed we were kind of stuck with all those cables.

"I PAY YOU TO FIGURE THIS STUFF OUT!"

Sometimes a printer jammed. That was exciting. The printers gave me a fair amount of trouble. I shook toner cartridges on a regular basis, because my boss-in-law was so cheap. And of course, there was the relentless love of the Savior that hemorrhaged out of Fanny every time I turned around. "Jesus loves you, Gentry!"

If Jesus loved me, then why was I there?

For penance. I thought of it all as penance. Penance for a night on a couch by a fire, just a stumble, I'd thought, not the fall that followed, just a small sin barely remembered by the two people who committed it.

But there were three people, there, not two. And for that, I would pay.

~

Even after living in Oklahoma for two years, even after getting married and accepting that I was going to stay married because this was what I deserved, even after taking that stupid job, Miriam and I still had "issues."

The hair was always an "issue" for Miriam. She hated my hair, always, she had hated it. But now, with the new job, she had what she considered a good reason to remind me how much she hated my hair on a daily basis. She was convinced that I would progress at work if I'd only get a haircut. "Where would I progress to, Miriam? I'm the entire department."

"You act like that job is HELL."

"It can't be any closer than the seventh circle. Maybe a haircut would earn me admission to the sixth."

"That's just like you, that English major garbage. You need to cut off that HAIR."

That hair? Or did she mean, MY hair, the hair on my head? I didn't want to cut my hair. I wouldn't cut my hair. I told her this, I said it, I repeated it. "I won't cut my hair."

Miriam railed for a few weeks, and the sheer volume would have defeated me on any other occasion. My ears rang with a steady indictment of my hair and everything it was costing us in the way of professional advancement and marital contentment.

It didn't work. Not with the hair.

She decided to try a new tack. She would approach it like it was a pleasant, exciting topic. She made it sound like a vacation. "Gentry's Hypothetical Haircut." Exactly how should I get it cut?

I hadn't known that there were magazines devoted to hairstyles for men. Somehow, I'd lived my entire life without coming across one of these magazines. And, since I was married to a certain type of woman, she brought one of these magazines home, and she made me look at one. Page after page of well-groomed men with alarming, Eve Mumford teeth, no one had any moles or bags under their eyes, with shiny, lacquered, mathematically precise hair. Unbelievable.

The little woman I was married to looked at me and smiled and said something that chilled me to the soles of my feet. "Well, you just pick one you like, or I will."

"Hey Miriam? Stop it."

"Stop WHAT?"

"Leave me alone about my hair. No, I mean it. Don't talk about it anymore."

"You won't even TALK about it? You won't even DISCUSS it?"

"No. It's not up for discussion. Put that magazine in the recycling."

It was true that I hated myself. Even so, I thought I'd been doing enough penance. I would remain married to Miriam. I would live in that house. I would drive to and from that job in that car, wearing one of those suits and those stupid shoes and socks. It was all penance, and I performed it. But I wouldn't cut my hair. Never. I made it clear that I would never cut it.

She heard me. She understood.

∽

I was sitting in my office on a Friday afternoon, staring at the clock on my computer, willing time to hurry up so I could leave. I was sending Phyllis an email every minute. I'd write, "Six minutes." She would reply, "No, five." I sent the one-minute email, and then my phone rang. Please, God, not Miriam. "This is Gentry."

"My parents want us to visit this weekend."

Thanks a lot, God. "Fine." At least someone would feed me.

"Well, I'm just not sure. I'll be fertile."

Did that take all weekend? "Do we have to talk about this on the phone, Miriam?"

"Fuck you." That was the end of the conversation. Which was fine because it was five o'clock and I could leave.

I walked out of my office. Fanny gave me a sendoff. "Jesus loves you, Gentry!" I looked at her and thought of ten ways that involved the wiring to make it look like an accident.

I left the office and drove home. I always drove the Toyota. Since I had a "good" job, Miriam had offered me the "good" car so as to enhance my professional image. I told her that the opportunity to drive a Taurus wasn't the enticement she imagined it to be. "Fuck you. Drive the SHITTY OLD CAR for all I care." I did. It was a penance to drive that car.

As I drove home, I divested myself of my professional attire. Miriam parked her car in the other bay of the garage, next to the broken Jeep. I parked in the driveway. When I got to my house, I usually emerged from the Toyota barefoot, in a T-shirt and my suit pants. That day, I made it all the way down to the boxers and T-shirt. I walked up to the front door in my underwear.

My neighbors probably wondered where I worked.

I waited on the landing, listening. I heard her grumbling in the basement, so I went up to the bedroom and put on my jeans.

"ARE YOU HOME? DINNER'S READY!"

I sat down at the table, which had a brass frame and a glass top. I found it strange to sit there and see our legs while we ate. It was like they were on display behind a window.

"I hope you're HUNGRY. I made a TON."

"Hm." I helped myself to a polite amount of something meat-free. I said grace over it, but that never helped. I took a bite of whatever it was.

And then, the next thing I dreaded. "How was your DAY?" It was never a question. It was always a challenge.

I made myself swallow. "Don't ask."

She threw down her fork. "THAT'S JUST LIKE YOU, TO SAY THAT I CAN'T ASK YOU HOW YOUR DAY WAS!"

My ears rang. "Hey Miriam? Do you have to shout *all* the time?"

"I don't shout ALL THE TIME."

"Yes you do. You hurt my ears."

She looked upset, but she brought it down a few decibels. "What's the big DEAL? Is this because you're not TEACHING? So you don't TEACH, so WHAT. You CHOSE not to teach anymore, Gentry, that was a CHOICE you made. That was totally your OWN decision. You can't blame ME, I didn't even KNOW you when you made that choice. You're just LUCKY to get this kind of a job. Aren't you an ENGLISH MAJOR?"

I thought about telling her that I got my master's in Education when I was twenty-one, and I didn't work that hard so I could sit in an office and listen to a raving lunatic tell me about her personal relationship with Jesus Christ while I prayed for work to do. But I didn't. Because I was tired.

Miriam made me so tired.

I decided to try to eat. While I moved around some rubbery chunks on my plate, she told me about her day, a series of slights, challenges, and betrayals. I didn't have to participate much in this conversation, just shake my head, "hm," pretend to listen, pretend to care. The world was lining up against Miriam, and all she required of me was the knowledge that I was on her side.

Of course I was on her side. We were married.

She gave me an encouraging smile. "Okay, I told you about MY day. So let's try AGAIN. How was YOUR day?"

"I told you not to ask."

"THAT IS JUST LIKE YOU!"

I closed my eyes and allowed myself to be washed over with memories of a dark wood table full of the best food I'd ever eaten, three soft female voices talking around me, one a little sharp, one a little smoky, one like the chiming of small silver bells. And Bosco under the table, waiting for scraps to fall.

Dear God in Heaven. What had I done to my life? I thought about my life. I remembered a fairytale, a girl with a mountain of mixed seeds and one night to sort them. Millet, wheat, flax. But she had help.

God, I needed help and I'd turned it all away.

"Gentry? What is WRONG with you? You look like you're going to CRY."

I opened my eyes. "I'm fine. Just fine."

"You don't LOOK fine."

"Okay. I'm not fine."

"What's WRONG? Is it because I forgot your BIRTHDAY?"

"My birthday?"

"Yes, you MORON. You're supposed to REMIND me. You're THIRTY, now."

I closed my eyes and the room spun around and started to tilt. But I put my hands on the table, forced myself into the here and now. "This has nothing to do with that."

"Well then what IS it? Is this about that little GIRL?"

I stood up and carried my plate into the kitchen. I ran dishwater and started chipping a layer of hardened meat substitute out of a pan.

She stomped in and picked up the phone, started punching in a number like the phone had offended her and deserved the abuse. "MOM? I'm so PISSED." The subject was me. Won't talk. Just watches TV or stares at the computer. Never listens. Doesn't appreciate. Hardly eats. Never sleeps. No libido. At this point, Miriam felt like the Grand Prize Winner in the Look Who I Married Sweepstakes. And her mother was hearing all about it.

"Hey Miriam? I'm right here in the room."

She slammed down the phone and glared at me. I finished the dishes.

~

Down below to my study. It was maybe the worst room in the house, cramped, windowless, always cold, but my computer was there, and she wasn't.

Hey, computer. Wake up, computer.

I looked up to see her standing in the doorway, staring at me with her arms crossed, the number eleven etched deeply between her eyebrows. "What the hell do you DO down here all night?"

A direct question. I tried to answer those. "I play games."

"You BETTER not be doing that ONLINE SEX STUFF."

Did she know me at all? I was mocked in college for what Sandy called my "monumental prudery," my "saintly dedication to the real thing." I couldn't look at anything like that. "Miriam, we aren't even online at home. I canceled it to save money."

She went back upstairs. I put my head down in my arms. She was right, Miriam was right, I was upset because I wanted to write to Gretchen again, but what could I say?

Hey Gretchen. I'm sorry for every single thing.

I had to let her go, because who was I, some lonely neighbor, a failure as a teacher, the pervert in her mother's mouth, kissing her sister, oh God, God, how did this happen? God, how did you let me do this? God, did she have to see everything, was this part of a plan?

Sedation. I wanted sedation. I went out to the wet bar and drank a little poison. I was trying to be careful, I wasn't headed for oblivion, but I needed something.

The television was so old that it didn't have a remote control. I had to select my channel carefully because if I did everything right, I'd be hard pressed to get up and change it within an hour. I stopped at a game show, but flipped the knob when I found myself shouting "What is the LIBRARY OF ALEXANDRIA!" at the screen. No, not going to do it. Game shows got the competitive blood pumping to the point where I was writing down the address for how to become a contestant rather than falling asleep.

I turned to another channel, one devoted to reruns. Reruns were soporific. I was tracing the history of sitcoms through reruns. I found that I didn't like any neighbor on any show. Anyone who lived next door was bad news.

The couch, the right channel, a bottle and a glass. Perfect. Soon, I was drifting off into a state of mild impairment that verged right on bliss, because I didn't feel anything.

"I AM JUST WORRIED ABOUT THIS MARRIAGE!"

I sat up fast, my heart beating so hard I thought it might pound its way out of my ribcage and land on the carpet. She stood there glowing faint and grey in the light of the television. She was trying not to cry.

And then she was crying.

"Do you know you haven't had sex with me ONCE since we were married, Gentry? Not ONCE? I just want you to come up and SLEEP with me like a REAL husband."

I stared at her. She had on a nightgown I used to like, the buttons down the front, how it stopped high on her thighs. I remembered reaching underneath it. I remembered when I wanted her. I had wanted her, I knew that.

My voice was rough from drinking. "Come here."

She did.

I reached up and gently pulled her down.

~

I fell asleep several hours later on my back on that couch, Miriam lying on top of me, her head on my chest, her hard little arms around my neck, quietly complaining that I needed to go take a shower. I stroked her backside and ignored her words. "Hush." Finally she wound down and gave up. We'd exhausted ourselves and I'd had too much to drink, and I knew the two were related but the sleep that followed was welcome and profound.

I woke up facedown on the couch in a silent house.

Our house was never silent. The television was on or she was using the phone or listening to music or complaining about something, or she was running the ancient dishwasher and the din of that was echoing throughout the entire main floor. But the house was silent. And I was cold. Well, no surprise there, I was naked, but I felt an unfamiliar draft on the back of my head. Was that from the air conditioning?

I reached up and touched my neck.

I rolled over and sat up. I looked down at the couch cushion.

I touched the back of my neck again, because I didn't understand.

I stood up, looked around. There was something on the wet bar next to a pair of scissors. It looked like the tail of a horse. I ran upstairs to the bathroom and looked in the mirror.

I wanted to yell her name but couldn't make a sound.

I went back downstairs. My clothes were on the floor, so I put them on. I wanted to put my hair on. It sat there on the wet bar, looking more alive than I felt. I didn't know what to do with it, what was I supposed to do with it? What was I supposed to do? Could someone reattach it to my head? I paced for a minute. I picked up my hair and put it in my office closet.

I found the car keys and left the house.

~

"What the hell?" The old man who had an open chair put a white apron around my neck. "A woman did this to you, ain't that right." I nodded. "I'm gonna tell you something right now, young man. You should never let a woman cut your hair. Even if she says she can, a woman cannot cut a man's hair."

I found my voice. "I was asleep."

"She did this to you when you were asleep?" I nodded. He shook his head. "I don't know how you pissed her off, but you're lucky she didn't cut anything ELSE off, if you know what I mean. Okay. She got you good up here. I'm thinking I can give you an inch, inch and a half on top, but I have to go closer on the sides." I nodded. "Okay. That's what we'll do then. We'll get this fixed up."

He went to work. I kept my eyes closed. It didn't take him long.

"This is as good as I can do."

I opened my eyes and looked in the mirror. My high school face looked back. The face of a boy who had to have his hair cut every three weeks because it grew so fast. A boy who loved God and his uncle and his dog, in that order. A boy who played soccer for all he was worth, who finally learned how to stop fighting, who knew he wasn't smart enough to be first in his class but tried, who hoped someday to lose his virginity if he could ever puzzle out exactly how that all worked and if God decided that would be okay, please, Amen.

A boy's face. Not a man's. The face that went with my first name.

~

I walked in the house and there she was, smiling, but when she saw me her face fell.

"Oh my GOD. That's not FAIR. You look even YOUNGER."

I pushed past her and went downstairs to find my duffel bag. I couldn't find it. Okay, then, my backpack. I started to look around. Where was it? I opened a desk drawer. My CDs were gone. Where were my Bibles? Where *was* everything?

And even if I'd had anything left to pack, where would I go? To Mel? I'd told him I didn't owe him anything. Could I go to the Sandersons, who had warned me, pleaded with me not to do this? Where could I go?

Paige had always kept trying. She wrote letters I never answered. She named her third son Emerson Gentry. There were two boys with Gentry for a middle name, then, Walter Gentry Gilroy and Emerson Gentry Sanderson. But neither of them were mine, God.

This was mine, this was what I'd chosen.

And my Jeep was broken.

∽

And so, God, that is how I stayed with Miriam.

I went to work and came home. I stayed downstairs watching television and playing computer games. I also drank. I spent my nights on the couch. And she let me know how she felt about it, repeatedly and at top volume.

Occasionally, to avoid the noise of her standing at the top of the stairs, blistering me with a litany of what was wrong with me, I'd rise up from the couch and climb the stairs. I'd walk down the hall, go into the bedroom, take off my clothes. I would lie down with her. I rarely spoke, we never kissed, but if the equipment worked, and it didn't all that often in those days, but if it did, I tried to put a baby in her. I did. I admit it. I tried. Because this was it, this was what I had left. Miriam, and the hope of a child of my own, someday.

This was it.

God, if You had wanted me to leave, if that were the plan, this would never have happened. That's what I figured out. I prayed for a path out and I came home to those letters. I saw no path, then. You wanted me to stay and so I stayed. She was my wife. That was my life. I submitted, I submitted to Your will, to all of it.

I had what I'd asked for. I had my own.

VII. RECKONING

The next morning is a doozy, in Lorrie Gilroy lingo. I go up and start the coffee. I know the drill. Pain, and coffee, and eventually it goes away.

I get into the shower and use up all the hot water. I have to rinse myself with cold water. That's okay. Mike has a hangover and a fat lip and baggy eyes, and cold showers are good for those things. I know this, because I'm the hangover expert. I could man a hotline, a 1-800-HANGOVER number.

I go downstairs to dress. When I come out, I check on Mike. "Mike?"

He appears to be breathing. "Growph?" I think that's what he says, but I'm not sure what it might mean.

"There's coffee."

"Hrashit." I hope he recovers his powers of speech.

There are benefits to learning to live with hangovers, after all.

Mike comes up looking so miserable and so old that I have to laugh, no matter what the cost to my head. "Do you want breakfast?" He makes a noise that I take to be negative. We sit at the counter, there are no tables in this house, and consider the day ahead. He looks worse for the coffee, if that's possible. Coffee's supposed to help. He's looking into the bottom of his cup.

"Gentry? How far away is the Cowboy Hall of Fame?"

"Miles, Mike. Miles and miles." I'm lying, of course. I hate to lie. "I have no idea where it is but I can find out. Did you want to go there? I'd take you, but I have to go in for a few hours."

"What do you do there?"

"I'm the LAN administrator."

He clears his nose drain. "You do the wiring?" I laugh. He knows what I do. "What does the company do?"

"They sell stuff."

"What kind of stuff?"

"Crap."

"Crap? Like fertilizer?"

"No. The other kind of crap."

He crosses his arms. "Explain this whole crap idea."

"You know when you go to a company event and you get a visor with the company name on it and a T-shirt, and you pretend you're happy to get it and then you can't figure out what to do with it after you get it home?" He starts to laugh. "Or you get a paperweight with the company name on it for Christmas? Or when you go to the doctor, and every pen has the name of a prescription drug on the side of it?"

"And the clipboards."

"Yes, the clipboards. Anything you can put a logo on. We sell stuff to people going to trade shows, that kind of a thing. This company is actually pretty big as far as sales volume. But it's all stuff that no one really wants."

"Why don't you teach anymore? Marci always said you were the best teacher she'd ever had."

I can't meet his eyes. "We needed more money than I earned as a teacher."

"A lot of good it did."

Yes, he's right about that.

∽

The office hasn't changed.

"Good morning, Fanny."

"Jesus loves you, Gentry."

I enter my office. Message. Already. I hate this job.

But this is a welcome message. On Tuesday, at Mike's suggestion, I put up a card in the break room concerning what he refers to as That Car. Today, the message is from one of the catacomb crew. He wants to buy the Toyota for his daughter, and he offers a sum near what I posted. This man must want to punish his daughter for something, that's all I can think.

I tie a rope around my chest and lower myself into the catacombs, and after several torturous circuits of the fluorescent gloom, I find him. He shakes my hand and pays me cash. I never have any money. There's not that much here, but it's money, and it's mine. I go back to my office. I spread the money out and look at it for a while.

This is boring.

I don't have one blessed thing to do. Why do I do this? I hate this job. My phone rings. "This is Gentry."

"DID YOU GET A HAIRCUT YET?"

"I, um, have to go." I hang up.

According to Bernadette, who cuts my hair, my hair grows a little more than an inch a month. This hair has taken a year of what she calls a "grow out plan," a system of haircuts designed to get my long hair back. Sounds like a zeugma to me, but it's worked.

God, Please. Let me have my hair. Amen.

I get to work. I have a big decision, today, whether to do "across" or "down" first.

My phone rings. "This is Gentry."

"Phyllis here. Did you get 12 across?"

"Harried."

"Oh, I had 'hurried,' and it screwed me up. Good." She takes a moment to get things corrected. "Are you busy?"

"Just with the crossword."

"Well, listen. Get in here and read this. But remember, you never saw it."

I hang up and break into her computer over the network. This is a good one. Someone filed a sexual harassment complaint against Terence, and she's writing a memo from the pen of the Big Hogan, himself, to the downstairs team leader. A copy is going to the attorneys. Phyllis, channeling Ben, is demanding that things be handled with the "utmost circumspection." I take her cursor away from her and change that to "utmost circumcision."

I can hear her laughing. I type "hush."

She types "get out of this document or I will circumcise you."

I add another magazine to my lap. I'm not paranoid, but it's definitely a double layer day.

"You're going to miss me when I'm gone," I type.

"No, because I'll die. If you leave me here, I'll wither and die."

I highlight and delete it all, and let her get back to work. But I read the document, and there are three different women complaining about Terence's break room conversation. The worst remark is to one of the account managers, about what to put in her coffee.

That's just sick.

Before I took this job, I'd never worked in an office. Ever. I pumped gas for one summer. I worked combine crews for twelve. I rolled around a cart and delivered mail at the college for five years. I taught at two high schools. I ran the computer lab at one vocational technical school. I find an office to be a strange and twisted place to work.

It's confined, restrictive. Everyone listens to what everyone else says, watches what everyone does. We develop zoo animal behaviors, I think, in response to the general feeling of captivity. We pace, we chew our hands, we fight over food. Some of us stack magazines on our laps. Well, one of us. There's an enormous amount of pecking, of throat baring, of posturing and display. It's disturbing.

The most disturbing aspect of working in this particular office is not the location, not the water tower. It's not the one-woman Jesus Patrol. It's not the barrage of hollering I face every day. It's not even the stupid suits. No, the worst part of an office is the sick undercurrent of sexual innuendo that seeps and oozes through the break room.

When I was a teacher and the kids talked like that, it was my job to make it stop and I did. Now, listening to grownups do it, I wish it were my job to shut them down. The idea of some of these people in any kind of a carnal capacity. Worse than peanut butter.

Terence is the worst offender and deserves to be fired. He starts every Monday morning by announcing to one and all, "Well, I got laid this weekend." I could have lived my entire life without knowing that. The things he says. "I'm the world's greatest lover." He tells people about his endowment. "Big enough to scare you, baby." He hands women the receiver of the break room telephone and says, "Be careful, the end of that is wet."

That was how I noticed Phyllis. She was looking for a paper napkin one day at lunch, and she was grumbling about it. "If Hogan's too cheap to buy paper napkins, then where am I supposed to wipe my hands?"

Terence looked at her and said, "You can always wipe your hands on me."

She looked him up and down. He stood there, grinning, sort of presenting himself. Finally, in an icy voice, she said, "I suppose I could, Terence, but that leaves us with the question of where I'd wipe my hands after that." I knew right then and there that I liked that woman.

Oh, I liked her before that. Phyllis cared about everyone in the office. She remembered birthdays and brought treats and let us all play with the toys on her desk. She was even nice to Terence. One morning, Terence came in looking so tired that Phyllis commented. "Terence, you look like hell."

And he leaned toward her, and he said, "Between this heat and having to have sex for hours on end every night, I really don't get enough rest." He walked on.

Phyllis looked at me and muttered, "Great. Now I won't be able to masturbate for months."

I was right there with Phyllis on that.

Ben knew what was going on, I think. How could he not? We all had to take a "sensitivity training workshop." A highlight, that workshop. Just the kind of thing I personally enjoy. It was taught by a glib, enlightened man and an angry, accusatory woman. It was like being back at that well-groomed therapist's again. For some reason they zeroed in on me, as if the quiet ones were the worst offenders. I hardened up my face, so I don't think I was broadcasting guilt. I have no idea why they picked on me. Maybe they smelled my fear.

The man was sincere, reassuring. He got us to loosen up. He talked about the natural attraction between men and women, sparks, currents, pheromones. I envisioned this chain of electrified hormones connecting everyone in the office. I was thinking about wiring all the time in those days, so that must explain my amusement.

And then, when we were all relaxed, the woman took over. And she got right up in my face, so close that she showered spit on me and I have a problem with spit and teeth so I shuddered and she yelled at me about what I was doing to half of the human race with my patronizing, degrading, dehumanizing attitude toward women.

Me? Why me? Was I doing that? Why didn't they go shout at Terence? And then the man said, "I want you to understand something. It's normal to notice how attractive your coworkers are, perfectly normal."

And then the woman said, "Do you think Sela is attractive? DO YOU?" Sela was as cute as a basket of puppies. If I said no, I'd be lying, and I might hurt her feelings. If I said yes, the woman might stomp me to death. They were trying to provoke me into saying something inappropriate. I started to panic, then hardened up my face and said not one word.

Eventually they moved on to someone else.

There was a video, too. I'd felt like scum since the day I got home from Hawaii, and that video didn't help. It escalated flirting into harassment into some sadistic, horrible, Marquis De Sade thing that left me sick at the injustice. I wanted to make a confession after that video, and I wanted a shower. A hot one, with plenty of soap. Lye soap. Forgive me God, for I have sinned. I have been male.

I was afraid to look at anyone after that video. We all were.

Everyone walked around and tried to talk about safe things for a week or so, safe things like each other's shoes. Hey, according to the talk shows I watched all night, there were people in this world for whom shoes were a charged topic. I thought we should do away with conversation in the workplace altogether.

I suppose I'm as bad as everyone else, now. I have conversations. Not conversations like Terence, but I do talk, and joke a little. And then I return to my office and wait for someone to call and yell at me. I know how to survive.

My desire for a snack begins the daily war with my distaste for Fanny. I want some pie. I know there's pie out there somewhere. My phone rings. Who can this be? I'll never get the crossword done, never. I hate this job. "This is Gentry." And I won't get a haircut.

"Hi. Do you know who this is?"

That's her voice. Oh God. You do love me.

"Gentry? Are you there? Do you want to talk to me?"

A noise comes out of my mouth, an incoherent sound. Does she understand this sound? Please, talk. Find words to say, because I can't speak.

"Gentry, do you hate me?"

"Oh, no."

"Are you mad at me?"

"No. Not at all."

I hear her cry. This child never cried.

"I'm sorry. I'm so sorry. Are you okay, Gentry?"

"I'm all right. Everything's all right." Now, now that I hear your sweet voice.

"Is Dad really there with you?"

"Yes. He came down Monday night."

"That's so weird." She laughs. I know I'm alive, because she's laughed in my ear again, finally, after four years, her laugh like bells. "I don't know what I should talk about."

"Just talk, okay? About . . . anything."

"Okay. It's sunny here today. And, I painted my room yellow. Oh never mind." She sounds embarrassed. "I went to a science camp, this special one for girls, it was really hard to get in, Gentry, you wouldn't believe how hard it was, but I made it. But that's pretty boring, huh."

"No, no, that's not boring."

"It is. I don't know what else to talk about. I went to the movies last night. I still take riding lessons but not so much. I might be outgrowing it, like Mom said I would. Oh! I'm studying Latin! For botany and biology, Gentry, I've been wanting to tell you that so much, that I'm taking Latin."

"Latin? I could help you with Latin."

"I could use the help. Languages are not my forte." We both laugh. "I wish you would visit us."

"You do?"

"Yes. I want you to come out here and visit."

"I could maybe do that."

"Soon? Mom wants you to come out."

"How is your mother?"

"She's fine. Married and boring and fat."

"I got fat."

"No way! Marci always said you would." There is a pall. I don't ask after her sister. "Well, if that's why you don't want to come out here, because you're fat, don't worry about it."

"You'll still like me fat?"

"I told you, dummy, I'll always love you, even fat, so don't stay away because you're all porky and huge." And I laugh again and I want to cry, because of what she said, and of how she said it, she sounded like, yes, exactly like, absolutely.

She sounds just like her sister.

"I mean it," she says. "I want you to come out and visit. I still, you know, love you."

"I love you back."

"You swear?"

"Swear to God."

"Are you sure?"

"Till I die."

"I'm sorry, Gentry."

"Me too, Gretchen. I'm so sorry." My heart will crack. I'm unraveled, unmanned by this girl. But I don't cry, I won't make her hear that. My boss comes in. He stands there, angry, listening. "Will you write to me?"

"Yes. I'll write to you today."

"Will you mail it today?"

She laughs. "I could do that."

"Good. I, um, have to go. Bye." I'm happy, God. So happy. I sit here, and I may levitate with my happiness.

Ben Hogan is not happy. Ben Hogan is never happy.

"I DON'T PAY YOU TO SIT IN HERE AND MAKE PERSONAL CALLS! YOU LOOK LIKE YOU SHOULD WORK IN THAT HARLEY SHOP, NOT THIS OFFICE, AND I WANT A PROFESSIONAL OFFICE! GET IT TAKEN CARE OF, TODAY! LEAVE THE OFFICE AND DON'T COME BACK UNTIL YOU CUT YOUR HAIR!"

He leaves.

Gretchen loves me.

Oh Dear, Sweet God, this is to give You thanks. Amen.

I go out to find Phyllis. "Hey Phyllis? Are you busy?"

"Busy? No. I'm just waiting for Diane Arbus to get here for the photo shoot." She looks around at the staff. "I think we're ready."

I pat her shoulder, and she looks at my hand in surprise. I think this is the first time I've ever touched Phyllis. She puts her hand on mine, squeezes it. "What do you need, hon?"

"I just spoke with Gretchen on the phone."

She cocks her head and looks at my face. "Did you now?"

"Yes. It was great to hear her voice."

"That's marvelous, Gentry." And she smiles, a warm smile. Phyllis has no idea who Gretchen might be. I haven't spoken her name since the day I received that letter. But Phyllis is happy for me anyway.

I had to tell someone.

∽

At lunch, the Toyota buyer comes up from the catacombs and gives me a ride home. On the way, I ask him to stop at Schuck's. I get everything, belts, hoses, a fuel line, new oil, an oil filter, a battery. I want to tell the man, look around, get familiar, this will be your second home, but I don't. He could still change his mind.

He comes in the house through the garage door, through the ratty family room, into my study. He looks appalled. I want to tell him, Hey, see, you work in the catacombs. I live in them.

I sign over the title with my initials and last name. I did take care of the posthumous legalities, I have no dead wife on this title. I send him off. I hope his daughter doesn't look at that heap and burst into tears. I hope she inherited his bad taste in cars and that somehow she'll appreciate that car. I'm done with it.

Now. It's finally time.

Mike sits at the counter shuffling around the piles of mess. "Hey, Mike."

He doesn't look up. "Hi. Did she call you?"

"She called me."

"Do you believe me now?"

"Yes."

"You can call her anytime."

"I'll call her. Every day, if I can."

"That'd be fine."

"Um, thank you." He's scowling at one of his calculator tapes. "Hey Mike? Could you help me with the Jeep in a minute?"

He looks up. Smiles. "Sure."

I have to go find some clothes I can ruin. I have only sweats and suits downstairs, and though I'd happily ruin a suit, I only have two where the pants still fit. I go into the second bedroom. There is nothing in here, the closet is absolutely empty, which confounds me. The weird stuff she bought for me used to be in this closet. When and how did it move? Did I move it? Did she?

I'll be brave, I'll go into the bedroom. I hate going in here. I refuse to remember.

I open some drawers in the huge 1970's dresser that Miriam had when we got married, the waterbed dresser I always called it. I had three drawers out of the twelve, and I mostly emptied them years ago when I stuffed everything into the closet downstairs. But there might be something.

There is nothing. Not even a pair of shorts.

There's nothing in here that will fit me, she got rid of all my baggy, disintegrating clothes years ago and bought this stupid crap that I would never wear and she bought it so much smaller, I'd put on these jeans and the whole world would know which direction I dressed, but I'm FAT now, it won't FIT now, it all goes over my shoulder as I dig deeper, there has to be something left, does anyone understand, what kind of a person would buy this ugly stupid crap she bought for me . . .

"Gentry?" Mike looks around the room. I look around the room. "What the hell are you doing in here?"

What am I doing in here? I never come in here, this was her room.

Where I found her.

The hair on my arms is standing up, the hair on the back of my neck.

"Are you all right?" He looks at me, he's coming towards me.

"Stop." I hold up a hand.

"Okay." He steps back, looks at the piles of clothes, looks at me. I can only see the bed, but I let them repossess the bed. There is no bed. I stand there, stroking my hair back from my face, looking at the bed that is not there. Her eyes slightly open, her head tilted back on the pillow, and that strong, strange medicinal smell.

I am losing my mind.

"What is it?"

"She got rid of all my clothes."

I sound weak. Weak and helpless and lost.

A voice of reason. A voice of sense and calm and understanding. "I remember your clothes, Gentry. I don't actually blame your wife for getting rid of them."

"Women have always hated my clothes." I stand for a moment, remembering. "I showed up to work at this farm one summer. In some old shirt." He stares at me, looking interested. "We were baling hay, and you end up taking off your shirt and tying it around your nose and mouth, so you want a shirt that's, um, worn thin. But the woman of the house was upset with me. Really upset for some reason. She said, 'That shirt's a disgrace. I wouldn't black a stove with that.' I had to go home that night and ask my uncle what it meant."

"Blacking a stove?"

"Blacking a stove." I stand there for a moment, everything in my body straining to tell more. To describe what it's like to combine, the symmetry of the fields, the gigantic machine under your control, working out the math of the swathe and the field and the turning radius in your small, cooled box in the heat and sun and wind of the prairie. I want it all to spill out of me like grain from the chute of a silo, to make myself heard and known and understood to Mike Mumford. I want him to understand me.

"Are you okay?"

"No." I go into the closet and start pitching.

"Gentry? This doesn't help." He starts to retrieve things from the floor, to fold them.

"Yes it does. Get some trash bags."

"What if you lose the gut? Won't you want this stuff?"

I hold out a shirt that Miriam bought for me. "I think we're safe getting rid of this."

He makes the drain noise. "That would be nice for Vegas."

"Or blacking a stove."

And so, we work in a purging partnership. I do the pitching, and he does the packing. He is constantly amazed by what he finds, especially the Speedo Miriam bought for me for the honeymoon. "Did she think you played water polo?"

"I don't know what she thought."

"Well did you ever wear this?"

"Of course not."

"Gentry, how about you model it for me?"

"No. Put it in the bag."

"I'll pay you. Cash. I'll pay to see you in this. Especially with that gut you have."

"I hate you, Mike."

"I know." He puts it in the bag. "Here's a question for you, Gentry. Why did she take off the tags on whatever she bought for you?"

I think for a second. "So I couldn't take it back."

"You're catching on."

"Well, I wouldn't take it back. I wouldn't want the clerks to know it was purchased with me in mind."

"You'd probably hit the clerks for suggesting it in the first place."

His lip looks better. "I'm sorry."

"Forget it. I deserved it."

We work, and what were supposed to be my clothes are in black plastic trash bags, where they belong. Which leaves hers. I start to pitch her old clothes out of the closet, and he does the same for the dresser. Mike holds up a tiny pair of shorts. "It looks like she was as little as Kathy used to be."

"She was bigger than Kathryn."

"Kathy has grown."

I step out of the closet. "Hey Mike?"

"I'll shut up." He pulls out one of her old shirts. "What a color."

Does he have to comment on everything? "She liked every variation of orange."

He opens a drawer. "Okay. Well. You'd better take care of this stuff."

I step backward into the closet.

"Gentry, come on." He comes into the closet and looks around. I've emptied it of all but the shoes. We returned sixty-two pair of unworn shoes on Tuesday, most costing well over two hundred dollars. But there is still a huge collection of tiny shoes in here. "I'll do the shoes. You go take care of that stuff."

"I can't."

"I swear to you that you can."

I step out of the closet and walk across the room to look down into the open drawer. These things. This is the first layer, all these soft, soft things. "I can't do this."

"You were her husband. Do it."

I smell her in these things. She didn't always smell like insecticide, like anger.

"For fuck's sake." He thrusts a garbage bag at me. "Hold this open." I do, and he empties the drawers in, one by one, three drawers full of all those tiny, soft things. I hold my face over the bag, I breathe her in. Sweat and sadness.

Mike closes up the bag and carries it down to the trash. I continue to stuff bags with less charged garments from the dresser, workout clothes mostly. He doesn't speak when he comes back up. I'm thankful for that. He goes back to finish the closet. I hear a thump, and then another. Two very familiar thumps. No. It can't be. I used to throw my boots at the wall in Detroit, one at a time, in protest, and they made those same thumps.

I turn around. There they are.

"They were back here under a pile of empty shoe boxes. I wondered why you weren't wearing your boots." I sit down and put them on. I may never take them off again. I look at him and he looks at me. "So now I have to ask you. What did you wear when you cut your grass?"

"I did it barefoot."

"You're insane."

"You're right." I send a quiet glance over to the corner of the room where the imaginary bed was. It's gone, but it might come back.

He looks around. "Is that her jewelry box?"

"No, Mike, it's mine. Full of my baubles and trinkets."

He clears his nose drain. "Let's see what you gave your wife." He looks through, whistles, holding up the chains and links and hoops that used to hang at Miriam's ears and flash against her wrists. "This is good stuff."

"I didn't give her any of that."

"I suppose you won't sell any of it, will you." He holds up her wedding ring. "You gave her this, right?" I nod. "Nicest thing in here. That's a helluva stone."

"Put it back in the box."

"You could . . ."

"Put it back in the box."

He does. I take it into the kitchen. But I look in there, and I find them, the gold hoop, the tiger's eye. Thank You, God, that she didn't donate them or throw them away or whatever she did with all my clothes, books, Bibles, and music. Every single thing I owned besides the Jeep.

But my boots are on my feet.

I go down the hall, pulling photos from the wall. Those go with the jewelry box.

The bathroom, I realize, is choked with her belongings. Her shampoo and conditioner are still sitting in the shower. I have moved them to wash the ledge and put them back in place for a year. I shake my head and open a trash bag. Her makeup, the little electrical thing she used to yank the hair out of her face, the boxes under the sink, that insecticide stuff next to them.

To the curb.

~

For once it's me calling the Goodwill, not Miriam. When the truck arrives, I recognize the drivers and they recognize me. They smile. I smile back.

I give them all "my" clothes, all the rest of her clothes, that waterbed dresser, this bedding and those towels, I'll drip dry rather than rub myself with satin butterflies again. And into the living room, whatever image she chose to desecrate a wall, the shelves of useless stuff in here, these books, what is this? Romance? In hardback? And look at these self help books, *Changing the Unchangeable Man, Men Who Hate Women, Turbocharging Your Marriage, Plotting The Path to a Man's Heart*, my heart? Good God, I'm sorry, God, but look at this crap, look at it, her classical CDs that she never even listened to, all this knick-knacky garbage that I hate, plumes and baskets and statuettes or whatever, what is this stuff? What is it for?

I clear the shelves, and then I give them the shelves. They carry it all out, smiling. They're happy for me. I'm happy for myself.

I stand at the front door, fighting an urge to wave goodbye.

Mike stands behind me. "Are you better?"

"As a matter of fact, I am. But I still have nothing to wear to fix the Jeep. You know what? I'm just going to do it in my underwear."

Mike bursts out laughing. "You would. Let me loan you some jeans."

∽

He frowns. "Those are too big."

"I like them too big."

He's irritated that his jeans fit me. He was hoping they wouldn't, he was probably enjoying the idea of my being that fat. I'm not that fat. But he wears jeans that zip. There is a limit.

Mike helps me out there in the garage. I have to tell him exactly what to do. He's as good under the hood of a car as I am with money. While we're working, Mr. Proffer, the dandy realtor, drops by. "Well, hey there," he calls, poking his head into the open garage door.

"Hey."

"How's it running?"

"We're still making a few adjustments." Actually, I am. Mike's job is to rev the engine, but he's helping, he really is. I tell him to cut it. It's ready, Oh Dear God, my Jeep is ready, but we have to have some dandy chat before I can take it out on the road.

"Dandy. That's a dandy Wrangler."

"This is a CJ5."

Hank Proffer has an offer. I don't believe it. Someone wants to buy this house? Mike intercepts the paper, scans it. "This offer is ridiculous!"

"It's twice what I paid."

"Gentry, don't be a fool. You put twenty down and the house appreciated. There's closing costs and the realtor's fees and then you have to pay off her doctor, her parents and her shoes. If you take that offer, you won't have more than six grand left after you clear your debts."

Six thousand dollars? How far away can I get on six thousand dollars?

"I accept."

Mike frowns. "Pre-qualified, as-is, no repairs, no allowances and absolutely no contingencies?"

Hank nods. "It's a great offer, except for the price."

Mike shakes his head. "What the hell, sign it."

I do, and the happy, chipper realtor tootles off in the Mercedes he earned by cheerfully ripping off desperate folks like me. As he leaves, I hear him whistling.

"You're getting reamed, Gentry. You had one asset and one asset only."

"Mike, really, it's okay."

"Six grand. Damn it to hell."

"I don't care."

"I care, you little dip. You put down three times that amount."

"Mike, think about it. Do you think I would survive showing this house to anyone else?"

He stops. "No." And then, he looks down at his feet. "I wanted to do better than that by you, that's all."

"You've done fine by me. Really." And we go into the house, and we wash up. I show Mike the hand cleaner, I can't believe he's never used hand cleaner before. Possibly he's never had dirty hands. "Are you hungry? Do you want me to cook, or do you want to go out?" I hope he wants to go out.

"We can go out. But I need you in the kitchen for a minute." Mike takes me in the kitchen and shows me what else he has done by me, today, while I was at work.

Dear God. This is to give thanks.

Mike transferred enough money into my bank account to pay everything off. Every penny. Every last thing is filled out and ready to go. All I need to do is sign the checks with my odd initials and my last name.

I sign, and I sign, and I have to keep wiping my eyes.

He seals all the envelopes, puts those return stickers in the corners. He found them in the desk, they have Miriam's name and this address. He has stamps in his expensive briefcase. He gets it all done and stacked up and ready.

I also sign a note of credit about owing him, paying him back. He says we don't need it, but I insist. He refuses to charge me interest. I want him to, but he rips up the note when I try to put something in there about that. So he makes one that says I'll pay him when the house deal closes, and it's so much, so very much, I can't believe how much it is. I shake my head, I have no words for this. "Why? Why would you do this for me?"

He puts a hand on my arm, tight. "Because you asked. And because I can." I pull my arm away. "Damn it. Listen. You needed a little help. Just a little. This was as easy for me to fix as that Jeep was for you to fix. It was less than nothing. And

I owe you. I'll owe you for the rest of my life, no matter how much money I loan you."

"What do you owe me for?"

He looks at me, puzzled. "Don't you know?"

I do know. But I want him to tell me.

"Okay, let's line it out. Kathy quit drinking because of you. She'd be the first to say it. And I understand that you got rid of that kid who was following Marci around, that fisherman. No one will tell me how you did it, just that you did. And Gretchen. Kathy left me when she was six months old. I could never find a way in with her. I didn't know her, I didn't know my own daughter, and you showed me a way in."

I nod. There's truth here. I thought I only hurt them. But I think he's right.

But I'm not sure what I did to Marci.

"Gentry, let's take a ride."

~

We take a ride in my Jeep, my wonderful Jeep that has never let me down. The Jeep shudders, grinds, and we're off. The top is off and my hair blows all over the place, whipping into my eyes. It's messing up Mike's coiffure, as well. I wish I had a cap, but at least I have hair.

We hit the open road, rattling and vibrating until our teeth hurt, bracing our feet on the metal floorboards when we hit potholes, and I hit potholes. Hard. I drive over every railroad track between the house and the post office. Fast. I love this Jeep. We rear and buck and shake. Mike grabs his equipment, laughs out loud. "Slow down, Gentry! This hurts!"

"It hurts GOOD!" I howl into the wind, and he just laughs. We drive to the post office, and we mail off all the mess. I'm free, finally, of all of it. The mess is over. This is to give thanks. Amen.

"Hey Mike?"

"Hi, Gentry."

"So, what did you get? To replace the Saab?" He tells me about his vintage Jag, then. I listen, nod. The Jag sounds expensive, and it does sound nice. And he tells me about Eve's new Lexus, and the new Suburban he drives when the Jag is in the shop. The Jag is always in the shop. That must be the point.

A Saab and a Jag. What is he thinking? "You should get a Jeep, Mike."

"Why would I want a Jeep?"

"Because a Jeep will never let you down."

"No Jeep. I'm a family man."

"A Jag is a family car?"

"The Jag is what I want. The Suburban is what I drive." And he gets quiet. "I want those jeans back. Those are my favorite jeans."

"Your favorite jeans have a zipper?"

"What's the problem with jeans that zip?"

"I was in a hurry once with jeans that zipped. And I've hated and feared them ever since."

He thinks that was funny. That was not funny. That was painful. "Go to a mall, Gentry, any mall, and let's get you some jeans that button."

But first, I take him south to Moore, and show him the water tower.

He howls.

∽

I wanted to grab a pair and pay, but Mike was fairly certain I should try on. Men don't try on. I hate trying on.

He was right.

This is a low point, here, in the dressing room. Mike, waiting outside, hears me groaning. He says, "You aren't that fat, you just have kind of a gut now, that's all." Well, thanks, Mike, but you don't and you're twenty years older than me, so you can afford to be nice, I guess, can't you.

"Mike, what size are these jeans? The ones I wore in here?" He brings me a pair. They're a little big, and since Mike brought his inseam, they're the length I like. And they button. Mike comes in, checks on me. I feel like a kid, like I did years ago when Mel would come in and check on me.

When Mel and I shopped, I always got the same things, every year. Every single thing on the list, everything I hated. I felt like a tiny grown man in those clothes. Only the sizes changed, and not all that much during my high school years. I grew about an inch a year. But Mel made me try everything on, and he checked on me, partly to assure himself of room for all that hypothetical growth I never achieved, and partly to make sure I wasn't just sitting in that dressing room, humming, making faces in the mirror, killing time and pretending to try on.

And here's Mike, doing the same.

Mike looks at me, frowns. "They're too big." And then, I can't believe this, he rips off all the tags, all the tags and stickers and crap, right off of me, ripping and popping, shaking me around.

"What are you *doing*?"

"You can wear them out of here."

We go up to pay, and Mike gets a bag for his jeans, and I start to pay for my tags, feeling like a stupid idiot. "Wait, um, I want some socks, too." I buy a few pair of socks, all the same, the sock purchasing system that Gretchen taught me. The clerk waits, grimly working over a piece of chewing gum to mask her impatience. But I am distracted from completing my purchase by a display of terrible shorts. I hate shorts like these. This is the kind of underwear my wife kept buying for me, and it is all I have left.

"Where is the, um, regular underwear?"

"Why don't you get these?" Mike studies them with mild horror. "Here. I think the alien faces glow in the dark." I pick up a pair to see, and he recoils. "I was *kidding*. You're not going to *buy* those, are you?"

"Miriam would have. She always bought me shorts like these. I think she did it so I would be afraid to drop my pants in front of any other woman."

"And that worked? Like chastity boxers?"

"I guess so. Here, Mike, let me buy a pair for you. They might help your marriage." I smile at him and lay a pair on top of my purchases. "Besides, I can't wait to see you in these." I wink at the clerk. "This man. He's so patient with the whole thing."

Mike smiles, I pay, and we leave.

~

I wanted to get Vietnamese, but he's too hungry to wait, so we end up at the mall's food court. I let Mike pay for my food. Mike has a salad. I want to tell him, be a man, have something greasy, be like me, have two gyros. But he and I wear the same size jeans.

"I see you no longer chain up your wallet."

"This isn't Detroit. And you know how much money I generally have in there."

He laughs, he likes that. Poverty jokes.

There are kids here. There are always kids at the mall, of course. I watch them, and I think of all the kids I've taught, all the kids I never will. I can't eat.

"Are you going to eat that?"

"No. Go ahead."

While he eats my second gyro, I watch a kid who reminds me of someone. Square glasses, a big smile, and a certain shark-like determination as he tries to flirt with a girl from whom no hint of intelligence shines forth. She reminds me of someone, too.

God, this hurts. So much, God. Right through me. "Hey Mike? Did you ever meet Vu?"

"Who?"

"Vu."

"You mean Hoan-Vu. Sure. Good kid. He got a business degree at PSU. He just graduated, but I'm not sure where he works."

"You should hire him."

"I should? What can he do?"

"Absolutely anything."

"I'll look into it. I can get his information from Marci." He frowns. "You never asked about her."

"Hm." I try to look like I would like to hear this. "How, um, is she?"

"Absolutely insufferable. She's up in Seattle doing an internship this summer, finishing up at the University of Washington. Grad school. Journalism. Talk about a useless degree."

Useless degrees. I think of my own degrees, both useless to me, now.

"Hey Mike? You're sure she never started seeing that kid again?"

"Which kid?"

"Garret Blount."

"That fisherman kid? No. As far as I know, Marci didn't have anything to do with him after graduation."

Okay. That's something. That's one thing.

One thing I did that didn't hurt her.

~

Mike packs. I try to get him to let me wash his jeans. I got grease on them and I have a system for getting out grease. He says not to worry about it.

I don't want to watch him pack.

I give him the letters. All of them, hers and mine together, except for the last one she wrote, of course. I put that one away. I'll never read that again, but I'll keep it. "Tell her I want mine back after she's done with them. The ones she wrote to me."

"I'll make sure she sends them back."

Mike writes out the addresses, his and Kathryn's, because Gretchen does a week at each, now. "Tell her I'll write. I promise."

I realize that I haven't had a drink today. I have a small one because I need it, but I don't want to be drunk. Mike finishes packing, puts his bag and his briefcase by the door. We sit in our sweats and watch television. Mike keeps patting me.

I keep letting him.

I hate Mike Mumford. I always have. He is a pompous, egocentric, rich jerk. Mike Mumford is godless. He cheated on his wife and abandoned his kids and he took my Gretchen away from me. I hate him.

I have always hated Mike Mumford.

"The plane leaves early. We'd better turn in." I nod. "Gentry, do you think we could turn off the TV tonight?" I turn it off and lie down on the floor below him. I'm as bad as Sandy's dad, now, locked in the basement with the television. Just call me Papa Hondo.

I'm ashamed, ashamed of all of it. Mike has seen my life. He knows how I live. He's had to put up with all of it, my drinking, my nightmares, sleeping with the television on, prowling around here all night. He must be insane with fatigue after a week.

Please, God, I'll find You, I'll find my church and I'll get things right, but please, don't let him tell anyone how bad it is, how bad I am, how I am, what I've become.

Please, God, don't humiliate me that way, too.

"Gentry? Are you asleep?" His voice is thick, exhausted.

"No."

We lie there for a minute. "How did she die?"

Oh God, I can't. "Hey Mike? It's a long story."

"We have all night."

"I don't want to bother you. I should sleep in my office."

"You don't bother me. I don't want you to sleep in there. Just stay there. You smell nice."

"What?"

He's starting to mumble. "Forget it. Go on and tell me about how she died. We have all night." I hear his breathing change. He is asleep.

I have all night.

VIII. REMEMBERING

We sat at the dining room table. I had a cup of coffee, and she had some brochures. On the cover of each were happy couples, cradling in their arms tiny, perfect babies. Inside were descriptions of what could be done to attain those babies. "Procedures." I hadn't read any of the brochures, but I would have put money on it that not one of the procedures involved having sex.

"Hey Miriam? Couldn't we accept this as God's will?"

"That is JUST LIKE YOU. There you go, getting CATHOLIC on me." She stared at me. I sipped my coffee. "I'm running out of time. We need to stop with our denial, Gentry. We need to recognize that we have a fertility issue and educate ourselves as far as our options. We need to get the input of a specialist."

"Do you think this is such a good time to think about kids?"

"I thought you wanted kids. I thought you wanted a baby more than ANYTHING." I'd thought that. At one time I had thought that. But I wasn't doing a lot of thinking at that point. I was drinking in order not to think.

I no longer wanted to think about children.

She started. We needed to go to this specialist, and determine the cause, and lay the blame. But we had no money for it, and our medical benefits didn't cover it. No problem, no problem at all, time to rack up more debt. Why not? We were in so deep as it was. It took every penny to stay afloat. "My parents will HELP with this." She watched my reaction. "Don't, Gentry. I see your face, just don't GO there. Don't be embarrassed by taking money from them. They have LOTS."

"I don't want to take money from your parents."

She shook her head. "Look, have you EVER gotten anybody pregnant?"

I shook my head.

"And you've never used birth control?"

"No." Some of the girls I'd been with in college used it, I knew that. But not me.

"Well, it's probably YOU, then. Because I've BEEN pregnant three times. Not just when we got married. Before that."

"Please don't . . ." But she did. She told me about the two abortions she had in her twenties. "It's not that big of a DEAL, Gentry." She described an abortion to me in scraping, painful detail.

I'd learned the hard way that as a Catholic man, I was not allowed to have an opinion on abortion. I'd been shouted down, shamed and shared with too many times in college to risk any reaction at all to what she told me. But my teeth ached from clenching my jaw.

She didn't notice. "So, anyway, we know I'M okay. So we need to find out about YOU, and see what our OPTIONS are."

I stared at the brochures, wondering about these.

Options.

"Hey Miriam? Can you be quiet for a second? And let me think?"

Miraculously, she was silent.

I spread my hand over the fan of brochures. I might have been trying to blot them out. Or I might have been trying to absorb their contents without having to read them.

I knew nothing of scientific remedies to infertility. My ignorance on this subject was chosen. But I'd spent quite a bit of time in the company of priests when I was an adolescent, priests who discussed the general and specific concerns of parishioners, including the desire to end marriages.

This is what I knew about infertility.

I hadn't been married in a church, but it still counted. I'd be married unless this marriage was annulled. If we couldn't have kids, I'd have a good reason for an annulment. I could leave this behind. And if I were the defective party, which it seemed I had to be, then Miriam would probably let me go without hunting me down and killing me.

But first, we had to find out.

"Make the appointment."

"What? You'll go?

"Yes."

"Without any kind of a fight?" She almost looked disappointed. She'd been looking forward to wearing me down, and I'd taken that away from her. "Seriously? You'll go to fertility counseling with me?"

"Yes. But I won't take money from your parents. I won't go if they pay for it." I stood up to go downstairs and add poison to my coffee.

She stood too, and wrapped her arms around me, too hard, too tight. I looked down, stroked her dark hair. She whispered into my chest. "I'm so glad." She sounded grateful and relieved. I could feel her heart beating against my stomach.

She was my wife, and she wanted my child.

I had a hole inside me where my heart was supposed to be.

~

We had an intake interview. Unfortunately, the nurse was pretty.

"How long have we been trying to conceive?"

Excuse me? The nurse said "we." Had she been in the room while we were trying to make a baby, is that why she said "we"? Had I missed her there in the bed?

"We've been trying for over TWO years."

Two? It seemed like ten. I looked around the office, which was nicely fitted out with the costliest of materials. I decided I hated everything about that office.

"Do we have any sexual problems besides the lack of conception?"

Was this the royal "we"? I assumed this was the royal "we." Because if it were not, I didn't know how I was supposed to know about this nurse's sexual problems, whatever she might have been referring to with her "we." If she'd been there, in "our" bed, she must have been aware of "our" humiliating struggles. So why did she need to ask "us"?

Miriam looked at me, encouraging. I stared at my feet. I wasn't going to say it.

She did. "Impotence." Ouch, ouch, ouch. "It happens at least HALF the time when we try. Maybe MORE than half." Miriam was not good at math. Seven out of ten. Seventy percent. That was easy, easy math. But who was counting?

The nurse smiled at me so sweetly. "That's very common in couples who are struggling with infertility. It's the pressure." Miriam gave the nurse a hateful look. "Did we want to discuss E.D. with the doctor, then?"

I finally had something to say. "What's E.D. ?"

"Erectile dysfunction. There are new options, it's . . ."

"No."

It was silent in that expensive office. I looked out the windows and saw a parking lot, some dry grass, an old Buick station wagon with a reflective shield set across the dashboard to keep out the Oklahoma heat. All the views in this city were bad.

I thought about the kitchen window in Oregon, how I would sit in a normal, regular kitchen, just an old kitchen like any other kitchen, and then I'd look out that window at the water and my heart would pull and strain and sing with the beauty of the ocean. I wondered whose feet Bosco was sleeping on, under the table.

"Well." The nurse broke the silence. "Let's see. Do either of us have any children with anyone else?"

No, just a little girl with white-blonde hair who should have been mine. I hoped Bosco was at her feet. Keeping her safe. Keeping her a child. Oh God. I had to stop this, I had to stop hurting myself with it. I pressed my hands into my eyes.

"I never had any children, but I had a miscarriage last year. And I had two abortions in my twenties." She sounded proud.

I took my hands away from my face and the nurse was looking at me, waiting. I shook my head.

"Nothing?"

"No. I have never fathered a child." I heard Lorrie's voice saying, *that I know of, kid*, and it almost made me smile. I never expected to miss him so much. Those mornings at the jetty, he always brought the bait and the coffee and extra hooks and I never thanked him. The sun rising behind his head, the smell of the water. The stillness.

"We have quite an age difference, don't we?" I thought, well, I don't know how old you are, Nurse, but Miriam and I, yes, we have an age difference. Not twenty years, though. And if twenty years didn't matter to me, I don't think six would.

Twenty years. I would never have guessed it was twenty years. I should have known, her daughter was seventeen, I should have done the math. She was so cold and small and beautiful. Her face lit by that window, all her attention focused on the crossword.

Not on me.

"Mr. Gentry?"

"Hm?"

"Did you hear what I asked you?"

"Gentry, stop DAYDREAMING." Miriam looked enraged. "He is MUCH older than he looks." Our pretty nurse's eyebrows went way up, then. She double-checked her papers. I felt like a preserved specimen. Maybe the alcohol was acting like formaldehyde.

She frowned. "Well, Mrs. Hirsch, it says here . . ."

"Could we get ON with this?" Miriam was losing her patience.

The interview went on and Miriam did all the talking. And then a different nurse came to get Miriam, and I thought my part was over. It couldn't be that easy, could it?

"This way, please."

We stepped into a little room with a television and a couch. She handed me a cup with a lid. What? Were we supposed to have a drink, take a nap, watch Oprah, what? What were we doing in there?

"This is just for today. In the future you can do this at home and bring it in, but for this initial count, we need accuracy. So we need you to bring your sample out to us as quickly as possible."

"My sample?"

"Your sperm sample."

"Sperm? My sperm?"

"Yes."

"How am I supposed to . . ." I felt a dawning clarity. "I'm supposed to . . . ?"

"Yes." She spoke carefully and sweetly, as if to a backwards child. "We need you to masturbate. Into the cup. And bring it out to us so we can get a sperm count."

"Are you kidding?" My face caught fire.

"No. That's what we do here."

"Oh." Of course. How else would they know?

And she prepared to leave us in there, the two of us, me and my plastic cup. She looked over her shoulder on her way out, smiling kindly. "Time is of the essence."

I see. This little reminder was intended to keep me from lingering there in a post-masturbational afterglow, having a cigarette with myself.

She closed the door and I shot the lock. I sat down on the couch.

It was important not to panic.

Right in front of me, fanned out neatly on a table, right there for my masturbational enjoyment, was an array of the kind of magazine guaranteed to shut me down. I never looked at this kind of thing, one more thing to laugh at about me, but I've always been careful of what I put in my head. I wanted to open a window and throw them out, but there was no window. I tried turning them over, but even the backs were bad. I finally stacked them up. There was a throw pillow on the couch. I set that on top. Was the throw pillow just a homey touch, or was I supposed to use it to muffle my cries of masturbational ecstasy?

God, I couldn't do it.

There was something so awful about the thought of all the other men who had sat there before me on that couch, looking at someone's daughter, their pants around their ankles. It was more than I could stand.

Every surface held a box of Kleenex. How thoughtful. In case I had bad aim, or something. I'd never actually aimed into any sort of a receptacle. A masturbational challenge, here.

Oh Dear Lord, Help Me.

I decided not to even glance at the television, not to look in the direction of the VCR. I had a suspicion that there were cameras in there. I lay down on the couch. It was a short couch but it was comfortable, and as always, I was tired.

I wasn't sure how long I slept.

There was a tentative tap on the door. "Mr. Gentry, are we all right?"

"We're fine, just fine."

God, will You please tell me how to get out of this room? What can I do? Can I just go out there and say I can't? Will they believe me if I claim not to know how?

There was only one way to get out of that room. And I decided I'd do it. Because I knew that the doctors would look at my sperm and they'd all have a good laugh. Miriam would be right. I could leave, and have this marriage annulled for infertility. I'd get out of there and away from her, so I would do it.

Great, "we" weren't working.

I decided I was out of practice. For some time, I'd saved whatever flagging desire I experienced for those rare, valiant and unsuccessful attempts to impregnate my wife.

But I'd always been good at this. Because privacy was fleeting, I did the majority of the work in my head, and that made the other part easy. But those private reveries were old, dim, foggy, faded. Worn out from over-use, probably.

Nothing. Not even Jillian worked.

Time for the sure-fire ammunition. I ran through the greatest hits of Becca. If Becca had known how she filled my conjugal bed, she would have been as disgusted with me as I was with myself. But Becca always worked, always. She reigned supreme. Every time I thought of Becca, she was an absolute revelation to me.

Nothing? Nothing.

I threw in a stray thought of Paige. Sorry, Sandy, but I was desperate. Nothing was working. I sat, contemplating that which didn't work. Hey there. Wake up. We used to have some fun, you and me. You, me, my brain, my hand, the occasional woman.

I was broken, God.

Dear God, I would never get out of that room. I would never get out of that life.

Another tap at the door. "Mr. Gentry? Are you all right?"

"Yes."

"Do you want your wife to come in and help you?"

I thought for a moment. "No, but you could."

Silence.

Well, that killed any hope. God, nothing was working. Nothing would do it. Unless I did the one thing I'd sworn never to do. I sat there and decided how badly I wanted to leave. I decided that I wanted to leave that badly.

It came down to one or the other. The mother or the daughter. Decide. One or the other. Which one, I had to choose, to pick one and do it. Just get it over with.

It was easy to choose.

I thought of her, the taste of her mouth, the smell of her neck, her legs around me, I'd already ruined everything by kissing her, how easy it would have been to finish the job and ruin her, too, she was so ready, begging, I wanted to, she wanted to, she was on fire, into her, oh, to enter her, to hear her, to feel her, to have her, to be ruined, finally, I'm ruined, oh here I am . . .

Time was of the essence.

I had what I needed to get out of my marriage. All it cost me was the last speck of self-respect I had in this world. I screwed on the lid, stood up, fixed my clothes and came out of that room. The pretty nurse was waiting, and she smiled. I held out the cup. "Take it. I don't ever want to see it again."

And that was the last I saw of it.

~

Three days later, we sat down with an actual doctor to discuss our test results. I got an "A." My half of this equation was praised for its powerfully concentrated quality. I had excellent motility and above-average volume, not to mention a count so high it could skew the mean.

Something was wrong with Miriam.

Well, a few things. Like her hormones. That, they could probably "address." "We can address the issues with your hormones. But there are some other problems, Mrs. Hirsch. Some serious conditions indicated in the scans. Your white count is high and during the ultrasound, your Fallopian tubes read as badly scarred. That's why we did the CAT scan. Your tubes are impacted."

Miriam was pale. "You're saying my tubes are infected?"

He smiled a cold little smile. "Impacted, not infected. You're a nurse. You know the difference." He seemed to like saying this to her. He wasn't being nice to my wife, and for that, I hated this doctor. "I'd say it's very unlikely that you were pregnant last year, Mrs. Hirsch. You don't have any sign of current infection for chlamydia, but you've been treated for it?"

She nodded.

"What is, um, chlamydia?"

He looked at me. "Don't worry, I ordered tests for you. We're going to make sure you're not carrying anything. The nurse will take care of you after we're done talking."

"Take care of me?" My stomach sank.

He looked back at Miriam. "You don't have any adhesions, but your uterus is only about the size of a lime, the angle is bad and you have some growths going on in there, probably fibroids but it could be adenomyosis. I'll leave the uterus in for now. But I want those tubes out. And if you go ahead with in vitro, it's going to be very difficult to implant, with the shape and state of your uterus. We're going to do our best, but first we'd better get those tubes out."

"You're taking my TUBES?"

"Mrs. Hirsch. Your tubes look like balloon animals, and they're possibly necrotic."

I turned to look at her face, and I understood something.

I understood that I was not leaving anytime soon.

∽

I took time off to take care of her after the surgery. She slept and cried. I didn't know this quiet, defeated woman who lay on her back in the dark, staring up at the ceiling, tears tracking out of her eyes and down into her ears, her hair. She was a stranger.

I learned all about making soup. "Miriam, please eat something."

"Just fuck off and die." She spoke so quietly that I felt the hair rise on the back of my neck.

I called her mother and sister. They came over clucking and reassuring, and ushered me out of the room. They closed the door. I stood in the hall with my forehead against the wood, listening to her cry through the hollow door. They came out worried. Two tiny women, one of them almost a twin to my wife, the other a preview of her future.

We stood by the front door. I looked at their faces, their concerned eyes. All three of them had eyes of that unusual reddish brown that looked orange in the sunlight. Their eyes looked so much like amber that I'd always look to see what was trapped inside.

I'd wondered if our child would have eyes like these.

"My little Miriam, such an anxious one she is," her mother said, clutching at her gigantic handbag. "She imagines you'll leave now. Like a man would leave his wife at a time like this." She put a small hand on my arm and gave me a wan smile. "Especially a man like you."

Evelyn's eyes brimmed. "Gentry, you won't leave, will you?" A stray piece of hair fell forward over her left eye. I had the urge to stroke it back, the way I used to with Miriam when her hair was longer. I fought it only for a moment until I reached over and smoothed that dark curl back behind her ear. Miriam's ear.

She shivered and bit her lip. I took my hand away.

Mrs. Hirsch squeezed my arm. "I know how much you wanted kids, Gentry." There were tears in her eyes, too, and something piercing. Her own pain.

I opened the front door for them. They held on to each other as they walked down the front steps and over to the car, their feet moving in matched, small steps. Miriam's steps.

A mother, two daughters. So much alike. So different.

I waited to die of the pain.

~

The room was dark, the shades drawn, the television on. I sat down on the bed and looked at her profile. "Did they finally leave?" Her voice was quiet.

"Yes." I stroked back her brushy hair.

She pushed away my hand. "I hope you're happy."

"About what?"

She put a hand on her abdomen. "This."

I put my hand over hers. "Why would this make me happy?"

"Because it's all me. You didn't have anything. The office called. You're just fine.

You don't have anything." Well, that was a relief after all that swabbing and poking. "Your God is punishing me, and I just hope you're happy."

"God would never do that."

"That's just like you, to talk like that. I bet you'll never have sex with me again, if a baby can't come from it. That's how Catholic you are." Tears fell from the corners of her eyes and tracked into her ears, into her hair.

"Come here." I held her, she pushed away but I held on and I was stronger. She gave in and cried against my shoulder, and my heart hurt. All this stupidity, this uselessness, two years of trying to make something out of nothing. Oh, God, it wasn't love, but it was something.

"I was so close," she whispered. "So close to having it all back. I wanted it all back."

I put my lips in her hair. "All what?"

"Everything. Everything I lost. I wanted it all back and now I'll never have it. I used to have a good life, you know. I did. I was a nurse, I owned a house, everything. But my whole life went to hell, and I knew I could never live with my parents. I was going crazy living with my sister. So I ended up next door to the Sandersons in that shitty little dump of a house. And I thought they were so perfect. I just thought they had it all. I'd look at them and think 'I'll never have that.'"

I knew how she felt.

"They talked about you all the time, it was Gentry this, Gentry that, what Gentry wrote that day, all these stories you told about the kids you taught and that little girl and the teachers you worked with. Some idiot who swore all the time. I would go over there at night, and Paige would be chatting with you on the computer, she'd read it out loud and Sandy would tell her what to say back, and she'd read what you said and laugh.

"The way they talked about you. You were the finest man Sandy had ever known. You were the best teacher in the world. You were the most beautiful man Paige had ever seen. That was what she said to Sandy one night. 'Understand this, Wilton. Gentry is the most beautiful man that God ever made, and that's all there is to it.' He just laughed. He didn't even care that his wife loved you like that because he agreed with her.

"You sounded so totally perfect. And then you wanted to move. I brought that job posting home to Paige, I helped find you that job. And you were going to work with me.

"I thought about you all the time. I couldn't wait to meet you. I don't know what I expected, maybe that you'd be like Sandy, but not so mean. It's so stupid, isn't it? I just knew you'd be perfect.

"I saw you drive up in your ratty old Jeep and thought, that's him? That skinny, beat-up looking guy is Gentry? He's supposed to be beautiful. And I just wanted to laugh. What a fucking joke. I thought they'd done the whole thing as a joke on me, making fun of me, so I didn't even go over there.

"I saw you later that day when you ran out there and cut open your mouth. I thought, that poor loser. How you looked, hunched over, holding onto that Jeep, barf in your hair. I went out there to help, that was how pathetic you looked. Just pathetic.

"But when you looked up at me and I saw your face, I knew they were right and I knew I wanted your baby. Children look like their fathers usually, did you know that? I thought if I could have your baby, then you'd love me back. But you've never loved me back. I've been waiting for years for you to love me. And I know you can, because I've seen love in your face. I see it when you look at Paige or Sandy or those brats of theirs. I've seen it in your face when you talk to your uncle on the phone. I saw it when you used to talk about that little girl or that dog, even. So I know what love looks like in your face. I've never seen that when you look at me. Never."

My throat contracted in pain. She cried and I held on to her, because I had no idea what else to do.

~

We moved on in a quiet way.

I went to work and she stayed home. She said she couldn't face going back there. I almost panicked because the bills took two paychecks and we only had one, then. But she stayed home. Her voice resumed its normal volume. She called me at work to yell at me about repairmen and give me shopping lists and to worry about what else might be wrong with her. And she typed on my computer.

Miriam took over my computer. She asked me to move it upstairs. I forgot, which was my way of refusing. I came home and sat in the family room and listened to her tap away on the keys, and I think that the normal thing would have been to wonder what she was doing. Normal is something I have never been.

She typed day in, day out. She typed all night. I let her clutter up my monitor screen with her crappy little document icons because she refused to put everything in a folder. I had a new monitor, I had RAM to spare. We were married, I was supposed to share with her, right?

She ignored me. She pretended I was not in the house. I stayed at work for twelve hours at a stretch. I drank my poison. I slept, in my clothes, on the couch. A part of me wanted to move to the office but I didn't, because Ben Hogan found out I slept there some nights and told me that was unacceptable. "THIS IS A GODDAMN OFFICE, NOT A GODDAMN HOTEL!" So I went home and lay on the couch and listened to Miriam type all night.

I lay in the basement in Oklahoma City, and I was not there.

I remembered a day years before. A woman cried to me because she said she felt invisible. She turned her cold, beautiful face to me, and told me her worst fear and her worst secret. *When he looks past me, it's like I'm not there. Like I'm invisible. I've been erased, Gentry, I'm not here.*

I lifted her onto the counter, fixed my eyes on hers, put my hands on either side of her tragic face. She shook her head, lay her hand across my mouth to let me know I was not to kiss her. I buried my face in the dusty smoke of her hair.

I carried her upstairs to a bed that was too small where I made love to her over and over again. I wanted to show her that she was there. But I traded my own existence for hers. She ignored me after that. I wasn't so much erased as obliterated until Becca loved me back to life. Becca was my maker, my creator, loving me back into existence, but it didn't last.

That is the problem with earthly creators, God. We can only remake each other in the mortal image of earthly life, and our resurrections do not last.

Only You can make something eternal.

~

One day I went home and all her documents were gone from the desktop. She seemed to be finished, then, and I felt relief at the thought of having my machine back. I sat down to play a game. Miriam put her head in the door of my study. "How was your day, Gentry?"

I was busy shooting something so I didn't answer.

"Didn't you HEAR me? I just asked you how your DAY was."

"Hey Miriam? What do you want?"

"I made an appointment for us to see the fertility people again."

Onscreen, I quietly died. Offscreen, too.

"Why?"

"I want to DO something."

I turned my attention to my wife. "What is there to do?"

"That is JUST LIKE YOU, to say that. There's still PLENTY we can do."

"Like what?" I'd been to the library for a refresher. Conception happened in the Fallopian tubes, and hers were gone. What was there to do?

"Listen to me, you OWE me something, after all of this, what I've BEEN through."

Did I? What did I owe her? "I'll go, Miriam. And I'll listen. But I'm still Catholic, I want you to remember that."

"I'd just like to know how the HELL I could ever forget that."

So we went again, it had been, what, three months? I didn't have to go in the little room that time. I might have preferred that, however, to what I had to do. I sat, listened. I took in enough information to understand the basic idea, and then I got Catholic on her. Big Time Catholic. I even swore. "No way in Hell am I going to participate in anything like this."

The doctor was angry. "This is a miracle, what we're offering to you and your wife."

"This is not a miracle. This is an affront to God."

He shook his head. "People like you disgust me."

I stood up and walked out.

∽

I waited in the car until she joined me, furious and silent, but not silent for long. She wanted to argue with me about it. After the house, and the job, and car, and the clothes, and the hair she thought she could get me to change my mind. She didn't know how Catholic I could get.

She found out.

It was a siege. The lines were drawn. On her side, she had her stentorian voice and a determination that had never failed to fuel victory. Miriam delivered a detailed catalog of my shortcomings and my failures. She demanded that I make a technological restitution for what a disappointment of a husband I'd been. The theme of the harangue was clear. Where man fails, let science succeed.

I wanted to say, "man" didn't fail. I didn't fail, it is not my fault. For once, something is not my fault. But I couldn't say that. It was too ugly to say out loud.

I thought I was a strong man, because I kept waking up in the morning long after I had any reason to want to. Somehow, I held on. I wondered how strong I was, after all. I wondered if I would break.

I went to work, and sometimes I'd sleep there because I couldn't bear to listen to her voice. If I did drive home, I stopped undressing in the car because if I got pulled over for drunk driving, I thought my chances of simulating sobriety were better if clothed. When I was home, I stayed out of her way. I refused to speak at all. I made her invisible. I went away. I prayed.

I drank.

∽

I came home from work and stood on the landing, deciding which way to go. There was a disagreeable odor in the air that I took to be dinner.

"Don't CHANGE, it will get COLD! It's your favorite." Favorite what? I walked upstairs and saw that the table was set. I would make an effort to eat, because Miriam had made an effort to cook. But first I had to wash my hands.

I sat. I took a bite.

"How was your day?"

I gestured toward my full mouth, shrugged. Silence, except for the sound of my chewing. I'd sipped a fair amount of poison in the car on the way home, so my taste buds were mercifully numbed. Finally I was able to swallow. "Fine."

"FINE?"

"Yes. Just fine." I mentally prepared myself to take another bite. I chewed away at the assortment of chunks and strings, unsure whether it was my tongue or a lump of meat substitute that I chewed.

She threw down her fork. "I can't eat, looking at you."

I set down mine. "Pardon?"

"I said I just can't EAT, when I have to LOOK at you."

"Am I chewing with my mouth open?"

"No, Gentry. Your fucking table manners are JUST FINE."

"Then what's the problem?"

She picked up her plate and jammed it against my chest. It stuck for a moment, then loosened and slid downward towards my lap. I pulled the plate away, leaving a gluey mass.

I put the plate back on the table and surveyed my suit.

"Will the cleaners be able to get this out?"

"Would you just LISTEN to yourself? The CLEANERS?"

I looked at her plate of dreck sitting on the table and imagined grabbing her by the back of the head and slamming her face into it.

Breathe, Gentry, breathe and count.

It was my intention to count to ten, but she burst in at five. "I NEED YOU, Gentry, I NEED you, and this is JUST LIKE YOU, to RETREAT like this, to FREEZE up."

I was no longer angry. I was tired. So tired. "Miriam, we have to stop."

"STOP WHAT?"

"This. All of it."

Panic rose in her face. "It's YOU. You just make me so angry, the way you are. You do it, you just make me angry. It's just something about how you are."

How I am.

I stood up, shook the dreck onto the tablecloth and removed my jacket, tie and shirt. And then my pants. I threw them all in the kitchen sink and put my shoes in the garbage can and started for the stairs, but she was in the way.

She put her arms around me, crying. I looked down at her head. She was so small. Why was I always surprised at how small she was? Miriam was tiny. Looking at her hair made my heart hurt. I put my face down to those soft, dark, damp curls.

She smelled like angry sweat.

"We have to stop. We're both going crazy." I spoke it into her hair.

"It's *you*. *You* make *me* crazy."

"Then I'll leave."

She shook her head. "You don't have to leave, Gentry. Because I've figured it out. I've called some agencies." She looked up at me, eyes shining. "Adoption agencies."

I moved her back a little, used my hand to tip up her chin as carefully as if it were made of eggshell. I stroked back her hair and looked in her eyes. I spoke clearly, slowly.

"Hey Miriam? I won't adopt a baby with you."

"I JUST CAN'T BELIEVE YOU WOULD DENY ME CHILDREN!"

I went downstairs and got a drink.

~

Miriam talked to me about adoption as if I hadn't already refused to participate. Sort of like she approached my haircut, which could have worried me. But I let her do whatever she wanted. I had a hunch I wouldn't wake up one morning and find a baby on the wet bar.

She wanted me to reconnect to the Net so she could research it all online, but I told her to go to the library because it was free. She did. She signed up for support groups and read adoption web pages. She retained an attorney. Her parents paid the fee and paid for a home study. A stranger came and looked through everything, made sure we had safety covers in all the outlet plugs, things like that. Miriam made lists of what I needed to do to the house. I did it.

I had no worries at all.

She filled out applications. I hate filling out forms, but Miriam loved it. She filled out form after form after form, in paper and online, throwing out personal information as far and wide as she could, as if it were a net that would magically draw in a baby. She attached photographs so that it would be clear that despite my name, we were not two women hoping to adopt. We looked terrible in the photos, but we looked pretty good on paper.

Still, I was not worried.

Dinners were spent eating food that tasted like cardboard and listening to her talk about the progress she'd made. Dinners were never my favorite part of any day.

Occasionally I had to answer questions about my past. I gave her basic information about where I'd worked, what I'd done in my life. Miriam ferreted out some additional information on my teaching career. "I never KNEW all this," she said, "You won all these AWARDS."

She asked a lot of questions about my high school. Had I really gone to an all-boys' school? Yes. Who paid for it? The Church. Was prep school as hard as they say? Yes. And did the boys get into each other's beds?

I shrugged. "I don't know what other boys did."

She squinted at me. "Were the teachers priests?"

"They were usually brothers."

"They were all *related*?"

"No, Miriam, monks."

She stared at me, silent.

Another night at dinner, she popped out with this. "You didn't date black women when you lived in Detroit, did you?"

Did three awkward attempts count as dating? I decided they didn't. "I didn't date anyone in Detroit."

"No one? That's weird." She looked uncomfortable. "You had girlfriends in Oregon, right?"

"Not really."

She kept staring at me.

∽

Another night, another plate full of something unidentifiable. Sometimes it was chewy but that night it was mushy. That was worse.

"Gentry?" Her voice was uncharacteristically soft. "Why won't you talk about your adoption?"

I frowned at her. "What adoption?"

"Paige told me you were adopted."

"Ah." I couldn't blame the Sandersons for their misinformation. I called Mel my uncle. People assumed he adopted me after some kind of unspecified upheaval in my life. Fictions sprang up around me. Most people were more than happy to provide their own details, but occasionally someone pressed to know the real story. I met those relentless Southern inquiries with polite smiles. "I'm not sure." "I don't remember." "I don't talk about that." My male classmates usually left me alone, but girls could be persistent. I found creative ways to make them be quiet, none of which I was currently interested in practicing on Miriam.

As my wife, she was probably entitled to more information.

Adoption. The word made me remember a long talk at the rectory table with the social worker in which Mel swore that if a serious challenge to his legal custody ever came up, if the Diocese lost patience with this unheard-of arrangement or some other amorphous, terrifying event that I wouldn't let myself think about occurred, that he would leave the priesthood and fight to adopt me legally. The social worker gently explained that he was too old.

I was sitting in the short hallway around the corner from the dining room on the floor and I heard those words, "too old." My stomach and fists tightened. I fought the urge to hurl myself at the stupid social worker. Mel was not too old, Mel was like God, he was going to last forever. I willed the fists go away and clasped my hands and bowed my head and sent up prayers, just let me stay with him forever, just let him be my uncle, that's all I want or need, God, just Mel.

I didn't attack the social worker. The Diocese labored along in disapproving participation. Mel lasted forever. And as long as I went away to school, as long as I kept myself from being expelled, as long as I stayed out of the way on breaks, as long as he took me away for weeks at a time on camping trips over the summer, he was allowed to oversee what was left of my ruined childhood. I wanted to stay with him more than I'd ever wanted anything I let myself remember.

But the secret was, I didn't want him to adopt me.

I sat at the table across from Miriam, my head hanging over a plate of inedible realigned soy, and thought about Christmases, summers. Our time, all we ever had.

I'd shut Mel out of my life completely.

"Well? What *happened* to you? Why won't you talk about being *adopted*?" She stared a little longer. Those eyes of amber held unforgivable speculation. "I think it's *gross* that they let a priest adopt a little boy. Even if he *was* your uncle, I think that's *wrong*. THINK about it, Gentry. Those NIGHTMARES you have."

I raised my head and stared at her.

It was quiet in our house. It was never quiet in our house.

I picked up my plate and went into the kitchen.

~

They had to interview us, of course. I came home from work fortified, but definitely still able to walk. Miriam met me at the door, hissed something at me and made me suck on an Altoid, which was a more intense flavor sensation than I could take when sober, but I handled it fine drunk.

She pasted on a smile. "Here he is! Finally!" A glib man and a suspicious woman waited in the living room. Names were exchanged, hands shaken, more Altoids passed my way. I was stuck in a glib man/suspicious woman continuum, trapped in it until I could somehow make it come out right.

I said very little past my initial "Hey." Everyone was so startled by the living room drapes that we moved to the dining room table, where we sat down. I sucked my mints and looked through the glass at everyone's shoes while Miriam described her perfect childhood. These people represented a private agency, and they wanted an assurance that if the hypothetical child they offered us was Jewish, he or she would be raised in the Jewish faith. "It's very rare that we get Jewish babies, and the parents really do care about this."

Miriam shot me a glare. "Of course." I nodded.

"But if we get a Christian baby, well, that's what we'll expect. That the baby will be raised in a Christian faith." The man smiled encouragingly. The woman took notes.

I nodded. Miriam fumed.

"Mr. Gentry? We started the background check and found that your childhood records are sealed. That happens with wards of the state. We tried to talk to your guardian? But he's . . . in a monastery? And we understand that you've spent a lot of time there yourself?"

Miriam's jaw dropped.

He leaned over the glass, almost reaching towards me across the table. I put my hands in my lap. "So, well, we were hoping you could help us fill in some of the blanks?"

"About the monastery?"

"No. About your childhood. What was it like?"

I thought for a moment. "I don't remember."

The woman cleared her throat. He looked over at her, blinking, drumming his fingers on the table. Maybe they had a nonverbal method of communication worked out, something based on blinks and finger taps. She picked up the thread. "Well, what you do remember, Mr. Gentry. You could talk to us about what you do remember."

"I don't remember any of it."

They exchanged a meaningful look, a couple of taps and tics. The man spoke again. "I see." His face looked somewhat dire. "Well, aside from all your speeding tickets, the rest of your background check looks good. Great, in fact. Your TFA background, your nonprofit work. You didn't write it down, but someone we contacted wrote us a letter about what you did at the monastery, what you did for them with the, ah, Internet, uh, and all. And your teaching awards. If you were still teaching, I'm fairly sure we could guarantee you a placement. Birth parents love teachers."

Miriam was frowning. "Well, I happen to be a TEACHER."

"Yes, we know. But Gentry taught high school. And the mothers who place their babies with us, they do it because they hope that life could be different. For the baby. And often that hope, that idea comes from an important high school teacher." He smiled.

I missed teaching at that moment. Missed it more than Mel, more than Bosco. More, even, than Gretchen. Why had I given it up?

The man looked over at his partner and tapped his fingers. The woman turned a predatory smile my way. "So on *paper*, you look fine, Mr. Gentry, except for this situation in Detroit. That's a little . . . questionable?"

Every reason I'd stopped teaching settled on me like a wet sheet.

I looked at my shoes under that glass tabletop. I hated those shoes. Hadn't I put them in the garbage recently? Why were they on my feet?

"Mr. Gentry? Detroit?"

"I have nothing to say."

"Nothing?" She looked over at him, blinked.

"Could you talk about it at all? Give us some background, some context for what happened?" He had that supportive, encouraging tone in his voice I associated with guidance counselors and therapists.

I remembered trying to do that for Rob Renton when he called me to interview me on the phone. Throwing up afterwards. "No."

"Why not?"

"Because it makes me sick." I scratched my head. "I really can't talk about this. I need a drink."

There was a long moment. The woman gave me a closed-mouth smile. "I think we're done." The man looked a little deflated, but not seriously. More like he'd lost a wager and would have to buy lunch.

Miriam showed them out.

I stood up, took off my jacket.

"HOW COULD YOU SAY SUCH A STUPID THING, GENTRY! WHY DON'T YOU JUST TAKE OUT AN AD THAT SAYS YOU HAVE A DRINKING PROBLEM!"

I started towards the stairs.

"WHAT IS THIS ABOUT A MONASTERY! I NEVER HEARD YOU TALK ABOUT A MONASTERY!"

She stood right in front of me, blocking the stairs.

"WHAT DO THEY MEAN YOUR RECORDS ARE SEALED! AND WHAT THE FUCK WERE THEY TALKING ABOUT A WARD OF THE STATE! I THOUGHT YOU WERE ADOPTED!"

She pushed a hand into my chest.

"AND WHAT THE FUCK DID THEY MEAN ABOUT DETROIT!"

I felt it boil up in me. No more.

I went around her and she followed, screaming, I was still half-drunk, not steady, and she pulled at me, I pulled away, and somewhere in the pulling it turned into pushing and I fell down those stairs, thumping down on my back, my feet flying over my head, finally landing on my tailbone and I thought, this is insane. She's insane but I'm getting there, I'm getting there.

"THERE ARE OTHER AGENCIES! LAWYERS! WE CAN ADVERTISE!"

She called this down to me there on the landing where I sat, pretending to have tripped.

How could I have ever thought we could be parents? What had I deluded myself into thinking, God, what was I pretending? Had it always been like this, was this the way it had always been? I couldn't remember anymore.

I had to get out of there.

~

Miriam took her revenge by shopping.

Before when she bought things, I could sort of follow the logic. Normal people would do it this way, she would tell me. Normal people buy houses, and then normal people fill those houses up with things. Normal people buy clothes for work, normal people spend money. I'd always taken her word for it, because I'd never been in the normal neighborhood, myself. But this didn't seem normal.

I didn't see the bills. I thought her parents were giving us money. I worried. But in my own mind, there was a tally running. How much I needed to fix the Jeep and buy the gas. It wasn't that much. I could have cashed one paycheck instead of putting it in the bank and I would have had more than enough to get on the road to North Dakota or Colorado. They would take me in, they had always taken me in. I had stumbled to the Sandersons back in college when I couldn't find my way back to my dorm. And Mel had always been my home in every way.

But I had to stop drinking.

I had two ways of drinking. In college, we'd all go out and I'd drink the most and have the most fun and get in the most trouble. I'd wake up the next day feeling like I had an ax sunk into my head. I'd be in bed with a pretty stranger if I were lucky, or on a couch or a floor with a black eye and no memory at all of how I got it if I were not. And I'd think, hey, idiot, better not do that for a while. And I wouldn't. Maybe a week, maybe a month, maybe two years. The other way I drank was the oblivion system. I used it to shut myself down for a week or two. A way to live through things. And then I'd be done, sick afterwards, but done.

Oblivion was not an option and fun was not the point. I had to work. I drank to maintain a mild state of impairment, of not-feeling, of not-remembering. Of not-knowing what Gretchen had seen. And I didn't seem to be able to stop myself.

Next week, I would tell myself. I was paid every other Friday. I'd poison myself through the week, cash a check, sober up over the weekend while working on the Jeep, and then take off Monday morning, heading wherever I decided to go instead of to the office. Friday night was always going to be the last of it.

I would drink too much that night, saying good-bye to my poison. And then I'd wake up feeling so sick on Saturday morning that drinking a little more was the only way to feel better. Except it only ever made me feel worse.

Weeks passed like this, weeks of intention and failure. Weeks of drinking to block out self-loathing over drinking, and then drinking to block out the self-loathing. I'd always been able to quit before. I'd just stopped. I got sick, yes, but that was over with pretty quickly. Why couldn't I stop? What if I couldn't stop? Ever?

And then one afternoon I came home from my awful job, in my stupid suit, I came home to the one room in which there was something I liked, and that was my computer.

My computer was not on my desk.

She had put some stack thing there, on the desk in my study, with some crappy inkjet color printer. Where was my computer, where were my printers, my scanner? Where was my new monitor, the one Mel sent to me, the monitor he paid more for than the whole ridiculous operation there on the desk? Coming home to that computer was like leaving home from Mike Mumford's house and coming home to mine.

She came into the study. "Do you LIKE it?"

"Hey Miriam? Where's my computer?"

"I could never get it to WORK right, so I just got something NEW."

"You got something stupid. Where's my computer?"

"I thought you'd be HAPPY to have something new."

"Where's my computer?"

She frowned. "Who CARES where that old computer is? Wasn't that the first computer you ever HAD?"

"No, it was the first one I ever built." I built and re-built my computer, I fashioned it, I had programs on it I'd written myself, I'd configured it, made it all the way I wanted it to be, just exactly how I wanted it. Yes, it looked old, but everything inside was the best there was.

I had to remain calm.

"If you want this one, that's fine. I can set it up for you upstairs. But I want mine. Where is it? Is it in the garage?"

"I donated it to the Goodwill."

"You *what*?"

"I DONATED it to the GOODWILL. They just came by and picked it UP."

"Get it back."

She started to yell. "You know, this is JUST LIKE YOU. NOTHING I do is EVER good enough. I TRY and TRY to make you happy, and NOTHING I do is ever GOOD enough."

"Get it back right now."

"NO!"

I hit her. Hard. Across the face. It felt good. So I hit her again.

It felt just as good.

She curled on the floor, guarding her face. I pulled her up by an arm and twisted it behind her back. I don't know what was coming out of my mouth as I pushed her upstairs, and I don't want to know. I took her into the kitchen and shoved her at the phone. She called them, sobbing and wincing as I twisted her arm to hurry her up.

She hung up. "They're bringing it back. They're bringing it BACK."

I let go of her. She could hardly walk because she was crying so hard. She went into her room and slammed the door.

I looked down at my hands.

∽

I waited in the driveway. The Goodwill men pulled up in their truck, they were laughing, they had seen it all before, they smiled and laughed at those crazy women, those crazy things they do, what does a man have to do to keep his stuff, I ask you, while we carried my equipment into the garage and loaded it into the back of my Jeep. My teeth were chattering. They got in their truck and drove away, waving.

I thought maybe I was going to throw up.

My duffel was gone, my backpack was gone. I went into the garage and found a box, took it in the study and threw whatever was left into it. I put the box in the Jeep, pitched my tools in there beside it. It took no time at all.

I decided I could do the rest of it in a garbage bag. I went upstairs, got a few things out of the second closet. When I opened the bathroom door, she stood there looking in the mirror. She flinched and put an ice bag over her mouth. I backed out and shut the door. I thought, I'm going to throw up now.

I was careful on the stairs.

I was in the Toyota getting ready to go to the auto parts store when the police car came down the block, lights on but no siren. It gently rolled to a stop across the end of my driveway. They got out with their hands resting on their guns.

I left my hands on the steering wheel and waited.

A small cop and a large cop walked over slowly, eyes down. They appeared to be inspecting cracks in my driveway and the state of my lawn care. They looked anywhere but at me. One finally spoke.

"We need y'all to get out slowly and stand right over here against the fender with your legs spread and your hands on the hood of the car."

I did as I was told.

The big one gently pushed me flat to the intense metal heat of the hood. He patted me, removed my wallet from my pocket, handcuffed me and pulled me up. "Watch your head." He tenderly guided me into the back of the car, where I saw that between the lack of door handles and the metal grid, I was in a cage.

The small one went through the Toyota, found the bottle in the glove box. He threw it in the trash. That was expensive poison.

They went up to the front door, rang the bell and waited, studying the porch railing and the welcome mat. The door opened, and they walked inside, eyes on the threshold.

It was unbearably hot in that car. I still had on my suit, my tie even. The plastic seat was hard. Static-filled jargon came over the radio in little bursts, and I jumped a little each time it broke the silence. My wrists ached. I finally wriggled my backside and legs over the cuffs so my hands were in my lap, and undid the tie and shirt. That was better, but it was still so hot. The air I took into my nose felt solid. I had to breathe with my mouth open, gulping it in.

The living room drapes opened like a play was going to begin. Miriam stood by the window and opened her hurt mouth wide. So wide that the cops, the house, the world, all the rest of it was all falling into that angry, yelling, bloody mouth of hers. She turned to the window and glared out at me with a look that could raise blisters.

A great wave of lassitude filled the car. Color went flat. I looked around at a world of bleached yellow, the color of Oregon sand.

Oh. I was going to Oregon. I let my head fall back.

My eyes sank shut as I washed out on that wave.

~

Someone slapped me across the face. "Pull him over here." Another slap. "Leave the door open so the poor bastard can breathe." I was yanked over, slapped again. "Sit him up. Wake up, Mister, do you hear me? Wake the hell up. Take those goddamn cuffs off him. Jesus."

I was almost to Oregon.

I felt the cuffs leave my wrists. "Don't make a run for it, now." Run? Sitting up was difficult. I looked around, blinked. My head pounded, my wrists ached. My hands burned, blood coursing into them with pain like flame. "We're letting you get some oxygen, but stay the hell in the car. We didn't know it'd take so long. That little wife of yours is a talker."

The smaller officer got behind the wheel and started the car, got the air blasting. He had my poison. He opened it and tipped it up for a delicate sip. "Nice." He had another. The car gradually chilled. So did I. He finally passed the bottle through the open door to me. I had a long, chugging pull. He took it away. "Henry, the air's working now, so why don't you stop cooling off the great outdoors?"

The big cop got in and shut the door. They sat there, trading respectful sips from the bottle and surveying the neighborhood. "These are some fugly front doors. I wonder if the builder got a deal because they're so ugly."

"Could be. Look, couldn't we get her for something?"

"There's no law against being her."

"There damn well ought to be." They looked through a code book, bounced different ideas around, brainstormed. I waited, teeth chattering, while the officers considered my fate and tipped my bottle.

The neighbors found reasons to emerge from their homes, get the mail, walk the dog, whatever, just to have a look at me. Finally, another cop car pulled up. The big cop hid the bottle, the little cop rolled down his window. They exchanged pleasantries with the cops in the other car, weather, that fire the night before in Bricktown, bugs.

The other car didn't stay long. "That little woman of yours called the cops," said the big one. "She called the cops on the cops to complain about the cops. Can y'all believe it?"

The little cop turned around and looked at me. "That's a fine little wife you have there. She said she wanted to spend the weekend getting rid of every single thing that's yours in that house, starting with your Jeep. Hey, easy now. Do you want the cuffs again?"

I sat back.

"Funny how you quiet ones can go off like that. I guess it makes you feel like a man to knock her around, huh. Maybe you haven't noticed she's twice your age and half your size."

"Leave him alone."

The bottle came around, probably for the last time. We'd almost emptied it. "Listen, I asked if her name was on the title for that Jeep. Turns out it isn't? So I told her if she gave it away that'd be grand theft auto." He shook his head. "I think she believed me. So don't worry about that. And now, I'm sorry, but we have to take you in."

It was silent in the car. Silent and cold.

"At least," said the big one, "At least she won't be there."

He had a point.

~

I went to jail to "cool me off," to "teach me a lesson."

I deserved it. I hit her.

I learned something new. I learned that you don't have to be charged with anything to be held overnight. An officer fingerprinted me and took my photo. Then she smiled at me. "You won't be long in here, don't worry. Women never press charges against men who wear suits to work."

I spent the night in a communal holding cell.

Jail was loud. It smelled like vomit, anger and unwashed bodies. A man sitting across from me took off his shoe and used it to beat himself in the face. He smiled the entire time he did this. Everyone seemed to either be psychotic or drunk. I had no idea how I appeared, maybe both, who knows. I didn't eat anything. I didn't touch anything. And I didn't say anything.

No one bothered me.

I sat down on a bench and leaned up against the wall and slept. I did wake up once. When I opened my eyes, everyone was staring at me, silent, so I guess I'd been yelling in my sleep. I apologized sincerely to all the psychotics and drunks for disturbing their ravings and went back to sleep.

I deserved this, because I hit her.

Morning came. The toilet was full to the brim and smelled so bad that I couldn't make myself use it. I sat back down on my bench and decided that if anyone ever locked me up again I would have to kill myself. God and I could sort it out when I got there.

"Gentry!" someone called out. I looked up. "This way."

Walking was hard. My arms and legs kept popping, jerking like they belonged to someone else.

∽

The officer who fingerprinted me came over and smiled as I signed for a plastic bag that contained my belt, wallet and car keys. "What did I tell you? Monday morning you'll be at that office in your suit! I told you that!"

Miriam waited by the door. I tried not to see it. A split lip. A bruised cheek. The way she favored her shoulder. There were no words, none at all, for how much I hated myself.

My shoulders gave a shake, my arm flying out beside me. I felt my knees buckle.

She frowned. "I'll drive."

∽

I fell down while trying to settle myself into the car, but eventually, while she stood there staring with her arms crossed, I got it figured out. She had to do up my seatbelt. My hands wouldn't work right. She got in and did up her own seatbelt. We sat there, silent.

Her fist landed hard and square in the middle of my solar plexus.

"Don't you EVER leave me, I MEAN it. I'll have you LOCKED UP. I MEAN it."

She started the car and drove us home.

~

My first stop was the bathroom. Then I ran to the kitchen sink and turned the tap to cold and let it run. If you let it run long enough, even that foul Oklahoma water would turn icy.

I put my face under the spigot and drank for a long, long time. When my stomach could hold no more, I bent back over the sink, retching and heaving and shaking. The water was still cold as it poured out my nose and mouth, and I was glad for that.

I wanted to throw up my life.

I got an armful of bedding and some clothes and threw it all down on the study floor. I loaded my computer out of the Jeep and put it back on my desk. I was afraid, pulling out of the driveway, but no police came. At the hardware store I bought two deadbolts and a drill-proof faceplate for the study door.

~

Every night, she gently requested that I open the door. "OPEN THIS FUCKING DOOR! YOU CAN'T HIDE IN THERE FOREVER, YOU ASSHOLE! THAT'S JUST LIKE YOU, TO HIDE LIKE THIS!"

Every morning, I dressed and left for work. I washed up in the men's room, ate from the machines and went to the liquor store on my lunch hour.

She kept me apprised of household events. "OUR WHOLE LIFE IS FALLING APART, GENTRY! I HOPE YOU'RE SATISFIED! YOU FUCKED UP OUR FINANCES TO THE POINT WHERE THE ACCOUNTS ARE FROZEN!"

At the end of the day I came home and locked myself in. She stood outside the door. I buried my head in my arms, in my blankets, in a pillow.

I could still hear her. Most of all, she wished me happiness. "I HOPE YOU'RE

HAPPY, YOU SON OF A BITCH!! I HOPE YOU'RE HAPPY ROTTING IN THERE, YOU SON OF A BITCH!"

Late at night, I'd creep up the stairs and sneak into the kitchen, open the refrigerator, eat a handful of cereal, drink a swig of milk, eat another handful of cereal, chug more milk. I didn't want to leave any dishes, any clues. I moved like a thief through my own home.

I thought I'd figured it out. I'd found, finally, the system to survive being Miriam's husband.

I knew I would die, someday. But not soon enough.

~

I hated having short hair, but I liked the woman who cut my hair. Bernadette. It was like being groomed by the Venus of Willendorf. I had my hair cut often, simply to hear her accent and have her fingers on my scalp.

I sat in the chair waiting for her, trying to figure it out. I kept trying to figure out the Jeep thing. How to get the Jeep fixed without Miriam knowing. She never left the house, so how would I do it? Thinking about it made me tired. But if I fixed the Jeep and got on the road early when I was supposed to be leaving for work, how far could I get before she called the office, demanded to know where I was, and found out I'd left?

The white apron flared out around me with a flutter and crack.

"Did I startle you? Sorry, Gentry." She said my name the same way Becca did. Gin-tree. If I got there early, I was instructed to "wait on the binch." When I signed the debit card slip, she loaned me a "pin" to write with.

She settled the apron, leaned me back. The hot water hit my head and a deep sigh escaped me. "You like that, don't you." She worked in the shampoo with her small, precise hands. I closed my eyes and surrendered to it. "Your hair's clean, but I'm going to lather you up and do you again, just to see that look on your face." It felt even better the second time.

Thank You God, I guess You do still love me a little.

"Gentry? Are you there?" I opened my eyes. Her face was grave and her breath smelled like peppermint. "Gentry, it's been two months since you were in here. What's happening to you? Your hair is dull, and your breath smells like booze, and your skin's grey. It looks like you're half dead. Are you all right?"

Ah, kindness. Undone. My eyes filled.

"Oh, Gentry." She kissed the end of my nose, then cut off all my hair.

~

I went back to work, and my boss-in-law was in my office hollering about something that had nothing to do with me but was my fault. I blinked, inwardly protesting, outwardly calm. I thought of how I could possibly divert his anger. Maybe by making him mad at someone else. Everyone else in the office did this, they all pointed fingers and offered up their coworkers to save their own skins. It was something like the McCarthy hearings.

And then he used a normal voice. "I'll see you at supper tonight."

"Pardon?"

"Supper. I'll see you there."

"Hey Ben? What, um, do you mean?"

"Miriam invited us over to supper tonight. Didn't she tell you?"

"It must have slipped my mind."

"Well, we've missed you on Sundays. It will be nice to see you outside this place."

I was always so confused when Ben Hogan acted like a human being.

He left, and I sat there, running my hand over my hair, feeling that stupid brushiness I could never accept on my own head. I thought about the indignity of having this man sitting across from me at a dinner table, harassing me about golf with that vein in his head throbbing through his thin hair.

I had limits.

~

Of course, I went home late. Of course, they were already there. I went upstairs and submitted to the comments on how "nice" the haircut looked. I didn't drink. I was starving because for weeks, I'd been living on poison. But when I looked at my plate, I wasn't hungry. None of us were that hungry, apparently.

Miriam scowled, watching her brother-in-law moving around what looked like a pile of dirty shoelaces with his fork. "Are you on a DIET, Ben?"

Evelyn gasped. "How RUDE. I just can't believe you SAID that."

"I was just ASKING."

"Well, he's NOT on a DIET. Ben doesn't need a DIET. He's just BIG-BONED,

Miriam, Ben is just HEALTHY. I mean, just LOOK at GENTRY. He looks like a SCARECROW."

They all looked at me. I looked at my plate. Ben cleared his throat. His vein throbbed. "When are we going to have that golf game, Gentry?"

I was silent.

Evelyn looked up and smiled. "We have some news."

Miriam stared at her sister. "No."

Evelyn beamed. "Yes! We're expecting!"

Miriam burst into tears.

∽

I was lying on the floor of my office. I wasn't trying to sleep. I was trying to do something else. Verifying, I guess. It was gone. All the way gone since that day at the doctor's office.

A knock on the door, a quiet knock, not a hammering. "Gentry? Will you open the door?" She waited. "Are you going to let me in?" I lay there. "I just wish you'd unlock this door. I *hate* locked doors, Gentry, I just *hate* them."

I had always loved locked doors.

She knocked again. "Please? Will you please unlock the door? Please, Gentry. I might *need* something."

I had a light on, of course. It was a banker's lamp that Miriam bought for me, even though I was not a banker. I considered the contents of that odd little room, wondering what she could need in there.

"Gentry? Did you say something? Gentry, I didn't hear you. What did you say?"

"I asked what you could need in here."

I waited to hear what she would say, what words might move me to throw those locks.

"You."

I'm not sure how long she stood there, waiting. It seemed a long, long time.

Eventually, she went away.

∽

The next morning, I woke to the smell of bacon. It was an emanation of my desire to eat, a food hallucination. I was going insane. I decided to take part of my poison allowance and go to a restaurant.

I got ready for work, hurrying because I had to get to a gas station to wash up. She knocked at the study door. "Gentry? Come out, please."

I stood on the other side of the door, waiting for her to go away so I could leave. But she wouldn't go. "Come up and eat, Gentry. I made you some breakfast."

My stomach twisted with a groan.

"Fried eggs."

I made a sound of lust.

"I even made you some bacon."

My mouth let go with a rush of saliva, and my knees buckled. I opened the door and stumbled past her up to the bathroom because it was an emergency. And then I sat down at the table and ate that breakfast.

"I'm sorry, Gentry."

I chewed.

"I mean it. I want things to be better."

I swallowed.

"I want us to work on our issues. I mean, we have a real communication issue, and we have all these sex issues, and then the issues about adoption." She took the rest of the bacon and put it on my plate. "Will you go back to counseling with me? To work on our issues?"

I looked up at her, at her amber eyes and dark eyebrows, the number eleven etched so deeply between them.

I got up from the table and went to work.

∽

That afternoon, my phone rang. "This is Gentry."

"My parents want to have us over for your birthday."

"Hey Miriam? That's six weeks away."

"So? They're old, they like to plan. My mother wants to know what you want to eat."

My stomach growled. "That beef stew with the dumplings?"

"Fine. I won't be able to eat it, but that's not important, what I can eat. Nobody ever takes me into consideration. That's just how it always is."

"I, um, need to . . ."

"What do you want for your birthday?"

A new life. "Dinner is fine, just fine."

"You never want anything, do you."

"Hm." Well, I actually did want a new life. "Hey Miriam? I really need to . . ."

"Aren't you forgetting something?"

I ran through the list of what I usually forgot. "What?"

"Our anniversary? It's coming up. That would be just like you, to forget our first anniversary." Had it been a year? It felt like five. "Well, Gentry, what are we going to do for our anniversary?"

"Cover the mirrors?"

"What?"

"Nothing."

"And we have something else to celebrate." Something else? This implied something at all. "Gentry, it's finally happened."

My stomach contracted in fear. "You're *pregnant*?"

The silence was chilly. "God, you're stupid. I mean it, you're so stupid it's insulting that I'm married to you. No. I'm not pregnant. I got an agent."

"For what?"

"For my book!"

"Your book?"

"Yes, I wrote a book."

"You wrote a book?"

"I just said that."

I thought about it. "Is that what you were typing? A book?"

"YES, and I found an AGENT who found a PUBLISHER!"

"Hm." What if it was a cookbook?

"Aren't you going to say CONGRATULATIONS? Don't you even care enough about it to say CONGRATULATIONS?"

"What kind of a book is it?" It had to be a cookbook.

"Are you LAUGHING?"

"Um, no, I just wonder what kind of a book you wrote."

"I wrote a book about our marriage, and everything we've gone through trying to have kids."

Oh, God, kill me now.

"Hello? Are you still THERE?"

"Um, isn't that kind of personal?"

"Yes, extremely so, and that was just what the agent liked about it. This agent says she's fascinated by the depth, the honesty. I mean, I really put it ALL in there, all the details, about what it was like and the problems it has caused for me, for you, for us as a couple, ALL of it. She said she'd just never read such a gripping, raw, real view of infertility before."

Gripping, real, raw? What was she talking about? How about sad, pathetic, lonely. That was how it was for me.

"Are you THERE?"

"Yes."

"You don't sound very excited." She waited. "This is just like you. This is just like giving news to a corpse."

"Hey Miriam? May I read it?"

"I can bring it over to you."

"That would be great. I could read it at work this afternoon."

~

Half an hour later, Fanny called me. "Gentry, you have the cutest little wife in the world out here waiting to see you."

I went out and there she was. The cutest little wife in the world. Smiling. "So THIS is where you work."

I looked at Fanny. I waited. She didn't say it.

Miriam held out a disc for me. I put it in my shirt pocket. People came over to get a look at my little wife, the underpaid ladies who made up most of the staff, harried account managers on their way out to make calls. Phyllis came over. People introduced themselves because I'm bad at introductions. Miriam smiled, she laughed, shook hands, nodded. And then she said, "Well, I better take OFF." She put her arms around me. I stood there, my arms useless at my sides. And she squeezed me, and smiled. "I have to GO, Gentry."

Everyone stood there looking at me, Fanny and Phyllis and the legion of near dead that populated the office. I didn't smile, I didn't move. Miriam waited, her smile turning to hurt.

Fanny said, "Kiss your wife good-bye, silly Gentry."

I turned my back, went into my office and shut the door.

~

The book was only fifty thousand words long, so it didn't take long to read. She'd come up with a unique approach to structure. Each chapter covered an event in our relationship. The more personal the event, the better. At the end of each chapter, Miriam put a coda in dire, descriptive language.

She had a unique approach to punctuation based on the overuse of the exclamation point. The dialog was mostly composed of dramatic shouting. If it had only been her speaking, this would have been accurate.

The book began with a summary of how perfect Miriam's life was until I stumbled into it, followed by a protracted scene in which I tried to take her to bed for the first time. I fumbled and flailed and apologized for my ineptitude and fell on my knees by the side of the bed and cried and apologized to God ("*Oh Jesus and Mary! Forgive me! You can see what we are doing!*"). She saved the day (that was the phrase she used, of course, *save the day*) with her calm experience and creativity, and some expository dialog ("*I can help you, if you will just let me! Let me just show you some things! Don't be afraid!*"). It went on for pages and pages and I actually had to laugh a couple of times.

And then came the editorial part.

When I met the tall, handsome man I would eventually marry, I was instantly drawn to his absolute pureness and complete innocence. But then I was deeply shocked to realize that he was still a virgin. Little did I realize that his total lack of sexual experience would mean that I had to take complete charge in bed. I tried everything to try and help him awaken, sexually. Nothing worked, and I tried everything. It was like sleeping with a frightened child.

That didn't make me laugh. That made me sick.

The second section charged from one hectic episode of sexual disappointment to another. I banged around for another couple of chapters, drinking too much, having car accidents ("*Oh no! Not another one! Miriam, I beg you to forgive me!*") and refusing to touch myself when I went to the bathroom ("*You make such a mess of the toilet!" "But I can't bear to touch myself! It is sinful!*"). But the Miriam of the book wouldn't accept defeat.

The years he spent being abused, by evil Catholic priests, probably accounted for his problems, but he refused to face up to what had happened to him. He was in total denial.

My total denial meant that I hit her repeatedly.

He became incredibly violent if I brought up the abuse. Finally, I insisted that we get professional counseling. He told me, in professional counseling, what had really happened to him. His years as an altar boy, were a never-ending nightmare that never ended, because they haunted his darkest dreams, and robbed him of his manly potency.

Finally, there was a chapter in which I achieved many important insights in therapy, thanks to her understanding and persistence. This was clear in the book, because after long, talky exchanges with a therapist (who delivered lines like "*It is time for you to stop living your life in denial and come to terms with the ways in which your religion has made your life into a living hell! Face the facts!*") I would turn to her and express my thanks ("*Oh Miriam! You have given me such insight! Thank you!*"). In gratitude, I rejected Catholicism and begged her to marry me.

Sadly, we were not out of the woods. That was the phrase she used in the book, of course, *not out of the woods*. Because I used all this newfound insight to become gay.

Nothing hurt me more than finding my husband in the arms of someone else on our wedding day. He had disappeared, and we needed to leave for our honeymoon, so I went and looked for him. I walked into my parent's bedroom, and there, to my total surprise, totally naked on the broad, wide bed, were my husband and our supposed best friend, our best man, locked in a passionate, sexual embrace.

I almost wanted to call Sandy and read that part out loud to him, to let him share in the details of our wedding day tryst on the broad, wide bed. Sandy would be reassured to know he was on top, of course, no wait, he was "*poised above*" me on the "*magnificent bed, his gigantic penis purple and waving.*" I felt relief that Miriam had interrupted this encounter while he was still "*poised above*" me, because that sounded a little scary. And of course I yelled at her. "*No one must know of my homosexuality! It is a crime against God!*"

I just can't describe my total anguish. He admitted his deep sexual conflicts to me, and begged for my understanding. I forgave him, but the bad mental image, stayed with me forever. He threatened me with serious violence if I ever told anyone. His menacing threats to violently beat me began that day, and my life after my wedding day, was totally colored with the fear of his physical violence. And yet I stayed, because I felt a strong moral obligation, to take care of him.

It was like I was his mother.

Again, I felt sick. And it wasn't just those commas.

We moved on, in Miriam's book, and recommitted ourselves to the marriage because she was so forgiving and we had such a good therapist. We decided to try for children. But we couldn't have them.

The doctors suggested, at first, that the fertility problem had to do with the extreme smallness of my husband's penis. He was just the size of a thimble, when erect.

Well, no wonder Sandy got to be on top.

The doctors explained to me, that the inadequate depth of penile penetration kept his feeble sperm from reaching the cervix. I tried to make him feel better about it, but he was too busy compensating for his small size, with violence, to let me through.

You know, I finally understood the toilet issue. Being that small, how was a person supposed to aim?

Eventually, my husband became totally impotent.

How would she be able to tell?

Our sex life, never good, became totally nonexistent. I just tried everything to arouse him. There was nothing I refused, to try and help him, but he was unable to achieve any type of an erection, after he found out how low his sperm count was.

Hey, now.

But then technology intervened, and we were able to scientifically compensate for my biological shortcomings. With donor sperm from my best friend.

I knew that it was my husband's inability to father a child, that drove him into his violent rages, but my self-respect wouldn't allow me to suffer the daily beatings at his hands. I was totally black and blue, before I finally called the police. And at that point, I had lost the baby. I forgave him, because I'm a forgiving person by nature, but he would never forgive himself.

So in this book, I was a murderer. A murderer who couldn't make a woman pregnant, a murderer who beat the child out of her that science and his gay best friend created.

There were scenes and scenes. Scenes at her parents, scenes at work. Through it all, she stood by me while I slammed her in the face and projectile vomited and wet myself and thanked her for her loyalty.

And then we accepted defeat.

My husband's issues about maturity, about his sexuality, his attraction to other men, all played into his unreasonable decision, not to pursue innovative conception options with me. His choice to return to the superstitious religion, that had done nothing but totally ruin him, was another culprit. I was totally devastated. We were then unable to adopt, once my husband's criminal record came to light. His many felony convictions disqualified him from adopting, and as a loyal wife, I also just had to try and live with this, as well.

Perhaps, he was just not meant to be a father.

And the best part of the whole endeavor was that my name, my stupid, humiliating name was on every page of that document, and I read it, over and over and over again.

∽

I picked up the phone. I dialed. "Hey Miriam? Someone actually wants to publish this?"

"Did you already finish it?" She sounded surprised.

"I have."

"Do you think I used too many commas? The agent says I use too many commas."

"Have you signed anything?"

"No. Not yet. Because of the content, they wanted you to just kind of, you know. Scan it beforehand. I have a release for you to sign."

"Those are some smart people."

"Now, the publisher offered me a huge advance, I sent them lots of pictures of you and they're talking about a book tour, we could go on the talk shows . . ."

"Talk shows?"

She cleared her throat. "It would be a chance for us to reach out to other couples who have had the same experiences as us . . ."

"What experiences are you talking about?"

She was quiet for a moment. "I know I exaggerated but I just wanted it to be EXCITING, you know . . ."

"Oh, it's exciting. It's so exciting to me that I'm leaving."

"WHAT?"

"I'm leaving. Today."

"You can't LEAVE."

"I can."

"Gentry, you can't LEAVE me. I'll call the POLICE."

"I'll call them myself and tell them to meet me over there."

She was quiet for a moment. "There is NO WAY you can leave me, we're too in DEBT!"

"We can go bankrupt for all I care. I'm going to leave today."

"That's FINE, it will make a great final CHAPTER."

"Oh no, no it won't. Because I want you to call these people and you tell them that I'll sue them if they print this."

"THIS IS JUST LIKE YOU, YOU'RE SELFISH, SELFISH, SELFISH! THIS IS MY ONE CHANCE TO DO SOMETHING IN MY LIFE AND YOU'RE TRYING TO TAKE IT AWAY FROM ME! I'LL JUST DO IT ANYWAY!!"

"Fine. Do it. This is libel. Do you understand that? I can get a lawyer and I'll win."

"I JUST CAN'T BELIEVE YOU WON'T LET ME TELL THE WORLD MY STORY!"

"Tell your own story. Tell any story. But you will never tell this story."

"WE NEED THE MONEY! THEY'RE OFFERING US A LOT OF MONEY!"

"I don't care about money."

She screamed in my ear. A true scream of frustration and rage. "YOU HAVE TO LET ME PUBLISH IT, YOU HAVE TO!"

"Why? Why would I let you do this to me?"

"GENTRY, YOU JUST HAVE TO!"

"No I don't."

"YOU HAVE TO! IF YOU DON'T, I'LL KILL MYSELF!"

"Then kill yourself, Miriam."

And I hung up the phone.

IX. RECKONING

"Gentry, wake up. It's time."

"Hm."

"You have to take me to the airport."

"Okay."

"Wake up there, fella."

"I'm awake." I am. Just . . .

~

"I hate to wake you up. You finally slept."

"No. Just a minute, just . . ."

"I could call a cab."

I'm instantly awake. "No, I'm up." I skip a shower, brush my teeth and throw on some clothes. Some terrible boxers, jeans that button, thick socks, my boots, oh Thank You, God, thank You.

Mike looks at me. "It's cold out there."

"It'll be a hundred and ten in a few hours."

"It's too cold for a T-shirt." He hands me a shirt. "This is what you need."

I like this shirt. It's faded flannel, thin in the elbows, way too big. Perfect. I put it on over the T-shirt and it hangs down to my knees. He looks at me, reaches to ruffle my hair, but I duck. He smiles. "A foot more hair, and you'll look like yourself again."

I put Mike's bag in the Jeep for him. It's still dark when we leave. But it's starting to get light. We drive along for a while. "I'm trying not to take it as a bad omen that I'm going down Amelia Earhart Way on the way to Will Rogers International Airport."

"Don't forget, we passed a cemetery."

"Better and better." Mike smiles at me and I have to look away. I look at God's arrows sunk into the earth, the two-story bronze arrows that, like the sunrise, are unexpectedly beautiful in a place like this. I've always liked those arrows. Mike looks at them, nods.

I'm glad he notices the arrows.

The sky is violently pink behind glowing, broken clouds. I can't keep my eyes on the road for looking at the sky. I've watched the sun rise so many times. It's the only benefit to insomnia that I know of. And it still inspires me to prayer.

Thank You. Amen.

"Look at that sky. My God, Gentry, that's something." His expression.

"Hey Mike? You know, right?" He knows my name, he must know everything.

"No. I have no idea."

"She killed herself."

His hand on my arm. "It's not your fault."

"It is."

I believe that. I always will.

∽

We get to his gate with a few minutes to spare. "So, did you learn anything about money this week?"

"Not really."

"Then you weren't paying attention. It's simple. When you need money, identify an asset. Then sell it."

I nod. I will try to remember this lesson.

We wait. I can't think of what to say. Mike didn't have to do any of this. Oh, I know he likes handling things, and he likes loaning me money, and he likes my gut. I can tell he really likes that. But all the rest of it. Sleeping in the same room, the drinking, the television, the nightmares, bagging up all those clothes, fixing the Jeep. The shirt. His lip.

I remember what it is you say to people who help you. "Thank you, Mike."

"You're welcome. You are welcome. Anytime." He gives me one of his bone-crushing hugs, and I let him. Then, I hug him back as hard as I've ever hugged anyone in my life. It hurts to let him go.

His face is full of emotion. "Why don't you just get on the plane with me. I'll buy your ticket." I shake my head no. "Why not, Gentry? What's keeping you here? Come on. Just get on the plane with me." I shake my head and drag my arm over my eyes.

He ruffles my hair. I let him. "Get something for those allergies. And come see us soon." He walks away down the corridor to the plane.

I watch him leave.

I watch the plane take off through the airport window.

I watch it get very small in the sky.

∽

"Good morning, Gentry."

"Good morning, Fanny."

"Jesus loves you, Gentry."

I think Jesus just wants to be friends.

I sit down on my desk and pick up the phone and hit her button. There's a smile in her voice when she answers. "Hello, darlin.' What can I do for you?"

"Well, it occurs to me that this is my life."

"Yes. I believe so."

"So, I was wondering. What's the point?"

And she laughs so loud that I can hear her, not just over the receiver, but through my door. My boss shoves into the office. "IS THAT A PERSONAL CALL? WHO THE HELL ARE YOU TALKING TO?"

Phyllis is laughing hard enough that I can hear her. Ben Hogan might follow the trail of her laughter, and humiliate her. "I, um, have to go. Bye."

He stands there, staring, red. "I CANCELED CASUAL FRIDAYS!"

Did we ever have casual Fridays? "Hey Ben, may I help you with something?"

He tells me that his new secretary can't figure out how to read or send email, and it's my fault. "I PAY YOU TO TRAIN PEOPLE ON THESE THINGS!"

"No problem." Mr. Hogan hires attractive but inept young women purely for their decorative functions, I think. But this is an opportunity to teach, so I'm ready to go. He takes me down the hall, to her area and I smile, because this looks so much like Tiffany, just exactly like Tiffany, this IS Tiffany, I think it is . . . no, just like her, though.

I turn to my boss-in-law and shake my head. "Hey Ben? Forget it, I tried with one like this. You'll never get your email sent. You should try hiring an assistant with basic office skills. They're pretty easy to find." He looks like he might have a heart attack.

I go back to my office. I get my solitaire going. I hate this job.

I start today's tick sheet, and give myself a bonus tick for making Ben angry. The phone rings. I don't pick it up.

I hate this job.

The message light goes on, blinks, blinks, blinks. I hate this job. The phone rings again and I ignore it.

Finally Fanny pokes her head in my door. "Pick up your line, you have an important phone call, silly Gentry."

"Thank you."

"Jesus loves you, silly Gentry." She withdraws her head before I can jump up and slam the door on it.

I look at the phone. Important. Hm. Maybe the house buyers came to their senses and decided to buy a Dumpster, instead. "This is Gentry."

"Mr. Gentry? This is Brooke Gilbert." I wait, because I don't know any Brooke Gilbert. "We haven't spoken before, but I was working with your late wife."

I don't remember anyone named Brooke at the school. "Which department?"

"No, not at the school. We were working on getting her book published."

"I, um, have to go."

"Wait, please . . ." And she addresses me by my first name.

"Don't call me that."

There's a silence. "What should I call you, then?"

"You can call me Mr. Gentry."

"Mr. Gentry, I'm in town and I wondered if I could I buy you lunch?"

I open my mouth to say no. "Okay. Where?"

"I'm staying at the Waterford. They have a restaurant."

Well, I'm glad she's buying, since she chose the Waterford.

~

When I arrive at the restaurant, I look around. I remember this place. Miriam wanted to eat here on her birthday because it was the most expensive place in Oklahoma City and had nothing I would like on the menu. I give Brooke's name to the host or whatever he is. He hesitates. He looks unimpressed with my attire. I extend the sleeve toward him. "Don't worry. This is a rich man's shirt." He takes me to her table. Brooke is pretty enough to make me hurt, were I able to hurt in that area anymore. But she's wearing a suit.

"Hey. I'm Gentry."

We shake hands. She's so pretty, even in that suit. She looks surprised. I'm not sure what I look like. I don't know what she expected. Maybe I don't look like a violent baby killer with an impotent thimble. At least I don't have on a stupid suit.

"Call me Brooke. I'm so glad to meet you, Mr. Gentry. I'm delighted that you decided to meet with me, especially under the circumstances. I imagine that Miriam's death destroyed you."

Nice icebreaker. "Um, yes, pretty much."

"How are you now?"

"I'm fine, just fine." We sit down. A menu, oh, my favorite thing in the world, a menu, sits here. There are poached and caramelized and seared things on this menu. There's nothing available with gravy. But I study my options so I don't have to look at this pretty woman.

She's talking to me about the book, about "what a gripping, timely, immediate tale it is, all the more so considering how, well, uh, er . . ." Her eyes shine with something sharp. "Her sister called me when it happened, and told me not to bother anyone. Especially not you. She wasn't explicit, but I was left with an impression that it was . . ."

I say these words for the second time in my life, the second time in one day. "She killed herself."

"Do you know why she did it?"

Can she truly have asked that? No one, ever, in this entire year, has asked me why Miriam killed herself. Not even her mother. Not even Mel. "I don't know."

"Didn't she leave a note?"

"She left a note." She stares at me, I stare back. Brooke, you're pretty on the outside, only. What is it that you see, when you look at me? I see a ghoul when I look at you, Brooke. A ghoul who feeds on what I say.

"How did she do it?"

"She had a lot of leftover pills from when she had her surgery."

She moves her hips in her chair. "She must have taken quite a few. What exactly was the drug?" The woman is squirming.

"I don't know."

The shine in her eyes. "And you found her?"

"Yes."

She breathes in sharply through her arched nostrils. "Tell me about that."

Her reactions are unmistakable. This is a unique experience for me. I'd laugh if I were not so disgusted. Which one of us I'm the most disgusted with, I'm not sure. Because it appears that I'm going to tell her.

"I came home from work and I went upstairs, and she was in her room. There was, there was something wrong." For as long as I'd known her, Miriam had looked angry. Even when she slept, she frowned. I walked in and saw her sleeping, and she looked calm, no anger in her face at all. How do I explain this? I can't. "I called for help."

"Was she still alive when the ambulance came?"

"Yes. She was alive for some time. In a coma."

"How long?"

"I don't remember." Twenty-nine days. Her systems shutting down, one by one, watching her face for even a flicker, staring at that monitor for brain activity, praying for a blip or a beep. They had a chaplain in there most of the time, they brought in a rabbi, they brought in a priest. All talking to me, reasoning with me, praying with me to understand God's will while my wife's body slowly ground to a halt and I clung to my Catholic hope.

They got Mel on the phone. He said he'd come down and sit with me. *I won't tell you what to do, my boy, I just want to sit with you right now*. And I said, *no. Don't come down here, Mel. You wouldn't be here when we were married. So don't come now, just stay away from this*. He said, *you're angry with me, my boy, go ahead and be angry. But know I am always, always here for you.*

I hung up on him.

Mr. Hirsch with tears in his eyes, saying, *Gentry, I know you believe in miracles, but Ruth and I, we don't. And this is our daughter.*

"They wanted me to let them turn it all off."

"And you agreed?"

"Yes. I agreed."

I press my hands into my eyes and remember.

I told them they could do it. They thanked me. I had to go out and sign something, and Mrs. Hirsch stood with me, that small, strong old man putting a hand on my back to steady me because my knees were weak and I thought I couldn't do it, but I signed the order with my full name.

I went back to her side. The nurses came in. I'd watched them care for my wife, I'd watched every moment, every movement because if anyone had been rough with her, if anyone had hurt her or touched her in the wrong way, I would have burned down that hospital. But they tended her as reverently as handmaidens. They gently slipped it out of her, freeing Miriam from what kept her alive.

I sat beside her and prayed. I prayed to the shape of her hand, curled into a cup.

I prayed to the locks of hair, curled around her calm face. If she'd fought it, if for one moment she'd stirred, complained, I would have had them start it up all over again. But she didn't fight. Life ebbed and left her peaceful. The monitor showed her slowing heart, the last part of her to give up. And then it gave up.

I closed her eyes. I touched her hair.

I shut her mouth.

"Mr. Gentry?"

I take my hands away from my eyes. "She died when they took her off life support. And then I ended up in the mental ward."

"You did?"

"I did. I thought I was signing myself in to spend a night, just to get some sleep. They promised they'd give me something to sleep if I signed myself in. But they took away my shoes. I knew I was in trouble." I spent three days in that place, with all the other crazy people, the man who crawled around all night on his hands and knees because he was afraid to fall asleep, the skeleton woman who wouldn't eat, the screamer, the crap thrower, and me.

I stood at the nurses station and quietly, calmly begged for my shoes. I told them I wasn't crazy but would be soon if they didn't let me out. They let me out for the funeral. And I went to the funeral, and I went back to work. I knew I would never break, never crack, never go back there.

I'll never go back there.

"Mr. Gentry?"

I'll never fall.

"Mr. Gentry, are you all right?"

I smile, blink my eyes. "I'm fine, just fine."

"I doubt that. How have you coped?"

"Drinking. Drinking and praying." I don't know why I can talk to her about it. I haven't talked to anyone about this, no one, not even Mel. But everything I tell her makes Brooke wriggle around in her chair, exuding heat, so I keep talking.

"You pray?" She likes things tortured and melodramatic, and I guess she sees the possibilities of my faith in that regard. "You've always been religious?"

"I considered the priesthood."

"I see." She's impressed. She's obviously not Catholic, or she would know that every little Catholic boy thinks about being a priest, and every little Catholic girl thinks about being a nun. It's like being a fireman or a doctor. But if she thinks this is impressive, if it makes her stir in her chair some more, well, fine by me. "I thought you were abused by priests." Ah, Miriam's theories.

I shake my head. "When I was eleven, I went to live with my uncle. He's a priest. He took me in when I was, um, orphaned." I'm not sure if this is the right word for whatever it was that was done to me, but Brooke likes it. "He took a year to help me get on track. Then I went away to school and he went back to his vocation. He never laid a hand on me in anger or in any other way but kindness." Mel's small hands.

"So you really didn't have any parents after you were eleven."

"No. I didn't have any parents before I was eleven, Brooke. After, I had Mel."

"Oh my." Her eyes shine and she shifts around, trying to calm herself.

All this before we order.

The waiter is intense, almost too involved in our food selection, even for me, and I usually appreciate the help. With his clasped hands, he looks like he's praying for our order. I pray not to look like an ordering idiot in front of this pretty, undead woman. We allow him to tell us about the various free-range vinaigrette pear-layered specialties, and then Brooke orders a salad. Doesn't she know that a salad in a restaurant like this could have *anything* in it? I order a steak. Every southern restaurant serves steak, even this one. It will be blackened, but it will be beef. The waiter seems disappointed that we didn't go with one of his intense suggestions, but he goes to put in our order.

I need a drink.

"I know you objected to the book. I understand that Miriam's version was, well, shall we say, informed by her need not to be at fault."

"Yes, Brooke. You could say that. Or you could just say it was a bunch of lies."

"Oh?" Brooke's eyes are open, and the glint is dulled by something wet. "Was it all lies?"

"It was," I have to think, "approximately ninety-two percent lies."

"Could you give me an example of something she lied about?"

"I'm not sterile. And she was."

"Really. How about the violence?" Is there anything she won't let herself ask? Is there no decency in this woman? And why does she have to be so pretty, I ask?

"I hit her."

"You did?" Oh, you like that, don't you, Brooke. "More than once?"

"No, it was just the one time."

"Even once was inexcusable." What a moralistic tone you take with me, sitting there on fire with your voyeuristic lust, Brooke. She leans forward, licks her lips. "Why did it happen?"

I try to think of something tortured and melodramatic to say. "It's because of my past. My life before I went to live with my uncle. I have violence in me."

Bingo. Her breath catches, she leans closer, she's mine. Her breath comes hard and fast. "Mr. Gentry, this is all so painful, so unbelievably tragic . . ." And then she relaxes. She looks at me, glassy-eyed. Is she spent?

This whatever it is stops for a moment, because the food arrives. I give thanks, and she watches. I'm used to that. I'm not, however, accustomed to having my grace be arousing to someone. I scrape a bunch of peppercorns off my meat and dig in. Black outside, raw and bloody within. Sort of how I imagine Brooke's heart. She picks at her salad. She's too worked up to eat that mess, I see. She watches me eat, women always watch me eat, why is that, I wonder? She nibbles, I chew. I don't talk while I eat. She might be picking up the tab, but I'm selling something for this meal and I want to enjoy it.

She bites her lip. "Mr. Gentry, I wonder about some of her other assertions."

"I have no felony convictions." I poke at the potatoes, sniff them, realize they're mashed turnips. I can't even recognize the stuff next to them.

The waiter comes over. "Is everything all right?"

I gesture to the gory heap next to the turnips. "What, um, is this?"

"Gingered Tomato Molasses Puree."

Why would anyone put something like that on a plate?

He leaves, I finish, she watches. "What about the homosexuality?"

This was a good steak. And the turnips were okay. "Miriam was, um, put off by some of my old friends, by the closeness of them, I guess."

"Closeness?"

"Old college friends. I guess she didn't have any, so she didn't understand."

"So you're not gay?"

"No."

She calls for the check. "Let's go to the bar."

~

Brooke gets a tab going. I order some nice single malt poison. Brooke has an expensive glass of French blood.

Hey, Poison.

We sit in a booth in a corner. Brooke slides close to me. Oh, I can't help it, to feel her thigh next to mine, I sit close, let myself smell her. Pretty, evil Brooke. She breathes her false concern all over me, and I like it. I like her beautiful face that masks her perversion, I like her breath that smells like salad and blood and the dirt from Miriam's grave, right up in my face.

Okay, enough.

Very few people in a lounge at one o'clock in the afternoon. There's a band. I guess any bar this expensive has to have music all day long to make up for the cost of single shot drinks. This band is an aging white man combo, playing slow jazz. "Mr. Gentry, do you want to dance?"

Me? I've never wanted to dance in my life. It's something I do only under the influence or under duress. But I take her out for a slow dance. We line up well.

I haven't been this close to anyone but Miriam in such a long time that I even enjoy being close to Brooke, a filthy vampire with a pretty mouth. Yes, move right up there, oh, that feels good to me. Do you feel me? That's at rest, and I can tell you like it. Don't get too hopeful, because I'm permanently at rest. Oh put your hand on me, Brooke. No one has touched me there in so long. I don't even touch myself. "So that was another lie?"

"Mm hm." I breathe this into her ear and she whimpers and puts her arms around my neck. Come here. Let me kiss your wine, and you. For a succubus, you kiss nice. I haven't kissed anyone for so long. You would suck me dry, wouldn't you.

I want to talk about money, so we sit down.

She sits close and lays out her proposition. The book, with a rewrite, a writer would work with me, and I would have co-author status with my dead wife. And the advance, I could live carefully for a couple of years on the advance alone. "And if I say no?"

The idea shocks her. "If you say no, we have to give you the book. You get it back as her heir. But the opportunity," says Brooke and her wet eyes, "what you'd be saying no to."

"What would I be saying no to?'

"Money, for one thing."

Money. There is that.

"We would fix the lies, Mr. Gentry."

"The book wasn't all lies."

"No?"

"No. One part is true." I reach under the table, take her by the wrist. I move her hand to where I want it, Oh, I want it. I hold it there. "Nothing happens for me anymore." She frowns, moves her hand. Disappointed.

"Are you sure? Are you sure that you're impotent?"

"Yes. Completely." Because if she could do what she just did to me under the table and nothing happened, I am dead.

"Then, because you've paid the price, I think you deserve some benefit from it, even if it is just financial." She breathes this in my ear, with her soft, soft, evil, pretty voice.

In my ear. Oh.

"If I let you put out my dead wife's book, I'd be doing it for the money. Just for the money. Do you know what that would make me?"

She looks in my eyes, she strokes, squeezes, she's persistent, this Brooke, she wants to make this work. Oh, I wish this would work. "Publishing the book wouldn't make you that."

"Make me what? Say it. Say what I would be."

"A sellout, Mr. Gentry." Not the word I had in mind.

"Well, then, what would it make me?"

"Money. Quite a bit of money." Ah, money. She's trying, I have to give her that. Her hand persists, her eyes persist, my deadness persists. But she knows what she's doing, and I give a little groan, I give her that. Because this feels so good. To be touched I need to be touched oh this feels good. "I tell you what, Mr. Gentry, how about we make a little bet."

"A bet?"

"A bet." And I moan, again, oh. She smiles. She likes this very, very much. "I bet you're wrong about being impotent."

"What are the stakes?"

"If I win, you let me have the book."

"If you lose?"

"I won't."

She takes the napkin from under her wineglass and wipes off her lipstick.

Under that red, her lips are pink. She licks her pink lips with her pointed, pink tongue. Oh. And her voice, her soft, soft voice, breathing in my ear. "Mr. Gentry? I have a room at this hotel. Remember that."

The sound I make must be heard by someone.

She begins the unbuttoning. It takes forever, jeans that unbutton. She would, she will, if I let her, she'll do it. She will, in this dark corner of this dark bar, she will take me into the dark grave between her lips. If I let her. I want to let her. I want her mouth as much as I've ever wanted anything.

There's a moment when her hand finds me, touches me, holds me. A moment when her face is soft with wanting what I want. A moment when I cup her under the chin, hold her face in front of mine, study it, look into her eyes, touch her pretty, hungry mouth with my fingertips, so soft, so ready. A moment.

Just a moment.

"All right. You be a whore first, Brooke, and then I will."

Ouch. That hurt. That sure won't work, Brooke.

And I think she knows, now. Nothing will work.

The book is a dead thing, like me.

~

Of course, I kick myself a million times over when I walk into the reception area.

Fanny waits, poised and starving. "Did you have a nice lunch?"

"Spectacular."

"What did you have?"

"A main course of prostitution, and some self-respect for dessert."

"Where do they serve *that*?" I can't help it, I actually roll my eyes. She lets out a giddy, maniacal laugh. "Jesus loves you, Gentry!"

I slam my office door.

My phone rings. I might as well pick this one up. "This is . . ."

"WHERE THE HELL WERE YOU? THIS IS THE FRIDAY I GIVE OUT THE EMPLOYEE OF THE MONTH AWARD! YOU MISSED IT!"

"I went out to get a haircut."

"Oh." He loses his yelling steam. "Well, I'm glad you got a haircut."

"I couldn't." I'm so bad at lying.

"What the HELL do you mean? You couldn't?"

"A haircut would be a violation of my personal moral code."

"WHAT?"

"Ben, are you Catholic?"

"You know I was raised Baptist."

"Well, Catholics have this, um, mourning tradition. We let our hair grow. To honor the dead."

"GENTRY, YOU'RE FULL OF SHIT!" He hangs up.

God, forgive me these stupid lies.

I'm losing it. I said no to walking out of here, that's what I did. I'd already dragged myself through the mud at that table, hadn't I? Just to watch her squirm. What a time to finally walk the stupid moral high road. I could be locked away in a beautiful room at the Waterford with a do-not-disturb sign and that beautiful vampire and her pink mouth, done with this job forever. I'm a righteous idiot. Oh, God, I'm a fool. I think about Mike for some reason, imagine how he would react if I told him what I'd done, or rather, what I hadn't done. He would accuse me of morality. He would laugh at me.

I want to swear.

The phone rings again. Might as well get it, I have nothing else to do.

"This is Gentry."

"Gentry? Michael said I should call you. He gave me your work number." This is a voice from the past, a voice I thought I'd never be able to hear again. Oh, this voice? This voice?

"I hope this is all right. Calling you like this." The person on the other line is not yelling. The person on the other end of the line has a calm voice, a removed voice, a musical voice that was once made low by too many cigarettes. But it's higher, now, her voice is higher.

"Kathryn." A whisper, not a word.

And she's saying kind things to me, kind things. "We've all missed you terribly, I hope you know that." Please don't be kind, please don't be kind. I can't believe this. Because, Dear God, Dear Sweet God I can't believe it, this kindness does not unman me. I'm remembering things, things we did together and Kathryn, the fine of your hair, the white of your skin . . .

"Gentry? Are you there?"

"Mm hm." Here I am. Right here.

"I hardly know where to start. It's been so long, but not too long, I hope." I make some noise, a groan or moan, because she sounds concerned. "Gentry, are you all right?"

"Mm hm." I'm *fantastic.*

She tells me about a job, there's a job, my old job, they want me to apply, putting in a lab at the middle school, new equipment for the high school . . . "New equipment, Gentry, everything is new and has to be installed. And you love to handle the equipment yourself, right?"

"Mm hm." Do I.

The school board says I can have it if I want it, I just need to call, just formalities, an emergency teaching credential due to the circumstances . . . "Does it sound good, Gentry, does that sound good?" Oh that sounds good, so good, keep talking, please . . . even if I don't want the job, they want me to at least come for a visit. "At least come for a visit. Can you take some time?"

"Mm. Not too much more time." Keep talking.

"I wish you would come, so much. Do you think you can come?"

"Mm. I think so . . ."

"Can you come right away?" I can come RIGHT NOW, Kathryn fire, the current, heat lightning, white hot, arcing electricity here I am, oh, oh . . . oh god oh god oh god I'm alive.

"Gentry? Are you going to come?"

This is a *miracle*. "I did. I mean, I will. Sunday, I can't leave until Sunday."

"But you'll come on Sunday?"

"I'll come whenever you want me to."

I can hear her crying. "I've missed you. Are you there, Gentry? Are you all right?"

"I'm here, Kathryn. I'm all right."

"I'm so glad you're all right."

"Me too."

"I'll see you soon, Gentry." She's crying, so she hangs up. I cup my hands around my parts as if to guard a flame while I wait for the return of mobility to the lower half of my body. Everything aches. But everything works.

Thank You, God.

Once I can walk, I get past Fanny as quickly as I can and spend some time in the bathroom, cleaning up. Considering what I just did at work, I realize I might be the stupidest person I have ever known in my life.

Back at my desk, I try to write a letter. I've been practicing for almost two years, now, so this should be easy. I can't get any further than, "Dear Ben." I consider handing him a sheaf of tick sheets, an entire desk drawer full of them.

I go down into the basement, climb up on top of Terence's desk even though he's sitting at it. The look on his face when I stand up on his desk, his papers, but I see her head. I find May and give her an address and tell her thank you, for lisping and for being sweet. Good-bye.

I leave those catacombs.

I find Phyllis and give her a hug. Thank you Phyllis, for feeding me those wonderful sandwiches. Here's the retro Swingline. I'd like to take it with me, but I'm going to confess everything and get right with my church and the idea of confessing stapler theft is a little too pathetic, even for me. Please take good care of it. Thank you for being intelligent. Thank you for being funny. Thank you for knowing about the Sensitive Plant, and for having read Gerard Manley Hopkins, and for even liking some of his work, or at least pretending to because you know how important he is to me. Would you please write my letter for me, I can't, and then would you give it and all these tick sheets to Ben Hogan? Will you do that for me? Please don't cry, please, or I will. Thank you for keeping me alive. Good-bye.

I go back to my office and look around. There's not one thing here to take with me. Well, I can fold up the newspaper and carry that out.

Fanny stops me with an envelope in her yellow-stained fingers as I pass the reception area. "Well, silly Gentry, here's your award."

"My award? For what?" I open it. Ah. A certificate signed by the mighty Hogan himself. And what do we have here, what is my prize?

One ticket to the Cowboy Hall of Fame.

I look up at her. "Good-bye, Fanny."

"Silly Gentry. Where are you going?"

"Heaven, Fanny. After winning Employee of the Month, where else would I go?"

And she looks at me and smiles her alligator smile. Don't do it, please, let it pass, one time, just once, Fanny. This is the last chance you will ever have to redeem yourself. Take it, Fanny.

"Jesus loves you, Gentry."

"Yes He does. And I love Him too."

Her mouth hangs open.

That was what I should have been saying to her, all along.

X. RESCUE

It's been almost a year now, Miriam, since you died, and I'm once again surrounded by this group of people who watch my nearness to the poison with hawk eyes, but I stay away from the poison. It does not call me. But I'm sure it remembers my name.

Help me, God. Amen.

"More coffee, Gentry?"

"Please." She pours it, I sip, and he watches with not a word. Mr. and Mrs. Hirsch are relieved. They've given me another chance and I'm behaving myself. This day of unveiling is more important to them than a funeral, and more important to me, because I'm expecting some help.

Yesterday after I left the office, I went home and slept for fourteen hours. Saturday morning I woke early and went to the Cowboy Hall of Fame, which is called something else entirely. It was pretty interesting. I stopped by a store to get some boxes, then came home to my ugly house and dragged a bunch of stuff into the garage. The orange couch, the console television, kitchen crap. I called Hank Dandy and he said he'd arrange to have it taken away.

I packed, then. I have everything ready to go out there in my Jeep. I can fly. But right now, I'll wear this stupid suit and suffer the presence of all these people and be polite, because I know it has an end, it all has an end, and I'm near it.

I came over early this morning. I called Mrs. Hirsch "Ruth," and I called her husband "Ira." They patted me on the back with their small, old hands. He told me, "I'm glad to see your hair, what a stupid haircut you had."

I brought the photos and the jewelry box. Ruth fed me an enormous breakfast. While I ate, she went through the jewelry and cried over what she found. There were family pieces in there. She tried to give me the wedding ring, but I told her what I really wanted was for Evelyn to keep that for the baby. Something from you, Miriam.

And I was relieved, because that was the last of it.

People arrived while I was eating. These people do not live in Oklahoma, they're all too smart for that. They greeted me as if I were your husband, not the man who got drunk and fell down the stairs after your funeral. No one mentioned how I yelled at your family, no one mentioned what I said to your mother to make her cry. No one talked about my sitting in the Jeep, drunk and raging and singing hymns until I passed out. Those were not the stories they told. They told stories about you, Miriam, laughing and crying over what you missed this year, cousins graduating, an uncle passing away, the birth of this beautiful baby, the center of this family, the future. They hugged each other and tried to hug me. But I couldn't bear that.

One of the cousins came over and took hold of my tie and fixed me with her eyes, which were brown, not the amber of yours but just brown, like mine. "It's the funniest thing. I can feel her here today. I keep expecting her to step out a door and start complaining about the weather, the catering, this ugly tie." She gave my tie a tug. "I just know she's going to turn up and open that big mouth of hers."

She smiled. I shivered. I went into the kitchen to hide.

Ben followed me in and shook my hand and thanked me for all the nice things I said in my resignation letter. Phyllis told him I was too emotionally overcome to deliver it myself. "I understand, Gentry," he said. "You've done a terrific job. You're leaving us in great shape. I mean that. And you come back if you ever want to. I mean that, too."

I sat alone in the kitchen for a while after that.

Ruth came in and gently put her hand on my head. "We have enough rugelach here to stock a bakery. And both kinds of babka. You like the cinnamon, yes?" I nodded. I did. "Will you take some with when you when you go home?" I nodded again, but I knew I wouldn't take anything with me when I left. She pushed my hair away from my face. "Such beautiful eyes you have. And so sad. That's what she told me when she first met you. She said Mama, I know he's too young. But this boy has the most beautiful, sad eyes. Wait until you see them."

I couldn't take it.

She pressed the heel of her hand against the center of her forehead, as if she were in pain. "Did you mean what you said last year? Do you really believe she went to Hell?"

"No, Ruth. I don't believe that."

"Good. She had enough Hell here on Earth, most of it of her own making."

"I'm sorry I said that."

I could see myself, hear myself, drunk, raging. What did I say? What set me off?

Two things. Someone I'd never seen before, a friend of one of the relatives, looking around at my ugly house. *If I'd had to live here, I might end it all, too*. That was it. It was just a joke, I knew it was a joke. A horrible thing to say, but still, a joke.

But one of the old aunts leaned over and said to one of the cousins, loud enough that I could hear, *it looks like he's shaved.* Of course I'd shaved. How was I supposed to know? I wasn't Jewish, I didn't know. But I was off. Turning to that cousin and shouting that Catholics are allowed to shave. Shouting to that person I didn't know that Miriam picked out that ugly house, I always hated it.

If I had only stopped there, I would have been able to forgive myself. But I turned to her dad and said that he made me kill her. That we all sent her to Hell, not just me.

Ruth weeping, Evelyn's voice sounding just like Miriam's, *do not DARE to come to my mother's home again. You are not WELCOME in my mother's home.* Her little hand snatching that torn piece of ribbon off my lapel.

I took off my jacket and threw it at her, told her to tear it to bits like a harpy, like her sister. I fell down the stairs and found a bottle and carried it out to my Jeep, where I waited for them all to go away, singing Catholic songs for my Jewish wife.

Miriam, I'm so sorry. I couldn't even mourn you the right way.

"Hey Ruth? I don't understand how any of you can stand to look at me."

"Ha. Looking at you, it's always been the easy part." She kept stroking my hair. "You were grieving. Grief does hard things to us. It makes us into lunatics." She smiled. "We were all crazy that day. You were just the one who showed it."

Unmanned.

She pulled my face to her shoulder. "Hush. Life, it goes on." She spoke softly into my ear. "You've been a good husband, Gentry. But you can marry again, now. It's been a year. You can move on. You can tell her good-bye." I took her hand, pressed it to my mouth. She looked down at her palm and smiled, then pressed it against her lips. She left the kitchen.

Miriam, I need to tell you good-bye.

~

We all went out to the little cemetery. I drove your parents' Lincoln. We saw the stone. It looked fine, just fine. I'll pay for that stone, and I'll pay for the funeral. I wish I had enough to clear the debt before I leave, but I'll carry the cost of burying you away from here.

The stone said your name, your dates. And not to nitpick here, Miriam, but you were six years older than you told me. Below that, it said *Beloved Daughter, Sister, Wife*. Evelyn looked at me and burst into tears. I knew she wasn't blaming me, no one blamed me for the fact that I couldn't make you a mother. No one but me.

I failed you in every single way.

~

Everyone else cried, but I didn't because I was near the baby. Her name is Miranda, and in some way this means she's named after you. Evelyn let me smile at her without whisking her out of sight. Miranda smiled back.

Miriam, she's beautiful. We would have made a beautiful child.

People put small stones on your grave. All the graves had piles of stones on them. I didn't ask why, even though I wanted to know. I was respectful. I was quiet. Everyone was relieved. I was the most relieved of all.

It occurred to me that everyone had forgiven me.

Everyone except you.

~

We're back at the house. I have been patted, hugged, and wished well by all the relatives. But they're tired, now, and starting to argue with each other about the past, the traffic, the babka. They're also eating and there will be talking with full mouths. And drinking.

Ben hands the baby to me. I carry her off into the kitchen, sit down on a bar stool and seat her on the counter, steadying the firm, heated bundle of her body with my hands so I can look at her. She's small, I think, and quiet, her eyes darker than yours but just as watchful. She has extensive little eyebrows. Her dark curls smell like baby products and something deeper, sweeter, a scent that lingers on her skin, soft baby skin that has the same golden hue as yours. I would like to take this baby with me when I leave, but she would probably be missed.

Miriam, if only you could see this baby. She's perfect.

Oh Miriam. Today is my day to grieve you, to lay you to rest, I'm so sorry, I apologize for marrying you and not loving you, for not being someone you could love, for hating myself, for hating you. My heart is hurting, I feel it, I'm sorry, wherever you are, please forgive me, Miriam, for your pain. I didn't mean it, Miriam.

I never meant for you to do it.

She presses her forehead to mine and coos a word I don't know because it's baby language, sweet breath pushing through round lips in urgent fricatives. Her starfish hands find my hair, and she pulls it around us, creating a private place. She smiles at this strange wonderful game and so do I. She continues with her words. What a miracle, that a baby can whisper.

She dips closer and presses her open mouth against mine. I've kissed every baby I could, but I've never had a baby kiss me. And there in our hair tent, I whisper something to her. I tell her that she wouldn't have made everything right, but she would have made everything worth it.

"THERE you are!"

Evelyn, Evelyn nervous, retrieving her daughter while I stand up, guilt and gratitude washing me over.

I excuse myself to change.

~

Ruth and Ira sleep in twin beds. Maybe we should have tried that, Miriam.

I changed clothes in here on the day I married you. I was drunk and scared and guilty and trying to do the right thing. I failed. This room has a picture in it from that day in which I have a black eye. I don't want to be remembered like that.

I take off that brown suit and wrap it around that picture and those shoes and the socks and tie it with the ugly tie and put it in the bathroom garbage where it belongs. I get dressed again. I don't like looking in mirrors, but at least I have hair again. No bruises. Some scars, but I've always had scars. Gretchen chose this earring because it looks like my eyes. That's the one I put in. I put the gold hoop in my pocket. I look like myself.

The doorbell. I check my cheap watch, remove it from my wrist and drop it in the toilet and flush. I leave the seat up.

What if it isn't him? What if I walk out there, and it isn't him? He promised he would be here to pay his respects. He promised. He has never broken a promise to me. He taught me what a promise is. But what if he doesn't come for me?

He's here. And so is she.

The girl of my memory is a white-blonde string of a thing, blue eyes, tall for her age but still a little skinny girl. How can this be her? I demand of You, where did she go? Where is her chapped mouth, where are her dusty hands with the bitten nails, her white braids? Gone. Dear God, how did Bosco let this happen?

Tell me the little girl I left behind is somewhere inside this young woman.

She moves easily into this room of exhausted, reproachful people like a cool tide, bathing everyone in reflected beauty. Jaws drop, voices stop, stunned into silence by this composition of pollen-dusted limbs, white-gold hair, and eyes like blue ice. All is made perfect. Even her blonde eyebrows are perfect.

"Hi, dummy."

She's in there. Oh, God, You do hear me, You do listen to me, You do love me.

Mel reaches out to me. I let him touch me, like I did all those years before. He lays one of his hands on my shoulder, one of his small, safe hands. She puts her arms around my waist, tight. They hold on.

They've come for me.

They have finally come for me.

Reader's Discussion Guide

1. Compare how we left Gentry in Book One to where is his at the beginning of Book Two. Was this inevitable?
2. Is Gentry's workplace a true Sisyphean nightmare or is he just exaggerating? Why does he perceive it as he does?
3. Why doesn't Gentry turn to Lorrie or Mel for help?
4. When Gentry finally has to ask for help, why does he choose Mike? What is Mike's reaction? Does this turn of events surprise you?
5. What do you learn about Gentry and his past from his interactions with Becca? Does this help you understand his actions in the first book at all?
6. How do the Sandersons feel about Gentry? What is this based on? How do they help him and hurt him?
7. Why does Gentry abandon teaching? Was this his best choice?
8. Why is Miriam so alluring to Gentry? It is clear she is physically attractive, but what are her other attractions?
9. In the first book, Gentry was often alone but rarely felt lonely. Why is he so profoundly lonely in this book?
10. Why do you think Gretchen stops writing to Gentry?
11. Who in this book cares the most about Gentry?
12. Why don't Gentry's friends save him from his terrible mistake? Do you think they try?
13. Is Gentry ever in love with Miriam? Is she ever in love with him?
14. Do you find Gentry's actions in Hawaii forgivable or deplorable?
15. When Gentry finally snaps, how did you react? Does he deserve what happens to him? Does he deserve worse?
16. Is Gentry a victim of domestic abuse, or is he a perpetrator of domestic abuse?
17. What do you think of Gentry's attitudes towards infertility treatments? Why won't Gentry consider adoption?

18. What keeps Gentry in that house, that relationship, that job? Are there moments when you think he might escape? What happens to keep him there?
19. Do you have a strong mental image of Gentry's home in Oklahoma? If so, which is the worst room? Should he have tried to fix the house? Why doesn't he try?
20. Where will Gentry go next?

About the Author

After a nomadic childhood that took her to South Dakota, California, Minnesota, Arkansas, Washington and Montana, Karen G. Berry settled in Portland, Oregon. She's stayed put for over thirty years, raising three daughters and walking many dogs. After graduating magna cum laude at age forty with a degree in English, Karen has worked in marketing. Aside from her novel endeavors, she is an extensively published poet, but tries not to let that sneak into her fiction.

Visit her at www.karengberry.mywriting.network/ to learn more.

79721108R00231

Made in the USA
San Bernardino, CA
17 June 2018